Bird
Song

S.L. Naeole

Bird Song

Published by Crystal Quill Publishing

S.L. Naeole

Visit my website at www.slnaeole.com
Visit the official website for Falling From Grace at www.GraceSeries.com

Bird Song

S.L. Naeole

To Rere ~ best friends forever.

"Ah, by no wind those clouds are driven
That rustle through the unquiet Heaven
Uneasily, from morn till even,
Over the violets there that lie
In myriad types of the human eye-
Over the lilies there that wave
And weep above a nameless grave!
They wave:- from out their fragrant tops
Eternal dews come down in drops.
They weep:- from off their delicate stems
Perennial tears descend in gems."

Valley of Unrest—Edgar Alan Poe

PREFACE

Loss is the catalyst to the weakening of faith. How many times have I lost, how much can one lose before faith becomes a dream; far off and out of reach? How much can I witness before my eyes finally stop believing and my heart finally ceases to hope?

I see him; Death is ready to take from me once again. How much more am I willing to sacrifice to keep my own wings above ground? Heaven holds no promise for me if even the rewards exact a cost.

FENCES MAKE FOR GOOD NEIGHBORS

The icy bite of the December air was a rude awakening for my barely conscious mind. If the sound of fluttering hadn't clued me in, the warm lips against my ear did as they encouraged my slumber to flee. I smiled at the soft words. "You keep kidnapping me and I'm going to have to start locking my window at night just to get some sleep."

"You know that won't keep me away from you."

"Mmm, promise?" I said sleepily, nuzzling the silky skin of his neck. "Where are we going?"

His thoughts told me were heading to the spot we always visited at this time of night—to his family's retreat. Robert Bellegarde, my kidnapper, was taking me, his willing victim, to view the sky before another winter storm rolled in and covered the ground with white and the sky with grey. The stars were always the clearest at this time of night, and he knew how much I loved to just stare at them while lying together, content to let the rest of the world spin around us.

"Why are your wings open?" I asked, picking up the sound of whistling as the wind sifted through his ebony plumes.

Robert smiled at me and answered quite bluntly, "Because you like them." And he was right. I did like them...very much. I'd told him many times just how much I envied them how he had something that made him different and yet so admired amongst his kind.

His kind…angels. The mythical creatures that have haunted our faiths and our fantasies since the beginning of time were real. And now they haunted my reality. I could never dream of going back to the semi-normal existence that I barely survived before meeting Robert.

His secret, his life had altered mine in ways that spanned the endless chapters that made up the story of me. And now it was the story of us; of how with the simple telling of one painful, black lie, he had lost his life. And with the forgiveness of truth, had regained it all back with the key to Heaven in his hands, and his heart in mine.

But, as with all great things, there was a price to pay for escaping death. And for Robert, his price was one that would have been the reason that life itself should have no meaning. Robert had lost the beating of his immortal heart.

Born without wings, as all angels are, and in a human body, Robert had needed a catalyst, a wing-bringer who would trigger within him what the angels called the change. He had searched and waited for fifteen hundred years, his ambition to ascend and receive his call his only driving force.

And then he met me. Simple, plain, unadulterated Grace Shelley, who would have given anything to simply vanish into thin air, rather than draw the attention of anyone or anything other than that of my best friend. But Robert saw—no, he felt something within me that acted like a magnet, drawing the two of us together.

Polar opposites on the playing field of everything that mattered in my world, he was beautiful, while I wasn't. He was popular while I was committing crimes with my lack of a social life. And yet, his perfection was merely a façade, while my perceived shortcomings were the veneer that covered who I truly was underneath. I was his soul mate.

I know that sounds ridiculously melodramatic, but when you're talking about angels, and dying, and growing wings, what else can you be. It's not like I'm talking about your typical high school romance here. In another life, that was all I ever wanted. But as soon as Robert's eyes caught hold of mine, the world and everything that I knew about it had changed. Girls who date high school kids don't get mowed down by cars, or nearly strangled to death by rogue angels hell bent on hurting your boyfriend.

And…girls who date high school kids don't end up sailing across the night sky in the arms of Death.

Along with Robert's wings came the one thing that all angels strive for, their destiny. It's a song, a never ending song of duty and devotion that they've named the call. It demands their absolute loyalty and they give it without question. For most, it's simply a duty of walking amongst us and ensuring that we remain faithful; mundane duties when compared to the darkness that consumes Robert's call.

He had hoped that his ability to heal the human body would have given him the call of a healer, someone who performed miracles for the sick and injured. Instead, the wickedness that is cruel irony sentenced him to the role of Death. He'd be taking life instead of saving it.

He won't tell me how many lives he's taken, how many souls he's had to help make the journey across time and physical boundaries to their final destinations, whether it be Heaven, Hell, or some place in between. But each time he returns to me, it seems like a small piece of who he is has been chipped away. The hope and optimism in him has dulled a bit and I often fear that he will come home to me one day unrecognizable, so consumed by the darkness of his call that he won't be Robert—my Robert. Instead, he'd become…Sam.

"Are you woolgathering?"

"What?" I looked at him, confused, his question catching me off guard. "Woolgathering—what does that mean?"

Even in the smooth flow of flight, his body shook with his amusement. "It means thinking, collecting your thoughts. You're quiet, and your mind is closed off which usually means you're thinking about something important. What is it?"

"Are you saying that my thoughts are like itchy sheep's hair?" I tried to sound insulted, but he could see right through me. There was no pretending when it came to him. "Okay, alright. I was just thinking about the past few months, about how so much has happened since September. I can't believe everything that's happened since I first saw you. It's overwhelming, and I'm not sure what else life has in store for me now."

Robert looked at me with inquisitive eyes. "You're not telling me the whole truth."

Of course I wasn't. I wasn't about to tell him that I was worried about his soul. He certainly knew much more about that than I ever would or could. My ignorance about much of the angel world was slowly diminishing, but I doubted that it would be completely eradicated in my lifetime. And of all the things that I was sure of, the very last thing I'd learn was the condition of the angelic soul.

"Robert, you worry too much," I chided and then changed the subject. "Do you think that the ground is going to be too wet to lie down?"

The warm air from my mouth forced wisps of vapor to float around me, and I continued to blow out streams of warm haze in a poor attempt to occupy my wandering thoughts. Robert was taking an awfully long time to answer my question, which was unusual, especially when a question can be answered with a thought…

Oh. I was blocking his thoughts again. *Sorry.*

I looked up to see him shake his head, sighing in amused frustration. *You're doing this much more frequently now. It's getting harder and harder to fight the shifting and stay where your thoughts are focused.*

"*This*" was a complication that neither of us had expected. While we both knew that I could intentionally keep his kind from reading my thoughts, it seemed that since I had turned eighteen nearly a week ago, my mind was shutting Robert out on its own more frequently. When given notice, he was able to follow the thoughts in my head so that he wasn't shut out. But it was becoming more and more difficult to differentiate when my thoughts were separating and when they weren't.

Sorry. There wasn't much else I could say. It wasn't as though I had wanted it to happen that way. I enjoyed the ability to keep some thoughts private; I am human, after all. But, there is also something incredibly intimate about being able to share one's innermost thoughts with another person.

As Robert slowed down, and the ground drew closer, I saw that the blanket of snow that covered the large field was not going to be bearing its stargazers tonight. "What do we do now?"

Robert's feet touched the ground and sank into the cold covering. I shivered just thinking about how it must feel to him. "It doesn't feel all that different than standing on a beach, actually," he said aloud, answering the question that I had not voiced.

I felt the line of dissatisfaction stretch across my face while I thought about that for a bit. "You know, you're not going to be winning many points with me if you keep on bragging about going to the beach when I'm stuck in Ohio during one of the worst winters in history."

He laughed out loud, his voice echoing around me, the sound a beautiful symphony of bells and brass and strings all blending into the only sound that could erase the very chill from my body. "You just say the word and you'll have your toes dipping in warm, Pacific waters in no time."

I shook my head. This was the hardest part when it came to what Robert was—at least it was for me. He wanted me to take advantage of what he was, use his abilities to help me, help my family out in ways that we both knew would be beneficial. It wasn't breaking any code, he had explained. I just didn't like the idea that by relenting, and allowing him the pleasure of doing this for me, I'd be using him.

I had argued that we had been getting along fine without him, his money, or his gifts, and we'd do well without it. I needed to be able to stand on my own two feet, I told him, because there was no other way for me to exist. It was why I had worked at the library. It was why I rode a bike instead of driving some used clunker. It was why I wore second hand clothes from thrift stores and garage sales. Everything that I did, I wanted it to be done my way.

"I'll be able to support myself," I had explained to him one night after he had argued against the possibility of me taking a job at the mall. "I don't plan on living at home once I go to college, Robert. After the baby comes, what kind of study time do you think I'll get?"

"You don't have to get a job, Grace. I'd be more than willing to support you while you go to school," Robert had argued. "Besides, you don't even like the mall. How will you be able to be in some store you can't stand and sell items to people you don't like?"

I smiled sweetly at him and replied, "The same way you angels can help people you despise."

It had been the wrong thing to do—Robert had been very sensitive as of late because of his call—but I couldn't take it back, and I wasn't going to either. Humans and angels weren't so different that they couldn't be just as deceptive as the other in order to achieve set goals.

There had been no winner in that argument. He couldn't forbid me from working, and I couldn't force him to like it. We were at an impasse in that regard, and I didn't mind it at all because the wall was on his side of the fence this time. He had set up so many boundaries and rules since the very beginning of our strange relationship that it was nice being the one with the gate key for a change.

I can hear that.

Of course he could hear it. I had allowed him back in. *And? It's true. You're the one who's set up all of these ridiculous rules, and I'm stuck following them whether I like them or not.*

He had walked over to our bench—where we had had our first real conversation, where everything began for the two of us—and used his wings like some kind of built-in broom to sweep the snow off the seat. "Why are you doing that? You won't get cold if you sit on the snow," I commented, watching him.

"Because I don't want to get my pants wet. They're new."

I rolled my eyes. Robert had discovered that being Death eased the restrictions on him that would have otherwise caused him significant harm. Lying, for example, would normally cause him extreme pain and eventually result in death if he didn't confess the truth. As Death however, some of the darkness that comes with the power to extend or take away life allowed for him to lie…a little, and Robert chose to use this leniency to joke around. He was like a kid with a new toy, but I knew that it wouldn't be long before it got on my nerves.

"You're not seriously trying to make me believe that you care about your pants?"

As he sat down, his wings retreated into the mysterious lines that crisscrossed his back, mirroring in some way the branches of a large tree with Robert as its trunk. I immediately felt saddened by their disappearance. I had definitely grown used to seeing them, and thought they were the most beautiful things to have ever been created. It didn't hurt that I was the reason for their existence.

"Grace, I don't care about my pants. I was just trying to get your mind off some of the trivial things. Like this gate or wall notion you have in your head. You know that the rules I have set up are to keep you and your family safe."

I shrugged my shoulders, knowing what he had said, but not appreciating the reason why he had said it. "Robert, you told me that I can never tell Dad about what you are. I said fine. You told me that Graham can never know. I said fine again. I've told no one about you; even Lark and I have never discussed it because you said it was uncomfortable for the two of you.

"But then you decide that I can't even say your real name, like I ever had anyway, and that I cannot discuss your absences with anyone, that I should just play dumb. I don't get that. It's not like I'm telling Madame Hidani that you're off in Swaziland ferrying souls to Heaven, Hell, and to Kosher Knishes for some lox and bagels. I'm supposed to be your girlfriend, and when I have to play dumb and say I don't know when people ask where you are, I feel like everyone is starting to feel sorry for me again."

I avoided mentioning the main arguing point, that neither of us had made any headway with…or concessions. Intimacy on a mental level was one thing. Intimacy on a physical level was something entirely different, and he had cut me off.

Robert's angelic lack of awareness when it came to feeling the physical touch that so many humans took for granted had made him ignorant to the simple pleasures of experiencing things, like a holding a hand, or kissing. As Robert's mother had explained, juveniles—angels without wings or a call—were more prone to experience physical pleasure through those of the humans they were with because that's the only way they could feel them.

And now that Robert had his call, his wings, now that he could feel, could enjoy the wonders of soft lips and smooth skin himself, he had chosen to abstain. And in doing so, had forced me to abstain as well.

"It's too much for me to deal with, Grace," he had explained when I had been particularly angry and hurt at being rejected yet again. He refused to go into it any further, and I was feeling too dejected to push it. Rejection was my forte, so I knew I could handle it quite well. He, on the other hand, couldn't. He just wasn't used to it.

Fifteen hundred years of living with the gift to charm people into doing what you want, to will them to bend to your whims had made him arrogant and cocky in some ways, and it took a simple seventeen year old girl like me to bring him down a peg. I admit that among all of my achievements in life—and there really aren't many—this was one of my finest. Even Lark, Robert's sister appreciated my doing so.

"What are you thinking about now?"

"Ugh," I groaned, realizing that once again, my train of thought had unknowingly left him behind. "I was thinking about your ridiculous inability to control yourself and how I'm being made to suffer for it."

Seeing his confused expression was almost enough to make me forget that his sudden vow of kissing chastity had also become mine by proxy. Almost. "Ugh," I groaned again, and shook my head at the impossibility of it all. How could I stare at such beautiful, mercury eyes and an impossibly perfect face and not want to attack it in a primal, feminine way?

"Ahh."

Well hooray. He'd finally gotten into my mind.

"You're thinking about that again? Why? I've made some concessions about this, Grace-"

I cut him off. "Yes. You agreed that while you wouldn't kiss me like a boyfriend would, you'd kiss me like my dad does. How utterly romantic of you, and how selfish of me to want otherwise." I felt my bottom lip slip out of its grimace, forming the pout that seemed to be ever-present now.

"Grace," he began, "you're being ridiculous, you know that? I'm trying to protect you. It's difficult for me to deny myself the same things that you want, but you have to be patient and understanding."

I threw my hands up, exasperated with his patience and understanding mantra. "It is ex-haus-ting, being so *patient* and *understanding*," I snapped, but immediately felt contrite when I saw the hurt spread across his face. "Robert, I'm not asking for you to make love to me in the snow, or anything even remotely similar. Although if you want to, I'm not going to object. I'm only asking that you not take away the only real form of physical intimacy we share."

I hadn't meant for it to sound like I was pleading with him, but that's exactly how it came out, and I hated it. I didn't think I was truly that desperate until the words were out of my mouth.

Robert sighed; the sound was sad and troubled, the same way he sounded after returning from answering his call. "Grace, please. Let's talk about this later, okay? I wanted to discuss something with you."

So he was changing the subject. Fine. I made a mental note that when we finally did discuss this, he'd be unable to discuss anything but.

"What is it?"

Holding onto my chin, he forced me to look towards the Gazebo that was nestled between two large trees. The last time we were here, a newlywed bride dipped her husband in an unconventional sealing of her wedding vows. That was the night I met the bride's grandmother, a kind woman named Ellie who had not only been an Electus Patronus, but also one of the few women who knew Robert in a more intimate way, a way that I never had. And with the way things were going, never would either.

"So what am I looking at?" I asked, taking note that the gazebo was shrouded in the white cloak of snow.

Robert grinned. "I'm going to set up a spot over there for us to celebrate the New Year. I've already spoken to your father and Lark is going to bring you here to meet me. I want you to wear the green dress again, if you don't mind."

"Why do I have to wear a dress?" I grumbled, not exactly enjoying the idea of being in the cold winter air in a dress that had only been barely tolerable when the ground still had some green to it. It wasn't that I didn't like the dress—the dress had been beautiful—it was more that it was…a dress. It had taken Robert actually purchasing it himself in order for me to put it on. It was the same night that I had told Robert that I loved him.

It was the same night that I had met Sam…

"Don't think about him, Grace. That's not how I want you to remember our first date."

"I don't think I can think about that night without thinking about him, Robert," I argued. "I'm not going to pretend that he didn't exist, that what happened…didn't. It did, and I can't forget it. The only thing I can do is hope things are better for us in the future."

Robert sighed before finally releasing my chin and wrapping his arms around me. He whispered into my ear, "So do you want to hear what I have planned?"

I shook my head. "Surprise me."

ARRANGEMENTS

The gross argument that friendship and dating go hand in hand is one that I had mistakenly adopted just a few months ago with my best friend, Graham Hasselbeck. He had abandoned our friendship after I had foolishly declared my love for him on the hood of his old Buick, and I fell headfirst into a deep depression that stained my life with the dark and lonely thoughts of being dejected for the crime of loving someone.

Fast forward four months and you've got an anxious me waiting on that very same hood for him to return from Christmas break with his mom. Lark, Robert's sister, had insisted on waiting with me, and so the two of us perched ourselves on the hood of his little green clunker, watching for the cab that would bring Graham and his mother back from their vacation in Florida.

"Have you ever been to Florida?" I asked Lark, remembering Robert's comment about beaches.

She nodded her head, her long hair that running like liquid onyx down her back and swaying ever so gently with the soft motion. "Sure. We've been to every state in this country, and almost all of the major continents. Robert thinks that North America holds the most promise though."

She looked slyly at me at that last bit, the silver in her eyes so light, it was almost colorless. I blushed, the heat of embarrassment at the innuendo burning the red into my cheeks. It didn't help that she could read her brother's mind and know what was hidden there. It bothered me though, knowing that she could also see that he was trying to remain physically distant.

"Grace, he's being a complete idiot. But he's doing it for the right reasons."

I looked at her and took note of her conspiratorial smile. "What are you plotting, Lark?"

She shook her head. "I'm not plotting anything. But I know someone who is."

I knew I could have asked her who it was, and she would have been nothing less than compelled to answer, but I couldn't abuse her trust in me like that. If something or someone was planning something, I'd simply have to wait to find out.

"Thank you," Lark sighed, having heard my reasoning. "Your difference never ceases to amaze me, you know."

Her comment annoyed me. Different was my least favorite word—especially when used to describe me.

"Oh let it go, Grace. You're going to have to face the fact that you are different. You're living in a small town which makes differences that much more noticeable. Everyone here is different. Stacy is different because she's the only girl who could kick every guy's butt on the football team. Graham is different because he's the most popular guy in the school whose best friend happens to be the least popular girl in school. Robert's different because he's dating you. I'm different because I'm blind."

"But, different doesn't have to be a bad thing."

She turned away then, a blush spreading across her face as she looked down the street. A yellow cab was heading towards us, and I could see that the conversation was over. "He's coming," she breathed, and I smiled at the tiny secret that she revealed with that subtle gesture.

The yellow sedan pulled up into the driveway fronting Graham's house, and Lark and I both sat up straight as we waited for its occupants to emerge.

Or...occupant.

"Hey guys," Graham called out as he stepped out alone. His hair had been cut since the last time I had seen him, and it had grown lighter; Florida sun would do that, I suppose. I felt a quick catch in the rhythm of my heart as he smiled, his evergreen eyes sparkling with satisfaction.

Where's his mother?

I looked at Lark and shrugged, the question hanging at the back of my throat was begging to be asked. I waited until the cab had left and Graham was standing in front of me before I did.

"She's staying in Florida," he answered me matter-of-factly, his face unaffected, his smile still sweet and genuine. "She and Dad aren't dealing so well together—well, you know that—so she's staying with my aunt down in Tallahassee."

"Oh," Lark and I said at the same time. Me by what I had heard him say, Lark by what he didn't.

Lark seemed quite uncomfortable at that moment, and started fidgeting with the buttons on her designer coat. Feeling oddly inadequate with my one size fits most jacket, I started preparing the list of questions I'd wanted to ask about his vacation, getting them mentally on deck so that perhaps the awkward silence that we'd given birth to would go away.

"I've got to go...powder my nose. I'll be right back," Lark suddenly blurted. She leapt off the hood and ran to my house in a slightly non-human burst of speed. It was only made more startling because Lark's supposed to be blind, and she did it without once opening up her walking stick.

"Wow. She must've really had to go," Graham mumbled, and then sighed. It wasn't a sigh of disappointment like I had partially expected. I might not have an angel's ability to read minds, but I certainly could tell when my best friend wasn't himself, and whenever he was around Lark, he was definitely not himself.

Sighing once again, Graham ran his fingers through his hair, now too short to be affected by the rough raking. "Look Grace, I didn't want to say this in front of Lark, but the real reason my mom's not here is because she's filed for divorce. She told me while we were in Florida."

Stunned, I sat there with my mouth glued shut. The entire list of questions I had disintegrated into a pile of dust as I understood what the ramifications of this sudden change would bring to Graham's life.

"When is she coming back?" I asked, thinking about Ivy Hasselbeck's cold, icy stare the last time I had seen her just a few days after the last day of school, when Graham had come over to drop off his Christmas present to me, and pick his up in return.

"She's not. She wants me to move down there with her, but I told her I didn't want to. I mean, we're halfway through the year, and it doesn't make sense for me to end up graduating from some school I'll have only attended for a few months," Graham rationalized, his hands shoved in his jacket pockets, pushing down on them like he needed to drive home the point more to himself than to me. I agreed with him; it made no sense. But it was different for me.

I couldn't picture—no, I didn't *want* to picture Graham out of my life once again so soon after he had wanted back in. That ache was still fresh in my mind, and I could feel the memories clawing their way to my heart, wanting to come out and rage at this new threat to our friendship.

"So, what does your dad think?" I asked, trying to distract myself from the burning need to hear him promise that he wasn't going to leave me again.

Graham's foot kicked the tire of his car as he stared up at the darkening sky. "He thinks that I should stay with him. But he's not taking the whole divorce thing so great. Sales at the store are down and he's had to let some people go. Add mom moving away on top of that, and then her wanting me to go with her and he's just become one big mess, Grace. I mean, he's been drinking like it comes out of the tap, and I'm just not sure I want to stay with him either. Not like that."

My heart hurt, literally ached at the thought of him being stuck in the middle of this little tug of war between his parents. I knew that neither Ivy nor Richard would have forced him to make a decision, but the fact that Graham felt guilty on both accounts must feel like he's being torn in two pieces.

"Hey, I didn't mean to upset you. Cheer up. At least I'll be staying at Heath, huh?" Graham said, punching me lightly in my shoulder and giving me a half-hearted smile.

"Yeah. At least..."

He straightened up as Lark reappeared, her face stony and her eyes lighter than usual. "So, you seem to have memorized your way around Grace's house pretty fast. How'd you do it? Braille for your feet?"

The look on her face gave me the impression that if she tried to smile, her face would crack into several pieces, the sound probably deafening the two of us while she stood there staring with her sightless eyes.

Taking my cue, I sighed and repeated the lie that Stacy and I had already said several times in the past few weeks regarding Lark's seemingly unnatural ability to find her way around while blind. "She's memorized the distance between each place, Graham. She counts the steps."

"Oh. Hey, that's pretty cool. You're going to have to teach me that sometime so I can find my way here in the dark."

Lark should have rolled her eyes. Lark normally would have. But this Lark wasn't doing anything but staring at me. Her face was void of emotion, of color, of anything that would suggest she was even alive. "Yeah. Sure," she responded finally when she realized that an answer was necessary before I had to start lying again.

Graham brushed his hands through his hair again, obviously not pleased with such a stoic reaction. "Um, so how was your Christmas?"

I raised my eyebrows. He hadn't asked that question of me. He had forgotten I was even there, because something he hadn't said, something that Lark had picked up on in his mind, made her smile. And how I felt when I looked at Robert, I was almost positive was the exact same feeling that was causing the ridiculously goofy grin to cross Graham's face.

"We spent it here, with Grace," she answered lightly, turning to smile at me. Gone was the stony expression, and her eyes were once again light gray, a slightly watered down version of her brother's. I saw a flicker of annoyance, and knew that my description hadn't pleased her. *Oh well.*

"That sounds like fun. Did her dad play that Christmas cat record again?"

I groaned as Lark smiled and nodded her head, knowing what was coming: my comeuppance. "Yes, he did. And Grace sang along. Quite loudly, as a matter of fact. And off-key, too, but that's okay. She didn't have the benefit of a drunken audience, so she was pretty brave, all things considering."

Graham's guffaw began deep within his chest, and barreled out until it was booming all around me. He laughed so hard, he was running out of breath, and the wheezing caused him to bend over. "I-can't believe you-you actually-you sang along?"

I felt my arms fold across my chest, and my lips purse in frustration. "You're not encouraging me to pursue my singing career, Graham."

He laughed even harder, and I could hear the duet of bells in my head as Lark began laughing as well. Great. Now the two of them were laughing at me. I felt my mouth twitch, my pursed lips traveling to the side in mock offense. In truth, I had been worried about the cold look on Lark's face. What had caused her to change moods so suddenly?

I stared at her, waiting for her to respond to my unasked question, but she continued to laugh, filling my head with a harmony of sounds that echoed in my mind. It was definitely a lot nicer than the icy sting that she could inflict with that very same mental voice.

"I'm sorry, Grace. Oh goodness, look at your face. You're so embarrassed, and I'm just acting like a complete jerk. You wanna tell me how your Christmas went? Besides the meowing?"

I frowned at the snickering—he tried to hide it behind his hand, but was failing…miserably—and sighed in defeat. "I think that this Christmas was probably the first and last time I'll ever play back-up singer to thirty-three cats, my dad, and Lark."

18

"Wait, Lark sang, too?" he asked—well, shouted really—and gaped at Lark, her face turning red from embarrassment. "I would've loved to have seen that."

Ah. It wasn't from embarrassment. It was something else entirely. I grinned at the cold stare she shot my way at my thoughts. This was going to be quite interesting, indeed.

"Grace, dinner."

I looked at the doorway of my little house and saw Janice standing there with her hand on her belly, my little brother nestled comfortably within. How odd, to call him my little brother. I had been an only child for so long; this entire experience should feel far more foreign than it did.

"I'll be there in a minute, Janice!" I called out to her, and looked at Graham, knowing I didn't even need to ask the question he had been waiting to hear. Instead, I turned to Lark, knowing that though she had been quite lax when it came to keeping some things about her a secret from Graham, there was still the need to keep up with the pretense of her being absolutely normal, in the incredibly beautiful, Greek goddess sort of way.

"Do you want to stay for dinner, Lark?"

She shook her head, and winked at me. "I've got to get going. I have some things I need to do, and I needed to speak to Mom about a few things."

The general lack of specifics in her answer was meant to keep her from having to tell the truth, but I detected something different. The void of details seemed like more of an...invitation?

"Hey, do you need a ride home, Lark?"

"Yes, actually, I do need one. Would you mind dropping me off?"

I watched the two of them, once again forgotten; I was the hood ornament on the green rust bucket while the two of them existed in their own world. It almost felt like I was standing outside of my own life and watching myself, only I was in Graham's body. His face held as much awe and interest as mine probably did when I had first looked at Robert.

"Um, Grace, could you, you know, get off my car?"

I stared into two green eyes and turned to see two pale gray ones. "Oh, sorry." I scooted off the hood and stood on the sidewalk as Graham opened the passenger side door for Lark. She stepped in gracefully, her lithe body sliding into the car like silk wraps around skin. I had never managed to do something like that; I always ended up looking more like wet burlap falling into a bucket.

"I'll see you tomorrow night, Grace," Lark called out after Graham had taken his spot in the driver's seat and started the car. I was about to ask what she meant by tomorrow night when they pulled off. She didn't even answer my thoughts.

"Well, isn't that interesting," I muttered to myself and headed into the house for dinner.

Dad and Janice were seated at the little table in the kitchen. I took my seat and picked up the fork, ready to dig into the mound of spaghetti and meat-like-balls that had already been plated for me.

"So, how was Graham's vacation?"

I looked at the food in front of me and sighed. I placed my fork down and raised my gaze up to Dad's. "His parents are getting a divorce."

Janice made a small moan of disappointment, while Dad's expression was uncharacteristically morose. "Did Ivy come home with Graham?" he asked as he looked at Janice's distressed face. I didn't understand what the reason for the look they exchanged, but I was fairly certain that I would in a minute or two.

"No. She's staying in Florida. She wanted Graham to move down there with her, but he told her no. School is almost over, and he doesn't want to switch schools for just one more semester," I explained, thankful that I got to keep my best friend with me for just a little while longer.

"Well, that makes things difficult for him," Dad muttered. Difficult would be an understatement. Graham had mentioned his father's drinking, and it was something that we all knew he'd had an issue with, but with the sound of glass bottles being tossed out more frequently coming from next door, half the street knew how difficult things were getting.

"James, do you think Graham should be staying with his father, knowing how he's been lately?"

I turned to look at Janice with my mouth hanging open in surprise. What was she getting at with her question? My head turned when Dad started talking.

"No, I don't. It wouldn't be healthy for that boy to be staying with Richard when he's not even taking care of himself. What do you suggest we do?"

As though I were witnessing a verbal tennis match, my head snapped back to Janice, and waited for her response. "I think he should stay here. I mean, he's over here most of the time anyway, we know he can be trusted around Grace, and it'll only be for a little while."

My eyes grew wide at the suggestion, and my head whipped back to Dad, curious to know what his reaction was. He was actually contemplating it!

"I think you're probably right, but Richard's gonna be upset. He's just lost his wife. I don't think he'll be so eager to give up his son, too."

"James, Graham's eighteen. He can make his own decisions; especially about this."

Dad sighed. He did not relish the idea of hurting his friend…but not as much as he hated the idea of his friend hurting his son with his behavior. "I'll talk to Richard. Grace, would you talk to Graham? It'd come off more helpful than custodial if you do it."

Pleased at finally being included in the conversation, I nodded, and finally dug into my dinner.

03

I waited out on the steps fronting my house until I heard the car grumbling up the street. When Graham had finally put the car in park and climbed out, a strange smile on his face, I called out to him.

"Oh, hey Grace," he answered, and smiled sheepishly. "What are you doing out here so late?"

I didn't know what time it was, but I knew why I was here. I reached my hand out, and he took it, knowing that there was something I needed to talk to him about, and it required him coming inside out of the cold and away from the prying ears of any neighbors who might have been awakened by the sound of Graham's return.

"What's up?" he asked as I pulled him inside. He followed me up to my room and said nothing as he sat down on my bed, watching me close the door as I did so.

When I was sure that we'd be left alone, I sat down on the bed facing him and told him of the conversation between Dad and Janice. I knew he'd be slightly upset that I had revealed his personal problems with my dad, but what I hadn't expected was the overall relief he expressed at not having to choose between either parent.

"You don't know how good that sounds, Grace. I didn't know how I was going to deal with it tonight. When I talked to my dad on the phone at the airport, he sounded so out of it. It's why I called the cab."

I frowned; if Richard was that bad, perhaps he needed to get some help. I silently prayed that he'd get it, that Dad would help him find it. Graham didn't need his father completely breaking down on in the middle of senior year. The fighting had been difficult enough for Graham to deal with, and now that his parents were living in completely different states, I couldn't imagine how he was feeling.

I could only relate to him on the level of losing a parent. He would still be able to see them, of course, and talk to them…but no matter what he did from now on, one was always going to be missing from his life. And if his father's drinking became worse, well…one might be missing permanently.

I frowned again, because that option would involve Robert, and the thought didn't sit well with me. Graham and Robert were finally getting along, things were going well. If Richard didn't get help…

"Grace?"

I blinked at the voice calling my name. "Yeah?"

He chuckled, "I lost you for a second. You totally spaced out. What's up?"

I shook my head, dismissing the thoughts that had taken me away from our conversation. "I was just wondering where you were going to sleep. Janice and Dad have already turned that teeny room next to mine into the nursery, and Dad actually parks his car in the Garage..."

Where *was* he going to sleep? Janice had said that they could trust Graham with me...she didn't actually mean that... "Oh please tell me no," I gasped before jumping off my bed. I raced to the door and flew downstairs to the kitchen, where Janice was cleaning.

"Grace? What's wrong?" she asked nervously, taking in my flushed face and my hectic breathing.

"Where's Graham supposed to sleep?" I panted, the anxiety in my voice apparent even to me.

As the seriousness of the situation finally dawned on her she smiled. "Oh Grace, he'll sleep on the couch! You didn't think we'd meant for him to sleep in your room, did you?"

I giggled nervously, sheepishly; foolishly. "Of course not!" Of course I did. She knew that. But she didn't know that the reason I did was because of something she wasn't aware of; I didn't want Robert to come into my room to see Graham sleeping in there. Even though they were friends now, I didn't trust what my boyfriend would do if he found another guy in my room in the middle of the night.

"Well, I'm done in here. You know where the sheets and blankets are, Grace. I'll let you take care of things. I'm going to bed. Goodnight." I watched as she left the kitchen, her head shaking at my obvious overreaction, her shoulders bobbing up and down with her quiet laughter.

Sighing with embarrassment, I went back up the stairs to my room. "Looks like you'll be sleeping on the couch," I said as I walked through the door.

Graham was sitting down on the corner of the bed, his hands holding onto something that appeared very fragile in his hands. It was pink, and shiny, reflecting the light from the ceiling lamp.

"I thought you might have thrown this away or broken it or something," he whispered as he rubbed an odd protrusion at the top of the largest part of the solid blob in his hands. I smiled, for in truth I had broken it.

For a while, it had lain in pieces on the floor. It represented, to me at least, our friendship...and me. The little, deformed object in his hand was a ceramic whale that I'd made in the second grade. It sported a large, green dorsal fin, the remnant of his own whale which had exploded in the kiln and melded onto mine.

I had thrown it against my dresser in a fit of rage a few weeks after he had ended our friendship; the head and tail broke apart cleanly, while other parts chipped and broke away, falling around it neatly. It was our life, my life, obliterated in one swift movement.

After that day, I hadn't thought about it. I didn't even try to find it after Graham had walked back into my life. It wasn't necessary, I had told myself. And that worked for me...until Robert had fixed it.

When he had somehow repaired the whale, and told me that it was stronger now than it had been before, I knew that he had been right. But I also knew that it wasn't meant for me, but for Graham. He was now the one who needed reassurances about the strength of the few ties he had to his friends, especially now that his family had fallen apart.

"Can I have it back?" Graham asked, never taking his eyes off the pink whale. "I should have never gotten rid of it."

"You're right. You never should have gotten rid of it. But, I'll let you have it back under the condition that when you use the bathroom, you put the seat back down after you're done."

He grinned at me, and I felt my heart skip—a faint reminder of just how much he still affected my flawed, human heart. "I'll try, but even Mom couldn't get me to do that."

"Come on, you gotta get home and talk to your dad, let him know what's going on. My dad went over to talk to him, but I don't know what happened. He didn't tell me anything when he came home," I explained as I pulled him up off the bed and out of the house.

We walked side-by-side, our steps silent on the lawn between our homes that had never been separated by fence or gates. The snow that had fallen the night before had melted quickly and left the ground soggy and dangerously slippery.

"Whoops!" I shouted, as I felt my footing loosen on a patch of grass that was exceptionally wet. I grabbed onto his arm as I nearly toppled headfirst into a planter sitting beneath one of the first story windows.

"God, Grace, you're such a klutz!" Graham kidded, though his tone was anything but amused. He was nervous, and I knew he was as apprehensive about this as I was. The house smelled like old beer as we walked through the door. That sweet, stale aroma that kind of reminds you that you need to wash your hair.

I don't remember the last time I had actually walked through Graham's house, but it wasn't like I remembered. Of course, I don't remember picture frames littering the ground, or beer bottles and empty liquor bottles covering every flat surface either. This was a recycler's dream. I tried counting the number of empty bottles as we walked towards the kitchen, but I lost track after I hit fifty. There were just too many and it felt like they were breeding, spawning as more appeared with each step, each movement towards the back of the house.

"Dad?" Graham called out. He flipped the light on and I groaned while he stood silent. The kitchen was disturbingly void of any space—each little scrap of spare air was occupied by a bottle of some kind or another, all in varying sizes. Bottles of varying sizes, shapes, and colors were stacked on the countertops, the kitchen table, the chairs, and the floor. It would have made for a great art piece if the reality of it weren't so tragic.

Graham turned away and walked past me towards the stairs. I started to follow him, unwilling to let him search upstairs alone, but he put his hand on my shoulder and shook his head. "I have to do this by myself, Grace." I opened my mouth to argue but he shook his head, and I bit my tongue to keep my words contained. What would he find upstairs that I couldn't see?

The smell in the house was starting to make me nauseas; I had to go and open a window before I lost my dinner. The kitchen window seemed the best place to start. I tried to raise it, but it was hopelessly stuck. Richard had neglected the house for so long, I was amazed that the door had even opened. How long had this been going on? And why hadn't Graham told me?

"He's not here," his voice said behind me. I turned around and saw the look of dismay on his face, mixed with confusion and fear. I knew that look so well. I had worn it myself. And I had been wrong—it didn't look good on anyone.

"Where do you think he is?" I asked as he once again took in the graveyard of empty bottles before us. He shook his head, not knowing and probably not wanting to even begin to think about it either. "Well, let's get your stuff then and head back to my house. I don't think I can stay in this funk any longer."

With what looked like despair and reservation, Graham headed back upstairs to pack a bag. I couldn't begin to think about what exactly was going on with his father, but the drinking, the enormous evidence of it was astounding and frighteningly real. This wasn't some after-school special, or a PSA on television. This was real life, and Graham had been living it for a very long time. And he hadn't told anyone.

He hadn't told me.

I shook my head at the selfishness my thought was laced with. Why did I need to know? Something this private and painful shouldn't have to be revealed to anyone...but the guilt from knowing that I could have helped him sooner and didn't was slowly starting to creep up in me. There was a lot that Graham didn't know about me, a lot that he'd be very upset about learning, so I couldn't hold this against him. He needed my support, not my complaints.

"Okay, let's go." I looked up and saw him standing next to me, his backpack slung over his shoulder and a baseball cap perched on his head.

We walked out of the house, Graham carefully closing the door, sealing in the stale air and the sea of glass behind us, and silently walked back towards mine. Graham laid his backpack on the ground next to the couch while I went upstairs to grab some pillows and a blanket for him to use. His mood was somber when I returned.

"I left him a note, letting him know where I was," he mumbled, the exhaustion showing on his face and in his tone. I wrapped my arms around him and squeezed him as tightly as I could.

"It's going to be okay, Graham. You're not alone in this," I said reassuringly, hoping that the words would find some place inside of him to burrow and take root.

I reluctantly let him go and watched as he plopped himself down on the couch and stretched his length out. He closed his eyes and I smiled. It had to be okay. Things weren't supposed to not work out for the people you loved.

I flipped off the living room light and headed up the stairs towards my room.

"Hey, Grace?"

I stopped on the fourth step and bent my head down so I could hear him better. "Yeah?"

"I love you."

I grinned. "Ditto."

RETURN

The feeling that I carried with me as I headed towards my room was completely different from anything I had felt before. It felt like completion. The final cracks had been repaired. It kept the smile plastered on my face as I went through my usual routine to get ready for bed.

When I walked into my room, Robert was sitting cross-legged on my bed, a slight frown distorting the beauty of his lips. He knew that Graham was downstairs on the couch, and he wasn't thrilled. "I don't want to hear your complaints about it, Robert," I whispered as I climbed into bed. I pulled the covers up over my bare knees and turned to look at him, ready to hear the arguments I knew he was going to make anyway.

I don't see why he couldn't stay at home. He's not being abused, and his father isn't even there right now. His guilt and your compassion shouldn't be enough reason for him to be here, Grace.

I felt my mouth push to the side, my expression doing nothing to fully convey just how annoyed I was that his mental spelunking hadn't been enough to help him root out the whole truth. "It wasn't my idea that he stay here, Robert; it was Janice's. The thought hadn't even crossed my mind, but I'm not going to let him stay in that house. You didn't see it. It's-"

Robert placed his fingers over my lips, silencing the slowly increasing volume of my rant. *I can see it in your head, Grace. It is disturbing, truly. I wasn't aware that he'd been going through so much. His mind is a lot like yours, only he uses random thoughts to hide how he really feels. I believe it's so he won't have to think about any of it. But, I won't tell you that I approve of him sleeping under the same roof as you are.*

I rolled my eyes at his thoughts. "You're acting quite protective of someone you treat like a little sister, Robert."

I saw his eyes flash with anger, and I admit that I enjoyed it. I was tired of him playing the good angel. Though I had been frightened and distrusting of his dark calling, there were moments I wish that a little bit of that darkness would come out so that he'd stop being so controlled and contained.

Grace. This isn't just about me, you know.

I snorted in disbelief. "Oh really? Then please, tell me how this isn't just about you. Tell me how I'm benefiting from this little arrangement because from where I'm sitting, it looks like I'm getting the short end of the stick."

Robert took my hand and placed it against his face, sighing with contentment. I sighed, too. It never felt normal, the way my skin tingled whenever we made contact. It always vibrated with an unseen energy that wound around and through me, a current of pure feeling that never felt like enough.

That is exactly how I feel, Grace. But it's worse for me, because I feel it from you as well. You don't know how incredibly blissful it is, to feel your softness, your warmth against my flesh. He held my hand still as he turned his face inward and kissed the palm of my hand. I heard the intake of my breath, but it fought for a spot with the pounding of my heart as it thrummed inside of my chest; the current rippled all through me and I had to bite my tongue to keep from groaning out loud.

"You're going to kill me, Robert. I swear on everything that's valuable, you're going to kill me dead."

Robert let out a snort, and I knew that my exaggeration had done nothing to sway him to my cause. *You can always agree to my changing you, and we won't have that problem.*

I threw myself back against my pillow and groaned. My head didn't even touch it as he snatched me mid-fall and pulled me against his chest. "Why are you bringing that up again, Robert?"

I felt him kiss my hair, felt the puff of air as he sighed. *I dream of waking up and finding you're not there. I fear the day when I hear the call...and it's because it's you.*

I felt that irritating sting of moisture prick my eyes; I had felt that fear manifest into something scary and monstrous in myself when he had been the one to die. To think of him experiencing that same pain himself was almost worse. I turned my head and placed my ear on his chest, the evidence of his death silent and still beneath the skin and bones that cradled it. I heard only the echo of breath in his chest, and I squeezed my eyes shut against the memories that leapt out of the dark recesses of my mind, taunting me with their hint at what lay ahead for me.

"I don't want to think about it," I cried into his shirt, my voice muffled against his chest. "I don't want to think about anything. I just want you to hold me, and tell me that you love me."

The circle of arms around me pulled me as tightly against his chest as humanly possible and he whispered the three words, while thinking them at the same time, my own personal echo. I reached my arms up to wrap around his neck and pull myself up, needing to feel something other than the rise and fall of his chest, or the strength wielded in his embrace. I needed to feel the unnatural heat from his lips, his breath tickling my skin, his nose nudging against mine.

I can't, Grace.

"Yes, you can. You just don't want to," I whispered as I inched closer to my goal. I needed to ease my way there, and I began by kissing his neck. The column of muscle that flexed there in distress seemed to beg for attention, and so I gave it. I kissed it softly, gently. My lips worked their way towards the curve of his jaw, and kissed along the ridge until I came to the dip between his lower lip and his chin.

I inhaled as he breathed out, and sighed at the sweet fragrance and blissful warmth that wafted over my face. I leaned in closer to breathe in the intoxicating aroma, allowing the tip of my nose to brush his, wanting that slight contact to draw out a reaction.

When nothing happened, I decided to tempt fate. I leaned in and lightly pressed my lips against his, feather light and soft. I took his lack of rejection as a positive sign, and applied my lips to his with more pressure, rubbing them against the heavenly friction that his offered. I knew I was dangerously close to overstepping the limitations Robert had set, but at that moment, I didn't care. I only cared about the heat that traveled from the point of contact between our lips to the sheets that hid my trembling knees.

How incredibly simple it all was. You read about passionate encounters involving enormous amounts of movement and contact, see the visions displayed in movies and on television, and yet, the simple act of pressing my lips against Robert's was enough to scorch my skin, and light my entire body on fire. My breathing quickened and my heart galloped at an unhealthy pace as I realized that though I had meant to lure Robert into my dangerous game, I had been the one who had been caught.

I pulled away, sinking back down his chest, the dizziness nearly drawing forth a faint from me, and smiled at my own foolishness. I attempted to take a breath to calm myself, but the force of Robert's strong hands at my face pulling me back up towards his lips sent every nerve ending in my body shooting out towards him, hungry for whatever he was about to give to me.

As his lips pressed against mine with force and clear intent, I whimpered. This was like no kiss we had shared before. It was as though he was starving, and the only sustenance he could find came from me in the form of kisses I was only too willing to give to him. My fingers thrummed with feeling as they tangled in the silk of his hair, while he covered my top and bottom lips with tiny kisses that each felt like a thousand little bursts of flame on my skin. He planted soft kisses in the corners of my mouth, and sighed at the excess of it all.

I could feel the blood start to leave me when once again, his lips pressed against mine with a firmness and a conviction like I had never experienced in him before. I pulled him towards me even as I leaned down, the urge to never break contact with his mouth blocking out anything that might argue to the contrary.

But I couldn't block out the strength of the divine. With a ragged cry, as though it physically hurt him to do so, Robert tore his mouth away from mine, his hands curled into strong knotted fists at his sides, his breathing erratic, his chest rising and falling like a stormy sea that mimicked my own.

"Why?" I breathed, gasping for air that didn't seem like enough, that couldn't fill that need I knew only he could. "Why did you stop?"

He turned away from me, his mouth pulled tight with a pained expression. *You know why.*

I grunted. "I only know what you want to tell me. There's more to this than you're letting on, Robert."

His gaze returned to mine and I could see the physical pain in his eyes now. I felt the sudden ache in me as I recalled the last time I had seen such agony in his face, and felt more confused than ever before. "You're not…going to die if you kiss me…are you?"

I breathed a sigh of relief when he snorted, a good sign during awkward moments like this. "Well then tell me what is wrong with the two of us doing something as simple as making out?" I grimaced at the sound of my voice saying those last two words. How cheesy it sounded. Making out was something you did with a part-time prom date.

Robert was my soul mate. He was the other part of me. There was just no getting around it, and I had cheapened it with that make out comment. I placed my head in my hands and groaned. "Ugh, I'm such an idiot."

Don't be embarrassed, Grace. It was insightful. It tells me that you're thinking about us in ways that go beyond just dating.

32

My head snapped back up. "What are we, Robert? What are we besides just dating? Soul mates don't just sit and search each other's minds all day, you know."

Don't you think I'm aware of this, Grace? I look at you and I see all the things I want for us. But there are limitations to what we have, what we are. You're human. You cannot begin to understand the complexities that are involved when humans and angels are together.

I felt my eyes lower into slits as I looked at him. "While you know it all." It sounded spiteful. It sounded jealous. It was how I felt.

I know enough, Grace, but don't make assumptions based on what little of my past has been revealed to you. You're the only person I have ever felt a physical and mental connection with. You're the only person I have ever felt.

I wanted to believe him. I wanted to trust that what he was saying was the truth, but knowing that he could bend the truth just a little bit-

I will never lie to you again, Grace. I won't do that to us, not again.

My eyes rose to meet his, and I felt the scars where my heart had mended itself after the only lie Robert had ever told me had destroyed it start to burn. He had lied to me when he couldn't, and was now promising never to lie again now that he could. I shook my head at the absurdity of it all.

"Okay, you won't lie to me again. So tell me now, what are the complexities involved between human and angels who love each other? Why is it that we're here together, and you want to treat me like my name is Hannah and you're Grandpa Bob?

He started to laugh, which grated at what little self-control I was holding onto. *I wouldn't kiss Hannah, Grace. Period. I would never look at Hannah the way I look at you, either. You make me question every experience I have ever felt through anyone else, because with you, it feels like I captured a star in the palm of my hand that's ready to explode, and the intensity of it has filled up every single part of me so much so, I feel as though I might burst before it does.*

When I touch you, I feel it to the very bones beneath my skin. He brushed my temple with an extended finger, the faint contact enough to feel the charge that flowed between us, confirming what he had just described.

I reached for his hand, and brought his palm to my mouth to kiss the longest line that ran down to the crease in his wrist. "I don't know how we're going to get through this if we both feel the same way about each other but one of us isn't willing to be close," I mumbled against his palm.

His arms encircled me once again, and I settled into them, feeling too tired to argue anymore. We were together, and we both knew that we affected the other profoundly. He hadn't answered my question, but if I had doubted how he felt when it came to me, it was long gone. I would get my answer. I could wait for it, if I needed to.

I closed my eyes and started to drift off to sleep, content to know that even unconscious, Robert was still with me, occupying my dreams. I fell asleep within minutes, but the sleep of the content never prepares you to be rudely awakened by a hand that was far less gentle when it was urgent than when it wasn't.

"Mmm…what?" I mumbled, rubbing my eyes and my mouth, the slight moisture that had collected in the corner cause for some embarrassment.

Graham came in here. He wanted to talk to you about my sister, but when he saw us, he left. I don't think he will say anything to your father, but his head is full of questions that he shouldn't be thinking about you. Robert's body was tense, his hold on me firm and protective.

I tried to digest what he had just told me, but it didn't seem right. Why would Graham come to my room in the middle of the night?

I told you, he wanted to talk about Lark.

I couldn't stop the small smile that formed on my face. I tucked my lips between my teeth to fight them from pulling into a full blown grin, and focused on what it was that Graham might have thought after seeing Robert asleep with me in my room.

You know what he was thinking.

I stared at him, my lids still heavy with sleep, and shook my head. I didn't know. I might know Graham better than anyone else, but if there was one thing these past few months have proven it's that I didn't know him as well as I had thought.

He thinks that you and I...

"What? He thinks that you and I what?" I managed to croak out.

He thinks that we're having sex.

I looked at Robert and felt the laughter start to ripple through me. It was soft, nearly silent, but it was there, and it was irking Robert, which suited me just fine. I wasn't interested in making him feel better about what had just happened, and what Graham had assumed was going on between the two of us.

What did it matter?

It matters to me. It's insulting to think that we'd behave in such a manner. You, and everything about you is paramount to me, Grace, and that includes your reputation.

I rolled my eyes at that. "What do you think he's going to do? Run around school and tell everyone that I'm sleeping with you? It's already difficult for most people to believe that you're even interested in me, let alone sleeping with me.

"And that's all this is between us, anyway. Just sleeping, because it takes a feat of superhuman strength just to get you to kiss me." I rolled over and turned my back to him, the conversation and the fact that he felt so insulted by the thought of people thinking that he wanted to be with me turning the blood in my veins to ice.

Grace, please stop jumping to conclusions. This is difficult for me to talk about. I've never had to before.

I snorted at that. "You've been around for over a thousand years, and you've never had to talk about your sex life? Give me a little credit, please, Robert."

I felt a swift movement behind me and fell onto my back, suddenly finding myself pinned beneath a very angry angel.

I give you all the credit in the world, Grace, but sometimes you have no idea how foolish you can be. I've never had to discuss this before because there's never been anything to discuss. I cannot believe that I have to discuss this with you now, like this, but so be it.

I have had many, many women and girls in my life. But I have never, ever been with them in the way that I hope to someday be with you. I have never felt this way about anyone, in fifteen hundred years of existing among your kind. I have never wanted anyone as much as I want you. But I have waited this long, and I can wait just as long for it to be right between us, to be safe between us.

There are some things in life you expect to hear, know that you'll hear, and know exactly how you'll feel when you do. Then there are moments like this, where what you hear is exactly the opposite of what you expected, and exactly the opposite of what you're prepared for.

"I...don't understand. Ameila said-"

My mother told you something that was only half true. I have been with many women and girls. But not in the way that you think. I've shared...thoughts with them, dreams of desires. But it has never been...physical, and never anything near as desperate as what I want with you.

The soft glow of light that surrounded Robert had changed from a muted black to a nearly brilliant blue as he saw the thought process in my mind run through the logical conclusions that were left to be made.

"So you're..."

A virgin? Yes. Just as you are.

I knew my mouth was hanging open in surprise; I knew that my eyes were wide with the full impact of this new fact about him. But the way my heart was pounding in my chest made it quite clear that there couldn't have been anything he could have told me at that moment that would have made me happier.

"Is that why you're treating me like some kind of nun?"

It is part of the reason. There's more, but I think I've done enough sharing for one night, Grace. I want you to think about what I have told you. I want you to truly think about it, and try to see why it is I am taking this as slowly as possible. With a swiftness that whipped my hair around my face and drew forth a quick gasp from my throat, we had reversed positions, and I was now atop him.

Sleep, Grace. I want you to think about all of this while you sleep.

"I'm not a child, Robert. I don't need to be told when to go to bed," I complained, refusing to lay my head down.

He placed a strong hand at the back of my head and gently, albeit forcefully, pressed my head down onto his chest. *Please. I'm sorry about what I said. We can discuss all of this later. Go to sleep, Grace. I'll be here in the morning when you wake up.*

The lull of sleep felt strangely appealing, and I closed my eyes in defeat. "Cheater," I mumbled, knowing that it had nothing to do with genuine exhaustion, but something else completely.

I love you.

"...love you, back."

SEX, TALK, AND VIDEO TAPE

I woke up on New Year's Eve feeling strangely relaxed and content. Robert's still form beneath me had a lot to do with it, but something else felt different. I looked at the morning light streaming through the window, at the dust motes that seemed to sparkle as they emerged from the shadows to dance in the sunshine, and I felt a glowing warmth spread through me, while my mouth curled up, the corners of my mouth tipping towards the peaks of my cheeks.

What's the smile for?

I looked up into Robert's silver eyes and allowed the smile full access to a grin. "I don't know, but I feel…good—like something good is about to happen."

I stretched to rid myself of the tenseness in my body—sleeping against something that felt like a metal beam could get uncomfortable after a while. I tilted my head down to check the time on the clock that was sitting on my dresser, and I groaned at the hour. "It's already eight," I complained, and rolled over towards the bedroom door. "Everyone's eating breakfast already—Graham's probably eating mine, too."

I suddenly remembered that Graham had come into the room last night. "Oh no. Graham! What must he be thinking?"

Robert's face lit up as now, after the sun had risen and the fog of sleep had cleared from my mind, I was fully aware of what had happened.

Vindicated. Robert was feeling vindicated.

"Stop gloating," I growled as I climbed out of the bed and walked to the dresser. I began pulling out the prerequisite jeans and t-shirt and stopped as something on my hand caught my attention. On the fourth finger of my right hand sat the ring that Robert had given to me for my birthday. It was meant to remind me of him while he was away, he had told me. Dark blue with a brilliant white star that was only visible when you looked at it directly, it was the most beautiful thing I had ever seen.

But today, the star was missing. "Robert…is the star supposed to disappear?"

Although I had left him lying on the bed, he was there before the question had even left my lips, my hand in his, his keen eyes scrutinizing the silver wrapped stone on my finger. *It's not supposed to…I don't understand.*

Rarely is an angel ever confused. You figure that out quite quickly after knowing one. They can read the minds of those around them, and some even have the ability to see into the future. So to see confusion on Robert's face wasn't comforting in the least.

"What?" I asked, making a mental note to pick up my thesaurus and figure out a different word to use the next time I needed to ask a question using only one word.

I don't fully understand the chemical makeup of gems, Grace, so I'm truly at a loss when it comes to explaining why the star is no longer visible. The inclusions don't just disappear, or fall out.

"The inclusions?"

Yes. It's what makes up the star. Every stone has inclusions in it, but they're usually cut away so that you don't see them in the final product. Star sapphires are unique in that the inclusions are what make them so beautiful, while in other stones, it makes them flawed. They're what the stars are comprised of. To not see any…

39

I walked over to the sunlight that now fully poured through my window and held my hand out in the warm light. The stone, while beautiful, now appeared naked—uncomfortably bare without the six-armed splendor that had represented Robert's divine nature far better than anything else ever could. What would I do now that it was gone?

The knock on my door startled me, and before I could answer, it opened, and Janice walked in, a plate balanced in one hand, and a bottle of water in the other. "Graham said you might not be feeling up to coming down for breakfast, so I brought it up to you. Are you okay?"

My head whipped to where Robert had been standing just seconds before, and felt immense relief that he had managed to disappear before Janice had walked in. It wouldn't bode well for me if two people walked in on us together.

"I'm feeling okay. I was planning on coming down in a few minutes." I pointed to my clothes that I had left on top of the dresser, and smiled apologetically.

Janice took everything in without missing a beat, and placed the plate and bottle on the nightstand next to the bed. She walked over to me and took my hand, examining the ring in the same manner as Robert had just moments earlier.

"This is a beautiful ring, Grace. I don't recall you wearing it before. When did you get this?" she asked, eyeing me suspiciously.

"Robert gave it to me for Christmas; it's his birthstone," I rambled quickly, being very careful not to let a stammer of nervousness break through.

Janice nodded her head, her lower jaw sticking out in the same way a disapproving mother's would. "At least it's on your right hand."

I giggled nervously. "Of course. It's way too early to be thinking about lifetime commitments."

I felt something tickle my ankle and I quickly lowered my eyes to the floor and choked back a gasp. Small wisps of black mist were curling around my feet. Robert hadn't left...he was hiding under my bed, and if

Janice were to look down, she's swear there was a fire beneath my mattress…

I quickly raised my eyes to hers and grinned. "So, I'll get dressed and we can talk about this downstairs?"

Janice shook her head and patted the bed. Oh-no. This didn't look good. "I think you and I need to talk about a few things, Grace."

Dammit. Damn-damn-damn that Graham and his big mouth. Damn that blond haired jock and his inability to keep his mouth shut.

"About what?" I sat down at the very edge of the bed, teetering on the verge of completely falling off both the bed and sanity.

"Grace, I know you're legally an adult now. I know that you're very responsible, but there's something that…well…gosh, this is difficult. I want to know what you know about sex."

I felt the blush rise in my cheeks, and I giggled nervously. It wasn't the giggle of an experienced eighteen year-old; I could tell that right away and, thankfully, so could Janice. "I know that I haven't had any, and I won't be having any for a while either," I answered truthfully after the nervous laughter receded.

Janice's face held a look of disbelief. "Well. I assumed that with how close you and Robert have become, especially so quickly…I'd understand if you've moved onto that stage-"

"Janice, I know what you're trying to get at, but please believe me when I say that Robert and I are taking things slowly. Very slowly. Almost too slowly." I felt the tickle around my ankle once more and wished I had a vacuum at that moment…being sucked through a HEPA filter would do him a world of good…

"Well, I think that's good, Grace. You're young, you've got a bright future ahead of you—you don't want to move too quickly on something that might only be a fleeting part of your life," Janice said, her smile sincere, as she reached for my hand.

I snatched it out of hers roughly. Her words hadn't been meant to hurt, but they did, and I didn't like the way that made me feel. "Janice, Robert isn't going anywhere, and neither am I. What we have isn't fleeting. He's going to be a permanent part of my life, just as permanent as you are in Dad's."

I saw her smile fade a little as she allowed my words to sink in. "Grace, please tell me you haven't started to think about a future with him. It's too soon!"

I swallowed down the bitterness and replied calmly, "I'm not talking about us getting married, Janice. But, I don't know…maybe in a few years that might happen. But even if it doesn't, Robert will still be a part of my life."

Janice once again reached for my hand, and this time held it firmly between hers, unwilling to allow me to pull away again. "Grace, you've got to understand that I'm only asking you about this because I care about you. Your father told me that he hadn't talked about any of this with you, and I don't want you to make any foolish and avoidable mistakes."

I understood what her reasons were, but I knew that my life wasn't meant to follow the same path that every other girl that lived in Heath's would. Robert entering my life had proved that.

I looked back at the ring on my finger and felt the need to ask the question… "Janice, what would you say if Robert said that he wanted things to be permanent between the two of us?"

Janice's face expressed a look of shock and alarm. Me and my big mouth. "Why, Grace? Are you actually considering it? Did he ask you to marry him?" Her thumb pressed the ring on my finger into my skin, and I could feel the circulation begin to cut off.

"No, Janice, he didn't ask me to marry him, but judging by your reaction, I can see that it wouldn't exactly be a good thing if he had." I knew that though my question had more to do with Robert's desire to make my life more permanent in the literal sense, she had taken it figuratively, and the ramifications were now starting to rain down on my head as she stood up and began to pace the small space between the wall housing my window and my bed.

"He's a nice boy, Grace, and I'm very glad that he's in your life, but I think this is all moving a bit too fast for you. You only just turned eighteen. You're still in high school. Who knows what will happen when the two of you graduate and head off to college.

"And what'll your dad think? You're his only daughter. He already thinks you two spend far too much time together as it is, and now with Graham here, what's Robert gonna think? What will he feel he needs to do to keep your eyes on him?"

I coughed as a bubble of laughter tried to break through. "Janice," I began, but was instantly cut off by her continued argument.

"Robert's not from here, Grace. He grew up in Europe. Ameila and I had a long conversation about his childhood. Europe has different ideas about relationships and sex. They're much more open there, much more...free. I don't want you to feel pressured into doing anything you don't want to. I know you said that you're taking things slowly, but what if he doesn't want to? What if-"

I'd had enough. She was speaking about Robert like he was some hormonally driven teenager. I wish!

"Janice, could you stop? Please?" I interrupted, upset—not at the fact that she was right, but because she was so wholly and unequivocally wrong. "Robert isn't the one wanting to rush things. *I* am. When I said that we're taking things slow, I meant that *he's* taking things slow." I stared down at the ground and saw the fading mist pull back beneath my bed. "He won't even kiss me without me putting up a fight. Sometimes it feels like he's allergic to me or something, and he doesn't want to get a rash."

Janice stared at me, stunned by my little revelation. "You..."

"Yes, me. I'm the one who's pressuring him! So you see why you have nothing to worry about?"

She nodded her head slowly, as though any quick and sudden movements would contradict the act itself. She had seen the disappointment in my eyes, and heard the rejection in my tone; she knew I wasn't just telling her this to get her off my back.

"Grace, I..."

"You don't need to worry about it, Janice. You're concerned for me. I get it. I just want you to know that there's no need to be."

I stood up to grab my clothes from off the dresser, a sign that the conversation was, as far as I was concerned, over. Janice understood and stood up, too. She walked quietly to the door and turned to face me before leaving. "Grace, if Robert wants to wait, I wouldn't doubt it's because he respects you. It's hard to find boys like that anymore...most boys are bundles of hormones wrapped up in pretty packaging. He's a miracle, Grace. I hope you realize that."

I watched as she left, closing the door behind her, and wondered whether she knew how right she was.

She has no clue.

I leaned back as Robert held me, understanding that I would need him right then. "She's right about more than just that."

I knew he was smiling. I didn't have to see his face to know. I could feel it in the way he brought me closer to his body, the way his breathing slowed down, the way he rubbed my arms and leaned his cheek against the top of my head.

"So, what time are we supposed to meet tonight?" I asked, needing the change of subject before I had to admit that he was right, too.

I have already asked Lark to drop you off at eleven.

Eleven. That was more than twelve hours away. I turned around to face him, knowing that in a few short minutes, he'd be gone. "I'm going to miss you," I whispered, and leaned my cheek against his shoulder, knowing that where he'd be going was a dark and twisted part of his life that I couldn't follow, even though a part of it always followed him home.

You are my home. Wherever you are, that's where I'm meant to be.

I smiled at the words that filled my thoughts. Feeling silly, I wiped at eyes that had started to dew up, and pushed away. "You should get going."

He nodded his head and headed towards the window while I watched his back move lithely and surely. Suddenly he was in front of me again, and his hands were on my face, his mouth on mine. It was a gentle, almost friendly kiss, but there were things happening between us that I knew would never happen with anyone else, or to anyone else. This was what miracles were. A kiss from nowhere, for no reason, that held every promise known to man.

I love you, Grace Anne Shelley.

I felt the glossy cover of my eyes finally fall down my face in ribbons of moisture. "I love you, Robert N'Uriel Bellegarde."

And then he was gone. Taking with him my heart, and my love, because what he now had to do went against everything the lifeless heart in his chest required. "Come home to me whole," I whispered as I touched my lips, hoping that this was a sign of things to come.

&#x03;

I brought my plate down to the kitchen after consuming the spinach omelet and tater tots that Janice had brought up, and cringed as the smell of burnt coffee and cold grease assailed my nostrils. I washed my plate, adding to the others that sat in the rack, and headed to the living room, surprised to find that no one was there; the blanket and pillows I had given to Graham had been put away, and Graham's backpack was nowhere to be seen.

"Graham?" I called out, half expecting him to jump out from some corner just to hear me yelp, but nothing came of my call. I walked over to the front door and turned the handle, pulling the door open to the crisp, morning air. The last morning of the year.

"Graham?" I called out again, and looked for the familiar green vehicle parked on the street. It wasn't there. "Where'd you go so early?" I asked myself aloud, and looked at the driveway fronting his house.

There was a white truck sitting there which meant that Richard was home. Following some stupid need to see if he was alright, I walked towards the house. The front door was locked. I bent down to lift the mat that sat in front of the door and grabbed the key hidden there, unlocking the door with it. The smell was even worse now than it was last night; I lifted the neck hem of my shirt above my face to block out the odor. "Mr. Hasselbeck?" I called out, my call muffled by the thin fabric.

I heard the sound of voices just beyond the entranceway, and I made my way towards the living room. The television was on, a home movie playing on the screen. I recognized it right away as Graham's tenth birthday. It had the prerequisite balloons and cake, but there had also been a very belligerent clown that taught us several new words that we had yet to learn but had a great deal of fun putting to use.

I watched the screen as ten year old Graham blew out his candles amid the cheers of everyone around him, including his mother who had been wielding the camera. I smiled as he called out my name and pulled the mousy creature that I recognized as nine year old me from the back of the crowd of kids. "You get first slice, Grace," he said cheerfully, and handed me one of the pre-sliced pieces on a character covered paper plate.

"Why did we invite Grace?" I heard whispered from behind the camera. The voice was slurred, and the way the camera shifted to the side a bit, I knew that its owner probably reeked of some alcoholic beverage or another. "She's a freak, Ivy. She doesn't belong here with the normal kids."

I recognized the voice as that of the clown, and wondered how close he was to Graham's mother to refer to her by first name. "She's Graham's best friend. He would have been miserable if she weren't here, and you know it. I don't care what other people say about her or the accident, Richard. She's a good friend to our son, and she deserves the benefit of the doubt, just like anyone else would want. Now go over there and start acting like a clown and less like a damn drunk."

I watched in muted shock as the belligerent clown suddenly appeared in front of the camera and started honking on a horn he pulled out of his pocket. "Hey-hey, kids! It's joke time! Wanna hear about the three guys who walked into the bar…"

The image started to fast forward and it was only then that I noticed Graham's father sitting on the sofa, a bottle of beer in one hand, the remote in the other. He was staring at me, no remorse or embarrassment on his face at having his opinion of me exposed like that. "What are you doing in my house, Grace?" he rasped, his eyes red and unfocused, his skin ruddy and blotched from intoxication still visible beneath the days' worth of growth that now made up a thin, salt and pepper beard.

"I came to see how you were doing, Mr. Hasselbeck," I answered truthfully.

I stepped back as he attempted to stand up, not wanting to relinquish either object in his hand and suffering from lack of coordination as a result. "You're a liar," he slurred, stumbling as he finally got to his feet.

I shook my head in denial, and continued to back away from him, his steps becoming surer, if not more determined. "I saw you were home. I wanted to make sure you were okay."

His hand flew out at me, the beer bottle that was in it whizzing past my face, and I cringed as I heard it shatter behind me as it hit the wall. "Get out of my house, you freak!"

I turned around and ran outside, stopping only when I heard the door slam shut behind me. I turned around again, shaking slightly from the entire episode. I had never known just how bad Graham's dad's drinking had been, or how long it had been going on. The video took it back at least eight years, but you don't get that way overnight.

I walked over to the steps in front of my house and sat down to wait for Graham's return. There was so much that he had gone through that he hadn't shared with me, and I was confused as to why. Was it pride? He couldn't have thought that I'd judge him based on his father's drinking, could he? Not Grace the Freak?

The afternoon sun was beginning to remind me of what spring held in store for us when he finally showed up. I waited as he parked the car and exited, taking a long look at the house that held his drunken father, and then finally walk over to me. "Hey Grace! The sun's out, pretty nice, huh? What are you doing outside?"

I motioned towards his house with my head and frowned. "I went over to see how your dad was doing. He's watching home movies and drinking. I don't think he likes me very much right now...or ever."

A nervous laugh that seemed to startle him came out of his mouth as he ran his fingers through his hair—he did that a lot, I noticed. "It's the alcohol talking, Grace. You know he loves you."

I shook my head at the obvious lie. "What I heard wasn't love. He called me a freak; he was right."

Graham's remorseful tone suddenly turned angry and my mind quickly jumped to his reaction when I had told him that I was in love with him. It had been such a quick turnaround, a nearly 180 degree reversal of emotions, and I had been shocked by it. This second time caused me to worry instead.

"Grace, you need to stop selling yourself short. You're not a freak. You're just a girl who happens to not be like everyone else in a way that people can see. I don't think you're a freak, and I definitely don't think Stacy, or Lark think so either," Graham grumbled, his voice rough with the anger that flashed in his eyes.

"Graham, why didn't you tell me about your dad? Why didn't you tell me about the drinking?"

I watched the dark ring of his irises thin out as his pupils widened, nearly swallowing the color completely in its blackness. "I didn't tell you because I was ashamed of him. I didn't want you to know, didn't want you to think of me the same way that I…"

I nodded my head, understanding. He didn't want me to think of him in the same way that he had thought of me…with pity. I rubbed the top of his spikes with my hand, needing to lighten up the mood a little. "Well, it doesn't matter anymore. We're going to get through this together now. You don't have to go through this alone."

He looked at me with confusion in his eyes, and pain surrounding his mouth. "Why are you just letting this go?"

I shrugged my shoulders and let out the breath that I had been holding in. "Because you're my best friend. You helped me through some of the toughest times in my life because you wanted to. I want to help you now, because I want to. No other reason."

48

Graham's eyes traveled towards the ground, and I could see his face twist up with some kind of unseen pain. "I also caused them. After what I did...to know that you'd still want to help me out...you're the kind of person I should have been happy to be with, Grace. I should have seen what you had to offer to an idiot like me and jumped at the chance. Instead, I acted like a jerk and hurt you in the process. I don't deserve your friendship..."

My head bounced in agreement as I replied jokingly, "You're right, you don't. But I'm giving it to you anyway because I'm stupid and I love you."

I saw him tense up again, and for a second, felt like I had once again tied the noose around my neck and felt the trap door open beneath my feet. Only this time, the door didn't open all the way.

"Grace, I gotta tell you something."

"O-kay," I said hesitantly.

He took a deep breath, his lips mouthing the words as though rehearsing what he'd say before the sounds actually came out. "I went into your room last night. I saw...I saw Robert in the bed with you."

So this was it. This was the moment that I had been waiting for, that Robert had warned me about, and yet, he seemed far more uncomfortable than I felt. "Okay..."

"I...I left as soon as I saw the two of you, but...are you, you know..."

I smiled at him, enjoying his discomfort far more than I should. "No. We're not."

A sigh of relief blew out of him in a large puff, and I couldn't help but laugh at the ridiculous expression on his face. His face grew beet red and I laughed harder, unable to contain the humor that I found in the situation.

"Well, I'm glad you can find something funny in this. I feel like a peeping Tom," he muttered, his thumbs burrowing into his temples as he fidgeted, a method of distraction to avoid having to look at me.

I grabbed his left hand and yanked it down, forcing him to look at me. "Graham, it's okay. You didn't see anything you weren't supposed to. Next time, though, could you at least knock?"

Shyly, he nodded his head, and turned away again. "So, why was he in your room anyway? How'd he get in?"

Now it was my turn to turn away, which I should have realized would only intrigue him and pique his curiosity. "He comes in through my window because he helps me sleep."

I had feared that the one sentence answer wouldn't be enough to quell his need for answers, but he sensed how uneasy I was with discussing the topic, despite the innocent nature of Robert's visits to my room, and he stopped. He reached for my hand and squeezed it. "I won't tell your dad."

And that was it. I didn't have to ask, and he didn't have to give it, but with those five words, he had given me a sense of security that I knew I'd never find with anyone else.

I nodded my head, and we sat there for the next few minutes, content with the secret shared between us, a new one to help cement our friendship once again, only stronger this time.

FASHIONABLY LATE

After lunch, Graham had gone back to his house to gather a few more things and speak to his father. He made me promise to stay home, no matter what I heard, and so I did. The silence that filled the house, with me and Janice staring at each other, waiting for Graham to return, could have suffocated a stadium full of people.

Janice kept looking towards the clock on the stove, while I kept flicking my eyes in the direction of the clock on the microwave. We took turns counting down the minutes, each one stretching out longer and longer until I felt I would scream if I had to listen to another sixty-second countdown.

Finally the kitchen door opened and Graham walked in, a duffel bag on his shoulder and another bag in his hand. His face was blotchy, his eyes red and puffy. I reached for the bag in his hand, while Janice helped him lower the duffel onto the kitchen floor.

"What happened, Graham?" Janice asked as she pulled out a chair for him to sit down in. His heavy form landed roughly in the seat, and I felt every ounce of hurt that weighed him down.

"It looks like I didn't need to tell him that I was going to stay here. He threw me out."

I heard my gasp before I knew I had even let one out. "But why?"

Graham's shoulders shrugged, his head heavy with disappointment. "Does it matter? I want you to know that I'm going to pay for my meals and for use of the couch, Janice," he said, gazing up at her with a half-smile looking very out of place with his stark eyes and ruddy cheeks.

I raised an eyebrow at him, the question unspoken on my lips. His half-smile grew into a full blown grin as he continued, "I got a job at the movie theater today. That's where I went this morning. I applied and they interviewed and hired me on the spot. Apparently I'm exactly the kind of guy who belongs taking tickets at the twelve-plex."

Janice reached out and hugged him, her voice sounding thrilled and hopeful as she congratulated him. "I think that's wonderful, Graham. But please don't worry about paying us for anything. You save that money for school."

The look on my face must have resembled one my father would have probably given under the circumstances, because when Janice looked at me, she burst out into hysterical laughter that grew infectious as Graham began to laugh as well. "Well, you know Dad will ask why can't Graham pay for food. He does eat more than the three of us combined, you included, Janice," I complained, my arms folding across my chest at their continued outburst.

It took nearly ten minutes before the two of them calmed down. Looking for a change of subject that wouldn't turn them into hyenas again, I asked them what their plans were for New Years. Janice patted her belly and sighed. "Unfortunately, heartburn and swollen ankles have made it nearly impossible for me to enjoy going out and dancing, so I'll be staying at home with your father and watching the ball drop on television."

I looked over at Graham and he smiled sheepishly. "What?"

"I saw Lark at the mall and she invited me over to her house to watch the ball drop with her and Stacy."

Now *this* was a surprise! "You're going to spend New Year's Eve with Stacy?" I asked incredulously, the image of a strangled Graham suddenly filling my head.

"And Lark."

I nodded. Of course. Stacy was the buffer. He was playing it safe, and what better way to do so than with the female bodyguard?

"Lark told me that Robert had some special plans for the two of you," he teased, pleased with the blush that bloomed across my cheeks.

"Yes, although I don't exactly know what it is that he's got planned. I told him to surprise me, and so he's going to. He's quite literal in that sense, I suppose."

"How romantic," Janice cooed, ignoring my rolling eyes and grunt of disapproval, especially after the conversation we'd had earlier that morning. "It's a lovely way to start the New Year off."

A sudden wave of panic filled me then as I remembered that Robert had told me that Lark would be picking me up. If Graham was at her house, how exactly would this work? And was he serious about me still wearing the green dress I had worn to the wedding?

"Grace?"

I looked at Janice's face and she cocked her head to the side, confusion covering her face as she saw the panic in mine. "What's wrong, Grace?"

I took a few deep breaths to calm myself and managed to somehow squeeze a small smile onto my lips. "Nothing. I just remembered that I had a few things I needed to get done before I start getting ready."

I turned to face Graham and said through my false smile, "If you want to take a shower before you head to Lark's house, I suggest you do that now. I'm going to be in there a while."

There are some faces that guys have reserved just for women's eyes. Graham made one of them at that moment. Perhaps it was the first time he tried it out, because it looked new—amateurish. It spoke clearly of how he did not want to know any details involving my bathroom activities. I probably should have been pleased that the idea of my taking a shower grossed him out to such an extent, but in truth, I felt offended.

I was, after all, still a girl with *some* pride.

As Graham went to gather his stuff, I went upstairs to my room to hunt down the items that Robert had requested I wear. After our first date, I had thrown the dress and all of the accessories that he'd purchased for me to wear at him, too upset with his behavior afterwards to treat them properly.

That was the first night he had spent in my room, and I had woken up to find that he had put everything away neatly, organized in ways Janice could have only dreamed of accomplishing. I didn't ask him where everything had been placed. I was content with the knowledge that I wouldn't have to put them away myself; I was so lazy when it came to cleaning my room that I was content to leave my closet looking like a war zone and my bed looking like a tornado had hit it.

After eliminating the obvious locations for the dress, shoes, and undergarments, I was left hunting for the amber earrings and necklace that he'd bought to compliment the stones that adorned the front of the dress. I found them in a box hidden in my underwear drawer, along with the dragonfly clips that he'd purchased that day as well.

I felt the blush that had spread across my cheeks earlier start to burn my skin again as I realized that Robert had gone through my underwear in order to place the box in there. "So much for innocent," I mumbled to myself, a secret smile causing the corners of my mouth to curl upward.

"Oh no," I gasped as I opened the zipper to the garment bag that contained the moss green dress. I hadn't realized the damage that climbing the gate to Robert's home had caused to the dress as I took in the torn chiffon and stained satin staring back at me, the sorry casualty of my own recklessness. The largest gems that were supposed to sit on the bodice of the dress were missing. "Oh dear bananas, it's ruined," I moaned.

I glanced at the clock and saw that it was only five. I had several hours before Lark was supposed to arrive, but what was I going to do about the dress? I could fix holes, sew a rudimentary blanket, but fix a dress that probably cost more than I made in a month of working at the library?

Well, there was nothing for it. Robert entered my life when I was wearing jeans and a t-shirt and had found that quite acceptable. He'd even kept that chili-stained t-shirt, for goodness sakes! I quickly went to my t-shirt drawer and pulled out one of the shirts he had given to me for Christmas.

"At least I'll be comfortable," I told myself, and laid the shirt on the dresser. A pair of jeans and my sneakers would complete the outfit. As much as I wanted to be normal Grace, instead of Grace the Freak, it didn't seem right that I start out the New Year dressed as someone else.

Ω

After a simple dinner of soup and cold turkey sandwiches, I felt the need to take a nap. I woke up a few minutes before ten, and rushed to take a shower. I threw my clothes on with very little care and felt very thankful indeed that I had decided on dressing normally. It had taken nearly an hour to get dressed for the wedding, and that had been with Janice's help.

Grabbing a jacket from my closet, I went to the window to wait for my "ride"; I leaned out and saw that Graham's car was gone, which meant he was already at Lark and Robert's house. What would he think when Lark stepped away for a while and left him alone with Stacy?

He'll think I'm being cruel and horribly unusual.

The hand that held onto my shoulder with a vise-like grip was the only thing that kept me from toppling out onto the walkway beneath me. The thought in my head had been just as startling as it would have had I heard it through my ears.

"Don't do that!" I hissed, more embarrassed than frightened, although my heartbeat argued to the contrary. "I cannot believe you invited Graham over tonight and then left him alone with Stacy. Do you think they'll be alive when you get back?"

She shrugged her shoulders and winked. "One of them will."

I shook my head and then looked at her more carefully. "How did you get in here?"

She pointed behind her and I saw my open door. "I came in through the door. What? Was I supposed to climb through your window, Rapunzel?"

My jaw lowered in surprise. "I thought you'd…you know, mist in or something. Like Robert does."

She rolled her eyes at me, the movement oddly graceful. "Please. Tonight is the one night in the year when everyone will be looking at the sky; I came on foot. Thank goodness you're wearing jeans and not a dress like my idiot brother wanted. He's *such* a guy."

I giggled at that little jab at her brother. As angelic as he might be, as dark as he might be, it was true. "Well, even if I had wanted to, I couldn't have worn the dress. It's completely ruined."

Lark looked at me quizzically and nodded her head. Her eyes flicked over to the closet, where the dress was hanging up, and sighed in disappointment. *It was a beautiful dress. Robert didn't tell you, but I helped him pick it out. He wasn't sure about the color, or the cut, but he knew you'd look good in green. Like I said, he's such a guy. He's got impeccable taste in jewelry, but clothes? Uh-uh. He should stick to dressing himself. That's his forte.*

I smiled at that, relieved that he hadn't chosen the items himself, especially the corset that had sent up warning flags of disapproval in Janice.

Yeah, I told him that would be a mistake. He said I needed to get everything you'd need for a dress like that, and it didn't matter what, as long as it made you feel beautiful.

The flush that spread across my face, accompanied by the wistful smile that grew on my lips spoke more than words could have that I felt beautiful because of Robert, and not because of some expensive piece of clothing, or jewelry. He saw me in a way that no one else ever had. To be thought of as beautiful—by someone who was far more beautiful than was humanly possible—was an incredible and heady feeling. To know that it wasn't something he was saying because he wanted something from me made it my own little miracle.

Well, let's go, shall we? I can only leave Graham and Stacy alone for so long before I fear they'll destroy my house.

I walked over to the window and waited for her to follow me.

Didn't you hear me? Everyone and their grandmother will be looking up at the sky tonight. Even with mist surrounding us, we'd still be highly conspicuous. We're going on foot tonight.

She grabbed my hand and yanked me onto her back. *Hold on very tightly. I will be moving very quickly. Keep your eyes closed, and don't make a sound.*

I nodded my head and wrapped my legs around her waist. She held my arms around her neck and before I had a chance to blink, we were outside of my house.

"Holy-"

I said don't make a sound. The thought came like a hiss in my head, and I cringed at the slight and unexpected sting that the sound caused in my mind. It was a familiar pain, but that did little to comfort me when I couldn't even rub my head to make the pain go away.

I'm sorry. I just don't like this method of traveling. It's far too primitive, and I'm not very good at it. I'll try not to get you scratched by anything, but please, no more talking.

I nodded my head once again, wincing as I braced myself for the thought-lashing I feared I'd get just for moving. Instead, I felt her body shake with laughter. She started moving again, and I did everything she told me to do, keeping my eyes closed until she told me it was time to let go.

Only then did I realize how sore my face was, or how my hair didn't seem to move when I moved my head. I raised my hand to the top of my head and gasped. "What happened to my hair?"

The wind had whipped my hair up into a massive mound of tangles and debris, leaves and dirt were caked between the strands. Now I know what the front end of a car felt like while traveling down the freeway. "Are there bugs in my hair?" I asked frantically, my hands weaving through the tangles, pulling and yanking at the knots, hoping that nothing that fell out had more legs than I did.

Lark's laughter echoed around me, and she doubled over from the force of it, my obvious discomfort and disheveled appearance being quite amusing to her. "You look so ridiculous right now."

Using my fingers, I tried desperately to comb my hair in hopes that it'd be somewhat presentable by the time Robert arrived.

"Oh cut it out, Grace. He won't care if you look like a Princess or a matted sheep dog. He only cares that you're safe, which you are, thanks to me. And now, I have to get back to my house before Graham starts to wonder where I'm at." Lark held her hand out to my hair and touched it lightly, dirt and leaves falling down around me. "There, all fixed. Now, Robert said he'd be here as soon as he could. Have a great time, and I'll see you next year."

I didn't have enough time to get a thank-you out before she was gone.

I turned around to look at the empty gazebo, the floor covered in leaves and slush. There was nowhere to sit in the gazebo, so I leaned against the railing and waited in the cold.

The jacket I had chosen to wear had no lining and I instantly regretted grabbing it while I watched with growing distress as tiny white specks started to fall from the sky.

"Just great," I muttered, tucking my hands underneath my armpits, and silently wishing that I had remembered to grab some gloves. The weather was turning bitter, the wind whipping up in angry howls with each passing minute, and I knew that it wouldn't be long before the sprinkling of snow turned into an all-out downpour of white.

"Where are you, Robert?" I asked out loud, knowing that no one was going to answer me, but needing to hear a sound other than the whistling of the wind through the branches, and the pattering of falling twigs and leaves as they landed on the roof of the gazebo.

The chill in the air turned my breath into white puffs of vapor, and my teeth began to click against each other as I fought the chattering that threatened to turn my entire body into a human jackhammer.

I knew midnight had come and gone by the colorful spangles and bursts of light in the sky that announced the end of one year, and the beginning of another. I felt my heart sink into my sneakers as the colors began to fade, the loud crackling and popping dwindled, and the smell of gunpowder finally drifted away while only the clean smell of snow and green remained.

"Well, there goes that idea," I muttered to myself, and slowly eased my frigid bones into motion. The lights that usually kept the gravel parking lot lit had not had their bulbs replaced since that last night I had been here alone nearly a month ago.

As I walked past them, the crunch of my sneakers against the gravel triggered the sharp memories of slamming into them to flash into my mind. I flinched at each sickening crunch, the sounds reminding me of the pain that had been inflicted on me by a jealous and ambitious angel—everything angels weren't supposed to be. I quickened my pace, desiring only to plant my feet on solid pavement for the long walk home.

By the time I reached the road, I could feel the sweat forming on my brow. "Some New Year," I snorted. At least last year, I was in the comfort of my own home, drinking flat soda and eating stale cheese balls from Christmas.

The wind was picking up and freezing the moisture that had started to pool on my face. I was going to catch one hell of a cold after tonight if I didn't freeze to death before I got home. I looked up into the sky to see how long the weather was going to hold up. I couldn't see the stars anymore.

"Just keep walking," I told myself, repeating it every ten paces or so, needing the sound, needing the reminder as each minute that dragged on left me feeling more and more exhausted. The cold was draining me of what little energy I had left.

Finally, I succumbed to the numbness in my feet and sank to the ground on the side of the road. My sweat and the cold had plastered my shirt to my skin, freezing it in place; the fact that I could no longer feel my toes moving was a very bad omen, and I silently cursed myself for not being better prepared...and thankful that I had not worn the dress after all.

"I'm going to kill you, Robert," I breathed before the shivering that started to creep up from my knees finally overtook my mouth, my teeth chattering like a hyperactive typewriter.

"Don't sleep, don't sleep, don't sleep," I chanted to myself. Robert was on his way—he had to be—and he'd find me. But if I froze to death, there wasn't going to be anything that he could do about it, and there was no way I'd let him off the hook for standing me up that easily.

I tucked my stiff legs up to my chest, and wrapped my arms around them, rocking to keep my body in motion. I tried to think of a song I could sing to keep my mind from drifting off, pulling my consciousness with it, but the cold was dimming my thoughts to everything.

"H-how l-l-ou-ousy t-to d-die f-f-from e-exp-p-p-posure, a-after s-su-survi-ving b-being h-h-hit b-by a c-c-car a-an-and s-st-stran-g-g-gled b-b-by a-a-an a-angel," I stuttered, each syllable wracking my body with violent shaking.

I knew I was hallucinating when the numbness turned into fierce pain in my hands and my feet. The cold was supposed to lull you to sleep, the numbness was supposed to be a soft lullaby that rocks you gently towards a frozen death. The pain—that's a sick joke on the part of your mind, I had deduced, and when it finally started to abate, I relaxed and welcomed whatever came next.

How could you give up on me so easily?

Definitely hallucinating.

You're not hallucinating, Grace. Open your eyes, please.

I shook my head. I didn't want to, didn't think I could.

I am such a terrible boyfriend. All of the powers I have, and you still end up with your life in danger.

I nodded my head this time, "A-a-and you always e-e-end up sa-saving me in the end. I-I think you d-d-do it on p-p-pu-purpose to keep things exciting—t-t-to m-muh-make yourself out to b-b-be the he-hero."

I felt his body stiffen, even as the warmth spread through me and the ebbing pain turned into intense tingling through my fingers and toes. "Oh dear bananas," I groaned as the sensation started to creep up my limbs, causing them to jerk around like suffocating fish on land.

I'm sorry, Grace. I didn't expect to take this long, and you almost…this shouldn't have happened.

I grunted in agreement. It shouldn't have happened, but it did. "You came, and I'm okay—I *am* okay, aren't I?" I waited for his nod before I continued, "Well, I'm okay, and you can now make up for being late."

It's a good thing that my legs were no longer numb, because I felt the ground coming a lot sooner than I had expected when Robert set me down with a roughness that I hadn't thought him capable of…not with me, at least.

"Why aren't you angry? Do you value yourself so little that you'd simply be okay with nearly freezing to death just because I'm the one who let it happen?"

I finally had the courage to look up into his face, and what I saw there was like staring into a block of ice; his eyes were flat and cold, colder than I had ever seen them before, and I felt the shiver run straight through me. He was angry.

"I was angry, but I'm not anymore. It's not like you did it on purpose. This is a part of who you are. I accept that part of you; I accept the risk and the consequences because loving you is worth it to me. Why are *you* so angry?"

He stalked away from me; I saw then that his wings were out, and I couldn't help but draw in a breath as I marveled at their delicate and yet powerful beauty. He was putting out a deep, red glow as his wings shook with his frustration at something I could not touch on. I reached my hand out to him, but he flinched away without even turning around to see me approach.

"This wouldn't happen if you would agree to being changed."

My hand dropped to my side, my mouth hung open in surprise, and my eyes grew wide with shock. He was angry with me because I turned down his offer to change me?

"Are you serious? You left me here waiting—nearly freezing to death in the process—and you're upset because I want to remain human? *That's* what's bothering you?" My mind raced through all of the different reasons why he'd be so angry, but there was nothing I could come up with. This was all too ridiculous for it to make sense. Unless…

"*Did* you leave me here on purpose? To prove a point?"

He whipped around to face me, his eyes wide with shock, the grim line on his face replaced with a snarl. "How could you think that I'd intentionally cause you harm?"

I shrugged my shoulders, trying my best not to show my fear and guilt at his reaction or my accusation. "What else am I supposed to think? I mean, you even told me to wear the green dress! If I had, I would have been frozen to death by the time you got here, Robert."

Robert shook his head. "I would have felt it coming."

"Felt what?"

His eyes grew sad as he turned away before finally answering, his voice soft with sadness. "I would have felt you dying."

"Oh." I kicked a rock that sat next to my sneaker and watched it fly out into the road. "Well, isn't that what you're supposed to feel? You are Death, after all."

I saw his head shake, and his thoughts came into my head. He didn't want to talk anymore.

You're a part of me, Grace; I told you. When you're in pain, I am as well. When others are dying, I hear the call in my mind; but…when you're close to death…it feels like something is being torn out from inside of me. You told me that your heart was mine. You don't know how right you were when you said that.

I felt ashamed when he turned to look at me again and there were crystal tears pooled in his eyes. Death was always on his mind, but mine was tugging at his heart, just as he being away from me tugged at mine. "I'm sorry. I shouldn't have said what I did. You wouldn't knowingly put me in danger, for any reason, and I should have known better."

He smiled for me, a genuine, brilliant, and beautiful smile, and I felt the residual chill leave my body as he reached his hand out to me. I took it—grabbed for it and clutched it for dear life is more like it—and allowed him to pull me into the shelter of his arms as the flutter of snow that had begun falling all around us when our argument began started to literally dump down on us.

And then we were up in the air, sailing back towards the gazebo. It was covered in snow and debris now, the railings bearing huge icicles that had not been there when I left. "Why did you bring me back here?" I asked, the location not holding as much interest for me as it had a few hours ago.

I had the whole thing planned, an event all set up and everything was pushed back, but I still want to get to the most important part.

I looked at him with a plainly confused expression on my face. What was so important that he couldn't have waited until we were someplace warm…and dry?

I watched, amused as kicked aside snow and leaves to clear a spot for whatever it was that he had planned. I folded my arms across my chest, the loss of his body pulling away my only source of warmth.

"Okay, I want to do this properly, so please bear with me," Robert said with a grin on his face, and I watched in absolute horror as he knelt down in the small circle that he had cleared in front of me.

"Oh goodness, no, Robert. Please don't do what I think you're going to do," I spit out quickly, hoping the words didn't jumble themselves together with the speed I had uttered them, the sound of Janice's voice droning away in the back of my head.

He waved my plea off with his hand, and then grabbed one of mine. "Grace Anne Shelley, I should have done this first. I didn't, and that speaks of poor manners that I assure you my mother has already chastised me for several times.

"It's probably redundant, but this has to be done right so that you know that my feelings for you are nothing if not genuine. I wanted to ask you if you'd allow me the privilege of courting you."

"I-" I was at a loss for words. This was unexpected. I had overreacted. And he knew it, too. He was enjoying my discomfort and embarrassment, but more than that, he was worried that I'd say no. I could see it in his eyes. He was afraid that after tonight, I might not want to continue our relationship.

I simply nodded my head, words failing me as I was overcome with emotion. He pulled me back into his arms and chuckled. "You're silly," he sighed as he kissed the top of my head.

I giggled. "I'm also freakishly abnormal. Every girl in Heath would give their right eye to have you get on one knee and propose to them, but not me. No, instead I freak out."

I felt him shake his head, and he pulled me away from him so he could look into my face as he spoke. "Grace, you're not abnormal, but you're not normal either. What you are is extraordinary."

I couldn't help but grin when he said that. Who else had ever called me extraordinary? "Can I ask you why you needed to ask me? I mean, I thought it was a given that we were dating. Why the need for such formality?"

He brought the hand that he was still holding to his lips, and kissed my fingertips, smiling as he did so. "I did so many things wrong when it came to you. I thought that if we started the year in the same vein, things would just become more difficult."

The tingling sensation that slowly crept up my arm, easing its way towards my heart, and kick-starting it into overdrive left very little room for coherent thoughts. I watched as he continued to kiss the tips of my fingers, the heat coursing in my veins hot enough to melt the snow around me, I was certain of it.

"I should get you home," he laughed as he took notice of my heavy breathing, and scooped me up into his arms. I locked my fingers behind his head and brought my face up to his, hoping, praying that for just this once, he wouldn't reject my kiss.

He didn't.

64

MISS MARJORIE MAY MULLIGAN

It wasn't until I was safely in my bed, tucked against Robert's chest, my feet smothered by my comforter, that Robert explained what had kept him away for so long. He had never talked about whose deaths required his personal attention before, and so I knew that whoever it was that left this world this evening was someone of great significance. Significant enough for him to tell me, anyway.

I don't want you to hate me, Grace, he had begun, his face searching mine for any sign of rejection.

I grabbed a hold of his face and stared into his eyes as deeply as any human possibly could. "I cannot hate you, Robert. I love you. You can tell me anything."

I know. I just needed some reassurance, I suppose. Tonight I helped the librarian you had worked with to cross over.

I hadn't expected the sob that spilled out of me, but when it came, I didn't try to hold it back either. "Miss Maggie? Oh no, what happened?"

Robert took my hand in his and weaved his fingers between mine. *She had cancer. She's been bedridden for months now, Grace. I thought you knew.*

I shook my head, because obviously I had no idea. "I don't understand. She seemed healthy the last time I saw her."

Robert's eyes narrowed as he thought over my last statement. *Grace, you didn't hear me. She's been bedridden for months. You couldn't have seen her.*

I sat up, the thought that he was questioning what it was that I had seen not sitting well with me. "I worked with her all summer, Robert. I saw her just a few weeks ago. She was perfectly fine."

Robert lifted his body towards mine and pressed his forehead against my own. I could feel him searching in my mind for the memories that I knew were there, and when he found them, it was though I could *feel* his disbelief.

I don't understand it. Your mind is clear of any deceit, but I also know what I saw in her mind. She's been unable to leave her bed since the end of May. There's no logical explanation for this.

The fact that Robert was stumped was enough to send the fear rippling down my back. "What do you mean, there's no logical explanation for this?"

What you saw was a very real person, Grace. You really saw Miss Maggie. The imprinted memory doesn't lie, but her memory, though foggy from pain and medication was just as clear. Perhaps what you saw was an astral projection, and she just had no recollection of it. The pain medication can do that to the human mind.

I looked at him, confused, skeptical, and still fearful. "Astral projection? Does that even exist?"

Robert pointed to his face and allowed a half-smile to breach the hard planes of his face. *Did you think my kind existed before you met me?* When I shook my head, his half-smile returned to a grim line. *Astral projection is real, although very rare. But that wouldn't explain what your mind saw. Astral projections are not material. They cannot hold onto physical objects, let alone replace them onto bookshelves.*

"Could it be that *I* imagined it all?" I asked, suddenly doubting my own mind.

66

No. I don't think so. Your memories have incredible clarity; it's almost like looking at my own.

"So how could I have seen her without her being there?" I demanded to know, the idea that perhaps I was going slightly crazy starting to sound much more plausible than that little old lady using astral projection to return books back to their places as defined by the Dewey Decimal System.

Robert had no answer for me, and that did nothing to ease my mind. *Would you at least like to know a little bit about who she was? It's a fascinating history.*

Knowing that he was trying to change the subject, and appreciating it, I nodded. He pulled my head back onto his chest, and laid down, his free hand rubbing my back as he began to tell me about the tiny, yet spunky librarian.

You knew her as Miss Maggie. Her full name was Marjorie May Mulligan. She was the eighth of ten children, and the only one to survive past childhood. It's the reason why she never had any children. Did you know that?

I shook my head. There was a lot that I didn't know about Miss Maggie, apparently.

She didn't want to have any children, and so she never married. It was very difficult for her parents to accept, of course, but she didn't care. She went to school to become a teacher, and eventually a librarian. She traveled all over the world, teaching children to read, and she met some of the most incredible people I have ever been witness to see. Some people only ever get to see the dark side of humanity, but she was blessed with the side of humanity that gives my kind hope.

But Maggie wasn't content to travel, no matter how many people she met, how many new experiences she encountered. Her first love was working with children. She wrote several children's books, and she helped spearhead the construction of that little library with the money she earned from them. When her parents died, she used the money she received in inheritance towards the library. She put almost every single dime she ever had into that library.

"Why?"

Because there was a need. She just didn't know what kind of need she was filling until you came along. Do you remember the first time you went into that library?

I nodded my head. "It was a few months after mom died."

His chest raised and then lowered significantly as he let out a long sigh. *Maggie was very taken with you. You reminded her a lot of herself. She saw you, all alone in a world full of people, and she knew that you were in need of something.*

I smiled as I remembered what that something was. "She gave me a little book filled with Irish folk tales."

Robert's body shook as a memory instigated a round of silent laughter. *Yes. It included a tale of Kelpies, if I'm not mistaken.*

I giggled as I realized what it was that had made him laugh. "Well, I told you that I was well read."

I realize that. I made sure to thank her for helping you along in that, just so you know.

I lifted my head to kiss his chin, and thanked him silently. He gently nudged my head back down, and rested his cheek against my hair as he continued. *She watched you grow up, alone except for Graham, and she worried about you. She prayed for you, prayed that one day God would come and help you see just how special you truly are.*

She told me that you coming to the library, your sweet spirit and love of books, your kind heart…all of that gave her reason to keep going to work every day, even after all of the other kids stopped coming, after the donations stopped coming in, and the new library opened up.

The mention of the donations stopping caught me off guard. "Miss Maggie told me that she had regular donors—she said that the library was doing well. I don't get it. Why would she tell me that if there were no donations coming in?"

She told you that so you'd work for her, Grace. She paid you herself. She viewed you as her own, personal angel, who saved her from the cost of her mistake of not having a family.

Shaking my head, I felt the irritation of tears start to form again, my vision becoming blurry with the liquid emotion. "So why didn't she tell me about her cancer? I would have visited her. I would have gone over every day."

I felt Robert rubbing my hair with the side of his face, his hand drawing slow, dizzying circles on my back that offered a sort of distracting comfort, and then he sighed, the answer difficult for even him to discern. *I don't know why, Grace. I think perhaps she felt that you had already experienced far more loss than any child should, and in such a personal way, too.*

"Or…maybe she didn't want me to see her that way, because she knew I'd be seeing her—or someone that looked like her—in the library," I announced, an idea starting to form in my mind.

I thought about how healthy she had seemed when I last saw her; she looked healthier than I had ever seen her, and she seemed so lively, so strong. She had been carrying several piles of books, which was highly unusual for such a small library—to have that many books out of place would have meant a backlog of books…

"It wasn't her, Robert. Miss Maggie would have never let that many books just sit off their shelves. She was such a stickler for neatness and order. Oh, why didn't I notice it then?"

Robert squeezed me and I felt his shrug as he, too, admitted that he was at a loss for an explanation. *I didn't delve that deeply into her thoughts, Grace. I wish now that I did, but that doesn't change the fact that she cared about you a great deal, and her last thoughts were of you. You've had a profound effect on her life, and it only reaffirms how special you are.*

There were words that could have expressed how grateful I was then to have someone like Robert in my life; someone who was able to share with me the intimate details of those who valued me as a person, as something more than just an oddity to discuss behind my back. But none of those words were available to me right then. Instead, what came to mind was the fact that Miss Maggie knew so much about my life and had felt such a great affection for me, but I didn't know anything about her other than her name and that she worked at the library. And now I questioned even that.

Grace, don't. She was never dishonest with you. She might not have divulged her life story with you, but she did give of herself to you. She gave you what you needed, and in return, she received what she needed. Isn't that enough?

I wanted it to be enough. But Heaven help me, I was greedy. "I'm tired of people window shopping when it comes to my life, Robert."

The gradual loosening of Robert's hold on me told me of his confusion and his disappointment at my answer. *I don't understand what you mean by that, Grace, but you could try to be more charitable about someone who was there for you during one of the most difficult times in your life.*

It was now my turn to be confused. "What do you mean? She wasn't-"

Robert's hand pressed against my lips as he quieted me. *You don't remember—you remember your first time in the library, but that was not the first time you met Maggie.*

The memory of my childhood was fuzzy and tainted with so much pain; I couldn't begin to sift through the different layers in order to find the specific event that Robert could see so clearly. It was too difficult.

Grace, you only have difficulties with the memories of events that had the biggest impact on your life. It's a defense mechanism for you, much like how your thoughts separate in your mind to protect them. This was after your mother's accident. Do you remember being in the hospital?

I remembered some things about the hospital, but mainly about the trip home. Robert had broken a few rules in order to allow me to witness what had happened when my mother had died, but nearly everything that happened afterwards was a mystery.

Grace, you spent nearly a week in the hospital after the accident. You were in shock, and the doctors couldn't get you to speak. You don't remember that?

With my head shaking no, and my mind racing to sift through the thoughts to try and find what it was that Robert was trying to get me to see, it was almost impossible to miss the fact that I really had no clue about what it was that Robert was talking about.

Maggie heard about what had happened to you and your mother. She came to the hospital room to visit you. She brought the one thing that she could relate to you with.

"She brought a book…"

He nodded. I felt the motion, knew what it was, and it felt like the acknowledgement flipped a switch inside of my brain. "It was a book, but it wasn't one that you'd find on a shelf. It was a journal… She wrote in it. I remember she had poems in it, some that she had written, and others that she had copied from other sources."

Robert shifted beneath me and raised me up above him so that he could see me better as I spoke. Or so that I could see him better. I nearly lost my train of thought just staring into the luminescence of his eyes. *Grace, do you remember what she read to you?*

I had to blink a few times, and finally closed my eyes to block out the silver glimmer that demanded my attention so that I could think. The book that Miss Maggie had held in her hands was old, some of the pages severely dog-eared and yellowed with age. I could hear the rhythm in her voice as she had read the lines that were written. There was a strange familiarity to the words that were muffled in my mind.

"I can hear the rhythm. I can hear it, but the words…they're lost on me."

It happened so quickly, I barely noticed the movement. Robert had sat up and left me to retrieve something, only to return to the exact same position, his arms holding me up, my face above his. Only this time, he was holding me up with one hand. In the other, he held a book.

"That's the book that Lark gave to me for Christmas," I noted, and reached for it; the leather cover was unmistakable, the smell of an old book just as intoxicating to me as a new one. I thumbed through the pages until I found the one that I had felt drawn to, the one that always pulled at me. "Al Aaraaf," I breathed.

The words that had had no structure, no form in my mind, suddenly gained an almost impossible clarity. This poem represented, in so many ways, the love I felt for Robert…

"But I don't get it. It's such an intense piece. Why did she choose this to read to me?" I asked, my fingers touching the words as though each letter connected me to Robert even more so.

Robert's hand covered mine and together we traced the lines that he had whispered to me on that first night he had stayed… I looked at him and waited for him to answer.

She did not know why she chose it. It just seemed to call to her. You needed an angel to help you, and she had nothing else to give, I suppose. Even she knew that I was your future.

"But why would I block that part out? Why would I choose to not remember something that significant?"

You chose to block out many things about that time in your life, Grace. It was the way your mind coped. But you see, Maggie wasn't just…how did you put it?

"Window shopping."

Yes, window shopping. Maggie wasn't just window shopping when it came to you. She was fully invested in your recovery, and your future. She might not have been as significant a…shopper as you would have liked, but she was still there.

I avoided looking into his eyes because he was right. He knew he was right; he had said it, and I couldn't deny that doing so meant it was the truth. Miss Maggie had, indeed, been a part of my life. That didn't mean I wasn't still bothered by it. It didn't seem right, or fair, that I had missed out on knowing her in the way that she knew me. I felt…robbed.

"I don't know why she didn't just let me in…" I finally muttered, more to myself than to anyone in particular.

Really, Grace. The woman has died, with no children or grandchildren, no family or any real friends around to mourn her, and all you can think about is yourself? He sat up with a huff, and I immediately felt guilty. I had been selfish and uncharitable, unwilling to empathize with the loneliness that Miss Maggie must have felt, and that was everything that an angel was not—I had offended Robert immensely.

"Robert, I'm sorry," I was able to get out before he left me alone on the bed to pace my room.

You were just told that someone you cared for has died, Grace. I told you that she cared for you a great deal, that she was there to help you when you were in need of it the most—she helped your father by doing that as well...and the only thing you can think about is how you feel, how you were denied something. Why? You give more care and concern for Graham's father, who's done nothing but treat you with contempt. Why?

Whatever charitable feelings I might have had disintegrated as he unleashed his thoughts on me. His eyes were cold, his face hard, and I couldn't find it in me to hold back the iciness that I felt in return.

"I feel more concerned about Richard because he's Graham's father. The only one he's got. He and I don't have the luxury of having parents who don't die, and we definitely don't have the ability to read their minds either, so when something is wrong, and they start hurting themselves or other people I care about, forgive me for giving a damn."

I didn't bother to stick around to gauge his reaction. I simply got up off my bed and stormed out of the room. I headed downstairs towards the kitchen, hoping that by the time I got there, I'd have cooled off enough to deal with him. Because I knew he was going to be there when I turned on the kitchen light.

That was very childish of you.

I scowled at him as I opened the refrigerator. I needed a distraction, and the leftover pot roast from dinner would fit that bill just fine. *No more childish than you leaving me on the bed.*

I heard the snort in my ears as well as in my mind and it felt like he'd taken a foam bat to my head and hit it...twice. *I did that to protect you.*

I slammed the refrigerator door shut at that comment and glared at him, my jaw hurting from jutting out at such an exaggerated angle, but needing it to do so to help emphasize just how angry I was. *Protect me*

from what? You? If I'm not mistaken, the only time I ever seem to be in any
danger is when you're not around, and you're not around a lot.

I shouldn't have thought it. The instant I did, I hated myself for
it, but it didn't matter. The hurt and guilt in Robert's face before he disappeared were enough to knock me to the ground. "Why do you open
your mouth?" I groaned out loud, and hung my head, too ashamed to do
anything but sit on the cold, tile floor, my knees throbbing, a small cramp
growing in my thighs, and the image of Robert just before he left staring at
me from every visible object.

"Grace? Why are you on the floor?"

I looked up and saw Graham standing in the backdoor, a concerned look on his face. "Just sitting here, thinking about how my mouth
always gets me into trouble," I muttered, taking his hand as he pulled me
up to a standing position.

"Well, you definitely do have to work on what you say to some
people—especially the stupid ones. We tend to lash out and hurt you," he
said, smiling half-heartedly as he implicated himself. "So what happened
this time?"

I shook my head, unable—no, unwilling really—to discuss Robert
with him as I sank back down to the floor. They might have hashed out
their differences, but I was still a sore subject with them. Well, with Robert at least.

"Did it have something to do with Robert?"

"I don't want to talk about it, Graham."

He shrugged his shoulders, and opened the refrigerator door, being
careful not to bang my knees in the process, and carefully removed a package of sandwich meats and a jar of mayonnaise. I watched in my awkward
position on the floor as he made himself a sandwich, whistling while he did
so.

"Here," he said as he handed me a triangle of bread and meat.
"Eat. You look like you need something on your bones other than Robert."

74

There was a time when something like that would have resulted in my reaching out a closed fist and punching Graham in the arm...or in this case, his face. But something inside of me failed to connect with that part of my reflex, and instead, I burst into tears—big, fat, embarrassing tears that I had never been able to shed in front of Graham, and yet there they were, leaving pools of saline on the floor and on my thighs.

Graham was squatting in front of me, his features twisted with concern and confusion. "It's just a sandwich, Grace," he muttered as he tried to wipe the moisture away from my face.

"Oh, I feel so stupid," I sniffled, and quickly shoved the sandwich into my mouth, hoping that I didn't choke on it...or maybe that I would. "Migh-shed-shumfing-bad-foo-shim," I mumbled, bits of bread tumbling out of my mouth as I spoke.

Graham laughed, his head cocked to the side in confusion. "You wanna try that again with less food in your mouth?"

After gulping down the remainder of the sandwich, I replied, "I said something bad to him."

"Aah." Graham nodded his head and reached for me, his arms circling wide around me in a strong, comforting hug, my shoulder pressed against his chest, the side of my head leaning in against the soft dip that rested between his shoulders. This was an embrace that felt...different. The depth of emotions that I could feel from it was the same, but they were just taking a different path. It felt like I was being hugged by a brother.

"I don't think he's going to forgive me," I told him, my voice muffled against his shoulder. "What I said was really bad."

"You want to tell me what it was? Maybe I can tell you if you're overreacting."

I allowed my head to move in a silent "no", and then felt him sigh, not liking that I was keeping a secret from him and that he was seemingly fine with it.

"Grace, he'll get over it. Let him cool off. He's a guy and we all get our egos bruised once in a while. Don't stress too much about it, okay?" He squeezed me, the way a brother would, and I nodded my head in confirmation even though I knew Graham was probably way off base.

"Could you at least tell me what started the argument?"

Wanting to be honest, I told him as much of the truth as I could. All five words of it. "It started with Miss Maggie."

"The librarian?"

I nodded my head and the grief that I had not yet felt, the grief that I had subconsciously put on the backburner because of my stupid selfishness, suddenly came running to the forefront of my emotions, and brought with it a whole new set of tears.

"You want to tell me what happened?" Graham asked, his voice soft and overflowing with concern.

But as much as I wanted to, I couldn't. I felt him exhale at my response, and the influx of tears only increased as my guilt and my self-hatred dog-piled onto each other.

I felt Graham's shoulders shake as he chuckled softly, finding some small amusement in my uncharacteristic behavior. "You must really like books to let Miss Maggie come between you and Robert."

I hid my smile on his shoulder. If he only knew the truth.

BOMBS AND BOMBS

Graham and I both went to bed right around the time the sun should have come up. I say should have because the winter storm that had made its appearance shortly after midnight continued to pour snow and the occasional balls of hail onto Heath well past dawn, completely blocking out any beneficial light. It was only when the pounding of hail went from sporadic to incessant that I finally woke up.

The gray glow that shined through my window deceived my inner clock when I looked at the actual one sitting on the dresser and fell back onto the bed with a loud grunt of dissatisfaction. "It's only nine-thirty!"

I rolled over onto my side and reached for the familiar shape that felt like it had always been there, as much a part of me as my own skin. But nothing was there. The spot on the bed where Robert normally slept beside me was empty, the void on the bed obvious by the lack of disturbance on the comforter or the pillow.

I hadn't expected just how bereft I would feel at the return of the emptiness that, until just a couple of months ago, had always been there. My fingers clutched at the empty space, my palm itching to feel the warmth of another's skin that it had grown accustomed to.

The tears that had flowed too freely just a few hours earlier renewed their path down my face as I felt wholly pitiful, Robert's absence filling me with more regret than I thought possible. I had to learn to control my mouth.

Yes, you do.

"Oh!" I exclaimed, and sunk my face into the covers of my bed. I didn't know where he was, but I didn't want him to see my face all swollen and puffy like I'd just been attacked by a nest of yellow-jackets.

I've seen you look a lot worse. I felt him seat himself on the edge of the bed, and with a speed I knew I shouldn't possess, I was against his chest, my arms wrapped around his waist, my face pressed up against the hollow of his neck.

"I'm sorry," I said in a low whisper, the sobs that I had barely held off finally breaking through and pouring out onto his shirt. "I shouldn't have said it. I shouldn't have been so selfish."

When his arms finally came around me, holding me as I did him, it should have been enough to calm me down. I should have been relieved, elated. Instead, the bawling only grew in intensity; the sobs turned into hiccups while my eyes, which had merely been puffy before, were now nearly swollen shut from the demands of so many tears. I couldn't breathe out of my nose, and I could tell by the warmth in my cheeks that I probably looked as red as a strawberry, with mottled seeds to match.

"And you're still beautiful," Robert sighed, his chin resting on my head, his arms squeezing me rhythmically, a calming pattern that slowly worked its way into my breathing. "And absolutely, ridiculously, and wholly silly."

I smiled, not caring what he said, as long as he was here to say it, here to hold me while saying it…just here.

"I'm sorry, Grace. I shouldn't have left like that. It was the wrong thing to do. I promise it won't happen again. We have to face our problems head on, otherwise this is what happens: We hurt each other."

Shaking my head I mumbled into his shirt, "I'm the one who hurt you. You have the patience of…well, an angel, and if I can make even you angry, then something is seriously wrong with me."

I felt his chest shake as he laughed, heard the deep timber of it beneath his skin. "Nothing is wrong with you. Everything in the world is right if I love you so much, you affect the way I think."

"Do I, really?"

His lips brushed the top of my head as he answered, albeit reluctantly, "Yes. You affect my entire world, Grace. The obvious changes are one thing, but it's the changes inside that prove to me every day how profound an impact you have had on my life. Fifteen hundred years of merely existing, feeling the same things, thinking the same things, dreaming of the same thing—and in less than half a year, you've changed everything."

For some reason, I apologized…again, which didn't seem to sit well with Robert. "Don't apologize, Grace. You didn't ask for me to come into your life and turn it upside down. Had I never spoken to you, you would have continued on your path, and I would have continued on mine."

There were times when I knew I needed to keep my mouth shut, to prevent myself from saying things that would only get me into trouble, and hurt those I cared about.

This wasn't one of those times.

"What do you mean, I would have continued on my path, and you would have continued on yours? What path was I on? Oh, that's right, the one where I had no friends, barely any family, and no you. And what about you? What would you have done for the next fifteen hundred years?"

Robert stiffened before shrugging his shoulders and exhaling. He pulled me away from him with little effort, despite my using all of my strength to hold onto him. "I would have continued to exist, never knowing what I was missing, and perhaps being all the wiser for it."

"Wh-what? Why?" I demanded to know. I looked into his face and, for the first time, saw a faint trace of disappointment…but for what?

"Don't worry about it, Grace. What's important is that I'm here, now. You are more than just a part of my life; you are my life."

I wanted to press the issue, as much as I knew he didn't, but as it always seemed, just when I was getting around to the most important of questions, someone knocked on my door. "Grace, can I come in?" I heard Graham ask on the other side of the door. I turned to look at Robert, to see if he didn't mind, but he was already gone.

"Sure," I replied. "It's not like you'll find me in here with any-one...brave," I mumbled under my breath as Graham walked in, dressed in a uniform of some sort.

"So, what do you think?" he questioned as he turned around, showing off the burgundy shirt with what I could only assume was a white, clip-on tie. His pants were a dark gray color with a matching burgundy stripe running along the side of each thigh.

"You look like a nutcracker. All that's missing is your hat," I commented, moving my hand to rest in the warm spot that Robert had recently occupied. It disturbed me how quick he was to run away, even now.

Graham took my motion as a cue to sit, and I snatched my hand out of the way before he crushed it with his weight. "Have you talked to Robert, yet?" he asked, his eyes filled with concern as he reached to push some of my matted hair out of my face. "You look worse than when I left you, Grace. You did talk to him, didn't you? Did he say something to hurt you?"

I shook my head, trying very hard not to let Robert's comments burn a hole in my head, itching to be filled with doubt and suspicion. "Don't worry about it, Graham. So, did you come in here just to show off your...uniform?"

He grinned, a hint of a dimple forming in his cheeks that made me blush. "I actually wanted to talk to you about something...important."

I turned my body around and pulled my knees up to my chest, resting my chin on them as I stared into his excited eyes. "Ok, shoot."

"Well—this is kinda difficult because of who she is, and who you are—see...I kind of like someone—God, how do I do this without sounding like a complete idiot—what I wanted to know is…do you…do you think Lark would go out with me?"

I felt my eyes widen but my jaw was held immobile by my knees. Instead, my entire face rose as I saw that he'd finally developed the courage to voice his feelings. "I think you'd have to ask her, but I'm pretty sure she'd say yes."

He breathed a sigh of relief that made his chest sink in and his whole body slouch over as the rush of air left his lungs. "I was planning on asking her out on a date after my first shift today." Graham took a look at his watch and jumped up, an expletive shooting out of his mouth as he did so. "Oh damn, I'm sorry Grace. I gotta get going. I start in less than twenty minutes and I'm supposed to be there ten minutes early so I can get a quick runaround of the place."

"Go on, then. You don't want to be late on your first day. We'll talk more about this later," I told him as I lowered my legs down to the floor and stood up. "What time is your first shift over?"

"Five. Are you going to come?"

I nodded and grinned. "I have to offer my best friend some moral support, right?"

He glanced at me sideways as he stood near my door, half-laughing as he said, "Are you sure it's not because you want to keep the peace between me and your boyfriend?"

The grin that had filled my face died away. "I don't know that I could actually do that, quite honestly. Things can get so up and down with Robert, but Lark has a mind of her own so I wouldn't worry too much about it."

He paused as he took in my response. "Is this going to cause a problem for the two of you?"

The rise and fall of my shoulders indicated that I didn't know, but deep inside I did. When it came to Graham and Robert, there was always a problem. This was only going to complicate things, but Graham didn't need to know that. I'd rather deal with Robert than with another Erica.

"Well, I'll see you at five then," he called out as he left, closing my door behind him. I sat and waited on my bed for Robert to return, bracing myself for the onslaught of questions and accusations that I knew would come. But he didn't show. After an hour of waiting, I finally gave up. He would find me sooner or later. My only hope was that we'd spend more time talking about what it was that he had meant when he said that he'd have been the wiser for not meeting me, but he was just as good at avoiding answering a question as I was at bringing it up. And now this…

଼

At four thirty, Stacy arrived to pick me up. I had called her to see if she wanted to go to the movies with me, but didn't tell her the real reason for going—she would have automatically said no. "So, what movie are we going to see?" she asked as she waited for me to pull on my boots.

"I don't know," I answered truthfully. What movies were playing anyway? I hadn't been watching the television at all, and couldn't remember the last time it was that I had actually gone to the theaters, much less seen a preview for anything playing there.

Stacy had a look of deep concentration on her face as she ran through what could only be a mental list of flicks she had wanted to see, finally settling on one with a curt nod. "Let's go and see the new zombie movie starring that hunky British sounding guy."

There was only one hunky British sounding guy I wanted to see, but he had avoided my thoughts and my room since his cowardly departure this morning, so I wasn't holding my breath. "Okay. Let's do that."

We climbed into her car and headed towards the theater, her radio on full blast. While most people chose to sing along to the melody, Stacy instead chose to sing harmony, complicating the song by alternating the highs and lows depending on what the backup track had chosen to pick. It was far more entertaining than the actual song, and I marveled at the incredible talent that she displayed.

"You can thank twelve years of piano lessons for my ability to pick out notes and make them work," she said in-between songs when she saw my expression. "I told my mom that I wanted to be a singer a couple of weeks ago, and she said that she wasn't working as a cook in a cafeteria so that I could be some American pop-tart."

The sadness in her eyes was one that I had seen before. The first time I had heard her sing, she had explained what her parents expected of her, their goals for her. Culturally, she was left with few options regarding her parents' approval, and more than making her own dreams come true, she wanted to please her parents. "That's what happens when both of your parents are traditional Koreans," she had explained a few weeks later when Lark and I had pressed the issue.

"But you're an American," I replied, feeling angry that her parents had come to this country because of the opportunities available to them and their children, and then denying them to her.

"I'm American by birth. For the rest of my life, I'll be their daughter, and I cannot just ignore that," she had said, the look on her face crestfallen.

"Well, I think you should tell your parents that you deserve to live your life the way you see fit," Lark voiced, her mood dark and spiteful.

Stacy had just laughed at Lark's comment, but it seemed to stick with her as she became more open about her singing, doing it far more often than she had previously. Now, in the car, she was belting out the notes, not caring about anything other than the improvements that she knew she was making to the song.

It was while parking the car that she brought up New Years at Lark's house. "Did you know that she disappeared for a while, and Graham did, too?"

I didn't have to feign shock. I had known about Lark, obviously, but not about Graham. I regretted that I hadn't even asked him about how things went at Robert and Lark's.

Gauging my reaction, Stacy continued. "Lark came in and acted surprised that Graham wasn't in the living room with me, but then he showed up a few minutes later, with that same surprised look on his face; I knew something was up. Do you think they're secretly dating?"

My head shook with the secret knowledge wedged deep in the back of my mind proving it to be the truth. "No. I know for a fact that they're not. Robert would know, and he would have told me—or complained about it."

Sighing with I could have mistaken for relief, Stacy turned the car off and turned to look at me. "It just seemed weird, the two of them disappearing at the same time. Lark told me later that she went to drop you off to meet up with Robert, but she can do that in just a few minutes. You don't think she found a way to lie, do you?"

"Stacy, you know Lark cannot lie. She told you the truth. She spent a few minutes talking to me at the gazebo. She came back as soon as we were done. I don't know where Graham was, but I do know that it wasn't with her."

"Oh," she replied, and a slight blush tinted her cheeks. "Well, okay then. Let's go and watch some zombies!"

As she opened her door and climbed out of the car, I was left wondering what had caused this sudden interest in what Lark and Graham were doing together. As we walked towards the theater, the thought seemed to reproduce like mice until my suspicious mind was filled with possibilities that bordered on the plain silly to the absolute preposterous. Stacy couldn't have an interest in Graham, could she?

The line for tickets was empty and we paid for a six-o'clock showing before heading into the theater's lobby. I quickly allowed my eyes to flick around, hoping to see a familiar face before Stacy did. I was far too slow for my own good.

"Graham works here?"

Stifling a groan of disappointment, I answered in the affirmative. "He actually got hired yesterday."

The look on Stacy's face was one of surprise and annoyance. I prayed she wouldn't put two and two together. My prayer was answered...in the negative. "Is that why you wanted us to come here? So you could see Graham?"

The twisting in my gut that always happened when I was about to lie felt like a vise was crushing my intestines, and I swallowed at the pain, bit it down, and answered. "No. I came because Robert and I had a disagreement and I needed to get out of the house so that I wouldn't sit and mope."

Strangely enough, the pain suddenly subsided; I had been partially right. I didn't want to sit at home alone, allowing my mind to run with scenarios that weren't healthy for a sane person dating a normal guy.

"You guys had a fight? Wow—I thought angels were supposed to be agreeable and pliant," Stacy said, amazement rather than sympathy filling her eyes.

"I don't know where you got that idea, especially knowing Lark, but agreeable and pliant they are not. They're angels by nature, sure. But angels by behavior? Not even close," I muttered as we approached Graham.

I took one look at the grim line that used to be his mouth and knew something was wrong. I turned to look at Stacy, but her posture indicated that she was not in the mood to be mocking or sarcastic. She looked just as nonplussed as I felt.

"What's up?" I asked him once I was close enough to do so without raising my voice. "You look downright sour!"

The harsh line of his mouth barely moved as he answered me. "The new manager is treating me like I've got a thing for his sister or something."

The best friend defense mechanism that was in me kicked on and I immediately demanded to know where this manager was. Graham motioned with his head towards someone who was approaching us, and I turned around to confront him, fully intent on chewing him out for whatever it was that he did to put that look on Graham's face.

"Hello, Grace," the manager said to me, because I couldn't find anything to say to him—not after seeing who it was. "If I had known you wanted to come to the movies, I wouldn't have agreed to a double shift."

Robert stood in front of me, disturbingly handsome even in his monkey suit of a uniform, and I couldn't breathe. I couldn't even blink. Surely this was an apparition of some sort, and Graham's boss wasn't my boyfriend.

Stacy, seeing that whatever truce that might have existed between Robert and Graham had suddenly flown out the window, decided that she had to choose a side...and quickly, and so she did the one thing I had never expected. "You look pretty good in that uniform, Graham. I didn't know you could clean up so well."

Graham's seething gaze shifted over to Stacy, and his eyes widened, as though he just noticed her presence. "Um—thanks, Stacy," he stammered.

She nodded her head and smiled. "No problem", she said with an amused tone as she inched closer towards him, and further away from Robert.

I looked the two of them over, and then flicked my eyes back towards Robert. "When did you start working at the movie theater?"

"Since yesterday," he replied in a curt tone that drew a swift intake of breath from Graham, which was a sign that he was trying to control his temper...and was probably failing.

"But you don't need a job," I pointed out to him, not wanting anything that was said today to escalate into something that would once again demand that I, too, choose a side. I might have known before which one I would have chosen, but not now. Not with the way things were at the moment. "And why did they make you manager?" I demanded to know. "Graham has been coming to this theater a lot longer than you've been here. He knows everyone in Heath. Why didn't he get offered the position if it was open?"

Robert grabbed my arm and pulled me towards the side, apparently not wanting what he had to say to be heard, which only infuriated me more. Wasn't he the one capable of communicating without making a single sound?

"Grace, you know how I got this job," he hissed. "Don't make me answer that question."

I raised my head up defiantly. *Then tell me why you got this job in the first place?*

Robert glanced over to Stacy and Graham, whose eyes were focused on the two of us, Stacy gripping Graham's arm with such ferocity, I could see the tips of her fingers turning white. Robert's mouth started moving, but no sound came out. He was mimicking talking to keep our conversation private. *Because I know what he feels for my sister, I've seen his thoughts. I've also seen his thoughts about you, and those two things do not sit well in my mind together, especially if he's going to want to date Lark.*

Exasperated, I threw my hands up, my eyes feeling as though they were bugging right out of their sockets. *You did this because he likes Lark? You're treating him like dirt because he happens to like your sister?* I turned to glance back at Graham, whose eyes were round with surprise, and I looked behind me to see what had caused that expression. Lark was standing behind Robert and me, a scowl etched on her lovely face.

The fragile beauty that belied the strength and the temerity that was Lark would fool anyone who didn't know who she was, what she was. I looked at her eyes, the nearly colorless gray eyes that saw more than they let on, and I could see through her just how juvenile the entire situation was becoming.

"Hello, Lark," I managed to get out before Robert was able to send out another thought. He turned to look at her, and the silent communication that went on between them was brisk and full of outrage. I didn't have to hear it to know. I could see it in the tenseness of their necks and faces, the steel iciness in their eyes.

Finally, after what had only been a matter of seconds, but certainly felt like half a lifetime, Lark turned to me and gave me a stiff smile. "Hey, Grace. I wanted to catch the latest Zombie flick, and had my mother drop me off. Robert told me I could get in free anytime I wanted, so here I am." *Stacy told me that the two of you were fighting—I didn't know it was about me. I'm sorry.*

I grabbed her hand, and pulled the walking stick out of it. She didn't need it, hated it, really, so I gave her an excuse to not use it as I placed her arm on mine and turned my back on Robert. "You're just in time. Graham is getting off from work in a few minutes, so we can all watch the movie."

The hiss that echoed in my head at that exact moment caused me to stumble; the pain was so acute, my mind flooded with memories of a similar pain that had lasted much longer, and had done far more damage than merely tripping me up. Though I had placed Lark's hand on my arm in the guise of helping her, she was the one who supported me, and kept me from tumbling down to the coke stained carpet.

I looked up to thank her, but her gaze was frozen on something else. Or someone else. I followed it, traced it back to its source, and saw that she was glaring at him. The one who had promised never to hurt me. And yet he just had. "Why?" I mouthed, but was dragged away towards a worried Graham and Stacy, lines of concern etched into their faces, before he could answer—before I could see him leave.

Graham reached for me and pulled my hand away from Lark's. He looked into my eyes and saw the hurt there, recognized it, obviously, but thankful that he hadn't been the one to cause it this time. He glowered at Robert, though his reasons were completely different, and asked me if I was okay.

I nodded my head, wincing as I did so, the pain that still echoed inside feeling as though it were bouncing around with each movement. "I'm fine. Just a bit clumsy," I said with a half-hearted chuckle.

He didn't mean to do it. Larks face was stern, her eyes flat and emotionless. *He's an interfering idiot who doesn't know when to leave well enough alone, but he didn't mean to hurt you, Grace.*

At the moment, I really didn't care. Too many things were piling up for me to want to rationalize anything. His behavior was odd, even for me, and I simply couldn't appreciate his reasons, however valid they might be.

Graham left to clock out, and Lark, Stacy, and I were left standing in the middle of the lobby. I knew that Lark hadn't shared a single thought with Stacy about what had transpired in those few short minutes between brother and sister...and me. I could only guess that it was out of respect for my privacy, as well as hers.

"So, you two don't want to share?" Stacy asked, her eyes hungry with need for information, gossip, anything that would at least hint to what was going on between us.

Lark shrugged her shoulders, and said in a monotone voice, "It's family business."

I watched for signs that Lark was lying—a twinge of pain, a grimace—but there were none, which meant that this was, indeed, family business. That I was considered family should have sent me over the moon. Instead, I was feeling even more confused than before.

"Okay, ladies. Let's go watch some Zombies," Graham said as he returned, his hands quickly divesting his shirt of the clip-on tie.

The reaction from Lark was expected. Her face was lit brightly, her smile radiant, making anyone who stood next to her appear quite plain. That meant, of course, that I became even more insignificant than I normally was.

But there was one exception; one highly unexpected exception.

"Stacy," Graham began, a sheepish grin on his face as he nervously shoved his tie into his pocket, quick to look around, making sure no one was watching. "I've got tickets to go and see that blues band that's playing in Newark next week. Do you want to go with me?"

Lark and I both stopped walking, our thoughts conjoined in mutual shock. *Stacy?*

"Uh...sure," she replied, her broad smile and bright eyes reflecting genuine pleasure. I turned to look at Lark, whose disappointment was plain, and tried to comfort her. Neither of us had expected this—why hadn't she read his mind beforehand?

I didn't want to know what he was thinking anymore. I wanted everything to be new… Lark's eyes suddenly grew very opaque and glossy with unshed tears. I looked back at Graham and Stacy, who hadn't seemed to notice that we weren't following them anymore.

I wanted to cry out to him, "How could you?" But, as they rounded the corner, I couldn't bring myself to utter a sound. I wasn't a part of that equation. Once again, the decision had been made for me, and the fact that this time, more than one person was hurt felt like I had stepped on a landmine of helplessness. If I stepped away, I'd be leaving Lark in the lurch. If I stayed still, the threat was always underfoot, just waiting.

"I'm so sorry, Lark. I thought…he told me-" I tried to explain, but Lark held up her hand and shook her head.

"No, it's better this way. No complications." She took a deep breath and pulled me forward down the end of the walkway towards the room our movie was playing. The landmine didn't go off…but it would. I was sure of that.

SETTLEMENT

The movie went as all zombie movies go—the only survivor was some half-dressed, hysterical, buxom beauty who was rescued by some big, burly hero who then showered her with kisses and professions of love. I gagged. Lark snorted. Stacy sighed. Graham squirmed.

As we filed out of the theater, my thoughts were running helter-skelter with uncertainty and confusion about what had happened in the past twenty-four hours. The lobby was nearly empty, everyone either on their way home or watching their select films, and the popcorn and beverage stations were closed, their lights turned off; I looked for Robert, but he was nowhere to be seen. I wasn't sure what I would have said to him anyway, my emotions were so twisted.

"Grace, are you riding with me or with Graham?" Stacy's voice broke through my confusion, and I shook my head.

"I want to wait for Robert," I answered, my gaze focused on a door I was certain would open at any minute, revealing the angel who could both heal and break my heart with a single thought.

"I'll wait here with you, Grace," Graham announced, seemingly oblivious to the inner turmoil he had caused that was exacerbating the jumbling of thoughts in my head. "I'll call you later, Stacy. It was good to see you again, Lark."

Lark looked stricken, but she managed to pull a smile onto her face, and began walking towards the exit, Stacy following behind, stopping only to wave shyly at us before disappearing. Part of me wanted to be the fly on the wall when the two of them got into the car, but I knew full well that Lark wouldn't be anything but kind and graceful to Stacy, despite how she felt.

"Can you explain to me why you asked Stacy out, when just this morning you were telling me that you were interested in Lark?" I barked as soon as we were alone.

The carefree smile that Graham had been wearing started to wear away, the person who had made it necessary no longer around. "I'm still interested in Lark. I like her, Grace. Really, *really* like her—it's scary how much I do. But...when I saw you and Robert arguing—by the way, you guys need to start getting loud so that we can hear you; it makes eavesdropping much easier—I thought about what would happen if things didn't work out between Lark and me. What would that do to you and Robert?"

"You've already had a hard time because of me. I didn't want to cause more problems. This way, if Stacy and I don't work out, it'll be just like normal, there'll be-"

"No complications," I finished for him, comprehension of what Lark had meant finally dawning on me.

"Yeah. No complications."

That's what comes from the foolishness of extreme like. You're willing to convince yourself that life gets less complicated if you stay away from the things you want, and settle for what you know you can live with. No one is ever happy that way.

"What time do you think Robert will be getting off?" I asked him, needing to change the subject before I started pushing him towards talking about things that neither of us felt comfortable discussing. Not yet, anyway.

"Probably in another twenty minutes. It's a weekday, so the theater closes early, plus he's not the regular nightshift manager, so he won't have to close."

Sighing, I looked towards the exit doors that led into the mall. Though the theater was nearly dead, the mall wasn't. After holiday sales were driving people to spend money they didn't have in droves. "You ever wonder what it must be like? Never having to do anything, work at anything, and just having everything fall into your lap so easily?" Graham asked dejectedly.

I turned to look at him, his face a mixture of sadness and defeat, and didn't understand what he meant by that. "Want to run that by me again?"

"I know you're thinking that I've had it easy, especially when compared to you; you're right about that. Things have been much easier for me than most, and definitely a lot smoother than they have been for you, but you have to wonder about people like Robert and Lark. They come here from another country, don't know anyone, they talk differently, have different ways of doing things, and yet everything just happens for them without them even trying.

"I mean, look at you. You've had problems making friends since I've known you. But Robert shows up and all of a sudden you're his friend, and now his girlfriend and I barely get to see you. He applies for his first job and he ends up getting a manager position, while I'm stuck making popcorn and cleaning booster chairs. And then there's Erica. I know—I know she was wrong for me, but I tried to get her to go out with me for over a year before she finally said yes—don't look at me like that; I'm sorry I didn't tell you about her—but Robert shows up and on the first day, she's ready to dump me for him.

"What is it about him, Grace? Can you tell me so that I can understand? I'm not jealous—really, I'm not. I just want to know what makes him so damn special."

I looked at my friend, and I did what any friend would do in that situation. I lied.

"Graham, there's nothing special about him, really. He's the new guy—he has that air of mystery around him because of where he comes from, but he's just like everyone else."

It hurt to do it. It physically hurt, and I knew it was because I had never done it before—not when I knew that the truth was what he was seeking, and not some generic answer to a rhetorical question. He wanted answers because he was hurting, he was angry, and above all else, he was feeling very alone. And yet, when he needed me to be his friend, the kind of friend I wanted to be...I chose loyalty to Robert instead.

I had to look away, and waited for his response. When none came, I knew that something had changed between us—he knew I was lying, knew that I had chosen.

With a large sigh, he finally spoke, his voice straining against the bitter sting of what I could only guess was betrayal. "I think that if I had been able to ask Lark out, we would have ended up just like you and Robert; defensive and protective of each other, no matter the cost. I've already made one stupid mistake. I'm not about to make another one."

That hurt. It hurt and he knew it did—he wanted it to. He didn't understand why I couldn't tell him the truth—not that I could have explained it anyway—and so he was lashing out.

"I think I'll head back to the house now. I'll see you there, Grace," he finally said in a rough voice. He coughed, and I looked up to see Robert approaching us, his tie in his hand, and a sad, half-smile on his face.

I whispered a faint goodbye as Graham stalked off, not knowing whether or not he had heard me, just knowing that he couldn't stand to be around me at that moment, and all those emotions that I had thought I was incapable of feeling again started to crawl their way back into my heart.

Sensing the emotion-induced paralysis that I was slowly succumbing to, Robert helped me to stand and supported me as we walked out of the theater. I felt him in my head, sifting through the many thoughts that I had jumbled up in there, wading through the nonsense and the empty pockets to find what he was looking for.

"Grace—you shouldn't have lied to him for me. Whatever I am to you, whatever you are to me, it doesn't change the fact that Graham is your best friend, and you should be honest with him."

I stopped walking, and looked up at him. We were in the parking lot of the theater, his bike only a few feet away from us. "I shouldn't have lied to him? What was I supposed to say, Robert? 'Sorry, Graham, the reason you aren't the most popular boy in Heath anymore is because Robert isn't human—he's the grim reaper'?"

Robert looked around us, checking to see if anyone heard what I had just announced, and he shook his head. "No. You know that's not what I meant."

Exasperated, I threw my hands up, my words coming out in great huffs of impatience and anger. "Well what do you mean then? That I tell him you're an angel? That you have wings and can fly? How about I tell him that you can read minds, and that you can also make people do things, alter their thoughts so that they bend to your will—is that what you meant?"

In the pale phosphorescence of the parking lot lamps, I could barely make out the slight glow that radiated out from his skin. I say glow, but the mood he was in caused his glow to look more like a shadow that enveloped him—my heart started racing.

"Grace, you're being ridiculous and you know it. You should have told him that you couldn't tell him the truth—it would have hurt a lot less than lying to him did. He knows you, Grace—you've never lied to him before. Being with me has turned you into a liar…"

Few things escape me—of this I am quite certain—but when I first saw the darkness that was Robert's glow, I was sure that he was angry with me for my outburst. Instead, I now realized that he wasn't angry with me; he was angry with himself.

"Robert," I began, trying to think of a way to say what I felt without him hearing the thoughts first, not wanting to be redundant. "You're under the impression that you're to blame for what I did. You're not. I lied to protect more than just your secret. I also lied to protect Lark's, and mine. And I did it for Graham, too. He deserves the truth, but he can't handle it right now. I don't know when he might be able to, but I know that telling him now wouldn't help anyone out, least of all him."

The frigid silence that separated Robert and I felt like it was clawing at me to say something, but I waited.

"Grace, you've been lying for us—because of us. This isn't a life meant for you-"

"What do you mean by that?" I interrupted. "What life am I meant for if it's not this one?"

"I don't want to have this conversation here, Grace. Get on the bike. I'll take you home."

Knowing that the conversation wasn't going to proceed any further, I capitulated and headed towards the motorcycle, Robert following me sulkily. It had been a few months since I had ridden on it but my legs' memory was very good, and the resulting hesitation was causing them to tremble.

Sensing my fear, Robert lifted me effortlessly onto the seat, situating himself in front of me with blinding speed, and then turned the key to start the monster up. Its rumble beneath us caused me to squeak. "Where's the helmet?" I asked him, feeling incredibly vulnerable at the moment.

I felt the tension within him recede as his body shook with laughter. "Grace, are you kidding me?"

I shook my head. Of course. I should have realized that there was no need to worry about safety whenever I was with Robert. What better person to save you from severe injury and death than Death himself?

Thank you.

I nodded and rested my chin against his shoulder, my arms wrapped around his waist in preparation of the quick leap into motion that I knew was coming. We took off through the parking lot and headed down the road towards my neighborhood. I counted the houses that still had their Christmas lights up, not wanting to have any type of conversation yet. I needed to go over what it was that I needed to say, what I wanted to know, and my mind's ability to focus on more than one thing at a time allowed me to do that, all while ensuring that Robert wouldn't know.

As we pulled up towards my house, I saw the light in my room was on. Graham was there, waiting. The tenseness that had permeated Robert in the parking lot had now returned. I felt the air leave my lungs with frustration. So much for getting down to the bottom of things with Robert.

"I'm going to talk to him," I sighed as Robert eased me off the bike.

"He shouldn't be in your room."

Knowing where the conversation would head if I tried to argue with him, I simply leaned into him and pressed my lips against his cheek. "I'll talk to you later."

I started to walk away, but he held fast to my hand. I could see his thoughts of remorse and I couldn't help but smile. "It's not easy for an angel to be so wrong so often," he mumbled as he pulled me towards him, wrapping his arms around me. "I love you, Grace, and I think that messes with my ability to see what's real and what's not sometimes."

"Do you know how comforting that sounds? Most people would tell me that you're not real, that this—us—we're not real. I grew up thinking that people like you don't exist, so for you to start having delusions…it completely helps to normalize me."

His hands made their way from my waist up to my face as he held me immobile. "Grace, I love you. That is real; don't ever doubt it. I know I have been behaving like an idiot lately and I apologize if I've hurt or upset you. That is the last thing I want to do."

The silver in his eyes were liquid, flowing in endless circles as he stared at me, waiting for my response. I raised myself on my toes, and with his help, I managed to press a quick kiss to his mouth. "Thank you."

He didn't let go of me, didn't want me to go at all. He brushed my lips with his and pressed his forehead against mine, his thoughts mingling with mine until I knew all of his hopes, and his regrets about this evening. It was difficult for him to deal with such human emotions when he wasn't one; a side-effect of being in love with one, he suspected. I laughed because it wasn't a side-effect that only affected angels. Humans experienced them, too.

"And who have you ever felt jealous of?" he asked as he pulled away, but not before I managed to steal one last kiss.

"I don't think it's jealousy, but I do often wonder whether or not we'd be more physically connected if I were as beautiful as some of the girls in school that follow you around."

I had touched a nerve, I could tell. He let me go with an exasperated sigh—I was very good at making him do that.

"Grace, you and I aren't just a pair of hormonal teens infatuated with each other. Do I think you're just as beautiful as those girls in school you're referring to? No. I think you're incomparable to them," he said smugly. He brushed the strand of hair that had fallen into my face, and made me look into his eyes, seeing my reflection in them in a way that I knew no one else had ever seen, or could ever see. In them, I was beautiful.

"You're just going to have to get used to it," he pronounced, his voice tinged with cockiness. I felt the corner of my mouth twitch at his sureness. I had been living in my body my whole life, and he already thought he knew me better than I knew myself.

He was right.

"Go on, Grace. He's waiting for you. I'll be here when you wake up."

I felt the warmth rise up in me, knowing that he meant he'd be *with* me when I woke up, and the thought filled me with anticipation. He clicked his tongue in disapproval at my thoughts, and I stuck mine out as I walked away, not needing to say goodbye because he already heard it in my thoughts.

The bike was gone by the time I reached the door, but whether it was started or pushed, I didn't know.

08

After bypassing the twenty-one question brigade from Janice, and mumbling a quick response to Dad's "how was the movie" question, I raced upstairs. Graham was sitting on my bed, staring out of the window.

"You really should knock," he muttered. He turned around and I could tell by the lines around his mouth that whatever it was he wanted to talk about wasn't going to be pleasant.

"I wasn't aware that I needed to knock when entering my own room. Besides, you're the one who's in here uninvited."

He tossed something at me, and with reflexes I know did not belong to me, I caught it. For a brief moment, a glimmer of surprise passed through Graham's eyes, but it was quickly replaced with the same despondent look. I cast a quick glance at the object that I had caught, and then looked back up at him.

"Where did you get this?"

He nodded his head towards the nightstand next to my bed. "I found it in the drawer when I was getting your phone out. I wanted to call Lark, to explain…"

He had found one of the crystal baubles that had fallen off my lone dress. Its amber color gave off a sense of warmth, despite its cold exterior. I held it up to the artificial light above my head to look at its gold and brown shimmer.

"Grace-"

I lowered my head to look at him, the tone of his voice sounding so…lost, I felt a pain in my throat as my breath caught.

"Grace, are we…friends?" he asked, and I nodded dumbly while moving forward to sit next to him on the bed.

"So, if we're friends, will you be honest with me when I ask you if you think I screwed up by asking out Stacy instead of Lark?"

I took a deep breath, because I felt the truth ready to pour out of my mouth. I forced it closed, biting my lips to keep them shut until I could organize my thoughts enough to make the words sound less abrasive and accusatory. Of course he had screwed up by asking Stacy out. But that wasn't what he needed to hear.

"Graham, I know you like Lark a lot, but you've only known her for a short while, and it's been even less time since you and Erica broke up. I think perhaps dating around really isn't a bad thing."

His snort told me that he knew I was trying to avoid answering the question, and was doing it badly to boot. I ignored it and continued, "I don't know what made you choose Stacy. She's Lark's friend, too, and I think you might have made things a bit more difficult by asking her out, but I don't think you screwed up. Not badly, anyway."

He flung himself backwards on the bed, causing it to bounce us up and down. I waited until we stopped moving before I asked him the one question I knew he probably wasn't going to answer. "Do you regret asking Stacy out?"

Shaking his head, he sighed. "No, I don't. Not yet, anyway. She's cool...in a sadistic, painful, scary way. But it'll be nice to hang out with someone who doesn't care about all that superficial crap, you know? I'll make things work, Grace. I won't hurt her. I've learned my lesson."

I nodded mutely, relieved that he would at least not take his mistake out on her, and threw myself back on the bed, the two of us lying in opposite directions, our feet dangling off the side of the bed. "You're going to be one weird couple."

"Oh, and like you and Robert aren't?"

I raised myself up on my elbows and glared at him. "What's that supposed to mean?"

He covered his eyes with the crook of his arm, and grit his teeth. "You know what I mean, Grace. I might be a guy, but I know that all the girls think he's the best thing since...well, me. And then there's you: you're a great person, Grace, and you're beautiful in your own way, but when the two of you are together, it looks...odd. Like night and day, black and white."

I couldn't argue with him there. I had made that exact same argument several times to Robert myself. "Well, it doesn't matter what anyone else thinks, Graham. We're not a pair of hormonally infatuated teenagers. I-" I had to stop to blink...hard. Hadn't Robert just said the exact same thing to me? I shook my head, and continued, "-love him, and he loves me—unconditionally. He knows my faults, and I know his, and we accept them." Boy, did we accept them.

Graham raised his arm and peeked out at me from beneath it. "You love each other *unconditionally*? Where am I? Some soap opera?"

I moved my leg and made contact between his head and my knee. "If we are, it's one of your own making. Falling into deep-smit with my boyfriend's sister, and then asking out her best friend instead? Really? Is that what you did in Florida during Christmas, Graham? Watch soap operas and take notes?"

Quickly, he reached over and grabbed my elbow and pulled it, knocking me down. "Actually, I thought of all the ways I would ask Lark out. I wrote it down, too."

Curious, I asked him if I could see what he'd written. "Maybe later," he replied.

I made him promise that he'd show me before he left to go and take a shower. As he shut my door behind him, worry took over any triumph I might have felt over being allowed to read what he had written about Lark. He had asked Stacy out on a date, which was just as good as dating, despite the fact that he had feelings for Lark...and none for her. What was going to become of all of us when the inevitable happened, and he and Stacy broke up? Did I even want to know?

QUEST UNLIKE

The first week of February brought with it far more snow than Ohio had seen in over three decades, and definitely more than we'd had the past two months, so when the sun miraculously appeared on the fifth day, it was no surprise that everyone in school was wearing tank tops and shorts. Everyone except me, of course.

Robert and I walked through the hallway looking as odd as Graham had described: him in a slinky, gunmetal gray short-sleeved shirt and khaki shorts, and me in a pair of jeans and a black t-shirt with a black and white long-sleeved shirt underneath. He had never complained about what I wore, and made it a point to compliment me when he picked me up every morning, but I couldn't help but feel a slight stab of self-consciousness as we walked by the countless girls who all insisted on saying hello to him while ignoring me. They were all dressed in a manner that would have complimented him, while I was merely a distraction.

"You're being silly, Grace," he whispered into my ear as we walked into French class. I stopped dead in my tracks, causing Robert to slam into me, which propelled me forward. Ungracefully, I landed on the floor. Robert was at my side in an instant, immediately contrite and apologetic.

"It's okay," I reassured him. "I was the one who stopped. There was no way you'd have known what I was going to do."

As he helped me up, making sure that I was genuinely alright, he asked me why I had stopped in the first place. Quickly, I pointed to the decorations on the wall and dangling from the ceiling. His gaze drifted up to the construction paper hearts and cupids that were hanging from ribbons and what looked like fishing line tied to them.

"Cherubim hate these things, too," he chuckled, and led me to my seat at the back of the class. "But, their reasons are far more different than yours, I'm sure."

I wrinkled my nose at the wash of pinks and reds that surrounded us. "I've never liked this holiday. I thought maybe it was because I never had anyone to celebrate it with, but now I know that has nothing to do with it."

He smiled at my disgusted expression and brushed my cheek with the backs of his fingers. "We really don't appreciate it too much ourselves. The cherubim especially despise it."

I looked around us to see if anyone was listening to our conversation, but thankfully, we were the only ones seated. "Why do you keep saying cherubim? And why wouldn't angels like Valentine's Day?"

Sensing my concern of being overheard, he reached for my hand. *Cherubim are angels who often get confused with those little fetuses with wings that Madame Hidani has glued to the ceiling. Humans call them cupids and cherubs, but I'm sure if they've ever seen one in person, they'd be quite surprised...and pleased.*

I raised my eyes up to look at a cut out of the "fetus with wings" and snorted. *But what about you? Why don't you like it?*

His eyes flicked towards the seat in front of me and smiled as the girl who took her seat flashed a full set of teeth in his direction, obviously pleased to have garnered any kind of response from him. Lacey Greene couldn't hold back any kind of glee that his attention had been diverted from me, and I would bet money that if she could have, she would have clapped.

I'm not a fan of any particular holiday that depicts my kind as anything but what we are. During Christmas and Easter, we're usually gowned in sheets, with trumpets in our hands...trumpets—ugh. But on Valentine's Day, they dress us in diapers, and put little harps in our arms, a quiver on our backs, and a bow in our hands. We're infantile, with no other purpose other than to infest your kind with hormone tipped arrows.

You'd think that humans would be a bit more creative...or generous with their depictions of us. Or, at the very least, a bit more accurate, especially given how much they do know about my kind.

He turned to face me, his eyes full of mischief as he leaned forward and unexpectedly pressed a quick kiss to the corner of my lips. *Then again, the human being's lack of creativity can sometimes make it that much easier to shock them with something as mundane as a little kiss.*

I raised my hand to my mouth and touched the spot that he had brushed with his mouth. *Sometimes I wonder about you angels, to think that a little kiss, especially one from you, could ever be considered mundane.*

The bell rang and I turned in my seat to see Lacey scowl. Obviously Robert had not been talking about me. He had read her thoughts, and needed to make it clear to her that he wasn't interested without actually telling her. It was a good tactic; I certainly approved of his methods.

As we listened to Madame Hidani discuss the merits of conversational French in the varying dialects throughout the world, a voice boomed in over the loud speaker.

"It's that time of the year again, Bulldogs! The annual Valentine's Day Dance! Tickets go on sale today during lunch, and they're expected to go quick, so get yours while they're hot!"

The bubbling of excitement nearly drowned Madame Hidani out as she began once again to go over today's lesson plan and I groaned as I realized that the class of all girls was excited at the prospect of asking one person in particular to the dance. Even Madame Hidani stopped speaking as all eyes turned to Robert; he glowed from the attention, and I felt terribly inadequate.

"I guess it's too bad that I'm scheduled to work that night," he said in a voice loud enough for everyone to hear, and the room nearly burst with the groans of disappointment that erupted from everyone there but the two of us and one relieved French teacher.

"So you really do have to work?" I asked, feeling incredibly relieved at the prospect of not being forced to attend any formal event in front of the school.

He nodded his head as he took out his text book and pulled my desk towards his. "I requested to work the closing shifts from now on."

Puzzled, I glanced at the text book. He had turned to a page regarding the different countries that utilize French in their daily administration. "Any particular reason for doing that?"

"Yes. This way, I'm not working during the same shift as Graham."

I felt my mouth turn up, a silly grin spreading across my face. "You did that for me?"

He nodded, pleased by my reaction. "Your happiness means everything to me, Grace. When the original night shift manager quit, I saw the opportunity to do this, and I took it. It didn't take much to convince the general manager to let me fill the slot. I might have cheated a bit, but it was worth it if you're pleased."

"I've turned you into a con."

He chuckled at that. "Maybe I conned you into thinking I was an angel or something."

I was about to argue with him when Madame Hidani called out my name. "Y-oui, Madame Hidani?" I answered, correcting myself before the English slipped out. As soon as that bell rang, Madame Hidani had a French only policy, and I had nearly broken the number one rule in her classroom.

"Which country has the second largest French speaking population in the world?" she asked me in French, a lone eyebrow raised in anticipation.

"Algeria, Madame Hidani," I replied, a smug smile sliding across my face as her eyebrow lowered.

With a determined gleam in her eye, she asked me another question in French. "And what type of dialect do they speak in Algeria?"

"Maghreb-French, Madame Hidani."

Satisfied—or defeated—she turned her back to me and started once again to go over today's lesson. I turned my head back to Robert and saw his wink, no matter how quickly he might have done it. "Thank you," I mouthed.

It was my pleasure. It's quite amusing, helping you cheat by giving you the answers. I might have to do it more often. He winked again, and then motioned to face the front of the class before we drew the attention of Madame Hidani once more.

When the bell rang to head to Calculus, I was overwhelmed by the crush of girls who surrounded Robert and me—well, mainly Robert—and I backed away towards the exit. He could take care of himself, so I simply walked out of the door, fully intent on waiting there until he exited as well. I should have known he'd be there already.

"Don't you think that the girls will be suspicious that one minute you're there, and the next, you're not?" I asked as we walked hand in hand towards Mrs. Hoppbakker's classroom.

"No. Humans like to believe what they want, no matter what the facts staring them in the face might be telling them. Besides, those girls were too busy sizing each other up to notice my departure. You, on the other hand, never miss a thing." As we walked through the doorway of our math class, we were once again inundated by girls who were determined to ask Robert to the Valentine's dance.

"Um, Robert…do you think you might be interested in going with me to the dance on Valentine's Day?" one girl named Jennifer Hall asked nervously. I almost felt bad for her, knowing what his answer would be. I say almost because as soon as she got the rejection she obviously had not been expecting, she shot me a look of pure venom.

"If you keep turning down girls, I might have to seriously start considering taking Stacy on as my personal bodyguard," I kidded as he led us to our seats.

106

"Would you rather I tell them yes?"

"Well, what if you didn't have to work that night. Would you say yes to one of them?"

He reached forward to touch the loose strands of hair that had slipped free of my ponytail and smiled. "Only if you asked."

I rolled my eyes. "Formal occasions aren't my thing."

He chuckled as he pushed my hair back, a soft sigh coming from his lips as he did so. "You're wrong. They are so your thing."

I raised my hand to adjust my hair and groaned as I realized he had fixed it for me. And probably in a much neater, and tighter ponytail, too. "Sure. The last time I went to a formal thing, I ended up hurting my hand, got grounded, and you nearly broke up with me."

His lips curled over his teeth as he hissed. I winced—the sound of his disapproval seemed to be bouncing inside of my head, nicking my mind; it hurt. His eyes grew wide and round as soon as he realized what had happened, his hands on my face, concern saturating his beautiful features. *I am so sorry, Grace. I don't know why this keeps happening.*

I shook my head at his apology. There was no need for it—he hadn't intended to hurt me. I knew that better than he probably did.

It doesn't explain why it keeps happening though. His eyes were filled with worry, and I nodded in agreement. It didn't explain why it kept happening, or what it meant. His thoughts weren't meant to be heard by me, but for whatever reason, I inexplicably had, and the result was painful. It was a testament to my humanity, I suppose.

As class started, the confused and self-deprecating expression that seemed tattooed onto his face only grew harsher and darker. I turned my attention to the day's work, intent on asking him what he was thinking about as soon as the bell rang.

Instead, as we filed out of the classroom an hour later, he quickly handed me off to Stacy and left, mumbling something about not wanting to be late for third period. I stood there dumbly staring after him, Stacy looking just as perplexed as I felt.

As Stacy and I walked towards the library for free period, I could still feel the mild tingling sensations in my head. Stacy, seeing my frustrated appearance, asked what was wrong. "I just have a headache," I lied, and cringed as the slight twinges increased in significance.

"Oh, well maybe it's math that did that. Calculus always gives me a headache."

I nodded, not wanting to say any more as we entered the library and headed towards our usual table. It was a shock to see Lark sitting there alone, an obviously phony smile plastered on her face. "What are you doing here?" I asked as we sat down.

"My British history class is here doing research on the King Henry VII, so I decided to wait for you two to get here so we can discuss what we're doing on the fourteenth."

I turned to look at Stacy whose face was suffused with a very intense blush—she looked nearly feverish. "I have no plans, really. Robert's working that night. What about you, Stacy?"

"Graham asked me to go to the dance with him. I told him I'd think about it."

Lark huffed. At least, it sounded like a huff. I turned to face her, and though she was smiling, I could see something else hidden behind it. She began discussing her plans with Stacy, but I didn't hear any of it. Instead, my head filled with her voice that spoke about something completely different.

Graham called me up three nights ago to ask me what he should get for Stacy for Valentine's Day. Can you believe that?

I blinked as her words registered with me. Why would Graham feel the need to discuss Stacy with her? What could he possibly have to talk about that wouldn't be awkward and misleading in some way?

I asked him why he didn't just ask you, since you're his best friend. He explained that I was closer to Stacy, that I would know better than you about what her likes and dislikes are. I tried to tell him that that was absolute rubbish, but I couldn't. Apparently I'm closer to Stacy.

My face twitched in acknowledgement of that fact. I highly doubted that had circumstances been different, Lark would have ever revealed to me that she was an angel. I only knew about her by default, which hadn't bothered me. Until now.

Oh please don't start feeling sorry for yourself, Grace—focus. My entire existence has been focused on what you humans feel, what you humans think. Let me have a moment for myself, will you?

Sheepishly, I nodded my head. It didn't go unnoticed by Stacy, whose eyes fixed in on my lack of communication. I quickly started fidgeting with my hair, tugging at the strands that were now so neatly confined in an impossibly tight ponytail—courtesy of Robert.

"What are you thinking about, Grace?" she asked, not buying my sudden distraction for a minute.

My eyes flicked around as my mind raced for an explanation. My hesitation only added to the obvious lie that soon spilled forth out of my mouth. "I was just thinking about whether or not Robert would take off from work to take me to the dance."

To my surprise, Stacy seemed to accept this explanation, and then began to question Lark about whether she knew if her brother was going to ask. As Lark answered, more thoughts that weren't my own filled my head.

You're a lousy liar, Grace. It's no wonder—you've surrounded yourself with people who are all unfailingly honest. Well…mostly.

I stopped a snort from coming out, knowing to whom she was referring. *Lying isn't something I'm used to doing. I hate doing it—even when it's to help you and Robert. I know it's not the same thing, but lying hurts me, too.*

Lark's physical voice continued to discuss Valentine's Day with Stacy, but her mental voice, the voice that sounded so much clearer and defined in my mind grew soft. *I'm sorry that you feel you have to lie for us, Grace. You're not an electus patronus—you weren't bred for this. You shouldn't have to be doing this for any of us—Robert included. We've ma-*

naged to exist without being discovered for centuries without your help. We can continue to do so.

I pursed my lips in annoyance as her words settled into my head. *For someone who can read minds, you sure are obtuse, Lark. I don't lie just to protect you and Robert. I also do it to protect myself and my interests. I'm finally happy, for the most part, and I don't want anything threatening my happiness.*

"Grace, what do you think? Do you think I should go to this dance?"

I turned to look at Stacy, her face earnest, the topic of discussion obviously having headed in a direction that had become less about partying and more about something else. "That's up to you, Stacy."

She threw her hands up, exasperated at my half-hearted answer. "You're no help! This is something major here—everyone in class has been talking about the "after" parties, and Graham being who he is will be expected to go. If I say yes to him, I'll be expected to go, too, and you know what happens at those parties."

Recognition finally dawned on me and I felt utterly stupid for giving her such an empty response. Everyone, even anti-social me knew what happened at those parties. They weren't called baby-maker bashes for nothing.

"I think…you should say no, Stacy," I answered, half-attempting to redeem myself, half-wanting to save both her and Graham from falling prey to the immense peer pressure that would be pressing on them should they go.

Lark nodded her head as she chimed in, "I think Grace is right. You should tell him that you've got other plans."

Stacy pondered our advice, leaving the table silent as Lark and I picked up where our conversation had left off. *Grace, there are times when it's okay to be selfish, but never when it costs you a part of yourself.*

My jaw jutted out in defiance. Lying is what had kept the most important part of me safe; I would do whatever it took to keep Robert safe—he was far more important to this world than I was…far more important to me than anything that I might "lose" as a result.

Do you really believe that?

I didn't have to say anything for her to know that I did. She had never spent a moment of her life as a human being, with the human emotions that separated us in ways her immortality and her abilities didn't; she would never understand.

Good grief, you're far more naïve than I thought. Grace, do you believe that losing the trust of people you care about because of your lying is worth it? The electus, they don't need to lie to their family because the electus is their family. They are born into that life, it's chosen for them. You've chosen this for yourself, and the consequences might not be something you can accept.

There was some truth to her words; I knew that the moment they began to fill my head. I simply couldn't accept them, though. The lying I had been doing was minor, even if it hurt me to do it, and I knew my dad—knew that even Graham would forgive me for doing it if it meant protecting someone far greater than any of us combined.

"Okay, it's settled then. I'm not going." Stacy's voice jostled me from my thoughts, and I turned to smile at her nervously.

"I've decided that I'm going to turn Graham down. I'd rather hang out with you guys than go to some silly dance. I mean, we've only been dating a month; that's too soon," she continued.

My nervous smile turned into a grin as I replied, "Well, what do you want to do then? Everyone will be at the dance, which means we'll pretty much have Heath to ourselves."

Lark snorted. "We always have Heath to ourselves. It's a small town."

I started to speak up when Stacy interrupted. "Actually, it's not as small as you'd like to think. Heath has over eight thousand residents, which makes it small in comparison to, say, Cleveland, but definitely not as small as some other town around here…and I'm babbling."

Lark and I both nodded.

She blushed. "I'm sorry. I've been doing that lately, haven't I?"

Lark and I nodded in agreement, and then burst out laughing at the frustrated look that spread across Stacy's face, further intensifying her deepening blush. "You're too easy, Stacy," Lark laughed. Stacy started giggling, knowing that it was true.

When the bell rang, announcing lunch, the three of us headed towards the cafeteria, bemoaning the gastronomical terror that awaited us. The heavy odor of grease and something rancid assailed our noses as we walked through the double doors.

"I've smelled many awful things over the past few centuries, but this—this stuff absolutely reeks," Lark grumbled, her voice muffled by her hand which she held above her nose and mouth.

Stacy and I mimicked her as we approached our usual table. Graham was already seated, a plate piled high with an unidentifiable mass of what resembled food, his mouth dutifully chewing as he waved at the three of us. If one paid attention too closely to his face, they'd spot the subtle differences when he looked upon each one of us. Seeing me, his eyes crinkled with mischief—the usual look that one gave his best friend I suppose. Stacy got an expectant smile, although the corners of his mouth didn't turn up nearly as much as I think they should have.

But Lark…there was something about the way his green eyes grew intensely bright, the color deepening to a rich hunter green, then quickly faded into a nearly dull, lifeless olive that told me far more than anything else that "like" wasn't what he felt for her at all. I felt my heart clench at that realization.

My head whipped around to Lark to see if she had heard my thoughts, but to my relief she had not. Instead, her face was riveted onto his, probably seeing the same differences that I had and drawing her own conclusions. But what would those conclusions be? Would they be similar to mine?

As the three of us sat down, Stacy taking her preordained seat beside Graham, I became aware of one important absence. The seat beside me that should have been occupied by Robert was conspicuously empty. I looked at Lark once more and thought of the question in a clear voice so that she'd hear it.

She turned to face me and smiled sadly. "Robert had an errand to run during lunch. He'll be back soon," she answered me, not realizing that I hadn't actually asked the question out loud. Thankfully, neither Stacy nor Graham seemed to have noticed as they were in the middle of a heated, though unusually quiet exchange.

They're arguing about Valentine's Day.

Lark hadn't pried into their thoughts. I knew she hadn't, but her ability to hear what others were saying, even at a tremendous distance, prevented any sense of discretion, although Stacy seemed to have forgotten that as she lowered her voice even more to a low hum. Lark shook her head and turned to face me, her expression one of dismay and hurt. For most normal high school kids, a month was more than enough time to get over a snub—even one as shocking and disappointing as the one Graham had dealt her—but for Lark, time passed by in blinks. It doesn't matter what you are: human or angel, hurt like that cannot fade in a blink.

You went from being wholly naïve to being surprisingly astute in the span of just an hour. I'm proud of you. A wan smile replaced the grimace that had marred the angelic beauty of her face and I smiled in return. I didn't know what else to do as we sat there, trying very hard not to listen to the argument going on right in front of us while also trying to pretend that we were completely oblivious to it.

"Lark, could you come with me to the bathroom, please?"

Lark and I both turned to look at a red-faced Stacy with Lark nodding a reluctant yes as she stood up. She and Stacy headed off towards the restroom and I immediately turned to glare at Graham.

"Don't give me that look, Grace. I didn't do anything but ask Stacy to the dance," he said, the scowl on his face mirroring my own. "How was I supposed to know you guys had plans?"

I feigned disgust as I processed what he had just revealed. Stacy had lied to him! I looked around us to make sure that no one was within earshot and then leaned in, my voice barely above a whisper as I spoke. "Why did you ask her in the first place?"

He shrugged his shoulders. "Isn't that what a boyfriend is supposed to do? Ask his girlfriend to some kind of dance?" He sighed and slunk down in his chair, his eyes flitting back and forth, the same concern for eavesdroppers apparently filling his own head. "Truth is, I wanted to ask Lark. I like Stacy—I really, really do—but she and I are just going to end up breaking up. You know it, I know it. Even Stacy knows it."

He didn't have to go any further for me to know that. I already knew what his mouth couldn't say. I wanted to encourage him to tell Lark how he felt, but before I could lean in even further, the hairs on the back of my neck stood up, warning me that something bad was about to happen.

I couldn't have been any more right.

FREAKS OF A FEATHER

I spun around in my seat as the screech reached us from across the cafeteria. It wasn't that the sound was nail-on-a-chalkboard piercing, or that it felt like it was bouncing off the walls—a testament to the sound construction of the school, or the universal disgust that had led most students to eat elsewhere—but rather the fact that I recognized it.

From a distance, it looked like some kind of gold and black striped fan was being waved around in the air as a pair of dancers circled the cafeteria floor. A quick flash of a hand, a swift lifting of a leg, and the blond half of the fan was on the ground while the shrieking grew ever louder.

"I'm going to *kill* you for that," the voice cried out as the golden arc stood up.

"Oh. My. God."

Erica Hamilton struggled to stand as the black haired individual laughed, the sound melodious, like a scale of bells ringing in unison. "I don't think so," Lark's voice chimed, and I turned to look to Graham, who watched with rapt fascination as the two girls once again began their dance. My only question was where had Stacy gone.

A figure stood up, as if to answer me and I gasped. Stacy's forehead was covered with blood, the unstoppable flow sliding down her cheek and onto the floor. I rushed forward and reached her just as a wave of dizziness hit her, causing her to lurch forward in a faint. Graham was beside me as I struggled to lower Stacy to the ground. He removed his button-down shirt and handed it to me. I balled it up and placed it beneath her head as he used his undershirt to dab at the blood that was still flowing freely from a gash on her forehead.

Behind us, the battle between Lark and Erica came to a halt. An angry Mr. Branke and an even angrier Madame Hidani were holding the two girls apart. Okay, so both teachers were holding a frantic Erica back while Lark snarled. Not a single hair on her head was out of place, her clothing lay smooth and wrinkle free on her body, while Erica's hair resembled a tumbleweed straight out of some old western movie, and her clothing showed some significant tears and staining.

"What's going on here?" Mr. Branke asked, taking a lazy blow to the side of his head without so much as a blink when Erica reached through her cage of arms to try to claw at Lark, another piercing shriek the only sound she seemed capable of making at the moment.

Lark tucked an invisible strand of hair behind her ear and motioned towards Stacy on the ground. It was then that everyone else noticed the three of us crouched on the cafeteria floor, a bloodied Stacy unconscious in my arms, a worried Graham dutifully pressing down on her wound with his shirt, a cold gleam in his eyes directed at his ex-girlfriend.

"Stacy and I were returning from using the restroom when Erica came out of nowhere and shoved Stacy into the doorway. Stacy hit the edge of the door and fell to the ground, and Erica tried to kick her while she was down. I wasn't about to let that happen, so I hit her." Lark's voice was flat, her demeanor nonchalant, but I knew by the way each word caused Erica to flinch that "hit" wasn't the only thing that she had done.

Erica's clawed hands turned into an accusatory point directed at Lark's head, howling as she did so. "She *did* something to me. I could hear her in my head. I think she drugged me!"

Lark rolled her pale gray eyes at the sudden outburst and I could have sworn I saw Madame Hidani do the same. "If you're hearing voices in your head then that surely explains a lot."

116

All around us, murmurs of agreement could be heard. The cafeteria was now full of gawkers and onlookers, curious to see who had drawn the wrath of Erica Hamilton this time. No one expected it to be Lark and the fact that—essentially—she was blind only fueled the growing disgust.

"You blind freak!" Erica screamed, drawing a collective gasp from the crowd surrounding us. "It's no wonder you're friends with Grace. Freaks! You're all freaks!"

Mr. Branke, finally tired of being pummeled by Erica's flailing hands, grabbed both of them and pulled them behind her, forcing her shoulders to hunch back and a cry of pain to disrupt her rant. "Come on, Miss Hamilton. I'm taking you to the Vice-Principal's office."

Madame Hidani, now accompanied by the school nurse, knelt beside me to see how Stacy was doing. I could feel the fear bubbling within me as I stood up and moved aside to give them room; she hadn't woken up yet, hadn't even moved. Graham, too, stood up to allow them room, and the two of us stood silently as they ran through a virtual checklist of things to see how bad things were.

I felt a strong hand grip my shoulder and I glanced up, but it wasn't Graham's eyes I was looking into. "Robert," I sobbed, and felt myself collapse into his waiting arms. "I don't understand why—Erica just attacked Stacy out of the blue, for no reason, and now Stacy won't get up." I fought back the urge to start sobbing, biting my tongue to distract me.

"Shh. It's okay, she's going to be fine," he whispered in my ear. I sighed with relief and eased myself away from him. Sensing my intent, his grip on me tightened. *Grace, I'm not going to do anything—I can't, remember?*

Foolishly, I had hoped that the little stipulation about him being unable to use his healing ability for anyone but me could somehow be put aside for a friend, but apparently the rules applied no matter the person. I nodded my head to acknowledge his thoughts and hid my face against his chest, not wanting to witness what was going on behind me.

"It's okay, Grace. She's waking up. Look."

Tentatively, I peeked out from the shelter of Robert's arms. Stacy's eyes were open. Well, only one eye; the other eye was sealed shut by dried, crusty blood. She was mumbling something to Lark who was kneeling beside her, her hands wrapped around Stacy's upraised one. Graham, still standing silently beside me, looked pale. I could only imagine what was running through his mind but whatever it was, it wasn't doing anything but adding to the difficulty he already faced with the battles going on inside of him.

"Okay, Stacy, the ambulance is here to take you to the hospital. Vice-principal Kenner has called your dad and told your mom about what happened, alright? They're all going to meet you at the hospital," Madame Hidani told Stacy as the crowd made room for two paramedics who were pushing in a gurney, a large, black bag resting in the middle.

"Hey, sweetie," one of them cooed as she wrapped a thick brace around Stacy's neck. The other paramedic wrapped a black cuff around Stacy's arm and took her blood pressure. Stacy answered every question, ever conscious of the audience that watched.

One of the paramedics grabbed a board that had been seated on top of the gurney and together with his partner they managed to place the board beneath Stacy. They lifted her up onto the gurney and after strapping her in, started their quick-paced walk out of the cafeteria, the entire student body of Heath High following in earnest, not wanting to miss a single thing.

The female paramedic had somehow managed to secure a bandage on Stacy's head as she walked beside her, the pad quickly turning red as Stacy's blood continued to pulse out. As they pushed the gurney against the rear of the ambulance, the legs popped and bent inwards, allowing it to slide into the back with ease. Lark stepped forward then and mumbled something to the male paramedic, who nodded his head and held his arm out, waving a path into the ambulance. Lark climbed up and sat down beside Stacy, reaching once more to hold her hand.

Next to me, Graham wondered aloud how Lark had managed to be allowed inside of the ambulance. I, too, felt confused. "I thought only family members were allowed in," I added to his question while the two of us watched mutely as the rear doors to the ambulance were shut, the siren and flashing lights turned on, and the vehicle pulled away from the school.

I felt the tug on my hand and struggled to maintain my balance as Robert pulled me towards his motorcycle parked towards the front of the parking lot. "Get on," he said quickly as he climbed on. I obeyed, my arms quickly encircling his waist. Graham, having witnessed our hasty departure, had taken the hint and was heading off towards his own car before the school staff could swarm down on us and prevent us from leaving.

The violent purr of the motorcycle's engine told me that it was more than ready to do whatever it was that Robert had planned to get us behind that ambulance. Squeezing tightly, I held on we took off, not daring to look at the gaping faces that watched us leave.

It took less than a minute for Robert to maneuver his way through traffic and land directly in back of the ambulance. We remained there as it turned into the hospital and emergency-vehicles-only lane.

Get off here and follow them inside. Robert held the bike steady as I did as he said. Lark waited for me and the two of us walked inside the emergency room's waiting room, our hands clasped. Stacy's parents were there as were her brothers, including her twin Sean, who hadn't been in school today for some unknown reason.

His face was paler than everyone else's and after taking one look at Mr. and Mrs. Kim, I could see why. He must have been reamed by them for not being in school and protecting his baby sister, like he was probably expected to do. I wanted to feel bad for him, but there was very little room in me for concern for anyone other than Stacy at the moment, and what space did exist was reserved for Graham, who appeared just as one of the emergency room doctors walked in to give Stacy's parents an update.

"So, this is the family for Stacy Kim?" he asked as he took in the seven Kims, cautiously looking over the five anxious and worried older brothers all standing with their arms crossed over their chests, already skeptical of whatever it was that he had to say.

Clearing his throat, he began to explain the severity of her injury, his tone growing graver as he mentioned their inability to stop the bleeding. He turned to look at me and blinked in recognition. "Your father isn't here, too…is he?" he asked nervously, his eyes searching even as I answered in the negative. "Are you sure?"

I nodded my head. "I'm Stacy's friend," I insisted, and stepped aside so that he could see that I wasn't lying.

He exhaled in relief as he accepted that my father wasn't going to pop out of some closet and start berating him like he had done after Robert had removed my casts…and forgot to put them back. I started to giggle nervously as everyone stared at me with unspoken questions written plainly on their faces.

"I guess I'm feared in this hospital," I explained abashedly, my face warming at my embarrassment. "My dad kind of went on a little rampage the last time I was here, and I guess they remember me."

Sean mumbled something that sounded a lot like "freak" while Stacy's mother made a soft clicking noise with her tongue at my admission. I had apparently committed some kind of Korean faux pas, though I didn't know what, and rather than try to apologize—like that would have helped—I sucked my lips in and bit them…hard; anything to keep from having the attention brought back on me again.

Clearing his throat once more, the doctor told us that as soon as they had the bleeding under control, only Stacy's parents would be allowed in to see her. Her brothers breathed a sigh of relief, obviously not prepared to see their sister in any situation where she would appear vulnerable. Lark stepped forward, her intent voiced to only me, and the doctor turned to face her, a pained look on his face. "And she wants to see you, too," he said, his voice barely recognizable as he stared into Lark's sightless eyes.

Graham opened his mouth to say something, but Lark turned around and shook her head. A silent warning that brooked no argument. Amazingly, Graham nodded. He walked over to a chair that was situated as far away from Stacy's brothers as possible and sat down. Lark walked over to Stacy's mother and began speaking to her in a soft whisper, the words foreign to my ears and I shook my head. It figures she'd be able to speak to her in Korean. Knowing that I'd be grossly inadequate amongst Stacy's family, I sat next to Graham, he the outsider for the first time, and me simply falling into place.

"Doesn't it bother you," he whispered as he watched Lark and Stacy's mother converse, "that you can't speak a single word of Korean, and Lark can?"

I shrugged my shoulders and felt one corner of my mouth twitch as I answered honestly. "It would if I thought it mattered, but it doesn't. Lark's unique, so it's expected of her to be good at just about everything. I'm about as abnormal as it gets, so if I find out I'm good at anything, it's time to readjust my view of the world."

A nurse appeared as I spoke and nodded to Stacy's parents and Lark; the three of them followed her as she led them through a set of double doors, disappearing behind them without a word to Stacy's brothers or us. I looked down at my hands and saw Graham had his gripped around his knees. I covered one with my own and squeezed. "It's going to be okay, Graham," I said softly. "A little cut on her head isn't going to keep her down."

Graham's head bobbed up and down in silent agreement. "I know she's going to be fine, Grace. It's what comes afterwards that I'm not too sure of."

"What do you mean?"

He glanced across the room and my eyes followed his gaze. Five pairs of eyes were staring directly at the two of us, scrutinizing our every move, and I realized that my hand was still covering Graham's. I slowly removed it, smiling as I did so, and said in a low voice, "They're not exactly the most cheerful bunch, are they?"

His grunt, an acknowledgement, his sigh a concession, and his slight chuckle a break in the tension as he looked up to see Robert walking in. "You ever notice that when your boyfriend enters a room, he looks like the angel of death? I mean, no offense, but he kind of has that quality about him…supernatural and…creepy all at the same time."

I laughed nervously, my eyes growing wide as I looked at Robert, knowing he had heard what Graham had said. The grin on his face did little to ease my fears. Of course *he'd* find it funny. The possibility of Graham ever finding out just how right he is was pretty non-existent, but that didn't stop me from fearing the consequences should it actually happen. Stacy had accepted Lark and Robert being angels quite well, but even she didn't know what Robert truly was…I dreaded ever telling her. And if Stacy, one of the most open-minded individuals I knew made me fearful of her reaction, what would happen if Graham found out?

As Robert sat down next to me, he nodded a silent greeting to Graham and removed my hand from my lap and replaced it back onto Graham's. *He's your friend. He'll understand. And if he doesn't, I'll kill him.*

I felt the nervous bubble of laughter start up again and I clamped my hand over my mouth to stifle it, glaring at Robert as I did so. He looked over at the brooding Kim brothers and shrugged his shoulders. "Hospitals make her nervous."

Robert wrapped his arm around my shoulder and pulled me in towards him, pressing my head onto his shoulder and sighed. "Sorry," he said soothingly. The one-word statement was nothing short of a blanket apology, but it accomplished its goal, and I mouthed a "thank-you" that I knew he felt from the movements of my lips and jaw, and had heard from my thoughts.

The hours seemed to slowly drag on as we waited for someone to reappear and let us know what was going on. I finally had had enough of the waiting and asked Robert to tell me what was taking so long.

Are you sure? He was hesitant, knowing that I had never used his ability for my own personal needs, never wanted to. It kept me normal…as normal as possible, anyway.

But this was different. I wasn't asking just for me. This was about Stacy, and Graham, and even her brothers, who had grown tired of trying to stare Graham down and had now moved on to simply trying to stay awake; two had already failed at that.

Robert searched my eyes, peered through my mind and saw that this was important to me. He smiled at this small concession I was making, and then closed his eyes for a split-second. He reopened them before I even had a chance to thank him, and his smile grew wider.

She's okay. They're done sewing her up—three stitches that she's already bragged about to her father…twice—and will be out as soon as all the paperwork is completed.

I felt the whoosh of release as the worry and stress left me. Stacy was going to be alright. Things were going to be okay. I turned to Graham to tell him, my mouth open and poised with the beginnings of the great news, but Robert's grip on my shoulder turned fierce, almost painful.

How will you explain to him that you found all this out because I read the minds of the people in the emergency room?

My mouth closed as I realized what I had nearly done. Robert had reassured me that Graham would be accepting, but I didn't possess as much confidence in that as he did and I knew that I didn't want to lose Graham over Robert—I had nearly done that once already and I didn't think I could deal with the consequences if I lost him completely.

It felt like a stab to my subconscious, the sudden and wholly unwelcome flashback of what Lark had said just a few hours earlier in the library. I wasn't capable of accepting the consequences that my lies and the subsequent truth would bring.

"Oh damn," I muttered.

"What?" Robert chuckled, his voice filled with humor, already knowing what my answer was.

"I hate it when she's right. It's just going to make her feel more superior," I groaned, sinking into my chair and burying my face into Robert's side.

He pulled me in closer and I felt his mouth press against the top of my head. "She may feel superior, but she's just as lost and naïve as you are," he whispered against my hair, his cool breath sending shivers down my spine.

"What time is it?" I asked, needing a distraction from the heat that was starting to build in me from the contact.

Without moving he answered that it was nearly five. I lifted my head with a jerk, my eyes round and large at the announcement. "Dad! Janice! They don't know! They're going to wonder why I'm not home yet, or why I haven't called—oh this isn't going to sit well with them. I've got to call them," I cried, and stood up, my body turning around in circles as I tried to figure out where the payphones would be located.

As if on cue, seven cell phones of varying makes, models and sizes appeared in front of me, all attached to the hands of their owners: Five Kim brothers, one boyfriend, and one best-friend. "Well...um," I struggled as I looked at each one like they were foreign objects, the business of how to use them fleeing from my mind in just that moment.

"What are you, some kind of cell phone magnet?" a voice asked behind me. I turned around to see Stacy being wheeled out of the emergency room in a rickety wheelchair, Lark standing alongside, Stacy's father holding the handles and pushing.

"You're out!" I shouted, reaching my arms out to hug her.

"Wow," she gasped as I squeezed her, my arms wrapped awkwardly around her and part of the wheelchair. "You've gotten pretty good at that. Now let go so I can breathe again."

"Oops," I squeaked, quickly loosening my arms and pulling them behind me. "So...what's the verdict?"

She pointed to the mass of gauze and tape that covered a third of her forehead as she answered. "I've got three stitches, *three*, and I didn't need any anesthetic. They marveled at my high pain threshold. I'll probably be a legend here." She took in the five pairs of rolling eyes and rolled hers in return.

"Anyway, the bleeding took a while to stop and I've got a nice concussion to boot, but other than that I'm fine. They insisted I be pushed out in a wheelchair—some stupid hospital policy that they wouldn't ignore—otherwise I'd have walked out on my own. I'm starving because they wouldn't give me anything to eat, and I'm so ready to kick Erica Hamilton's ass."

She turned her head to glare at Graham as she continued. "I don't know what you ever saw in her, but whatever it was, if it was in her face it'll be gone come Monday."

"Stacy," her father chastised, but his gaze was fixed on Graham. The look wasn't hard to read. It said quite plainly that Graham wasn't good enough for his daughter. Especially if his ex-girlfriend was attacking her and sending her to the hospital; Graham looked down at his feet and said nothing.

"What? I'm not going to do much damage, but Bimbo Barbie is definitely not going to be going out on many dates when I'm through with her. Who'd have thought I'd be taken down by that walking peroxide bottle?" Stacy grunted, ignoring her mother's hissing and her father's groan of disapproval.

Sean laughed at his sister's comments. "Maybe hanging out with the freak and the hottie threw off your sense of equilibrium."

It didn't take much to figure out who the "freak" and who the "hottie" was, and I genuinely wasn't bothered by it, but it took even less for him to quickly blurt out an apology as both Robert and Graham released menacing growls at the insult. What did bother me was that I knew that Graham had been more insulted by the quip referring to me, rather than it being an insult to Stacy. It shouldn't have been that way.

"Oh please," Stacy laughed. "We're all freaks. But at least we can get dates, unlike you, Casa-no-game."

This time, the laughter spread—with the exception of the parents…and Sean—and the tension that had been thicker than wool was finally lifted.

Lark helped Stacy to stand, her face still filled with concern, though not to the same degree as it had been at the school. "Are you sure you want to go home? You could stay here for the night, you know. The doctor did recommend it."

Stacy jeered at the suggestion. "I'm not an invalid. It's just a stupid concussion. I'm going to be fine and I'm definitely going to school tomorrow; I don't care what that man in the white coat says, I'm not staying home."

Stacy's mother launched into a rant entirely in Korean, with words that I was certain weren't meant for innocent ears, judging by the wincing and cringing that came from her sons, as well as by the way Lark's perfect upturned mouth shaped itself into a perfect line.

The yelling continued as everyone walked out of the waiting room towards the elevators that would take us to the parking structure. I stood with my hand firmly clasped in Robert's, frequently turning my head to look behind me at Graham, whose face held a wide mix of emotions, the least of which was amusement.

"Are you going to follow Stacy home?" I whispered to him, and frowned when he shook his head. "Why not?"

Seven heads whipped around, seven pairs of eyes all glaring at me, as though I had committed some heinous offense for even bringing the subject up—another faux pas.

"Grace, just go home, okay? I'll be alright. In fact, Lark, I think you should catch a ride home with Graham while I deal with…this," Stacy said with frustration. "I'll call you guys later on tonight."

That short, seven word sentence set off another barrage of foreign words as the Kim family entered the elevator, completely filling it to capacity. As the doors shut, I felt an urge to giggle at the ridiculousness of it all.

"What floor are you parked on?" Graham asked Robert, breaking the unnecessary silence that remained long after the elevator doors had closed.

"Third. You?"

"Second."

The ding of the bell announcing an empty car quickly ended that short-lived conversation, and the four of us piled into the elevator. I pushed each respective floor button and waited in silence as the elevator lurched up. It remained quiet until we came to a stumbling halt and the doors dinged open again.

"I'll see you at home, Grace," Graham said softly as Lark filed past him, her walking stick conspicuously absent from her hands. It was the first time I had noticed it was missing, and I prayed that it wasn't absent on purpose. My thoughts must have been heard, because I soon recognized the clattering sound of her folding stick opening up.

"Okay," I replied, lifting my hand to wave good-bye but having the doors shut on us before he could see.

"So what gives?" I asked as the elevator started rising again.

"What do you mean?"

I turned to face Robert, my arms folded across my chest, and cocked my head to the side. "Why didn't you complain or argue or something when Stacy suggested that Graham take Lark home?"

"Ahh. What would be the point in complaining? If I had, Stacy and her family would have gotten the impression that I didn't trust Graham around my sister, and vice versa, and that wouldn't have helped Stacy out now would it? You saw how they looked at Graham. He's popular in school, and pretty much what every parent hopes their daughter brings home to date. But..."

"Not with Stacy's family," I finished for him.

"Exactly. He's not what they expect for her. If I had given them any reason to doubt him even more, it would have just made things harder for Stacy, and that's not what she needs right now."

I followed him as we walked out of the elevator, our hands still joined. "Thank you."

He stopped and looked at me, his pewter eyes turning molten with pleasure. "You're very welcome, although I don't know what it was that I did."

I stood up on my toes and pressed a quick kiss to his lips. "For at least pretending that Graham is trustworthy with your sister."

He laughed softly, brushing the back of his fingers against my cheek. "I do trust him, Grace. Don't think that I don't. But...well, you saw how Stacy's brothers were with him; I feel the same way, only I can read his thoughts," he explained as he leaned down, his intent quite clear.

I laughed as comprehension finally sunk in. I lifted my head up to accept his kiss and far too quickly, we were once again walking towards his motorcycle. "What's going to happen to Erica? And Lark?"

"Actually, I have a feeling that you're going to be a part of that equation as well, so I'd start wondering what's going to happen to you, too."

He helped me climb onto the seat behind him as I allowed his words to sink in. "What do you mean, I'm part of the equation?"

Over the roar of the engine, his thoughts filled my mind, settling into every empty crevice. *You've received part of the blame for Erica's behavior. Your dad's probably already received a phone call from Vice-Principal Kenner, so be prepared to tell them nothing but the truth when I get you home.*

I gulped at that bit of news. After having a fairly boring and overall quiet high school career, my senior year was quickly turning into something that I wouldn't have believed had someone predicted it just a few months ago. Dad had received not one, but two phone calls from the school this year about me. The first one because I had left school on the first day during lunch and hadn't returned. Who knew what this one detailed.

As Robert pulled into my driveway, the front door flew open and Dad came rushing out. "Are you okay? What happened?" He reached his arms out and pulled me off the bike, his hug nearly squeezing all of the breath out of me.

"D-Dad…what's the matter?"

He pulled away and looked me over, his eyes red from…crying? "The school called…they said that someone had been knocked unconscious and that she'd been taken to one of the emergency rooms. They didn't tell me who, or where. I called every single one asking if you had been admitted, and they all said no. Janice is on the phone with one of her friends who's a supervisor at the hospital in Licking; they were trying to find out if you had been admitted under a different name."

I heard Robert walk up behind me, and I leaned back to put some distance between Dad and me. "Dad, I'm okay. Stacy was the one who was hurt."

"Stacy? But...I don't understand. The vice-principal called-"

I held up my hand to quiet him. "Dad, apparently Vice-Principal Kenner thinks that if Erica hates someone enough to hurt her, it must have been me. Erica pushed Stacy while she and Lark were coming back from the restroom; Stacy hit her head against the doorframe of the cafeteria." I continued with describing the entire ordeal, finishing just as Graham arrived.

"Is this all true?" Dad asked Graham as he walked up.

"What happened today? Yeah, pretty much," Graham replied.

Dad shook his head in disgust. "I don't know what you saw in her, Graham. That's some freakish behavior she displayed today. You should be glad you're rid of her. You don't need freaks like that in your life."

I saw Graham's mouth twitch, and I knew what he was thinking— it was my thought as well. Robert concurred. We waited until Dad announced he was going back inside to fill Janice in, and then we burst out into laughter.

"Can I tell her that your dad called her a freak?" Graham guffawed, his head thrown back in a full bodied laugh.

I nodded, too amused to do anything else.

SPEED BUMP

As with all things high school, the incident between Stacy, Lark and Erica turned into a she said, she said battle for supremacy. Erica's crony Becca insisted that she had witnessed Stacy instigate the entire affair, although several people had already given statements that Erica had been completely alone when she pushed Stacy. It wasn't until I was called into the office during lunch that I learned the truth of school politics.

"Well, Miss Shelly, I suppose you know why you're here," Vice-Principal Kenner told me as I sat down in front of his desk. He was a short man, slightly balding with a thin, wispy mustache situated off center, directly below his nose. He wore thin-framed glasses perched midway on his nose and though he smiled often, you just knew that it was out of habit and not from genuine happiness.

"It's because of what happened yesterday," I replied, watching as he brought out a folder from under a large pile on his desk. He opened it and pointed to a few things with one of his stubby fingers.

"Yes, it is. I'm afraid that there is some confusion as to what exactly started the whole mess, but your name was brought up by Miss Hamilton, and I'm going to need to hear your side of the story."

"Okay…"

130

He started to read from the top sheet, a basic laundry list of incidents that led up to yesterday's fight. "Basically I'm being told that Miss Hamilton's intended target yesterday wasn't Miss Kim, but rather you. It took much coaxing on my part for the truth, but Miss Hamilton seems to feel that you have wronged her in some way. I want to know what exactly it was that was said or done—from your own point of view—that could have triggered such an uncharacteristic outburst."

I felt my jaw drop. "Erica's blaming this on me?"

"Please, let's not focus on that right now. I just want to hear your side of the story."

Accepting this, I began. "Erica hates me. I don't know why. I've only spoken to her twice. She used to date my best friend, but they broke up almost four months ago and now he's dating Stacy. I thought that was why she went off on her."

Vice-Principal Kenner leaned back in his chair and pressed his fingertips together, forming a pyramid beneath his chin. "That's the same story that Miss Bellegarde and Miss Kim told me, as well as Mr. Hasselbeck. Unfortunately, Miss Hamilton's version makes mention of your relationship with Mr. Bellegarde as one of the reasons she feels such ill will towards you."

I frowned, the direction his tone had taken sounding more like an accusation. "Well, I certainly don't know why. She made Graham end our friendship because she hates me; this was before school had even started, before I had even met Robert. Whatever her reasons, if Robert is one of them, it's definitely not the main one."

"Miss Shelley, certainly even you can see why she'd feel so…put off by your relationships."

I shook my head, the reasoning completely lost on me. He smiled and turned the folder that was in front of him around, his fat finger pointing to an image printed in the bottom corner of the top page. It was of me. "Take a good look at this picture, Miss Shelley and-" he reached to the side and pulled out another folder and opened it up, revealing an identical sheet of paper, the image at the bottom now replaced with Erica's "-look at this one. Do you see the difference between the two?"

I nodded. "Yes. One is of me and the other is of someone completely off her rocker."

He clicked his tongue, shaking his head in a grandfatherly sort of way. Well…it would have been grandfatherly if it didn't feel so condescending. "Grace—do you mind if I call you Grace? All this formality is wearing on me. Thank you. Grace, you're an intelligent girl. Your grades are always top-notch, and your academic future is definitely promising. But that's to be expected for girls like you.

"What do you mean, 'girls like me'?" I asked as I felt my hands clenching against my knees.

"Don't take this as an insult, Grace, because it's not. You're the kind of girl that has to do well in school because you're just not cut out for other things that require the assets that someone like Miss Hamilton has. She's popular and attractive, her family is well-known, and her status in the community is above par, while you're-"

"A freak," I finished for him.

"I wasn't going to say that," he insisted, but I shook my head at his denial.

"Yes you were; don't try to insult the intelligence that you just said I was expected to have, Mr. Kenner. I'm not conventionally beautiful—I already know that. The whole school knows that. I'm different, but you know what? I'm okay with that now. I wasn't before, I admit it, but I am now, and so are my friends.

"I don't have to be beautiful to warrant the same kind of admiration that you seem all too eager to give to Erica, but if that's what it takes then I don't want it. Yes, Erica is beautiful and popular, but she's also mean and spiteful. She's a vindictive person who cannot accept that she cannot get everything she wants."

"And you know what she wants then, Grace?" he asked, leaning in this time, anxious to hear my answer.

"Of course I do. She wants Robert."

132

He smiled. It was one of satisfaction; I recognized it right away. "And are you willing to give her what she wants?"

I snorted at his question, the notion too ridiculous to even consider. He didn't approve. "Grace, I'm almost certain that you've spent quite a deal of time questioning why someone like Mr. Bellegarde would be with someone like you in the first place. I know that I certainly have, as has pretty much everyone else here at Heath. It's not that you don't deserve to be happy, it's just he's out of your league, and-"

I'd had enough. "And what? Where are you going with this, Mr. Kenner? What does any of this have to do with Erica attacking Stacy?"

He seemed pleased that I had cut through the unnecessary conversational filler and got right down to the point. "Erica has agreed to take a suggested suspension for her—error in judgment if you agree to break things off with Robert. If you don't, she's going to sue the school for discrimination."

Reflexively I pounded my fist onto the desk. Mr. Kenner didn't even flinch. "I'm being blackmailed by proxy? On what grounds does she have to sue?"

"Her father's attorney mentioned the fact that both you and Stacy are of Asian descent and that your actions haven't received any form of punishment, while hers has. That screams discrimination, don't you think?"

I heard my voice rise, and I knew that anyone outside of the office would hear everything that I was saying, but I didn't care. "I have done absolutely nothing to Erica. From the moment this year has started, she's had it out for me. She attacked Stacy because of me, and now you're telling me that she's blackmailing the school, too? Whatever it is that she's accused me of, whatever *truth* you think you've received from her, it's all a lie and I refuse to sit here and allow you and Erica try and dictate who I can and cannot date. I'm through."

I stood up, prepared to storm out of the office when he mentioned something that left me unable to move. "Grace, are you aware that two days after the start of the school year, Mr. Hasselbeck and Miss Hamilton both filed a complaint against you?"

I couldn't say anything. I simply stared at him mutely. "They both insisted that you had made threats against Miss Hamilton, that you were so distraught over your friendship ending with Mr. Hasselbeck that you had cornered Miss Hamilton in the restroom and threatened her with bodily harm. Miss Rebecca Muniz corroborated their story, stating that she had been in the bathroom during this incident.

"It seemed so uncharacteristic of you, and I was willing to dismiss it. But then I remembered how you left school on the first day without authorization," he said as he lifted the top sheet from the folder containing my school record and pointed to the date that I could never have forgotten.

"Have you asked Graham about that so-called incident recently? I'm fairly certain that he'll tell you he was simply doing it because Erica wanted him to, and that nothing like that happened at all," I argued.

"And what does that say about him if that were true, Grace? That he's weak, and susceptible to the charms of a beautiful woman, that's what. Either way, it's not going to help you out. You've got a decision to make. What's it going to be?"

"Tell Erica to sue the school. I'm not breaking up with Robert because she doesn't want to accept responsibility for assaulting Stacy. And," I paused as I walked towards the door to leave, "I'd be more concerned about Stacy suing the school for discrimination.

"She was physically attacked to the point of needing to be hospitalized by a student on campus, and instead of punishing the person responsible for it, you're telling me to break up with my boyfriend. I hope you're camera ready, Mr. Kenner, because I have a knack for getting other people into the paper, and that's exactly where you'll see your name if you go through with this."

I stormed out of his office, out of the office period, and entered the hallway where an anxious group awaited my return. Lark and Robert were both trying to mask the anger they felt—they had heard every single

134

word—while Stacy and Graham held nervous expressions, the verdict still unknown.

I focused my attention on Graham, the fresh knowledge that he had actually filed a complaint with the vice-principal against me tattooing my mind with the latent betrayal. "How could you?" I whispered, unable to say anything else.

Robert placed a comforting hand at the small of my back and I felt I could lean fully against it and never fall. I needed that support right now. "It's going to be okay," he said to me softly, his hand moving in small circles.

Lark spoke up then. "Come on; let's go somewhere else other than the hallway. People are staring."

"They're always staring," I muttered but allowed Robert to push me forward as we walked towards the front entrance of the school. The crisp winter air was a welcome change to the stifling warmth of the school's hallway.

"Now, tell us what happened," Stacy insisted as she sat on one of the outdoor tables, patting the space beside her.

"I don't know where to start," I grumbled, my eyes glued to Graham's. He couldn't have known what I was about to reveal. Good. Let everyone be shocked. "Erica's trying to blackmail me into breaking up with Robert. She told Mr. Kenner that if I didn't, she'd sue the school for discrimination."

Robert and Lark remained quiet while Stacy managed to muffle a very nasty expletive. Graham never took his eyes off me. "I told him that I wasn't going to be blackmailed, not by Erica, and definitely not by him. And that's when he told me that Erica had filed a complaint against me at the beginning of the school year."

"For what?" Stacy hissed.

"For threatening her. She had a co-complainant."

"Who?"

I looked at Graham. His face already spoke volumes. "Your boyfriend."

Stacy turned accusatory eyes towards him, her mouth open with shock. I felt my own eyes start to burn at the confirmation I could see written in his face, the guilt that could not be hidden.

"Grace…you had been acting so strangely after—well, you know. When you ran off that first day, it wasn't like you. You don't run. I knew something was wrong, so when Erica told me that you had threatened her in the bathroom…Grace I didn't do it to hurt you, I swear.

"I thought that if I filed that complaint someone would talk to you. You needed someone to talk to and I couldn't be that person for you. Not then, anyway. Please, please say you believe me," Graham said imploringly, his eyes full of hurt that mirrored my own.

Stacy reacted before I could.

"Ow!"

"That's what you get for being such a simpering, stupid jerk!" she shouted at him while rubbing her fist, her knuckles sore from the angry punch she gave to Graham's chest. "She was your best friend, you idiot."

"I know. God, don't you think I know? I feel like a complete jerk; I deserve to be punched—but not by you, Stacy…not again anyway— Grace, say something. Here-" he lowered his head to mine and turned his face to the side, his finger pointing to his cheek "-hit me. Punch me right here, blackout my eye."

I could feel the fingers of my hand twitch, itching to do just that. Instead, the cool hand of someone slid between them. I looked up and saw Robert holding my hand against his chest, a smile on his face. "You'll regret it later if you do. You know you will."

I returned my focus to Graham's cheekbone, and envisioned my fist making solid contact with it. I could do it: I had resumed my Tae Kwon Do lessons with Stacy and could land a fairly decent hit. "Grace…"

"Fine!" I cried, throwing up my free hand in exasperated disappointment. "Graham, stand up straight. I'm not going to hit you. Robert's right. I'd end up regretting it later. But *only* because my hand would hurt."

"Thank you."

"Can I hit him?"

I turned to the voice that asked, and felt a smirk pull at my mouth. "Sure, Lark," Robert said from beside me. Even Stacy held her arms up, her posture like that of a prize presenter on a game show. I watched as Lark slowly walked up to Graham, her face absolute deadpan, and swing her arm behind her.

"No!" I cried out, leaping in front of the flying fist, knowing what it was that was hurtling towards Graham, and knowing that he had no clue. The pain didn't set in at first, and for that I was grateful.

But when it did...

"Why did you do that? You could have been seriously hurt!" Lark complained as she tried to hold me up. Robert was at my side just a split second after the blow landed on my shoulder which forced me into Graham, the two of us falling onto the pavement. Graham had managed to crawl out from under me as Robert gingerly turned me over, his hands immediately healing what I knew was a dislocated shoulder.

"You were going to hurt Graham," I wheezed, the pain constricting my chest and making the simple task of talking a painful venture. "He doesn't know..."

"I don't know what?"

"That Lark's been taking lessons with me," Stacy stepped in, her voice pitchy and nervous. Did I sound like that when I lied, too? If I did, I really was a bad liar.

"Lark's been taking lessons and she's really good...for being blind. She's very advanced—she might surpass me, and I can see. And she's really coordinated, too," Stacy continued, obviously having inherited the "I'm-so-nervous-I-can't-stop-talking" gene.

"Oh." That was it. Graham didn't question it. Had I said it, he would have automatically known I was lying—I had inherited that same gene, after all. Instead, he accepted Stacy's explanation. I didn't know if that was out of guilt or genuine naiveté but it would bother me for days afterwards.

Graham's attention turned back to me, amusement and concern blending together to distort his features. "Are you okay? I'm sorry…"

I shook my head at his apology. "Don't. I'm fine. It's just a little bump. See?" I pointed to my shoulder, now nearly pain free and mobile thanks to Robert's unseen ability. "It'll be gone by tomorrow."

He snorted, his gaze turning back to Stacy. "You're a lot stronger than this, Stace—there isn't even any bruising. You've knocked me flat on my rear-end; Grace looks like she was bitten by an ant."

It was as close to a compliment as I had heard him pay her and I wasn't the only one who noticed. "Thanks," Stacy murmured, her face growing red with embarrassment. Or was that pleasure?

"Okay, now that we've established that I'm a complete weakling, can we get back to the issue at hand?" Lark asked, her head tilted upwards, her eyes blinking rapidly.

I felt my heart skip and threw a quick look at Robert. He had the same concern and quickly stood in front of his sister, blocking her from view. It took less than a minute, but when he stepped aside, I knew that the danger of Lark's crystal tears falling in front of Graham had passed.

Unfortunately, he noticed the silent exchange and stepped forward, his hand reaching out to comfort her before dropping to his side limply just before it could have brushed against her face. "Are-are you alright, Lark?"

She nodded stiffly, something that resembled pride taking over her demeanor. "I'll be fine. Let's get back on topic, okay?"

His head bobbed up and down but the concern remained even as Stacy began asking about what else had happened. "Did Mr. Kenner threaten you, Grace? Did he actually threaten to blackmail you?"

I shook my head. "I didn't give him the chance. I-I think I ended up blackmailing him…"

The incredulous looks on Stacy and Graham's faces were almost enough to have made my threat worth it. "You blackmailed the Vice-Principal?" Graham gasped, voicing the question that I knew was poised on Stacy's lips.

"I guess I did," I said, giggling nervously. "Oh dear bananas...I blackmailed the vice-principal."

Robert grinned. "I think I like this side of you"

"What side of me? The side that's going to get me suspended?"

"The side that's proving to everyone just how special and unique you truly are," he said behind his grin, his eyes crinkling with amusement at my resulting scowl.

"Fat lot of good being special and unique is going to do me when I'm not only Grace-the-Freak, I'm also Grace-the-girl-who-got-the-school-sued."

Stacy placed her hand on my shoulder, a comforting gesture that only made me feel worse. "Oh geez, Stacy, look at me. You're the one with the concussion, and I'm here complaining."

"Don't forget three stitches," she said mockingly before laughing. "Grace, what did you say to Mr. Kenner exactly?"

I repeated the entire event, the words spilling out without any effort, the final sentence barely leaving my mouth before Stacy launched into a tirade that rivaled the one she displayed in the emergency room. "I'm going to destroy her—physically, socially, and then physically again," she seethed. "Well, my parents are definitely going to sue the school now. This isn't going to fly; my dad is going to have a field day with this."

Lark, finally able to express her anger over the situation had her teeth bared in a silent snarl. "She's got a death wish. She doesn't know who she's messing with."

Robert's stoic features belied the low, rumbling growl that he emitted, while Graham looked disgusted.

"God, I didn't think I could feel any more sorry, be any more sorry than I already am, but man, Grace...I am so—oh God, I cannot believe this—I am incredibly sorry for ever getting involved with someone like Erica. I had no idea that she'd be this vindictive," Graham said as he shoved both hands through his hair, turning the tame hair into a field of twisted spikes. "I wish I could go back in time and change everything."

"Ditto," I muttered. "Look, it doesn't matter anymore whether or not you used to date her. Erica hates me and has it out for me for some unknown reason, so whatever it is that I do won't matter." I turned to look at Robert, wrapping my arms around his waist and tilting my face upwards so that I could be sure he saw the truth in my eyes as well as my mind when I said, "I'm not breaking up with you. Not for anything."

It would have sounded like typical high school ignorance to anyone else listening. If I had heard it uttered by someone else, I probably would have rolled my eyes and made some kind of off-hand comment about the stupidity and cluelessness of the statement, but I wasn't talking about someone else. "Not for anything," I mouthed.

"So what's the plan?" Robert asked Stacy just before he pressed his lips against my forehead. "Are your parents going to confront Mr. Kenner? The Hamiltons?"

"The plan right now is to get through the rest of the day without me killing Erica, and then I'll tell my dad about what happened. Grace, I think you should tell yours, too." Graham stood beside her, his hand awkwardly pressed against her back as he attempted to give her the strength that she clearly did not need, but judging by the look on her face, greatly appreciated.

"We'll talk to our mom about the Hamiltons. They're a fairly important family here from what I know about them, but they'll be quite surprised to see just how important the Bellegardes are as well," Lark said smugly. She had her arms folded across her chest and I imagined Erica slowly suffocating in her arms. This thought brought a smile to Lark's face. "She has no clue what's coming to her, does she?"

I shook my head. No one did. As the bell rang, signaling the end of lunch, I wondered if anyone ever would.

LOOKS AND DAMAGES

I felt incredibly anxious during fifth period as the clock's second hand ticked slowly around the dial. Each minute movement seemed to cause my emotions to flip flop, changing from angry to fearful. Sixth period loomed ahead, with the one person who seemed most intent on ruining my life in every way possible.

She had attacked Stacy thinking it was me. She had somehow managed to convince Mr. Kenner that blackmailing me was somehow a good idea. What was there left?

When at last the bell rang, and the class gathered their things to leave, I felt all the suspense leave me. I grabbed my backpack and headed towards the classroom exit, searching for the pair of silver eyes that I knew would be there waiting for me.

"I didn't see you after fourth period," I said as Robert grabbed my bag from my shoulder and hefted it onto his own. "Did you have to…"

"Yes. I was hoping that you'd have met up with Lark afterwards, but she's left campus."

"Why?" I asked, half-knowingly.

"She's upset with herself, and with you," he answered. He placed his arm over my shoulder and pulled me against his side. The closeness helped disguise the next few minutes as he shared with me what couldn't be said out loud.

She attacked Graham, not to hurt him, but to incite you to feel concern for him, remind you that despite his many flaws, you still care for him. She didn't expect you to jump in front of him at all—hurting you upset her greatly today, and awakened some of that compassion that she's kept tamped down for the past century or two.

I immediately felt quite, well…stupid. *That's why she only dislocated my shoulder, instead of tearing it off.*

He nodded grimly. *I suggest you never do that again, Grace. I don't like seeing you hurt; it was very difficult for me to not hurt Lark in return, or even Graham for that matter when I felt the pain in your mind, saw the injuries to your shoulder.*

The thought that Robert had to struggle to keep from harming his own sister because of my foolishness compounded the guilt that I felt for upsetting Lark. *Wait, you said injuries. I know she dislocated my shoulder—she didn't break it, did she?*

No, she didn't break it. Like I said, she had no real intention of hurting Graham. Not severely anyway. The angle at which you were hit is what caused the dislocation. The other injury was dermal.

Dermal? You mean skin, right?

He smirked. *Do you really hate Mr. Branke's class that much that you'd need to ask that?*

I pictured myself stomping on his foot and smiled when his smirk disappeared and was replaced with an apologetic frown. *Sorry. Yes, dermal as in involving your skin. No one could see it except me, but it was there, Grace.*

The word "it" shouldn't have meant anything to me. It shouldn't have, but it did. *That awful bruise I got on my hand at the wedding. You mean that was on my shoulder?*

He shook his head slightly, and pulled me in even closer to him, steering us towards a small alcove between some lockers. He pressed me up against the side of them and placed his hands beside my head, his arms trapping me between him and the cold metal behind me. *It's everywhere, Grace. It's…all over your chest. I stopped it from spreading down your legs but there's some faint lacing of it crawling up your neck and down your arms.*

He traced his finger along the column of my neck, the touch causing me to forget everything he had said, everything I had been thinking of. All I was able to do was fight back the need to groan as he traced the path that led up to my pulse and then back down to the collar of my shirt.

Grace, focus please.

I shook my head. *You started it.*

I need you to listen. The bruising is very unique in appearance, Grace. It doesn't look like a normal bruise. You remember-

I remembered. Despite the delicious feeling of having him so close, I remembered everything about that bruise. I had punched Lark playfully in her arm, the contact brief and painless for the both of us. It shouldn't have been for me because according to Robert, the chemical makeup of an angel's skin was like that of spider's silk: it was unbelievably strong, like steel, but felt like the exact opposite. It was soft, smooth and supple…deceptively supple. The brief connection between Lark's arm and my fist had broken every single bone in my hand, and turned my flesh into a veritable palette of blues and blacks.

But, while the bruising, the breakage, and the fact that I didn't feel a thing was all incomprehensible enough on their own, the pattern of the bruising is what had left Lark and Robert with little in the way of explanation. I quickly lifted my arm and pulled at my sleeve, gasping as I saw the familiar markings. My arm looked like a purple and black honeycomb, the hexagonal shapes fading gently down my forearm and disappearing shortly before my wrist.

I quickly yanked my sleeve back down and stared, wide-eyed at Robert's face. *What am I going to do? I can't go home like this—Dad'll freak!*

Robert's eyelids lowered as he thought about what it was that could be done to quickly heal the bruising that was slowly going to reach my hands and demand an explanation to the unexplainable. I grinned. I more than grinned; I nearly whooped for joy.

Grace, be serious here. This is to help heal you. It will only be for a little while, and we do not want to gather too much attention because of it.

I turned my head to look at the mass of students that walked by, each one stealing a quick glance in our direction and then looking away, embarrassed that they had been seen looking in the first place. *If you don't want us to gather too much attention, I suggest you hurry up and kiss me before the bell rings.*

As he leaned in, his method of healing now the only thing I ever wanted to think of ever again, I felt the familiar stumbling of my heart as it sped up and lost control of its rhythm. I held my breath, held myself completely still while his painfully slow approach increased the building anticipation within me.

When his lips finally, softly pressed against mine, the first time he'd ever actually done so in school, the self-control that I was holding onto so desperately broke free. My hands flew to his face, wanting to hold him there forever. I felt his mouth turn up into a smile against mine as he heard my thoughts.

"Is that a promise?" he whispered, his breath sending every nerve I possessed into a frenzy as it hit my skin. I relished the way his breathing sounded as ragged as my own, the short connection between us doing just as much damage to him as it had done to me. "Damage? I thought I was healing you." He leaned in and brushed my lips with his again…once, twice…the third time was done with as much pressure and insistence as I knew he was capable of before he lost his composure.

When at last he rested his forehead against mine, I answered his question. "It's damaging, being so close to you, needing you so much and not being able to do anything about it."

"Yes. I suppose we are doing some serious damage to ourselves then, aren't we?" He pulled away, his arms dropping down to grab my arm. He lifted my sleeve and smiled at his handiwork. "No more bruis-ing."

I didn't look down. I didn't want to. I could only see the disappointment in his eyes that contradicted the smile on his face. I wanted to ask him, needed to know what caused it, but as usual, my timing was all wrong; the bell rang, sending the remaining students in the hall into a mad dash towards their classes.

Robert took a firm hold of me and stepped out of the alcove. Although I knew that we weren't anywhere near our class, we still ended up standing in front of the door in the same amount of time it would have taken any normal person to have exited our little hideaway. He opened the door for me and gently coaxed me inside, his hand on the small of my back offering tremendous comfort as I realized that, with all eyes on the two of us, our exchange of affection had been witnessed or relayed to just about everyone possible in nearly no time at all.

And you thought your ability to share thoughts was fantastic. I thought to Robert, smiling. *Nothing beats the speed and accuracy of high school gossip.*

"Okay Mr. Bellegarde, Miss Shelley. Take your seats please," Mr. Danielson called out to us from his office. "We'll be starting in just a few moments so I think I'll excuse your…tardiness."

The giggling and snorts of amusement that echoed around the large, auditorium-like classroom was enough for me to understand why we had never done anything like this until today, and why we probably wouldn't do this ever again.

I wouldn't say that.

My head turned slightly to acknowledge his thoughts as we sat down in our seats. *Oh? Why?*

Just that it was worth all of this discomfort.

I felt my eyes narrow as I looked at him, his features giving away nothing. Almost nothing—I saw it then: the slight twitch in the corner of his mouth told me everything I needed to know. *You didn't need to do that, did you? You could have healed the bruising the usual way.*

The twitch grew until his bottom lip looked like it was trembling from trying to contain the grin I knew was threatening to break free. *You little sneak! You did that to distract me!*

He nodded, the silver in his eyes shimmering with liquid heat. I had to blink before I lost my train of thought.

It worked, didn't it?

This time, it was my turn to nod, and I turned around in my seat in a huff, miffed that he couldn't have simply said that he wanted to kiss me. *You're enough of a distraction. I don't need subterfuge to kiss you, Robert.*

He turned in his seat to face me, and leaned forward, his elbows resting on his knees, his hands held out for mine. I pretended I didn't see them. *Grace, you need whatever distractions you can get right now, but you still need to be able to focus. If I had simply told you that I wanted to kiss you, two things would have happened. The first one being that you'd want us to leave, and the second one being that you'd become very disappointed when I said no.*

I felt my bottom lip push out. He was right.

And, even if I hadn't said no, you would have still been very disappointed when I wouldn't let you get carried away. At least here, there was a double reason for maintaining your self-control.

I snorted. *Self-control. Hah. You were having some difficulties yourself, Robert. You specifically chose the environment to help keep you in check; not me.*

His face paled at my words, his lips pulling into a surprised smile. *Well, I suppose you're right. I do have a problem with my own self-control around you, you know that. It's becoming more and more difficult to reign in, but I've got time. So…forever, eh?*

I glared at him. *Don't change the subject!*

He chuckled softly as he motioned towards the front of the class with his head. *I don't think I have a choice.* Quickly, very quickly, he reached for my hand and pressed a warm kiss to my palm, replacing my hand without anyone having seen a thing.

146

The start of class wouldn't be ignored today as Mr. Danielson began handing out packets of paper: our next classroom exercise. I took mine without bothering to open it up, choosing instead to watch as Robert leafed through his lazily. I knew he'd have thoroughly finished reading it before I even completed the first paragraph of instructions, so I simply waited, my eyes scanning the classroom carelessly. Instantly my gaze stopped on the only other pair of eyes that chose to ignore the packet.

Erica's eyes were narrowed into angry slits, her mouth ironed into a harsh, aging line. She was glaring at me with an unbelievable amount of anger and vehemence; I felt the hairs on the back of my neck stand up again.

She looks like she wants to kill me. I didn't need to do or say anything. Robert had his hand protectively at my back, the room suddenly growing still and cool. Mr. Danielson walked over to the thermostat to adjust the temperature, just enough of a distraction to cause Erica to point her gaze elsewhere.

Her mind is clouded with rage. I've tried several times to pinpoint the source, but she's so angry, so full of hate for you, I don't know which end is up. It's rare to find someone so focused on something so destructive, it blocks out all other thought and memory. Robert's thoughts told me nothing new. Her face said everything. She hated me. Hated me without any room for rhyme or reason, and I still had no clue as to why.

I will find out, Grace. I will get to the bottom of this before she tries a repeat of her attack on Stacy.

I smiled sadly and wondered when exactly had my life as being nobody's friend turned into being someone's mortal enemy.

ADMIRERS

As the days dragged on, the same scenario repeated itself: I'd flow through the first five classes without incident, and then enter sixth period with Erica's dagger-like stare stabbing me at every possible moment, ending only when Robert caused an environmental or emotional diversion, or when Mr. Danielson finally had enough of being ignored. Robert could only see black rage in her head, and it was affecting his moods, so he simply stopped delving into her mind. Lark became extremely protective over Stacy, even as she and Graham appeared to grow closer.

By the time Valentine's Day rolled around, we had entered into a routine that would have seemed very ordinary if it weren't for the building tension between what had by then become known as Team Stacy and Team Erica. No one else in the school knew that Stacy's attack had been meant for me, and Stacy and I both agreed it should remain that way. Erica had yet to be punished, and while Stacy's parents worked on a litigation strategy, Stacy, Graham, Lark, Robert and I made it a point to always keep Erica within our sight to prevent anything else from happening.

Of course, the arrival of flowers put a kink in things. I say flowers, but in truth, it seemed like an entire forest had sprung up around Lark as one by one, she was inundated with bouquets by boys who had chosen to spend their hard earned allowance money on her. We had barely made it to our table, her arms full of roses and carnations, the heady aroma thick enough to make even the diehard flower fanatic nauseas, when yet another round of boys showed up with flowers for her.

"You should re-sell those flowers," Stacy suggested as Lark quipped about how not even she could carry all of the bouquets and singletons that covered the table and spilled over onto the floor around us. "It looks like every florist in Heath owes their day's profit to you."

I smiled at Lark's frustration, thankful for the single lily that Robert had presented me with this morning. "You know, I think we're the only two girls here who actually feel sorry for you."

Lark huffed. "If you felt sorry for me, you'd help me carry some of these around."

Stacy shook her head while laughing. "I don't think so. Graham didn't even bother to get me a card, so suddenly walking around carrying twenty bouquets of roses and baby's breath is going to feel even more awkward and inadequate."

Lark turned her head to me, the question on her mind sounding like a mournful song in my head and I almost relented. Almost. "I'm sorry Lark, but I have Biology next, and all of those flowers will only get in the way of trying to keep Mr. Branke's hands to himself."

Lark pouted, the face so unbelievably precious it drew forth another round of flower-laden boys, each one professing their extreme like, lust, love, and one even admitted to her being an obsession. Each time she graciously thanked them and then turned down their requests for dates. All around us, I could feel the air of jealousy and envy growing thicker and thicker. "I can see now why *you* hate this holiday," I murmured as I pulled some of the flowers out of her arms.

"It's more than just this," she responded as she sighed and dumped the rest onto the seat beside her. "I mean, these boys cannot help feeling the way that they do. It's part and parcel to what I am, and so a great deal of their behavior is involuntary, which makes it far less flattering than all of those girls believe it to be." She nodded her head towards a particular table several feet away from us filled with just girls whose eyes were all glued to the stunning and ethereal Lark.

"Human males aren't capable of telling me no, and they certainly cannot help themselves when it comes down to a choice between me or their girlfriends. It's not something I say out of ego, because it's not me, Lark, that that they're interested in. It's the hidden divinity that draws them in. It's the same thing for Robert. He's got no control over the way girls react to him; they never tell him no and it's that power that gives us the ability to pretty much live and do what we please. Very rarely will a human ever defy us, which is why you're pretty special, Grace."

I felt myself flush at the compliment. "You didn't think so when we first met."

Lark laughed at that as we both recalled the short confrontation that had occurred. "You're right. You caught me off guard. I hadn't expected Robert to have told you so much so soon, and yet you weren't trying to suck up to me like I had expected. I think that angered me more than anything else. I don't like being surprised."

Stacy chuckled, her head bobbing up and down in agreement. "That's true. I can't even begin to imagine what that must feel like for you; you know what everyone is thinking, and then Grace shows up throws something at you from out of left field...that's a total mental plot twist!"

"What's a total mental plot twist?"

The three of us looked up at Graham. And his tray of food. "Are you actually going to eat all of that?" Stacy asked as he sat down and we took in the enormous mound of unrecognizable mush that he had piled on his plate.

"I'm hungry. Besides, your mother made this, although I'm definitely hoping that your cooking skills aren't as bad."

Stacy's lips pursed, the insult taking a stronger, tighter hold on her than the hint of a possible future together. "My mother didn't cook this slop. She makes the desserts, like that piece of pie that she wrapped up for you." She reached over and snatched the plastic-wrap covered plate from his tray and placed it in front of herself. "But, if you think that she's such a lousy cook, I'm sure you won't mind if I eat this instead."

She pulled the plastic wrap off and, using her hands, lifted the pie to her mouth and took a large bite out of it. Graham was left gaping at her, his fork poised in mid-air, the "slop" oozing from between the tines.

"Now *that* is good pie," she said after swallowing the last bite. "It's too bad that the desserts are usually the first to go, otherwise you'd be able to go back and get another slice."

Lark and I couldn't help but laugh as Graham looked dejectedly at his now cold lunch, the spot where the pie had once sat seeming to shout out its emptiness, and sighed. "I deserved that, I guess. Sorry."

Stacy shrugged her shoulders and reached into her backpack, pulling out a brown paper bag. "Here," she said as she tossed the bag to him.

He caught it just before it landed in his food. "What is it?"

"Just open it."

He pulled the bag open and let out a whoop of joy as he pulled out another plastic wrapped piece of pie. "Thanks, Stace!" He jumped up and placed a quick peck on her cheek before returning to his seat to quickly devour the dessert, sighs of satisfaction the only sound out of him for the next few minutes.

"You're welcome," she said in a soft voice. His reaction should have made her smile, blush, something…instead she seemed disappointed, sad even.

"So, what's with the garden?" Graham asked when he was done inhaling his pie. "Did somebody die?" He looked at the flowers that surrounded Lark, wrinkling his nose as the smell began to mingle with the odor that emanated from his lunch tray.

"It's Valentine's Day. Guys do this sort of thing on days like this when they like a girl," Lark replied, her voice annoyed.

Graham snorted. "Yeah. Right. It's more like this is the sort of thing that guys do when they want to get into a girl's pants."

"Oh really?"

Graham's face grew ashen as he turned around. Robert was standing behind us, his arms crossed over his chest, his expression stern, though upon closer inspection a slight twitch of a smile could be seen at the bow of his mouth.

"Well, it's not like you got Grace anything," Graham pointed out, the flowers in my hands all bearing tags that read Lark's name quite obvious to anyone who was looking.

Robert slowly lifted the cellophane and tissue paper wrapped bundles out of my hands and placed them onto the ground behind me, leaving one ribbon wrapped stem lying in front of me. He picked it up gently, turning it around and staring at it, the sheer, sapphire and silver ribbons dangling well past the stem. I hadn't noticed how well it complimented the ring that glinted on my finger, the deep blue stone still void of the once brilliant star that had once occupied its center.

"You got her that?"

Robert nodded, his hand gracefully laying the flower into my own. "It's not an entire florist shop, or a piece of pie, but it's something I know that Grace would appreciate."

I lowered my head to hide the flush on my face. Robert sat down beside me, his hand lifting my chin to look into my eyes as he continued. "And while some boys do use gifts to try to lure their paramours into giving up certain liberties, most don't. I don't. I wouldn't know what to say about you since I'm fairly certain that you haven't given Stacy a gift yet, but if you truly believe what you say, I suppose it's a good thing that Stacy's been left wanting this year."

My eyes grew wide at the insult, the insinuation. I heard Stacy gasp, felt the shock in Lark's mind as her thoughts stung my mind. What I didn't hear was the rebuttal from Graham. He should have been livid. He should have jumped to defend himself, or at least defend Stacy.

Instead he apologized, grabbed his tray, and left without saying another word. *How could you do that?* I glared at Robert, my eyes having never left his. *How could you embarrass him like that?*

His eyes turned into cold steel and the temperature in the air around us changed to match. *He's embarrassed because he knows I'm right, Grace. He left because he couldn't face that fact. His comment was asinine and his behavior unacceptable. But I didn't say what I did to hurt him, or you. Sometimes people need to have their mistakes pointed out in order for them to be rectified.*

I opened my mouth to say something. Anything. But what could I say? He was right. And I was angry with him for that.

"The fact that you two are so eerily silent should be enough to clue me in that you're fighting, but if you don't mind taking it off mute so that I can defend myself if my name happens to come up, I'd really appreciate it." Stacy looked at the both of us. She could have been quite calm, or she could have been furious; I had no clue as to which because the look on her face was totally unreadable.

"I'm sorry," I apologized. "I-we weren't…"

She waved her hand in front of me. "Look, I know it was one hundred percent about Graham, so don't get all freaked. Robert, I appreciate what you said, but I don't need you to defend my honor, or whatever it is that you were trying to do. I can take care of myself, okay?"

Robert nodded, his mood lifting somewhat, the air slowly warming around us. "I guess I overstepped my bounds. I forget that not all girls are damsels in distress."

"No one here, anyway," Lark snarled. "If you're feeling useless, why don't you go out and flick someone in the head? Create a nice little head wound that you can try and heal so that you keep your nose out of other people's business?"

She stood up, the movement so quick her chair went flying out behind her and slammed into the back of the cafeteria wall. The sound caused everything else around us to stop. "You might think you're perfect, Robert, but you're not. Remember that."

Stacy and I looked at each other as Lark stalked off. We both could almost see the thoughts running through each other's mind, and instinct took over all other form of judgment. I looked at Robert apologetically, looked at the stack of flowers piled up all around our now empty table, and turned to follow his sister.

To my and Stacy's surprise, she hadn't disappeared with the speed that she was accustomed to. Instead she stalked towards her locker at the leisurely pace of someone like…well, me. She had foregone the walking stick, instead choosing to vocally count out any steps so that should anyone ask how she managed to make it to her locker without it, she'd be able to answer truthfully.

Of course, the attempt at human actions ended as soon as she reached her locker. Without a second thought, she ripped the combination lock cleanly from the door, the mechanism holding the lock seemingly melting like butter. Her door opened with a lazy squeak, and Stacy and I witnessed something that we both knew no one had ever seen before.

Lark's hand was shaking. I stepped towards her and took her hand into mine. It felt unnaturally cool, as though her icy demeanor had transferred into her flesh. I followed her gaze into her locker and felt the catch in my breath even as I recognized the very same one in hers.

A pink box of charcoal sticks was propped upright; a sheet of paper covered with tiny bumps lay at its side. Lark's free hand reached inside to retrieve the note while I released her other hand so that she could skim the surface with the pads of her fingers. "I wish that these came in different colors so that you could feel the colors that you've brought into my life. Until then, at least you can use these to show others what you feel," she read, the sheet of paper starting to flutter beneath her fingertips.

"Who is it from?" Stacy asked as she peered at the blank sheet. "Does it say?"

Lark shook her head. "That's it. It has no name on it."

"A secret admirer! Well, this is much better than flowers, I'll give you that," Stacy said, her nose wrinkling at the residual smell of the numerous blooms that clung to us as we stood alone in the hallway. "I wonder who it's from."

I remained silent, as did Lark. How does one go about telling their friend that their boyfriend, who hadn't given them anything for Valentine's Day, was the secret admirer of another? I looked at Lark's face and tried to gauge what her emotions were. She looked ethereally beautiful as always, but there was something I couldn't detect hidden in her eyes. It was like a fog had rolled in and blocked everything from sight.

"It doesn't say who it's from," Lark said softly as she folded the sheet of paper up and tucked it back into her locker. She closed the door gently, pressing it in when it wouldn't seal properly, and then simply walked away. I started to follow her when the bell rang. Soon she was swallowed up by the masses of bodies that filled the hallway; students trying to rush to class in a mad dash at trying to forget what it was that had been labeled "lunch".

"You don't think that she's upset about what Graham said, do you?" Stacy asked as we walked towards our respective classes. I shrugged my shoulders, not wanting to look into her face for fear that she'd be able to see the lie that I couldn't voice. "I would be if it had been me. Robert was right. It is a good thing that Graham didn't get me anything. I mean, we're not really that serious anyway. Not like you and Robert. You're all in love and crap. I like Graham, but I don't think I know how to get past that and into something more. Like isn't really enough...you know?"

"Yeah," I answered.

"I mean you and Robert—you two were meant for each other. It's like when Robert was born, God had you set up on a shelf for later, the yang to his yin. Graham's not my yang."

I laughed in spite of myself. "No, he's definitely not your yang. I don't know if he's anyone's yang, but then again I was stupid enough to think that maybe he was mine, so what do I know?"

As we neared Mr. Branke's class, Stacy turned to face me. "Grace, you made the classic mistake of falling for your best friend. It's perfectly normal and doesn't mean you don't know anything about who is and isn't meant to be with each other."

She waved goodbye as she walked towards her class, leaving me to ponder what she had just said. I couldn't help but smile. She had said that I was perfectly normal. No one had ever said that before.

At the end of the school day, when everyone else's heads were full of dancing and party dresses, mine was filled with chocolate covered raisins and a gross-out comedy fest at the theater. Robert had managed to save my flower from the mountain of blossoms that Lark had left behind in the cafeteria and I carried it safely in my bag as we rode home on the back of his bike.

So have the plans changed?

The plans…*No, the plans haven't changed. We're still going to the movies.*

So, when are you going to tell me?

I felt my head jerk back at the question. *Tell you what?*

As we approached my house, I saw that the driveway was empty. Janice's car wasn't in its usual spot, and I knew that Dad wasn't home either. Robert pulled the bike into the drive and turned off the engine. "Why you lied when you told me you didn't know why you didn't like this holiday."

I started to stutter, the words unable to form anything but incoherent sounds in my mouth. I looked at him and saw the pained look in his eyes. I had hurt him. I quickly turned my head away as I tried desperately to climb off the motorcycle without killing myself. I walked towards the front door and fumbled with my key ring—it looked ridiculous and plainly obvious that I was stalling since only one key occupied the ring—my heart was pounding a thick and heavy beat as I felt his shadow cross over mine, blocking out what little light there was from helping me see what I was doing.

"Grace, don't run away from me," he said, his breath blowing across my ear; he was a lot closer than I thought.

I turned around to face him, knowing that I'd never be able to open the door or avoid answering him. "I'm sorry," I managed to say in a low mumble. I stared down at my boots, afraid of seeing any more hurt in his eyes and knowing that I was the cause.

His hands cupped my face and lifted it, forcing me to look at him. "I don't need you to apologize. I just want you to be honest with me. I know this is difficult for you, but I'm not going to hurt you for being honest. I love you. I've always loved you, even before you existed."

The warmth in my cheeks flooded his palms and he smiled. I sighed at the sight. "Okay, truth?"

He nodded his head. "Truth."

"I think this is ridiculous, since you already know; I hate today because today is when my mom died. I hate the decorations, hate that every single year it looks like someone's throwing a party on a day that I think should be reserved for mourning."

I shut my eyes, hoping to block out the painful images of seeing my mother's last moments before she died—moments that I had altogether forgotten until Robert helped me to remember on my urging.

"I can usually push it out of my mind and forget about it, but sometimes the blatant reminders just make me want to curl up into a ball and hide until February fifteenth. Today is the day I became Grace the Freak, the day I'm at my most freak-like, and I don't know how to be anything else."

Robert sighed softly as he pulled me against him, his arms wrapping securely around me. "You're not a freak, Grace, and no matter how many times you try to attach that label to yourself, it'll never stick. Not to me, anyway. I guess that's one reason why we're so perfect for each other; we both loathe this day and yet, we're both tied to it for some inexplicable reason, although yours has far more merit."

I sighed into Robert's chest. "I'm sorry I lied to you."

His arms wrapped around me tighter, his chin resting atop my head. "You don't have to apologize for this. I understand your reasons, and support you. I just wish that you could trust me enough to tell me anything."

"I'm working on that," I mumbled, inhaling the intoxicating scent that was starting to overwhelm me.

He laughed as he felt my mood change and pulled away slightly. "So where is your dad? Janice?"

I turned around in his arms and finished opening the front door, pulling him inside and quickly shutting the door behind us with my foot. "Dad is where he always is on this day; he'll be at work until four, and then head off to the cemetery until it closes at six. I don't know where Janice is, but if she's with Dad, they both won't be back until six-thirty at the earliest."

"So we're alone, then?" he asked, his mischievous smile turning my stomach over deep within me.

"Um…I don't know. Graham might be coming home, soon," I said nervously, silently praying that I was wrong. Oh so very, very wrong.

"He won't be. His shift started five minutes ago."

"So we're alone, then," I whispered, marveling at the idea.

Robert brought my hand against his lips, his breath against them causing the faint hairs on my arms to stand at attention. "What do you want to do now that we have this house all to ourselves?"

"I-I…" I couldn't say anything. I looked at the stairs, wondering if saying that we could go to my room would seem too forward.

With blinding speed, Robert scooped me up into his arms and raced up the stairs, my door opening and closing so quickly, I would have sworn we walked through it.

"What makes you think we didn't?" he chuckled as he sat me down on the bed, lying down next to me. "You have so much faith in me; I don't know why." His fingers pushed aside a fallen lock of hair from my face, his thumb brushing the outside corner of my eye, tickling my lashes. "I often wonder what it was that I did to deserve you, to be so blessed with you, with knowing and experiencing you."

"I do the same thing," I whispered. He had moved his hand to my neck, his fingers grazing the pulse-point and slowly dipping into the hollow at the base of my throat.

158

"Yes, but my kind views blessings far differently from yours. We have so much in the way of abilities and power. When you take into consideration what it is that we're capable of, and what it is that we do, there really isn't much that humans possess that can give us cause for appreciation.

"But with you, whenever I'm with you, whenever I'm able to touch you and smell you, hear your voice, your thoughts I feel like I've never truly known what being blessed was. And when I hear this, feel this-" he laid his head on my chest, directly above my heart "-I understand what it means to experience a miracle."

We remained that way for some time, his head pressed against my heart, his hand against my throat, feeling the pulse there as the journey of the life that my heart pumped into each vein repeated itself over and over again.

"Robert," I said softly as the sunlight that had been shining through my window started to recede. "Is…is this all that we're going to be doing until it's time to leave?"

His head lifted and he smiled at me, a heart-stopping, breath-catching smile that would have made me forget what I had just asked had it not also sent my stomach into a fit of urgent dancing. "This is all that I trust myself to do, Grace. I feel very roguish, being all alone with you in this house, laying here like this knowing that there isn't anyone around to walk in. It tempts me to do…other things, but I know I have more control than that."

I felt my heart stop when he said "other things", but I also knew that no amount of cajoling was going to get him to do anything more than this. It was more than I expected, and enough to make me realize that I was doomed if I ever had to choose between self-control and letting go when it came to Robert.

"You're silly," Robert laughed, his fingers moving towards the bottom of my chin, tickling me and causing me to giggle. "And I love you."

"I love you, too."

He raised his head and shifted his body so that he was nearly fully on top of me. "Really?"

I rolled my eyes. "Of course, really. You know when I'm lying. You proved that today."

"True. I guess I was kind of hoping that you'd say something utterly human like 'how can I prove it to you' or something along those lines."

I stared at him, at the incomparable and undeniable perfection that was Robert, and started laughing. "You wanted me to do what?"

"What? It's been my experience that when questioned about what they say, human girls will go out of their way to prove it to be true. I was just hoping that perhaps you'd simply follow type," Robert said, laughing along with me.

"And what exactly were you hoping I'd do?"

He placed his hand in mine, lacing his finger with my own and pressed them onto my pillow above my head. "I was hoping that you'd go more into detail about wanting to hold me forever."

I let out an exasperated sigh. "It was a figure of speech, Robert. I'm not planning on living forever."

He leaned his face closer to mine, nudging my nose with his as his breath caressed my face. "Are you sure?"

I took a deep breath, inhaling the perfumed aroma of his skin, his breath, everything that I imagined made him what he was. "Y-yes," I replied, ignoring the wavering in my voice.

"Is there anything I can do to convince you to change your mind?" he whispered as I felt his mouth graze over my cheeks, the loose wisps of his hair brushing across my lashes, causing me to blink rapidly. "I'm open to suggestions." His lips traveled to my ear, and I knew my eyes crossed when I felt his mouth find the soft flesh of my ear, felt his teeth nibble and pull at it gently, each tug loosening any resolve I might have had…

"No," I managed to say, grasping desperately to the last shreds of my willpower.

Slowly, almost unbearably, he left a trail of small, almost feather-soft kisses along my jaw. He stopped when he reached my mouth; I felt him smile against my chin as he felt my body tense, saw me lick my lips in anticipation. "Nothing at all?"

I wanted to say no but I couldn't remember what it was that I was saying no to. Robert's mouth was poised directly over mine, his breath blowing across my lips in a teasing dance that tempted me to succumb to their owner's wishes. I took a deep breath and closed my eyes, willing to give him whatever it was that he wanted if only he'd finish what he started.

"Ahh…" Robert sighed, victorious. "Ahh, bloody hell."

My eyes flew open.

"Lark, you have incredibly horrible timing."

I peered over Robert's shoulder and felt the blood drain from my face. "Um…hi, Lark," I squeaked, mortified to have been caught in such a compromising position.

"Am I interrupting?" she asked sweetly. I detected a hard edge to her tone despite the softness in her voice and I groaned.

"Yes," Robert growled.

"No," I mumbled as I tried to sit up. Robert looked at me, disappointment flooding his face and I felt it wash over me, leaving me equally disappointed. Perhaps more so.

"Never more than I," Robert said with a sigh and helped me up. "I guess I'll be going now. I'll see you tonight." He pressed a quick kiss to my forehead and disappeared, the slight wisp of midnight smoke slowly fading from my window.

"He's right. You have really horrible timing," I grumbled as I pulled my hair back into a ponytail. "I'm finally making headway with him and then you show up. How did you get in here anyway?"

Lark remained silent as I completed my rant, her face impassive. "Are you done?"

"I am now," I snapped.

"Good."

"Fine."

"Are you done acting like a third grader?" Lark asked, the mocking tone to her voice emphasizing the same hardness that I knew was still there.

"That depends on whether or not you're going to tell me what's going on. You walked away today, didn't tell me anything about Graham's-"

She held up her hand, cutting me off. "I didn't tell anyone about Graham's gift. And how did you know it was from him?"

My eyebrows raised in surprise. "Because only Graham could possibly know what you would do with something like that."

"Oh. I thought that he told you in advance."

I shook my head. "He hasn't told me anything lately."

She looked at me skeptically and then sighed. "He probably thinks that whatever he says to you will end up getting back to me. If only he knew that you don't have a choice."

I glared at her. "You know, if you're that interested in what he thinks, why don't you just search his thoughts instead of mine? Cut out the middle man entirely. That way I don't get blamed when you say or do something that tips him off."

Lark looked away from me, but not before I caught a flash of anger in her eyes. "You think it's that simple, do you? Would you have wanted to look through his mind after he dumped your friendship for Erica? Would you have been able to?"

"No, of course not."

"Of course not. See, it's simple for you. You don't have to fight it; it's not a choice for you. I'm constantly struggling to keep from hearing Graham's thoughts because I don't want to see him thinking of being with someone else. And I hate the fact that that someone else happens to be Stacy.

"But the hardest part, the worst part is knowing that there might be a part of him that is thinking, not about Stacy, but about me, and knowing that there's nothing that either of us can do about it. If you've ever wanted to hurt me, Grace, forcing me to sift through Graham's thoughts would be it," Lark explained as she tried very hard to mask the crack in her voice. She failed.

"Why don't you just tell Graham about how you feel? Tell Stacy? What exactly is keeping you from telling them the truth? Isn't that what you're supposed to do anyway?" I said sarcastically.

Two soft thumps alerted me to the fact that something had changed. My eyes traveled down to the carpeted floor and I felt a wave of guilt wash over me. Two small, teardrop shaped crystals lay at Lark's feet.

"I'm sorry, Lark. I didn't mean to make you cry. Oh dear, oh dear bananas, I'm sorry," I stumbled, reaching to grab a tissue and hand it to her.

"And what exactly am I supposed to do with that?" she wanted to know.

I brought my hand back, staring at the tissue dumbly before tucking it into my pocket. "I guess it wouldn't have been much help. I'm sorry; I'm not used to this. I'm usually the one crying, so giving tissues is kind of an automatic response."

"Of course it is. Sometimes it's easy to forget that you're human with human sensibilities," Lark acceded. "I'm not used to all of this...emotion. And the worst part is that I don't even know what it is that I'm feeling! It's maddening, not being able to understand what's going on and yet having to control it so that I don't let it overtake me."

My head cocked to the side. "What do you mean you don't know what it is you're feeling? About Graham?"

She waved her hand in the air, as if to brush away my question. "No. I know what I feel about him—it's not that difficult to figure out considering Robert went through the same things. It's what I feel about Stacy, about not being honest with her. I cannot explain it. It's not painful. It's more...confining, like I'm stuck in neutral; I can't go forward, I can't go back, and the worst part is I can't make it go away because it just keeps growing."

The need to be supportive crushed down my desire to laugh. "What you're feeling is called guilt, Lark. You're feeling guilty for not being honest with Stacy about your feelings for Graham."

She scoffed at my simple answer. "Guilt? I give you insight into the unknown emotions growing inside of me and you give me guilt as the explanation? Is this some human trick to make me feel incompetent?"

"I'm sorry, but when was the last time you were human again?" I questioned sarcastically. When she didn't answer me I continued. "You've never been human, never known what it means to feel emotions that are a result of disappointing someone because you've never had to until now. You're feeling guilty, Lark. There's no science to figuring that out."

Lark slouched to the floor, her head pressed up against the wall beneath my window. "How do I get rid of it? What do I do to stop feeling like this?"

The frown on her face as I told her the answer did nothing to mar her beauty, but did a great deal to leave me with questions of my own. What would Stacy do when she found out, *if* she found out? Would Lark actually find it in her to do what was right? More importantly, was telling Stacy really the right thing to do?

"It's nearly six. Stacy will be here in a couple of minutes so we'd better get going," Lark said with a sigh.

"Great try on changing the subject. Very human of you," I joked as I dug around my backpack for my wallet. Finding it, I shoved it into my back pocket and headed towards the door. "I suppose you're going to make some kind of comment about how you wouldn't stoop to that level, huh?"

I turned around to see her reaction but she was gone.

"Hurry up, slow poke!" I heard her call from outside. I rushed to my window and looked outside. She was standing by the curb, a hand resting impatiently on her waist. "Well? Are you coming or not?"

"Show off," I mouthed.

I heard that.

THREE BLIND HUMANS

Stacy showed up ten minutes late, her face sweaty and pale. "Sorry guys. Practice ran late today—you're going to make up for missing it to-morrow, Grace," she called out from her car as she pulled into my driveway.

I swallowed the fear of what it was that Stacy would put me through for missing practice. I had honestly forgotten, but that wasn't an excuse according to Stacy and my shins usually paid a price for it. Lark pulled the front seat of the car forward so that I could climb into the back, a smirk plainly visible on her face.

"Oh sure, you smile now," I quipped, glad that at least someone was amused.

As soon as Lark was seated and the door closed, Stacy was gunning it towards the theater. "So, are we eating out after the movie's over or are we heading to someone's house to eat?" she asked as we rounded a corner. "I've got to call my mom and let her know so that she's not worried about me being out with serial killers or something."

"We could eat at my house," Lark announced, ignoring the serial killer comment. "I'm not exactly a fantastic cook, but I'm sure I could get my mother to make something."

I wrinkled my nose at the prospect of eating anything that Ameila made. "If she's as adept at making dinner as she is at making Jell-O molds then you might as well be out with serial killers."

"What was wrong with my mom's Jell-O mold?" Lark snapped.

I rolled my eyes. "Oh come on! That thing was harder to chew than an old belt. And it was JELLO!"

Lark turned around in her seat to glare at me. "I don't know what you're complaining about; I was able to eat it just fine."

"Oh sure. *You* were. Humans don't have the ability to chew through rebar, Lark, and we don't especially like testing that theory out either."

Stacy's giggling, accompanied by the random snort broke through our argument, causing me to realize just how ridiculous it was. "If you two only knew how hilarious you sound," she gasped, tears causing her eyelashes to spike. "I mean, it's probably only funny to me because let's face it, your mom's supposed to be this perfect angel and she can't even make Jell-O! And Grace actually had to eat some of it!"

Lark groaned as I, too, started to laugh. "Humans have such low standards when it comes to humor."

"Oh quit complaining," I said between laughter. "You're best friends with a human, your brother is dating one, and for all intents and purposes you're pretending to be one so obviously your standards have lowered, too."

We continued this way for the next ten minutes while Stacy maneuvered her way through the holiday traffic. "I don't think I've seen so many cars on the road here ever," she griped as she pulled into the darkening parking lot. "I am so ready to see something unromantic, unfunny, and totally gory. Oh, and something my mother would definitely disapprove of."

"Here-here!" Lark concurred.

"Are we actually going to find something like that on Valentine's Day?" I asked as I climbed out of the backseat. I stretched my legs and shocked myself by wishing that I had chosen to arrive on the back of Robert's motorcycle.

So when did your dad start letting Robert pick you up on his bike? Lark wanted to know.

"There's always at least one horror flick playing on Valentine's Day, Grace," Stacy confirmed.

I looked at the two of them, each one staring back awaiting an answer.

"Okay, Stacy. You're the Zombie expert," I said quickly. *My dad had a change of heart after talking to your mom about Robert's bike. She told him that he's very careful, has never had an accident, and feels more comfortable on it than driving the car. My dad said that for short trips, like to school and back, I could ride the bike.*

We entered the lobby of the theater, the smell of popcorn and hot dogs hitting our noses like a combination punch. I glanced at the marquee, browsing the different titles in search of the one that Stacy would most like to see.

"See, there it is, just like I told you," Stacy pointed out. The title definitely jumped out at you. "Black Bouquet. It's supposed to be the greatest slasher-flick in over a decade. It's going to spawn some serious sequels, although I'm pretty sure that some of them will go straight to DVD."

I simply stared as she pointed to the movie poster that hung between two obvious romantic comedies. A bouquet of black roses dripping with the deep burgundy of blood set against a backdrop of pure white velvet stood out among the posters full of beautiful, laughing faces. I shook my head, wondering when it was that I had graduated from Rocky Horror to actual horror.

"Hey, do you think you get a family discount?" Stacy asked Lark as we walked up to the ticket counter. "I don't get a girlfriend discount so I don't think Grace would get one either, but maybe you do."

Lark looked at Stacy with a quirky smile crossing her lips. "I've never had to pay for a ticket in my life and I don't plan on starting."

She smiled at the lady behind the counter, a brilliant smile that made the woman beam. "I'd like three tickets to see Black Bouquet, please."

The woman, her eyes still gleaming, her smile broad and full on her face, waited for the tickets to print out and then handed them over to Lark. "Enjoy the show," she said cheerfully.

Lark thanked her and then turned around, handing Stacy and I each a ticket. "See?"

Stacy's grin was nearly as wide as the woman's. "Wow! Why didn't you say something the last time we were here? Is this okay, though? I mean, you won't get in trouble, will you?"

"Is this even legal?" I asked worriedly.

Lark turned her back to us and pointed at the star of the most recent hit movie. "See that woman in that poster? She made more money for a ninety minute movie than all the teachers in school combined. Her latest boy toy is starring in the movie we're about to see, and he got paid twice as much as she did. I think it's perfectly okay if we take three tickets worth of money from their bank account."

Stacy nodded, obviously agreeing with Lark's contrived argument. I was interested in something else entirely.

"Lark, are you allowed to do this? I mean, if it's not okay to lie, why would it be okay to steal, because that's what this amounts to: theft."

She laughed at my concern. "Oh please spare me the moral lectures, Grace. I may be blind, but I'm not stupid. Just enjoy the perk of having me for a friend and let's go and get some popcorn."

"I don't like popcorn," I admitted.

"You don't like popcorn?" the two of them gasped.

"Yeah, she hates the stuff," Graham said from behind me. He placed a hand on my shoulder and smiled reassuringly. "Always has. I always say more for me, but some people find it odd."

Stacy looked away while Lark smiled. "Odd? I'd say you're the perfect person to have come with you to the movies. You can buy a bag of popcorn for someone who likes it and then they won't look like a pig to everyone else. You're a popcorn junkie decoy!"

"O-okay."

"So, what movie are you guys watching?" Graham asked, looking over my shoulder at the ticket in my hand. "Black Bouquet? A horror movie? Why not one of the rom-coms we have out?"

"Why not? It's not like any of us feel exceptionally romantic tonight," Stacy bit out. "A horror movie is just what we need to keep us in the mood."

I looked at Stacy quizzically. Mood? What mood?

"What mood?" Graham asked, as though he plucked it straight from my thoughts.

"Unromantic."

"Oh."

Lark crept up beside me as Stacy and Graham's conversation quickly escalated into an argument.

"I don't get why you think it's perfectly alright to complain about my lack of romance when you're the one who turned me down when I asked if you wanted to go to the dance tonight! We could be surrounded by stupid flowers and balloons right now, swimming in *romance*."

Stacy dismissed his statement. "I didn't want to go to some stupid dance where everyone's competing for who has the best dress, who has the best dance moves, who has the best corsage. That's not romantic. That's commercial."

Lark pulled me several steps away from the growing dispute, and I glared at the crowd that had gathered to watch. *Did Stacy tell you the real reason she didn't want to go to the dance tonight?* Lark wanted to know, her eyes flitting around, listening to the thoughts of the people surrounding us.

I shook my head. *She reveals more things to you than she does to me.*

She told Graham no because she thinks he wants to have sex with her and she's not ready.

I slowly closed my mouth and looked at Stacy and Graham closely, ignoring the redness of anger that disguised their faces from those who truly knew them. *Wow. Did you tell her she has nothing to worry about?*

Lark gave me an exasperated look, as she shook her head. *How would I explain that to her without revealing a thing about Graham? I couldn't do that to her. It wouldn't be right.*

"Do you two mind telling me what's going on?"

I turned around to see Robert standing behind us, mild anger crossing his features. "They're arguing," I answered, ignoring the obviousness of my statement.

"I see that. Will either of you explain to me why?" he asked as he crept closer to me, his gaze never leaving my face.

"Um...I really don't know. I think it's about the fact that they're not at the dance tonight. And why are you asking? Couldn't you just...you know."

His hand rose to gently touch the side of my face. "I could, but it's much more entertaining to hear other people's perspectives. Especially yours."

I couldn't see it, but I knew that that slight contact between our skin had left my face bright pink with the blush of remembrance. My lips pursed as I looked at him through the corners of my eyes. *You cheated.*

He didn't say anything. He merely winked at me and walked over towards the arguing couple. I nearly leapt after him, some strange feeling of protectiveness washing over me that I had not expected but I didn't know who it was for. He spoke in a low voice—so low I couldn't make out what he was saying—to Graham and Stacy before nodding his head and turning around, a stiff smile on his face.

"Everything's okay. Why don't you ladies go and enjoy your movie," he said to us when he returned. "I'm sure that it's about ready to start."

I opened my mouth to ask him what he had said but he brought his finger to his mouth, a sign. I didn't feel ready to leave him yet but he appeared ready for me to be. "But…we don't even have any popcorn," I blurted.

"But you don't like popcorn," three voices around me announced.

ᘓ

I sat through the movie, oblivious to what was on the screen. Beside me, Stacy was laughing at each scene, the imagery apparently amusing to her. Lark, on the other hand, was thoroughly annoyed. So annoyed in fact that she didn't care that she was supposed to be blind.

"They call that a wound? Look at the skin! Saw blades tear at the skin. That skin is smooth, like a scalpel sliced through it. You'd think with such a big budget, these special effects artists could at least have done some research on the way actual skin looks when damaged. And the blood! Who believes red corn syrup is actually blood?"

As the minutes ticked by, I felt myself sinking deeper and deeper into my seat. People around me were trying to forget about being in love, wanting love, looking for love. They were absorbed in gore and guts, escaping the mad, flower and candy heart laden world just beyond the theater doors.

But for the first time in eleven years, I longed for it. The sounds of screaming and slashing, of bodies piling up were causing my mind to recall images I did not want to see. I looked at Stacy; she was so into the movie I probably wouldn't have been able to glean a response from her if I set her clothes on fire. I turned to look at Lark. She seemed far too engrossed in the inaccuracies to hear my thoughts. As a precaution I started to jumble my thoughts, filling my mind with them, pulling away at just the right moment and finding a quiet corner to focus on what today had meant for so long.

The excuses I made for disliking Valentine's Day had all been a way to avoid the real reason. My mother's death, the car accident had been the death of one Grace and the birth of another. The sweet Grace that had been accepted, been welcome died that night along with my mother and in her place, the Grace that survived an exploding car, that couldn't remember a single thing, the "freak" had been born.

I hated that night because I couldn't remember what had happened, couldn't recall anything, not for anyone. Dad had asked me over and over, the police had questioned me, too. Therapists had tried to coax the secrets from me, but nothing worked. Until Robert.

He had shown me, physically taken me there to see, to remember. My thoughts brought to life in front of me and I was finally able to understand what had happened to me. I had accepted it, embraced it because for just a brief moment, I was reunited with my mother and I could now look back on those short, precious minutes and know that I had been blind to the truth not because what people had been saying was true. I had blocked out the truth because I couldn't accept it until Robert was with me.

I shuddered as I thought of what my life would have become had I succeeded at pushing him away after finding out what he truly was, what his call was. Simply imagining it left me feeling cold and empty.

"The main character should have been dead three scenes ago! How unrealistic are they trying to make this movie be?" Lark complained.

I braced myself for the protest from another member of the audience but none came. I slyly peeked around me and nearly fell out of my seat. We were the only three people in the theater!

"Can you believe her? Like any normal person would go and meet some stranger in the middle of nowhere!"

Seeing my opportunity to leave without being too distracting, I crept out of my seat and slowly ambled towards the aisle. I turned to see if Lark and Stacy had noticed my departure and smiled when I caught Lark's hand poised to throw some popcorn she had found on the floor at the screen. She might think we had low standards but Lark was every bit as much a human as we were.

I entered the hallway between theaters and headed towards the lobby, my nose following the pungent smell of burnt popcorn. It was fairly empty—most of the movies were currently playing—so I walked over to the door that read "employees only" and stared at it, thinking of his name, picturing his captivating eyes staring down at me.

"You're going to go cross-eyed if you keep staring at that door, Grace," Graham called out to me from behind the concession counter.

"Maybe it'll help me out in the looks department," I replied. I continued to look at the door, wondering how long it would take before he showed up. "Where is he?"

"Probably ordering us some more popcorn, or something along those lines. He's always in there. I'd start to wonder about him if I didn't see the way he looked at you all the time." Graham frowned as he said that, his forehead wrinkling with the thought that formed in his head. "D-do I look like that?"

I stepped away from the door and walked over to him. "Do you look like what?"

"Do I ever…have you ever seen me have that look on my face?" he questioned.

I watched him, saw the nearly pained look he had in his eyes as he awaited my answer. "Actually, yes, I have."

It was an honest answer, and it was one that I freely gave. It didn't matter who he was looking at when he did so, it only mattered that he was capable of doing it.

"Grace, do you think I'm unromantic?"

I held my hands up at that question. "Whoa, just because I told you I was in love with you, that doesn't mean you get to ask me all these emotional questions," I kidded, winking at him when it took a bit longer for him to realize that I wasn't being serious.

"Graham, I know you're not exactly the romantic type. You're Mr. Football, not Mr. Flowers and Candy. But I do know that you've got a sentimental streak to you, and when you show it, man…it ends up being one of the most romantic things I've ever seen."

The slight smirk on his face told me that I was convincing him, reassuring him that he wasn't whatever it was that he thought. He stuck his hand in his pocket and pulled out a little white heart. He handed it to me and I examined it in my palm. It had two little words inscribed on it.

"Best Friends."

"Yes we are," I agreed, and popped the little heart into my mouth, nearly gagging at the chalky, peppermint sweetness. "But next time, write it out on a post-it or something, okay? I think it'd taste much better than this."

He laughed as he watched me struggle with the candy and handed me a cup of water. "Sorry. I guess I still get a kick out of watching you eat whatever it is I give you."

"That's because you're a sadist," I stated, gladly accepting the cup of liquid relief.

"Well, that's true," he agreed. "But you're not exactly an angel yourself, you know."

I coughed, nearly choking on the water. He whacked my back a few times, slightly amused to be doing so and slightly concerned as to why he needed to in the first place. "None of us are angels, Graham," I managed to choke out before a fit of coughing took over.

He removed the cup from my hand and thumped my back a few more times until I settled down. "Geez, Grace. You're too serious tonight. It's no wonder Stacy likes hanging around you and Lark. The three of you make a scary trio sometimes."

"We do not!"

He snickered at my response. "You are! Just think about how intimidating you three are. You stood up to Erica during the soliloquy, totally destroyed her in under two minutes. Then there's Stacy, who got knocked out and came back to school the next day like some kind of superwoman. And then there's Lark, who's so beautiful everyone forgot about Erica today and gave their gifts to her instead."

"Even you," I said softly. I watched his reaction, his expression change from surprised to defiant. I was pleased.

"You know then. She told you."

I shook my head. "She didn't tell anyone. I was there when she found it, Graham. I knew who it was from the minute I saw what it was, and I have to say, that was pretty slick, typing the note in Braille. When did you learn how to do that?"

He smirked at the praise. "The girl who cuts my hair has a sister who's blind. I was telling her my idea, since I know that none of you know who she is, and she mentioned her sister and suggested that she write the note. So...what did she say?"

I wanted to say that she liked it, that she was over the moon, but she hadn't said anything about it. So that's what I told him. I almost wished I had kept my mouth shut when I spied the disappointment flash in his eyes and pull his carefree grin down. Almost. Whatever the fate of Graham and Lark, right now Graham was dating Stacy. He shouldn't have been giving anyone Valentine's Day gifts if he hadn't given her any, and so I told him that.

"I know, Grace. It was stupid and dumb, and I suck at being a boyfriend but I didn't really think about *not* getting Stacy a present, if that makes any sense to you."

The conversation paused as Graham helped a kid who went to our school with his drink and popcorn order. The kid looked at the two of us and shook his head. I couldn't help myself. I winked at him when he looked one last time and laughed when his face distorted with shock and disgust.

"Am I really that frightening?" I asked as the kid left. I looked at my reflection in the chromed frame of the popcorn maker and stuck my tongue out. "Well...am I?"

Shaking his head, Graham replied, "Of course not. You're just not what a lot of we guys are used to, that's all. None of you are."

I raised an eyebrow, my silent cue that he should elaborate.

"I told you, you, Stacy and Lark are intimidating. Yeah, guys all follow Lark like she's got them on leashes or something, but they talk about you, too. I hear them, Grace. I know what they say about you, the good as well as the bad. The story about your mom...that kind of freaks a lot of people out because they can't picture it in their heads, but the guys that can get past that see you as someone who'd rather talk about stuff than trying on clothes at the mall. They always thought it was cool that you'd come to the games and knew what was going on.

"That's one of the most awesome things about you, Grace. You're just like one of the guys; you're approachable and if they ever stopped to actually talk to you, they'd understand why you're my best friend."

I blushed at the compliment, knowing full well that no guy would ever truly understand. It just wasn't possible. "Look, Graham, I get that you think I'm someone that guys would like. I don't necessarily understand it, but then again I don't understand how you can eat so much food and not look like the Goodyear blimp either. I'm never going to be *that* girl, the kind that guys flock around and talk about like they do Lark and Erica. I know my limitations, Graham."

"I would beg to differ," I heard voiced behind me. Robert placed a hand on my waist and turned me to face him. "I talk about you all the time. You're the only topic of conversation I'm ever interested in." He lifted my chin with a finger and pressed a quick kiss to the corners of my mouth.

"Why aren't you inside watching the anti-Valentine's Day movie with Stacy and Lark?" he asked when he realized I was alone aside from Graham. "How long has she been here?"

Graham looked at the large clock on the wall. "About fifteen minutes," he replied. "She likes campy horror stuff, not the hardcore guts and glory kind of film that Stacy's into. Speaking of which, are we on next week for some RHPS? We haven't done that in a while, and since I'm staying on your couch, there's no real excuse for not doing it."

Robert looked at me and raised a curious eyebrow. "RHPS?"

I laughed at the puzzled look on his face. "You honestly don't know?" When he shook his head, I felt something akin to…pride. "I actually know something that you don't? Oh wow, I need to savor this moment for a bit. Hold on."

"Holding," he said, laughing as well. "You let me know when you're ready to let go of the smugness."

Graham rolled his eyes at the two of us, a loud groan of discomfort spewing from him. It only made me laugh harder.

"Okay, okay. RHPS stands for the Rocky Horror Picture Show. It's a ritual with us. We watch it on the last Friday of every month. Well, we *used* to anyway. We sort of stopped doing that after-"

"After I made one of the biggest and dumbest mistakes of my life," Graham interjected quickly.

I nodded and continued. "We get kind of goofy, and call each other the names from the movie all day. Whoever forgets and says our real name first gets punched."

"You watch a B movie, call each other names, and then hit each other as a ritual?"

"Yeah. I said it was goofy," I said defensively.

Robert glanced over at Graham who seemed to be trying very hard to appear as though he wasn't paying any attention to the conversation. He was failing miserably. "I think that's actually a great idea. I'd like to participate."

"You what?" Graham and I uttered at the same time, our jaws hanging open in shock.

"I'm interested in everything that you do, Grace. If this is something that you like to do, I'd like to do it with you."

Graham objected first. "Look, Robert, I've got nothing against you, man, but this has been our thing since Grace and I were kids. You hear me? Our thing."

I held up my hand to stop Graham from continuing. "Robert, I don't know if this is something that you'd really enjoy. Are you sure you want to?"

His hand lifted to cup my face, a soft and gentle touch that spoke of comfort and tenderness. "I want to."

I looked over and Graham who threw his hands up in the air, defeated by three little words. "Sorry," I mouthed to him and cringed as he threw his hands up once more, exasperated by my weakness.

You are mine as well.

I turned my head to face Robert and felt the warmth of unrestrained affection flood my cheeks. How was it possible for him to not say a single word out loud and yet still cause my heart to flutter like some spastic bird's wings? I shook my head at the inconvenience of the moment and pushed my face deeper into the palm of Robert's hand as his fingers cupped my ear and his thumb gently stroked the edge of my cheek.

"So, are you planning on staying out here until the movie is done?" he asked when Graham's angry banging and annoyed grunting became too loud to hear even the silent thoughts in our heads.

"I'd like to. Graham's right about my not liking all that gory stuff. I'm perfectly content to stay out here and inhale the scent of stale popcorn and cola stained carpets."

He looked over at Graham who had suddenly quieted, his face turned away but one lowly ear conveniently pointed in our direction. "Do you want to come into the office with me? I've got some paperwork to fill out but we could talk in there."

I nearly burst out laughing as I watched Graham's ear turn a bright shade of crimson. "I think I'll stay here and keep Graham company. Maybe I can convince him that you joining us won't be such a bad thing."

Robert sighed in defeat and playfully tousled my hair. "Fine. I'll see you later then." *I love you.*

I beamed at him, all teeth and gums. *I love you, back.*

He nodded his head to Graham and headed back to his office, his movement so swift and catlike, I knew that he wouldn't be in the office for long. Whatever it was that he had planned for me had I said yes was now put on the backburner.

"So, are you going to stay here until closing again, or are you heading off someplace else with Stacy and Lark?"

My attention returned to Graham, his question barely registering with me as I worried over who it was that Robert was having to help cross over this time. "What was that again?" I asked, knowing that I probably looked like a lovesick fool but not caring a whit.

"I asked if you were going to be staying until closing like the last time, or if you were going somewhere with Lark and Stacy."

"Oh. We're probably heading back to the house to eat. I don't have the cash to go and eat out, and although Stacy might not know it, Lark's mom is a horrible cook—real cafeteria grade material."

That seemed to cheer him up a bit. I realized my gaffe too late and couldn't take it back. "Sweet. I call dibs on your leftover meatloaf, though. Janice said she was cooking tonight, which means it's all healthy and junk. I swear I've started having dreams that I'm a horse and she keeps trying to shove oats into my mouth."

The sound of my laughter filled the empty lobby. I hadn't exactly taken a liking to Janice's choice in menu as of late either, but I knew that she was doing it because of the baby. I wanted to tell her that my mom ate junk food throughout her entire pregnancy with me, but that wouldn't have been the truth. I didn't know what my mother ate while pregnant with me, and I had certainly never asked Dad about it.

"You know, you've got to start learning how to cook for yourself, Graham. That way, you won't have to eat bean sprout omelets and turkey bacon," I chided as he threw a handful of popcorn at me. "I'm serious! You could do with learning a few recipes!"

He walked around the counter with a broom and long handled dustpan in his hand and shook his head. "Uh-uh. I'm going to marry a woman who can cook like Julia Child so that I'll never starve and never have to learn how to boil water."

I moved my feet around as he swept the popcorn from between them. "Have you even tried a recipe from Julia Child?"

"No. But the way she talked always sounded like she had some food in her mouth, so I guess the food has got to be good, right?"

There was little else to do with that comment than shake my head. "You're hopeless, Graham."

He straightened his posture and looked at me forlornly. "You're right."

The lighting quick change in his mood acted like warning flares telling me to back off, but I ignored them. I stepped in closer and looked at the hard lines that had formed around his mouth and across his forehead, their paths burrowing deep as he tried to maintain a rocky silence.

"What's wrong?" I asked, concerned and almost fearful.

"It's just...I don't think that it's supposed to work out for me, you know?" he answered, pain and discontent written plainly on the lines that pushed his eyes downward. "It feels like I've inherited the reasons why my parents' marriage didn't work out, only I'm twenty years younger."

"That's ridiculous," I objected, "You're only eighteen. You're too young to even be thinking about marriage, much less having problems in one that doesn't even exist."

He laughed mockingly. "'It's never too early to start planning for the future.' That's what my dad said every single day last year as he drank away most of his paycheck. He and mom were always fighting, Grace—always. Oh, they didn't do it in the conventional way. No. Mom was always the one to start it. She'd give everyone the silent treatment, even me, and then she'd sit at the table and mumble under her breath about being unappreciated, unloved, take for granted...it never ended.

"Dad would come home and the two of them would just walk around each other, mumbling about how the other one was worse. They never yelled, they never argued out loud. They just mumbled. It got to the point where the only way I could hear anything either of them was saying was to talk to them on the phone."

He stopped talking and went behind the counter again. I opened my mouth to ask him to continue but soon realized that his internal clock had rung some silent alarm as the sound of doors bursting open echoed throughout the lobby and a rush of people filed out of a theater, empty popcorn and drink containers in their hands.

I stepped out of the way as several of them walked up to the counter to purchase additional drinks and snacks. Soon, the crowd dissipated as they headed towards their cars. Graham rushed from behind the counter once more, the broom and dustpan in his hands, and began to sweep up the shower of trash that the moviegoers had left in their wake.

"Do you need any help?"

"Sure. Go and grab that extra broom and butler under the counter over there and get that side of the walkway, will ya?" he answered, never looking up from his task.

I walked behind the counter and looked beneath it for the broom. I found a short handled one next to another long handled dustpan. "Isn't it against labor laws to keep a butler beneath the counter?" I quipped.

"The dustpan, Grace," Graham said, annoyed.

"The dustpan, Grace," I repeated mockingly. "You know, it's not nice to annoy the boss' girlfriend. I might make him schedule you for longer shifts."

Graham stopped sweeping and stomped towards me. "I think you need to get out from behind my counter and go back and finish watching the move before Lark and Stacy notice you're missing."

"I'd rather not," I disagreed.

"I'm not asking."

Realizing that I had worn out my welcome, I shrugged my shoulders and left him standing in front of the counter. I stopped before entering the hallway that would lead me back to my theater of gore and turned around. I walked back to him and stopped with just inches left between us.

"You know, I hope that one day you realize just how fortunate you are to have seen firsthand the mistakes your parents made in their relationship so that you can stop yourself from making the same ones, like not communicating with the person that you love."

I didn't bother to wait for a response. I simply headed towards the theater where I knew Lark and Stacy were still busy tearing apart the movie, oblivious to my absence. I could only hope that Graham wasn't oblivious to what I was trying to say to him.

PUT A SPELL ON YOU

When we left the theater that night, it came as a surprise to me when Lark insisted on being dropped off at home first. "I have a need to eat some of my mother's cooking," she said acerbically when asked why by both Stacy and I.

"I'm sorry if I offended you, Lark," I apologized but she held up her hand in rejection. I looked at Stacy's reflection in the mirror and saw her smirk. Lark's head whipped around to face Stacy.

"You think this is funny, too?" she snapped, shocked that her only other ally had turned against her mother's cooking.

"Well…Grace isn't exactly known for lying, and I don't see any reason for her to insult your mom's cooking other than because it was genuinely awful," Stacy struggled to answer as she fought with a bubble of laughter that seemed stuck in her throat.

"I don't believe this. Two humans are insulting an angel's cooking," Lark shook her head disapprovingly. "You two just wait until I get my wings and my call. If I'm called to be a guardian angel, you can forget asking me for help."

Stacy and I locked eyes in the mirror once more and we both burst into amused hysterics while Lark unceremoniously crossed her arms across her chest and huffed, her lips forming a perfect pout.

The laughter had died down a little when we reached the house with the white walls and ironic angel guardians standing in front of the large, wrought iron gate. Lark climbed out of the car without saying goodbye and disappeared into the night.

"You think she'll forgive us?" Stacy asked in between chuckles. As she pulled out, I crawled up to sit in the front seat.

"Oh, she will. She's probably just as amused by this as we are," I replied, watching the gate disappear behind us.

We rode in silence for a little while, the radio's music substituting for conversation. I looked at the time and sighed. "It's nearly ten. Are you sure you want to come over to my house for food?"

She nodded her head emphatically. "Actually, I'm sort of glad that Lark's not here. I needed to talk to you about something…private."

The way she said "private" made my ears burn, as though it had just heard something it shouldn't have. I nodded hesitantly and remained silent the rest of the way to my house. The lights inside were off, but the front door light was blazing a bright creamy white when Stacy pulled up into the driveway.

"What time does Graham get off?" she asked when she noticed that his car wasn't parked in its usual spot.

"He'll be off soon but I don't think he'll be in any rush to get home."

"Good," she sighed and unbuckled her seatbelt. I did the same and exited the car. I reached into my pocket to pull out my key and fumbled with it in my gloves as I tried to unlock the door. After a few moments, I succeeded and we quickly rushed in from the cold.

"You ever wish you could be able to handle the frigid cold like Lark and Robert?" Stacy asked as she removed her gloves to rub her hands together. "I mean, they never look cold. They dress the way they do because they need to fit in. They can be sitting butt naked in Siberia during a blizzard and it'd feel like a tropical day for them."

I smiled at the image and then shook my head. It was starting to feel quite tropical in here!

"I've only ever wanted to be considered normal," I confessed. "I've never wanted to be something as unique as an angel."

Stacy shook her head at my response. "You're crazy then. I'd give anything to be one of them. To be immortal, never sick, never weak…how can you not want something like that?"

I didn't answer until we were in the kitchen and I had placed a bowl of what appeared to be warmed lentil soup in front of each of us. "It's not all it's cracked up to be, Stacy. You see the things that we cannot do and you think that's great, but they have their weaknesses, too."

She nodded as she ladled some soup into her mouth with her spoon. "I know that. The whole lying thing and the secrecy issue. I just think that if there was some way for me to change into one of them, I'd do it in an instant."

I dropped my spoon in shock. "You don't know what you're saying," I gasped.

"What? You mean there *is* a way?"

I sucked in my breath at the revelation that Lark had kept this from her…and I had now revealed it. "N-not exactly. Let's just forget I said anything," I said quickly. I picked up my spoon and focused on eating my soup, hoping that Stacy would let the subject die.

I should have known better.

"No. I want to know. Is there a way?"

I shook my head. "No. There isn't a way for humans to become angels."

She frowned at me, obviously doubtful of my reply. "So why did you even mention it?"

I didn't want to lie to Stacy. The lies were piling up one on top of the other, and I couldn't add this one to it. "It's the truth, Stacy. There isn't a way for humans to become angels. Angels are born, not made."

Her frown deepened. "So you're basically telling me that there's no hope in me ever becoming immortal?"

I opened my mouth and then closed it, unsure of how exactly to proceed with this topic of conversation. I wasn't exactly clued in on all of the specifics myself, so what could I say to her that wouldn't get her hopes up or dash them away completely?

"You're going to have to talk to Robert or Lark about that," I finally said. It was the best that I could do.

Stacy bobbed her head up and down in silent acceptance and we finished our soup in the quiet of the kitchen.

After cleaning up, we headed up to my room, the whole purpose of Stacy coming over having not yet been addressed. I closed the door quietly behind us and then sat on the bed with my back facing the window.

Stacy sat next to me, one leg dangling off the bed, a shy blush spreading across her face as she struggled with the question she had wanted to ask me before we became sidetracked by the immortality discussion.

"Grace…this is kind of personal, so if you don't want to answer I'll understand. You and Lark are my best friends, but Lark's not into guys. At least, not to my knowledge, so I couldn't ask her this question, but you and Robert are joined at the hip so I know that you'd be able to."

I watched Stacy's hands as she rambled through her introduction; her fingers were flying through the air as she fidgeted with her nervousness and unease. I knew exactly how she felt.

"What I wanted to know was if you and Robert have…you know, done it yet."

I nearly choked on my own tongue as the shock of the question took control. It prevented me from recovering in time to reassure her that I wasn't offended as she started to apologize profusely, her hands flitting around like nervous birds.

When I had regained my composure, I grabbed her hands and pulled them down, pinning them to the bed. "Stacy, it's okay. I wasn't expecting this, but I'm not offended. Just shocked."

Stacy nearly started apologizing once again, her stammering voice contradicting the strong and self-assured person I had always known her to be.

"Calm down, Stacy," I said reassuringly. "Calm down and I'll answer your question."

186

She stopped talking, her hands quit fighting against mine, and she waited with an almost instantaneous patience for me to answer her. "I guess the only way to go about this is to be honest. The answer is no, Robert and I haven't...done it."

Her face showed shock, her eyes wide with surprise. "You haven't? But you two look so...close, like something intimate has happened between you. I thought..."

I nodded, understanding what it was that she had assumed. "We haven't done anything other than kiss."

"What kind of kiss?"

It was my turn to blush as I realized that I was about to admit to Stacy just how chaste my relationship with Robert truly was. "The kind you'd give your brother...if he was unbearably handsome and you were madly in love with him."

"Wow."

"Yeah."

Stacy looked out the window, her gaze focused on the empty space on the street down below. "I was going to say—I didn't know what I was going to say. This is all so weird for me. I mean, I've never had a girlfriend, someone I could talk to about this kind of stuff before, and now that I have two...one can't talk to me about sex and the other hasn't done anything more than kissing."

I couldn't prevent the sad smile from forming on my lips as I acknowledged just how woefully ignorant I was when it came to topics like these. "I'm sorry that I don't have the, uh...experience that you're looking for. I guess that's one less thing we have in common, eh?"

Stacy chuckled. "I don't have any experience in that department either, Grace. I just wanted to know what exactly it was that told you, if you *had* done it, that it was the right time."

"Oh. Well. That's something different," I mumbled, embarrassed at my incorrect assumption.

"Tell me about it. How pathetic are we, huh? Two inexperienced know-nothings thinking the other had some knowledge about sex."

I felt my head nod at her overwhelmingly accurate statement. "What made you ask anyway, if you don't mind me asking?"

Stacy sighed and leaned back on her elbows as she wore an invisible pattern into the carpet with her toe. "I kept thinking about what would have happened tonight if I had gone to the dance with Graham. Would I have been able to think nothing of it and just go along with the crowd? Just do it because everyone else is? I mean, don't get me wrong; I've never thought of it as something special, you know? It's not like my parents ever stressed remaining pure or anything like that, so I have to wonder if the reason I simply don't like the idea of it is because if I did do it, it'd be with Graham. Does that make sense?"

The idea of Graham having sex with anyone wasn't exactly my idea of appealing conversation, but I couldn't just ignore Stacy's need to talk or the fact that although she could have gotten far more sage advice from Lark, she had chosen me to open up to.

"I think that the longer you are with Graham, the more you're going to start questioning everything about your relationship until you come to a decision about what you really want." There. I planted the seed I didn't know I had.

Stacy's head tipped up and she stared at the ceiling as my words began to sink in. "I guess you're right. I don't know what it is I want, but I do know what I *don't* want. I don't want to end up a stupid statistic for some Government Health Agency because I caved in to peer pressure. I don't want to say that my first time was with someone I didn't love. And most importantly, I don't want to do it just because it feels good at the time, like I'm under some stupid spell or something. I've got enough brains to say no."

She was right. I marveled at how right she was. "It looks like you don't need to worry about what it is you want, Stacy. Your don'ts are just as good."

Stacy brought her head down to look at me, confusion and disbelief layered onto her face. "You sound as though I made a decision for you, too."

"You sort of did," I replied as this time, it was her words that sunk in. "I've been so stupid."

Intrigued by my admission, she sat up. "What do you mean?"

I sighed, the relief of finally being able to talk to someone about it almost dripping from the sound. "The reason Robert and I haven't…you know, is because he's not ready while I've been more than ready. Or so I thought. The feeling I get when I'm with him is incredible. It's euphoric, and all-together consuming and I can't help but want to feel more of it and I realize now that it's because of what Robert is. He insists that I'm not susceptible to his 'charms', but now I know that I am. At least, when we're that close I am. "

Stacy's mouth was poised to speak, her face surprised at what I had revealed about the intimacy of my relationship with Robert. Obviously Lark had been keeping a great deal from her.

"Angels don't get by on just their looks, Stacy. They radiate a type of divine charm that makes people automatically like them. You cannot help but be drawn to them, attracted to them. Most of it is artificial but it affects us all the same, and we become so enchanted just by their aura, we'll do whatever they want, even without the mental interloping they're capable of.

"Robert and Lark both thought it wasn't possible for me to fall under their—how did you put it—spell, since I defied both of them with every chance I got, but it looks like they were wrong. I'm just like everyone else."

I looked at my reflection in the mirror facing the foot of the bed and sighed at the sullen expression that now tattooed my features. "I should be happy that I'm starting to resemble someone normal."

Stacy rested her hand on my knee, the soft touch comforting. "So why do you look so down?"

I shrugged my shoulders and sighed, a half-hearted smile forcing itself onto my face. "I guess because now I'm going to start second guessing every single emotion I feel when I'm around Robert, try and decipher what's genuine and what's a product of his innate charm."

"You love him, Grace. I've seen the way the two of you look at each other. It's not the kind of look that makes you sick from the syrupy sweetness. It's the kind of look that makes you envious of what the two of you have, the connection that goes deeper than anything most people have ever felt with anyone else, much less with the people they're with now, myself included."

I looked into Stacy's eyes and saw the genuine gleam of envy in them. It was almost laughable that someone like her would be envious of me.

"I know I love him. I think I was probably born knowing it and it just laid dormant until he came into my life, as stupid as that sounds. I just don't know if what my body feels is what it would were Robert human and not…well, him. I mean, I know he's not making me feel that way. Not on purpose anyway.

"And I feel incredibly stupid now because I've been pressuring him into being more physical with me even though I know he's not ready. I feel like the abusive girlfriend and I, too, have enough brains to know how to say no, and yet I won't take it for an answer."

Stacy giggled as the words that came out of my mouth painted me more and more like the abusive girlfriend I had described. "I wouldn't worry too much about abusing Robert, Grace. Something tells me he can handle himself."

I nodded in agreement, giggling despite myself. I glanced at the clock on the dresser and sighed once more. "It's getting late, Stacy. Graham will probably be home soon, and Robert might stop by, too."

She cocked her head to the side, the part about Robert obviously not what she was expecting to hear. "Your dad lets him come over this late?"

I shook my head and raised my finger to my lips. "No one knows. Well, Graham knows. He came in while we were asleep and saw us together."

Stacy's mouth made a slight popping sound as it hinged open in shock. "He sleeps here with you?"

"Robert?"

Stacy rolled her eyes at that. "No, Ghandi—of *course* Robert! Lark didn't tell me that he was spending the night here with you! And you two haven't...wow. That's one patient angel, Grace."

I laughed as I stood and helped her up. "I'm the one with the patience, remember?"

She nodded, laughing right along with me. We walked downstairs and headed to her car. "I'll see you tomorrow at school then," she said before she climbed into her little car. "Thank you, Grace, for everything." She reached up and wrapped her arms around me, a quick hug that carried with it a great deal of friendship and affection that I knew I was not entirely deserving of.

I returned her hug and then waved as she drove off, waiting in the icy air until the red glow of her taillights were gone from my view. I walked into the house and quietly closed the door. I turned around to walk towards the stairs and nearly screamed when I saw Robert standing in front of me, a smirk lifting up one side of his face into a beautiful, yet crooked line.

"You scared me!" I whispered fiercely. "Why are you down here? What if my dad or Janice comes down and sees you here?"

His smirk turned into a grin and he swooped down, my feet leaving the ground in the living room and then being placed back down in my bedroom with incredible speed I would have sworn up and down that I hadn't even been in the living room to begin with.

"There, now there's no need to worry about that, is there?" he said smugly as he placed his hand at the base of my collar, his hand skimming the slight hollow that appeared between my shoulder and neck.

I pushed his hand away and turned towards my dresser, intent on searching out for something to wear to bed, but more interested in a distraction from the warm tingling that insisted on turning into a small crackle of sparks. "That's not the point," I managed to say, though my voice sounded winded as I struggled to keep pace with my rapid breathing.

He chuckled, silently moving up behind me and placing his hands on either side of my hips. "Why so nervous? Is it because you're afraid that my charms might make you do something you don't want to do?"

With remarkable speed, even for me, I whipped around and started to hit him with a pair of boxers. "You were listening!" I accused. "That was a private conversation between Stacy and me! I cannot believe you did that!"

He held his hands up defensively even though he knew that he'd cause more damage to the clothing than it would him, and I stopped hitting him. "I'm sorry. I didn't mean to, but I'm not going to say that I'm not glad I did. It was very insightful. Your mind has been shutting its door to me quite often these past few weeks and I'm beginning to feel like I'm not welcome in there anymore."

"Well, if you keep pulling stunts like this, you won't be," I muttered and turned around to finish grabbing some clothes to sleep in. "I'm going to change," I announced before I left the room. I stomped—softly, of course; I didn't want to alert Dad and Janice to any trouble—to the bathroom and nearly slammed the door before realizing that doing so would shake the entire house.

I quickly changed clothes and brushed my teeth, hoping that counting to a hundred would be enough to calm my nerves. I hadn't planned on talking to Robert about this until much later. I had wanted to plan out what I was going to say, needed to actually think about what all of this meant to the both of us, but that was obviously not going to happen tonight.

"You chose this life," I said to my reflection before flipping the light off and heading back to my room. It was empty.

I spun around, half expecting him to appear from some corner in yet another attempt to change the subject or distract me from my intended goal, but when I didn't see even a hint of smoke or silver, I relaxed. I sat on the edge of my bed and saw the fluttery movement of a piece of paper that had been left there.

"Something came up. I'll be back before you wake."

"Oh sure. How convenient that something came up," I muttered before crumpling up the note and throwing it on the floor. I crawled beneath the covers of the bed and turned my back to the window. After what only amounted to a few minutes, I crawled out of the bed and fumbled in the dark for the note. I did my best to iron it smooth with my fingers and then placed it gently beneath my pillow. I laid back down, this time with my face pointed towards the window.

SHOES

The week following Valentine's Day was as up and down as it could possibly get. Graham and Stacy alternated between fighting, arguing, and waging an all-out war. Lark appeared unmoved by it all—a front she put up to keep her true feelings from being exposed again—and chose to remain neutral when asked for her opinion about certain arguments by Stacy.

I felt like I was being pulled in three different directions by Lark and Stacy, who each felt it imperative that they give me their take on the situation. And by Graham, who hadn't spoken to me since our conversation in the movie theater, but to whom I felt a loyalty that I simply couldn't ignore because of the silent treatment.

The only one who kept me from pulling all of my hair out was Robert, who didn't understand how such trivial issues for him could be so stressful for me, but remained supportive as I vented and railed, ranted and cried about what this quadrangle was costing everyone.

Things came to a head during lunch, when Stacy and Graham began arguing about the virtues of French versus Steak cut fries. It was as ridiculous an argument as you could start, but anything could turn into one with them and they made it a point to prove it. I had always felt grateful to have a table with friends to sit down with during what could have been a very isolating time for me, but right now, all I wanted was to become invisible.

Every eye was trained on the two people sitting directly across from me as their voices reached a crescendo of substantial proportions. Their voices bounced around us, echoing off the walls and filling every table with enough gossip to last until the end of the quarter. This was better than television for most of them, and I hated that I was sitting front row, center.

"Will you two just break up, already?" Lark finally hissed at the two of them. Her face was a deconstructed study on anger. She was so beautiful that it was nearly impossible to detect the rage that lurked just beneath the surface, but I knew. "You guys do nothing but fight and yell and scream and shout. You're making complete asses of yourselves.

"Either make good on your equal hatred of each other and break up, or get it over with and sleep together because I refuse to listen to another ridiculous and inane argument about potatoes, or clouds, or grass or…whatever it is that you two find so important you have to disagree about it."

She stood up and stormed out of the cafeteria, the doors blowing open before she reached them. I watched the faces of those who had witnessed this and sighed with relief when they seemed too preoccupied with what would happen between Stacy and Graham now.

Stacy's face was a beet red as she noticed the eyes focused on her. She looked at Graham and his expression was one of shame. I immediately felt a need to jump to their defense but Robert's hand stayed me. Stacy quickly mumbled an apology and ran off after Lark, too confused and upset to deal with Graham at present. Graham, in turn, fell back to his old stand-by. He reached for Stacy's lunch and began to finish it off.

I turned to look at Robert, needing his reassurance that things were going to be okay, that my semi-normal group of friends wasn't going to begin tumbling down around me. He smiled and shook his head. I felt a bit of relief at that, but couldn't quite build up enough of it to make any headway when it came to easing my fear.

The clangor of the end of lunch broke through my melancholy, and I glumly stood up and prepared to head to biology. Robert carried my bag and kept his free arm wrapped securely around my midsection, the brace for my wobbly and unsteady frame to lean against as we walked towards my dreaded class.

The door was wide open and the smell of formaldehyde instantly clung to my skin and clothes as we approached. "Thank you," I whispered to Robert as I looked inside, dreading the next hour.

"Anytime," he said smiling and pecked my cheek in that same, chaste manner that I had described to Stacy. I couldn't help but feel more depressed as I lumbered into the classroom and sat down on my stool, my bag tossed haphazardly onto the exam table.

The chatter around me did nothing to help lighten my mood as I caught snippets of names that I recognized, little bits of conversation that were focused on what had occurred during lunch just a few minutes ago. It was on everyone's mind, and their eyes kept flicking back to me, the friend who had done nothing to stop it, done nothing to prevent it either.

I shook my head as the guilt that I knew I shouldn't feel began to grow inside of me, each layer being placed by each lingering stare from all around me. The whispered words and snickers were starting to sound like a trance beat inside of my head, and I placed it down against the cool surface of the table, hoping that I might get some relief from it. At the very least, I'd be able to shut out half of the noise.

"Grace, could you come here, please?" I heard being called out. I cringed as the thick voice of Mr. Branke said my name once more, insuring that if no one had heard him the first time, they did the second.

With resignation, I stood up and began the short journey to the front of the class where Mr. Branke had a stack of papers to pass out. I was two tables away from reaching him when my boot made contact with a substance on the floor that caused me to lose traction and I fell, quite quickly, to the cold linoleum beneath me. My head made a loud cracking sound as it hit the ground and a high-pitched hum began to fill my ears.

There were spangles of black and white that appeared in front of my eyes as I tried to focus on something, anything. I could barely hear the murmur of activity around me as people began crowding over me, their voices a dull buzz, their faces blurred and spotted. I moaned when I tried to raise my head and felt something push me back down.

"Don't move, Grace," I heard someone say, but the voice was indistinguishable. "You hit your head very hard on the ground. Just lay there while someone gets the nurse."

"I need Robert," I mumbled as I closed my eyes, knowing that no nurse would be able to help me the way he could. "Get Robert."

There were giggles. I heard them as a female voice said snidely, "I'll get him, alright." I wanted to say something in reply but a sharp pain slashed through any intent I might have had. I could feel the throbbing on the side of my head now, a steady base beat that pounded its rhythm permanently into my mind.

As the buzz of voices grew more intense, I felt the need to see what was going on around me. My eyelids lifted and I was staring at a pair of gray pant legs. I lowered my gaze to their shoes and felt my breath catch.

They were brown.

With black laces.

My lungs began to fill with an intense pressure and I blinked, hoping that what I had seen would simply be a reaction from hitting my head. I blinked twice, three times, and the shoes only became clearer. They were a bit more worn than I had remembered them, but they were the same shoes that I had seen that night I had been mowed down.

Even the color of the pants was the same. I exhaled and inhaled at a rapid pace, knowing that I was setting myself up to begin hyperventilating, but not caring. I just needed to get away from this person, whoever it was.

"Grace? It's okay, Grace. The nurse is coming."

I shuddered as I recognized the voice that was attached to those shoes as belonging to Mr. Branke. I flinched when I saw his feet tip forward, he knees bending as he knelt down to touch my hair and my shoulder. "It's okay. You're going to be fine," he said, his voice wanting to be comforting but failing miserably.

"Grace?" I heard being called out and my heart leapt as I recognized it. "Grace, it's Graham. Oh God, what happened?"

"Graham! I slipped on something and fell; I hit my head pretty hard and they won't let me sit up," I managed to squeak out. I wanted to shout to the world—or at least to the class—that Mr. Branke was the man who'd run me down a few months ago, but I was too afraid, the horror of that night replaying itself in my mind like a movie stuck on repeat.

Graham grabbed my hand, his grip firm and reassuring. I felt instantly safer and nearly blurted out to him what I had discovered when the sound of more activity shook the two of us apart.

"You're quite the little disaster magnet, aren't you?" someone said as a cold hand pressed against my wrist. "You've been hit by a car, your friend was shoved into a doorframe, and now you slip on the floor and have probably given yourself a nice little concussion. I'd be worried if I were your friends. Keep this up and you might end up knocking on Death's door."

I couldn't help myself as I started to laugh. "He climbs through my window," I snickered, the pain of my body shifting with each chuckle causing me to take in deep gulps of air.

"You're going to have to stop doing that if you want us to get you up and out of here, dear," the voice said again. I nodded and then groaned at the sharp pain that caused. "I told you."

I laid still for the rest of the examination while the nurse made sure that I hadn't broken anything on the way down and could still use my legs and arms to stand up. When she was sure that I would be able to, she and Graham placed their arms around mine and helped me to a standing position. I felt woozy, the outlines of everything around me blending into each other and forming their own abstract shapes.

With tentative steps, the three of us walked out of the classroom and down the hallway towards the nurse's station. After carefully maneuvering through the doorway, Graham and the nurse helped me to one of the two beds that were crammed into the tiny room. "We don't get many of you in here at any given time, so they gave us a closet," the nurse mentioned as she placed a sheet over my legs. "This will keep you warm until we can figure out what we're going to do with you."

She whispered some instructions to Graham and then left the room. Graham sat on the bed opposite of mine and started chuckling. "You know, if you wanted to give the school something to talk about besides Stacy and me, you could have just ran through the classroom naked. It would have saved you all of this pain."

I glowered at him from beneath heavy lids. "I didn't slip because of you. Something was on the floor when Mr. Branke-"

I stopped speaking and Graham's head snapped to attention at my sudden silence. "What's the matter, Grace?"

"Mr. Branke. He's the one who ran me over," I breathed, the image of his shoes once again filling my mind. I could hear the crunching of asphalt as the shoes began to walk away, leaving me on the cold, empty road alone and broken. "He...he's the one who left me there. I saw his shoes today, they're the same ones."

Graham moved quickly to the floor beside me, his face rigid with shock. "Are you sure? I mean, your vision is kind of blurry—you did hit your head pretty hard—maybe you made a mistake?"

"No. I know those shoes, Graham. They were right in front of me," I protested, afraid that he'd crack some joke about my being obsessed with shoes or something in an attempt to change the subject.

"Okay, okay Grace. What do you want to do about it?"

"I don't know," I whimpered. After all this time, I had no clue what I wanted to do, or what I should do. I had given up on ever finding out who it was and now that I was sure, I didn't know what the next step was.

"Well, I think you should call the cops," Graham said as he held my hand in his. "We're not a very big town. Finding Mr. Branke should have been a piece of cake for them."

The thought of having to tell the police, having to face Mr. Branke afterwards brought on a wave of panic that quickened the pace of my breathing once again. Graham squeezed my hand to calm me, his free hand patting my shoulder in a comforting gesture that did nothing to calm or comfort me.

"I don't know if I can do this," I said. "The last time I spoke to those cops, they treated me as like I was the one to blame; that I had rode my bike in front of the car on purpose."

Graham sucked in his breath as he heard this for the first time. "Why didn't you tell this to me? Did you tell this to Robert?"

I shook my head and then moaned in pain—it felt like my brain was bouncing around the spiked cavern that was my head. "My dad was pissed, but they said they needed to know that I wasn't partially to blame, and that my reaction was enough to convince them that I hadn't been at fault. But they didn't apologize, and kept looking at me as though they didn't believe me."

"Why haven't you told Robert about this? I know his family has a lot of money. That would have greased the wheels a bit, you know? Made this more of a priority with the police."

I sighed and closed my eyes at the suggestion. "I don't want him to use that money on something like this. The police didn't have a lot to go on and I mean, all I could remember was a pair of brown shoes. There are over eight-thousand people living in Heath. How many guys own brown shoes?"

"So what makes you so sure that Mr. Branke's brown shoes are the ones you saw?"

I felt myself shudder as I saw the shoes once more behind closed lids. "I just do."

Graham patted my shoulder once more and we sat in silence for the next few minutes until the nurse returned with an ice pack. "Okay, Grace. I've called your dad and he's on his way to come and get you. Graham, I think you need to get back to class. I'll write you a pass and you can give it to your teacher."

I heard her leave and opened my eyes to look at Graham still kneeling beside the low lying bed. "How did you know I had fallen anyway?" I asked.

He shrugged his shoulders, confusion written plainly on his face. "I honestly didn't. I got a strange feeling that something was wrong, like a prickly feeling on the back of my neck, and then I heard this voice in my head that told me to get up and to check on you. It was like my conscience or something was warning me that you had hurt yourself. I didn't think much about it, but now...well, now it freaks me out."

My eyes bulged at his description. He didn't notice and continued. "You'd think that the voice of your conscience would sound like yourself, you know? But mine didn't. It sounded metallic at first, like those cartoon aliens we used to watch when we were kids, but then when it got clearer, it sounded like..."

"Like what?" I wanted to know.

He grinned guiltily as he answered, "Lark."

I groaned once again. "Oh dear bananas," I murmured as I rolled onto my back and stared up at the popcorn ceiling. "What else did she...um, your conscience tell you?"

Graham stood up to stretch his legs and looked up as well, the grin never leaving his face. "I cannot explain it, Grace. I mean, it felt like Lark was in my head telling me that you needed my help, and it kept repeating over and over again until I got to you." He lowered his head to look directly into my eyes. "It sounds crazy, doesn't it? I mean, it does to me. Why would I hear her voice in my head? And why would her voice be telling me that you were hurt?"

"I don't know," I said softly, hating myself, hating the lie. I turned my head away to stare at the cement wall beside me—it couldn't make me feel guilty, too.

"I'm not going to lie to you, Grace. I wish it hadn't stopped. I hadn't felt that at peace inside of my head before. Even if the only thing I could think about was you being hurt, it was like her voice made things okay…and I hate it," he admitted sadly. "Look, I'm going to get back to class. I'll see you after school, okay?"

The shuffling of his feet was the only clue to his leaving. I waited until I heard the soft thump of the door closing before I turned around and focused on what Graham had told me. For whatever reason, Lark felt it was important that Graham come to help me, and she had gone against her self-imposed ban of entering his thoughts to do so.

I tried to understand why, but aside from him being my best friend, there wasn't any reason why he would have a need to be there. I raised my hand to the side of my head and felt around gingerly for the spot that I had hit on the ground. The lump that met my fingers was larger than I had anticipated, and felt like a cucumber was protruding from beneath my skin. "Ugh, now it'll look like I've got a horn shooting out of the side of my head," I mumbled to myself.

"No it won't," the nurse said as she walked in with my dad right behind her. "Although, it doesn't add to your looks either."

Dad pushed past her and, with ungentle haste, he picked me up from the bed and cradled me in his arms like he used to when I was a little girl. "Grace, I don't know what I'm going to do with you if you keep giving me scares like this," he said, his voice muffled by my hair.

"I'm okay, Dad. I just slipped," I said as sincerely as I could. His burst of emotion had made me weepy and I didn't particularly like it. Not when I had the pressing issue of Mr. Branke and his shoes on my mind.

"Listen kiddo, you're the sole reason why my hair is mostly gray and thinning. How am I supposed to face the new one without a full head of hair?"

Dad pointed to the spot at the top of his head that had been thinning out since I was thirteen. I rolled my eyes, wincing at the pain that caused, and then reassured him once again that I was fine. "I'm going to have a headache, but I'm not nauseated or anything. My vision has improved, too. I can definitely see that you've got more than enough hair to greet little Matthew with, so I don't see how you can try and place any more guilt on me than I already have."

"Nevertheless, I'm taking you to the emergency room and have you checked out. The doct-"

An unintelligible sound shot out of my mouth, cutting him off before he could finish his sentence. "Dad, you can't! They remember you there. They might lobotomize me if they see you again!"

He brushed off my concern and patted my head, my role as helpless daughter going to his head. "You're going to be fine. They'll just check you out, and I'll stay out of their way. I won't complain or accuse them of doing or not doing anything. I promise."

I eyed him skeptically, not believing him for a second. He laughed at that and patted my head once more. When I winced his laughter silenced and a contrite look spread across his face. "Oh, your head. I'm sorry!"

I squirmed out of his arms and planted my feet onto the ground, determined to walk out of the room on my own. "Well, let's get this over with then," I sighed.

"Alright. Oh, hey, before I forget, your biology teacher met me outside to explain everything before I showed up so that I wouldn't frighten you with my concern. I think you should thank him for that because I might have ended up making things worse...you know me," Dad said as we exited the nurse's station and headed towards the school's main entrance.

I stopped moving and turned to face him, shock and fear overtaking the pain the sudden loss of motion caused. "I can't, Dad," I gasped. "I can't."

He gripped my arms in his, my change in mood transferring my fear onto him. "Why? What is it, baby?"

I looked into his eyes and I could see my reflection in them, I could see my pupils dilated in fear. "He's the one." Those three words left my lips in a breathless whisper, almost silent and imperceptible, but he heard it, and he knew what it was that I meant.

This time, it was his mood that changed rapidly. His face lit up like a red beacon of fury as his hands loosened their grip on me, his arms dropping to his sides. I grabbed for him, knowing what it was he was intent on doing, fearing that nothing good would come of it. "Come on, Dad. We've got to call the police," I said in a much firmer tone. I pulled him away from the direction I knew he was fixed on heading.

He followed, somewhat unwillingly, saying nothing until we were in the car and leaving the parking lot. "How long have you known?" he finally managed to say after all we could see of the school was its outline in the rearview mirror.

"Not long. I realized it after I fell," I answered softly.

"I'm going to call the police as soon as we get to the hospital. This is going to be finished today. I promise you, Grace," Dad said determinedly. "He smiled at me, actually smiled at me when he saw me. That bast-"

"Dad!" I yelled as he raced towards a stoplight on the red. Dad's foot slammed on the brakes and we screeched to an undignified halt. I braced myself against the dashboard, one hand over my fluttering heart. My head began to throb again and I moaned as the pain grew worse.

"Dammit, I'm sorry Grace," Dad said as he fidgeted with one hand to comfort me and steer with the other. "I'm not good at this emotional driving thing. I must have been a woman in another life."

"Dad," I grumbled beneath heavy lids. "That's not nice."

He chuckled at my complaint and patted my leg. "Well, when you learn how to drive, you can prove me wrong. Grace?"

I mumbled something incoherent as the black and white spangles returned to my vision. I tried to rub them out, my hands pressing against my lids, but they remained steadfast. "I think you'd better hurry up and get us to the hospital, Dad," I managed to get out before everything turned black, the high-pitched hum returning to my ears and blocking out any other sound.

೧೫

It's something quite surreal, waking up in a strange room, surrounded by strange people who are all talking and the only sound you can hear is the pounding of your own heart, out of synch with the moving lips, yet creating an interesting beat all its own. The feeling of something cold rushing up my arm and the painful pinch in my hand told me that Dad had made it to the hospital, but being unable to hear anything made me question whether or not my lobotomy theory had been proven true.

I opened my mouth to say something but the words held fast to my tongue. No one above me seemed to notice as they continued to work. There were some familiar faces and some that I didn't recognize from the many recent trips to the emergency room I had made over the past few months. Someone flashed a bright light into my eyes, moving it from side to side; my own personal light show.

The doctor that had treated Stacy looked at me with a blank expression on his face. He said something to the nurse standing next to him, but his words contained no sound.

And yet, I knew what it was that he had said. I could hear the words in my head, like a little song that flowed in time with the beat from my heart. He was asking for ammonium carbonate. I recognized that from chemistry class the year before as smelling salts. The nurse handed him what looked like the wrapping for a suppository, which he opened. He then leaned in towards me, his hand extended out farther till it was directly beneath my nose.

The intense odor that felt like my head had been dunked into a bucket of cleaning solution hit my nose like a sucker punch. It stung and burned and I could do nothing to get away from it.

"Atta-girl—wake up, Grace," I heard as his lips moved once more, his voice actually coming through this time. "Well, hello. Welcome back."

I blinked as he pulled the vile little package away and pressed something cold and wet against my upper lip. "I haven't left," I muttered against the dripping cloth.

"You suffered a nasty fall I heard. You've got a concussion, and you'll probably be a bit woozy for the next couple of days, but now that you're awake I think you're going to be just fine," he explained.

"Where's my dad?" I asked, knowing he must be frantic with worry somewhere; hopefully not restrained and locked in a dark closet.

The doctor nodded to the nurse standing beside me who left with a wink. I frowned at that little gesture, it saying more to me than anything she could have uttered.

"What did you do to my dad?" I demanded, trying to pull myself up. "Where is he?"

The doctor stepped back and allowed me to sit up, a look of panic written clearly on his face. "He'll be here in a minute. He's fine, honest!"

I tried to climb off the bed but the sharp pull of the IV that was hanging from a rod attached to the bed prevented me from doing so. "He's fine? If he's fine, why isn't he in here? What did you do to him?" I demanded once again as I struggled with the valve that attached the tube to the needle that was taped to my hand.

"He was frantic and he wasn't allowing us to do our job, so we gave him a sedative. It was a mild one. He's asleep in the children's ward, perfectly fine. I promise."

I calmed down as the explanation sunk in. "Oh, I knew this was going to happen," I moaned. I sat back down on the bed and shook my head. "Ow."

The doctor approached me hesitantly, but I did nothing to wave him away. He placed a cold hand against my head, his frigid skin offering a great deal of comfort to my throbbing head. "I apologize for having to do that to your father, Grace. If it could have been avoided, I would have gladly appreciated it but unfortunately there was no other recourse."

I sighed and gently nodded my head. "I know. He's never been good with hospitals, and until my baby brother is born, he's only got me to focus all of his worries on. I just—I warned him that this was going to happen. Well, not *this* exactly, but I knew he'd end up freaking out or something. Thanks, Doctor…"

The doctor chuckled at my confession. "I'm Ambrose. The nurses here call me Dr. Bro because they think I don't like my name, but to tell you the truth, I do."

206

"I do, too. Ambrose…like the Saint?" I asked, surprised at my question.

He grinned and nodded. "Yes, actually. Not many people know that. He's not exactly one of the more well-known Saints, but my mother, she wanted me to grow up to be a great doctor and so she named me after one of the 'doctors of the Church'. She couldn't read very well so she didn't know that Saint Ambrose wasn't a medical doctor, but the end result is still the same. She's got her doctor son named Ambrose. How do you know about him by the way? Your dad doesn't strike me as Catholic…"

I smiled. "No, he's not Catholic. We're not very religious, actually. I do like to read a lot, though. I suppose I read about him at some point, but don't ask me when because I probably couldn't remember. Not now, anyway."

He chuckled but then quickly sobered as a question formed in his head. "The police are waiting outside to ask you some questions. Do you know why?"

I looked at the ground and took in Dr. Ambrose's shoes. They were dark blue clogs, comfortable looking and very plain. "They're here to ask me about the man who ran me over."

He nodded solemnly and walked over to the doorway to peer out into the hallway. "Do you have something new to tell them? Is that why they're here?"

"I know who it was," I answered quietly.

He turned around and looked at me in surprise. "You do? How do you know?"

"I saw his shoes."

His head quickly dropped to his own feet before snapping back up to look at me once again. "Who is it?"

"That's exactly what we want to know," a stern voice concurred through the doorway. An officer with a pen and pad pinched between his fingers stood between me and the only exit. I glanced from between the officer and the doctor and knew that whatever came out of my mouth was

207

going to set into motion a set of actions that I couldn't take back, for better or for worse.

I took a deep breath and began...

GAMBLE

As all things go, the ordeal of having to explain to the police what had led me to believe that Mr. Branke had been the one to run me over was a long and involved one. As soon as Dr. Ambrose gave me the all clear, I was whisked away to the police station to give my statement.

Although Dr. Ambrose—probably out of guilt—argued that I should be able to give a statement at the hospital, or at least wait until Dad arrived from the children's ward to be with me, the police in turn stated that I was now a legal adult and didn't need my father to be with me when they questioned me. And so I was placed into the back seat of a very dirty, off-smelling police vehicle and made the relatively long journey to the Newark police station.

Once there, I was seated in front of a desk littered with stacks of papers and fast food wrappers. The officer seated behind the desk was a portly man with dark, greasy stains on his already dark uniform. His nametag had a dollop of what looked like dried mustard on it, and he had the remainders of what had probably been a pizza clinging to the cleft in his chin.

"Okay young lady, you're going to write down everything you've said to the officers in the hospital and then you're going to sign it at the bottom of this-" he placed a lined sheet of paper in front of me "-form and date it. When you're done, you'll be free to go."

I blindly accepted the pen he handed me and began to write. All around me, the business of law enforcement seemed to revolve around answering phones, rushing out, stomping back in, and the filling of endless amounts of paperwork.

"How much time do you guys actually spend outside?" I asked as I neared the end of my statement, checking it twice before signing off on it. I dated it and then handed it to him before the officer finally answered.

"It depends on what our assignments are. Some of us get stuck on desk duty for one reason or another. I was wounded while on duty, so I'm on desk duty until I get the all-clear from my doctor," he garbled, his lips getting in the way of fully articulating his words.

"Wounded, Charlie? Tell that girl the truth! Listen, little lady, Charlie over here 'wounded' himself by throwing his back out when he bent down to pick up some Skittles he dropped on the ground," a female officer laughed from the desk across from us. "He's been on desk duty since before you were even born and will probably be there till he retires. Wounded while on duty. That's a good one, Charlie!"

I turned to look at Charlie and immediately felt sorry for him. "I like Skittles, so I don't blame you for getting hurt. Nothing sucks like a wasted candy."

He smiled at me and took my form, looking it over to make sure that I hadn't missed out on anything important. "You're a good kid, Grace. I hope that we catch this S.O.B. so that you can stop worrying about him. That wasn't right, running over a kid and then leaving without helping."

I nodded as he stood up and walked over to an office that was surrounded by glass and wood panels. A man inside stood up and peered out of the glass, his eyes focused on me. He nodded his head and then picked up the receiver of the phone on his desk.

Charlie turned around and walked back towards me, a smile on his face. "They're calling it in. He'll be brought in within the hour, if you want to wait so you can identify him, although we won't necessarily need that."

Was that what I wanted? To be sitting here while they brought Mr. Branke in handcuffed? I shook my head. "No, I think I'll go and wait outside for my dad."

The officer nodded and then thanked me. "You stay safe, now."

"I'll try," I said and headed towards the exit, trying my best to remember where it was. When I stepped outside, I realized that I had left my coat and gloves at the hospital. The cold, February air still had a vicious bite to it and I knew I'd freeze to death if I remained out dressed the way I was.

With rushed steps, I hurried back inside and sat on a bench that was bolted to the floor and wall. It was a full thirty minutes later before my dad finally showed up. He was so angry he blew right past me and was halfway down the hallway before he heard me calling out to him.

"Grace!" he shouted. He ran back towards me and wrapped his arms around me, his breathing heavy and erratic. "I'm going to kill that doctor for putting us through this. If I ever see him again, that's exactly what I'm going to do."

I giggled as I really couldn't find any fault with his reasoning for it. At least, not when it came to him. I took a look at his face and then burst out laughing. "Dad. Um…have you taken a look at yourself in the mirror?"

He growled and nodded. "Yes. That twisted so-called doctor drugged me and left me in the Art room in the Children's ward."

He raced to a display case and inspected his reflection while I snickered behind him. He turned around and I burst out into loud laughter once again. It appeared that, while passed out, the children in the Children's ward had felt a need to use Dad's face and hair as their own living canvas.

Half of his face was painted a bright purple with orange spots dotted below his right eye and at the corner of his mouth. The other half of his face had been painted with alternating black and white stripes, followed with what appeared to be hot pink glittered glue. His hair had streaks of yellow and green paint, and the slightly bald spot that neared his hairline had been filled with the same hot pink glue, although he must have moved while it had been drying because it clumped over to the side.

Dad tried to grit his teeth but even that failed when they squeaked from the crayon that had been rubbed against them, making them a streaky olive-green. "Is this what I have to look forward to with Matthew?"

I nodded between laughs, pressing against the tightness that was building in my side. "Boy am I glad I'll be away at college when that starts."

He sighed, my words a sobering reality that neither of us had been ready for, despite my utterance. "Just a few more months, kiddo," he said resignedly. "A few more months before you're on your own. You're not my little girl anymore."

"Aw Dad," I groaned. "Do we have to do this in the middle of a police station?"

He immediately straightened and, as if suddenly remembering why we were here in the first place, became intensely serious. "What happened? Tell me everything, give me the names of the officers who questioned you, everything."

"I'll do it on the way to the car," I promised, and so I did, leaving out nothing except the part where the officer named Charlie had said that they were bringing in Mr. Branke in less than an hour.

CB

It would be less than twenty-four hours later when the news we hadn't expected threatened to tear apart the little bit of security that had been formed knowing that Mr. Branke would be behind bars.

"Grace," Dad called out from downstairs. I stood in front of the bathroom mirror, my mouth full of toothpaste foam.

"Wha?" I shouted, spraying foam all across the reflective glass.

"Come downstairs. Now."

I quickly rinsed out my mouth and rushed downstairs to see Dad and Janice sitting on one side of the sofa, Graham's pillow and blankets all piled on the opposite end.

In Dad's favorite chair sat one of the officers from the hospital, his hat in his lap. The look on all three of their faces told me that something wasn't right, something was not right at all.

"What's going on?"

Dad glared at the police officer while Janice shook her head disapprovingly.

Taking a deep breath, the officer began to repeat to me what it appeared everyone else already knew as I suddenly became aware of Graham stomping around in the kitchen.

"Grace, as I told your parents already, I'm afraid that after speaking to Mr. Branke and following up on his statement, it appears that he has an alibi for the night you were hit. We also examined his car and there's no damage to it. At least, nothing that would result from hitting someone on a bicycle. He's not the person who hit you, Grace."

The weight of his words seemed to transplant onto me as he sighed from the release of them. I shook my head in denial. "I know what I saw. I saw his shoes. They're the same shoes, the exact same shoes," I argued.

The officer nodded in understanding and offered me a hand for comfort but I jerked away. He sighed once more and tried to explain. "Grace, I know you want to believe that it was Mr. Branke that did this, but please understand that we checked and double checked his alibi. He was teaching a weekend biology course at the community college. There are fifty eye-witnesses that place him in class. He didn't do this, I'm sorry."

I didn't want to believe it. I couldn't believe it. "When you brought Mr. Branke in…was it while he was still in school?"

The officer nodded. "Yes, actually. He was in the middle of some kind of afterschool science club meeting. There were quite a few angry students there, I must say."

213

I groaned as the repercussions from my implicating Mr. Branke became clear to me. As creepy as Mr. Branke might be, he was a respected teacher by many kids, and I had just accused him of nearly killing me and leaving me on the side of the road to die. I had sealed his reputation to those who had already disliked him and tarnished it to those who didn't.

"Oh no, what have I done?" I moaned, the pounding in my head returning. "Oh, what have I done?"

Graham came out of the kitchen and grabbed my arm, yanking me up the stairs and towards my room. "Don't worry about it, Grace. I'm not going to let anyone use this against you," he vowed as he sat me down on my bed. He walked to the door and shut it so that they couldn't hear us downstairs. "If you still believe that Mr. Branke did this, we'll find a way to prove it, Grace. But…do you? Do you still think it was him? I won't question you if you don't."

I looked at him through foggy eyes. "I don't know. I don't know anymore. I saw his shoes and I could have sworn that he was the guy. I felt the connection there, Graham. I know I did."

He sat down beside me and placed his arm around my shoulders, giving them a gentle and reassuring squeeze. "You did the only thing you could do. I'm not that bright, but I can see that and so will everyone else."

I nodded but felt unsure. I didn't know what Mr. Branke's arrest had left in its wake, and I was terrified of finding out. But more importantly, I was afraid of what would happen when I would eventually see him in class. I would have to apologize to him—I wanted to apologize to him—but I didn't know if I had the courage to do so.

"Hey, where's Robert been? Shouldn't he have stopped over or something yesterday?" Graham asked.

I stared at the empty wall near the door and shrugged my shoulders. "I don't know."

"Well, I'll take you to school today then. I'll stick by your side like glue all day, okay?"

214

The thought of Graham being permanently attached to my side would have probably made my day if I were any other girl, but I wasn't just any other girl. "I'll be fine, Graham. But I'll accept your ride to school."

He nodded and stood up. "Well, if I'm going to be playing body-guard, I need to fuel up. Janice made some real bacon today, so I'm going to stuff my face while you get ready."

He left, quietly shutting the door behind him, and I waited until I could no longer hear the thumping of his heavy footsteps before I turned around on my bed and opened my window. I looked at the police car parked conspicuously in our driveway; saw the faces of the neighbors who had gathered across the street to point and whisper behind raised hands about why it could possibly be parked there.

One of them, a Mrs. Gladys Fallacci, saw me peering from out of the window and she waved, embarrassed that she had been spied gossiping yet smug all the same because the car wasn't parked in front of *her* house.

I quickly shut the window and yanked the curtain closed over it. "Every single time I think I'm getting close to being normal, something comes up and changes everything."

I rummaged through my drawers for something to wear to school and settled on a pair of old, camouflage pants and a plain black t-shirt. I was heading into battle; I might as well dress like it. I was pulling on my boots when Graham knocked on my door to see if I was ready to leave.

"I'll be there in a second," I called out in response and began to tie my laces. I looked over to my dresser and saw the picture of Robert and I that Janice had taken last October. "Where are you?" I asked silently.

With a heavy heart, I grabbed my bag and hoisted it onto my shoulders. I opened my door and did my best to put on a brave face as we walked downstairs together. I grabbed my jacket—Dad had remembered to grab it from the hospital—and walked with Graham to his car, ignoring the officer and the concerned looks on Dad and Janice's faces.

He was in the middle of unlocking the passenger door when the sound of an engine revving behind us alerted us to the presence of another person.

"Your boyfriend is here," Graham snapped as he fumbled with the keys in his heavily gloved hands.

Robert's black motorcycle stood out against the white of the snow covered street but it paled in comparison to the jet of his hair. His gray eyes were like cold steel as they glared at Graham, but turned molten the minute he looked at me. "Are you okay?"

I nodded, immediately feeling calm and relaxed. "I'm okay."

Graham snorted. "Of course she's okay. She wouldn't be heading off to school if she wasn't." He looked at me and grunted as he shook his head. "Whatever it is he has on you, I hope it's good, Grace. He should have been here today. He should have been there yesterday, too, instead of me."

With a negligent wave of his hand, Graham climbed into his rusty green Buick and drove off, leaving a cloud of brown smoke trailing behind him.

I knew there was no point, but I couldn't help but yell for him to wait. I looked at Robert and sighed. "You always have a way of making things instantly easier and more difficult without even saying anything. Is that another one of your charms?"

Robert's face didn't alter in its concern. He reached for me instead and pulled me into him, his chest my buffer. "I'm sorry. I'm so sorry that I wasn't here for you. There are a lot of reasons, but none of them are good enough. None of them will ever be good enough."

I inhaled the scent of him, drugging myself, numbing myself to anything else. "There isn't a way you can reverse time, is there?" I asked him.

He held me tighter and shook his head. "If I could, I'd have come back when you were born."

Strangely, this comforted me. "What am I going to do, Robert? I might have ruined an innocent man's life. Ugh—why can't I just be normal and not such a colossal screw-up?"

Robert looked down at me and he frowned. "This isn't your mistake, Grace. If I had been there, if had not been…elsewhere, I would have been able to tell you what you needed to know and then none of this would have happened. This is my fault."

"Don't try and take away my guilt, please. As much as I would like it, it's not what I need. I just wish that this were easier. I messed up and now I have to fix it, but it's Mr. Branke. How can I apologize to *him*?" I eased myself out of Robert's arms and sighed. "Whatever the solution, we've got to get going or else we're going to be late. I'm already in enough hot water. I don't need to add tardiness on top of everything else."

Robert flashed a grin in my direction as he climbed onto the bike. He held out his hand and helped me to seat myself behind him. "I'm glad you have your priorities in order."

"Ha-ha."

With a turn of the key, the bike started up and we were flying down the street. I had forgotten to put my hair up and it whipped around my face, lashing at my wind-bitten skin.

I felt Robert's hand grab mine and pull it into the confines of his jacket. With movement that I could not see, he had somehow removed my glove and my bare hand pressed up against his abdomen. I could feel the warmth through his shirt and my fingers itched to be closer to the source of that heat.

Robert's hold on my hand allowed him to push it inwards and I nearly fainted when I felt it slip between the edges of his shirt and touch the bare skin of his waist. The immediate jolt of electricity between the two of us caused Robert to swerve the bike and instinctually I held on tighter. This sent my hand deeper into the pocket he had created in his shirt and I felt the sinew of his belly clench as he moved to control the bike's actions.

The contact, like any other flesh-to-flesh contact between us, sent an influx of thoughts and visions into my head, but I had learned to stave them off over time. This contact wasn't meant to share his visions with me. It was meant to heal me, reverse the damage that might have been caused by my fall as well as from the short ride to school.

But I would have gladly gone to school looking like some royal brat's whipping girl if it meant I could remain this close to Robert for a little while longer. I'd gladly endure it and I knew that despite my earlier revelation, this had nothing to do with Robert's angelic charm.

As we pulled into the school, Robert took a detour that brought us into the faculty parking lot. I didn't need to ask to know what his intent was. We hadn't shared a single thought about what I would do once we got to school, and yet he knew what I had wanted. *I have to know what you want, Grace. Your happiness and well-being are paramount. If you're not safe and content, I can't be.*

With a defiant sigh, I pulled my hand out of his shirt and allowed him to put my glove back on, then climbed off the back of the bike. *He's in the alcove to the left smoking a cigarette. I'll be waiting right here if you need me; I can hear everything that's going on so if he tries to harm you in re-taliation, I'll be there in less than a nanosecond.*

I nodded and looked towards the alcove that Robert pointed to. I could see a faint puff of smoke trailing out from behind the wall and started walking in that direction. I began to repeat a silent mantra, imagining myself as the little apologizer that could, focused on forgetting my own self-consciousness and instead remembering that I had hurt Mr. Branke and insulted him with my accusation. Whatever it was that I was feeling was nothing compared to what he must be going through.

As soon as I could make out his outline in the shadows of the al-cove, I began to rehearse my opening lines. "Mr. Branke, I wanted to apologize for what happened yesterday. I was wrong and I will do my ut-most best to ensure that everyone knows that you had nothing to do with what happened to me."

It sounded good.

Too bad though, because it was looking like I wouldn't get a chance to say anything. As soon as Mr. Branke saw me approaching, he flicked his cigarette onto the ground and gave it a quick stomp before rush-ing towards the side entrance, his hands rammed deeply into his pockets.

"Mr. Branke!" I called out, my pace picking up to try and get to him before he could escape me into the crowded halls of the school. "Mr. Branke, wait!"

The doors closed just as I reached them and I could make out Mr. Branke's silhouette through the glass as he continued to walk very briskly down the hallway, finally disappearing around a corner.

"Damn," I exclaimed.

I turned around and headed back towards Robert. I felt my shoulders hunching down in defeat and disappointment, and when Robert stood up to comfort me, I knew I wasn't imagining it. I had lost a couple of inches in height.

"He doesn't want to have anything to do with me," I mumbled into Robert's jacket. "He ran away from me, Robert. You'd think I was infected with the plague or something, he was moving so fast."

Robert's hand pressed against the back of my head, he pressed a kiss to my ear and laughed softly. "I cannot exactly feel too sorry for you. You always did want him to leave you alone. Now you've gotten your wish, albeit not exactly in the way you probably wanted."

I said something that was so muffled by my close proximity to Robert's chest, I was certain he didn't hear it, but he did. Of course he did.

"That wasn't very nice, Grace."

"Sorry."

He chuckled again and then gently pulled me away from him. I tried to hold on with all of my strength, but I might as well have not been trying, his motion so effortless. "You're a brave girl, Grace. I don't understand how you could possibly think that you're susceptible to my, how did you put it, 'angelic charms', when you're far more often trying to be as rude as possible to me."

I watched as he pushed my hair back with his hand, his leather gloves so well made, they were like a second skin. "There. All fixed. Maybe you'll be less frightening to Mr. Branke now that your hair looks less like a wild animal and more like something that belongs there."

"Oh, you-"

This time I shouted the word that I had said into his jacket and laughed at his wide-eyed expression. I was definitely being as rude as possible, that was true. It might have been something that wasn't entirely a normal, human thing to do, but my body was still human and I couldn't outrun an angel no matter how hard I tried and as a result, Robert caught me around the middle as I tried to flee, the two of us laughing and appreciating the break in the residual tension.

"I don't know why you're so obsessed with being 'normal' when the version of 'normal' that you seem to be basing this whole artificial goal on happens to deem you anything but," Robert said as he lifted me back onto the bike. He climbed on swiftly and started the bike with a purr. We traveled the incredibly short distance between parking lots at a leisurely pace, each passing stare causing me to grow redder and redder from the guilt that I had yet to appease.

"Let's take a look at some of these people, whom you would describe as 'normal', shall we? Donovan Gleason over there is what you would deem 'normal', right?"

He directed my attention to a red-headed boy in our senior class who was on the basketball team and the swim team, not to mention one of Graham's closest male friends. I nodded when I thought of how normal his life was. He and his girlfriend Kendra had a fairly solid relationship spanning our entire high school career, and he did fairly well in school, though not so well that he'd get singled out for it. He was always where the crowds were, always up for anything, and was never looked at as anything *but* normal here in Heath.

"Would you believe me if I told you he was gay?"

I felt my jaw drop. "What?"

He nodded his head. "How 'normal' do you think his friends would deem him if they ever found out about that? How 'normal' would he be if they learned that he listens to the same bands as they do because he's attracted to the lead singers?"

I honestly did not know the answer to that. I had never thought of Donovan as anything but a guy. "I don't think he's any less of a great guy, though," I said as I remembered that he had been the one who helped me bring Graham home one night during our junior year after Graham had snuck a bottle of his father's whiskey to a study session at the library. He had put up with my panicking and even said that he thought it was 'cool' that Graham had a 'chick' for a best friend. "Donovan hasn't changed in my opinion. He's still a normal guy."

"Yes, but would he be normal to someone like Kendra?"

I looked over to Donovan's girlfriend and shook my head severely. "She'd call him all sorts of names do her best to ruin his reputation both at school and in town."

Robert nodded, glad that I was now seeing his point. "Normal is a relative thing, Grace. What's normal to you might not be normal to someone else, yet that very person is whom you're basing your definition of normal on. I have to tell you, who you are 'normally' is exactly what I love. Why would you want to change that?"

I looked at Donovan and Kendra again. They were reading something that I hadn't noticed until just then. It was the local paper and Mr. Branke's face was plastered all over the front page.

"That's why," I said, pointing to the paper. "A normal person wouldn't have done something like that."

Robert pushed my hand down and sighed. "Grace, what you're going to have to learn is that normal people play it safe in this world because they're afraid of the risks involved with being different. It's a gamble. You gambled when you agreed to get on my bike. You gambled again when you decided to keep my secrets. You kept on gambling even after I hurt you, and Graham hurt you, and life hurt you because you knew that the rewards outweighed the risks.

"Would you take any of that back?"

I looked at Mr. Branke's school picture staring blankly back at me and knew that there was only one thing that I would if possible. However, angel at my side and all, that was impossible.

BLANK

For the next two days, I failed to get Mr. Branke to speak to me or acknowledge me at all. I even doubted that he checked my name for attendance when I showed up for class. He refrained from any contact with anyone during class, the lessons dull and flat, his monotone voice a complete shadow of his old one.

The negative reaction I had expected from the small faction of students who hadn't doubted Mr. Branke's innocence never appeared. With his demeanor so withdrawn and sullen, his hands were kept to himself, which pleased everyone. I had suddenly become a sort of hero to the girls of the school who had endured, some for years, the constant touching that went hand-in-hand with being a pupil at a school occupied by him.

Of course, any benefit I might have received from this was lost in the fact that for better or worse, I had been wrong about Mr. Branke. My mistake was now fodder for a new wave of gossip and bathroom conversation. I was now not only a freak, I was a liar as well. It didn't matter that I didn't lie; the end results were just the same.

I tried to speak to Lark about Graham and what he had told me, but she shut me down with each attempt. I tried to talk to Graham about anything but he avoided me with nearly as much determination as Mr. Branke, which was quite a feat considering that we lived together.

Sitting in fifth period English reminded me that today was the last Friday of the month. It didn't look like there'd be a renewal of our RHPS tradition. How could there be when he wouldn't even speak to me? The thought was enough to bring that annoying burn of tears to the edge of my lids, but I fought with them to stay inside. I had cried enough over Graham for one lifetime.

As soon as the bell rang, I was out of the door. I looked around for Robert but he wasn't there and I knew the reason for it. At times I would wonder when it would be that the reality of what he did finally hit me, but today wasn't one of them. I simply sighed and walked towards Mr. Danielson's class.

"So now everyone knows you're a liar. How well do you think that's going to go over with Mr. Kenner and your little threat?"

I felt the burning of bile as it rose in my throat. I turned around to look at Erica, her face smug with satisfaction. "I'm sorry, who are you and why are you relevant again?"

She laughed a throaty, deceptively beautiful laugh. "My-my, you've developed quite the backbone haven't you, freak?" Her eyes narrowed as she stepped in closer. "There's something very off about you, and I'm going to find out what it is. And when I do, no one is going to want to even admit to knowing you. Not Graham, Robert, or that Glamazon he calls a sister."

She shoved past me, her shoulder roughly pushing against mine as she walked through the classroom door. I stared at the wall directly across from me and tried to calm myself, tell myself that there was nothing that she could learn about me that would cause the people I loved the most to turn away from me.

I steeled myself against the growing fear inside of me and walked into the classroom, determined not to let her see any type of reaction at all. She had chosen to sit in the seat I normally occupied, the one immediately next to her reserved by her overly large and obnoxious purse. She smiled sweetly at me and I smiled back. If this was going to be a battle of wills and wits, I was determined to prove that she had come unarmed.

"Hey, Grace! Come and sit by us!" a voice called out from my left. Shawn, one of a group of three friends who referred to themselves as Chips, Dip and Salsa waved at me and pointed to a seat next to him that was vacant. I grinned and headed towards them.

As soon as I sat the door to the class opened and Robert entered, looking for all the world like he'd just stepped out of some black and white epic. His gaze never veered in the direction of our normal seats. Instead he made a beeline for me, a broad smile on his face.

"Hey guys, thanks for taking care of my girl for me," he said as he greeted the three characters around me. They all started speaking at once and their words were lost in the confusion, though Robert heard every word, every sentence.

"So we're taking a tour of the classroom I take it?" he said, his eyes flicking quickly to look at Erica who fumed in the corner next to an unoccupied seat.

I nodded. Robert reached for my hand and for reasons I wouldn't understand until much later, I pulled my hand away. "Not now," I whispered, hoping that those two words would be enough. His smile slowly disappeared and I saw his eyes turn to steel as he turned his head to look at Erica.

I don't know where this desperation is coming from. I don't see a source for such vindictive hatred.

The tone of Robert's thoughts felt heavy in my head, like thick syrup, and it coated each word with confusion and irritation. I didn't know what it was that he saw in her mind, and part of me didn't want to know either, but the way he looked at her—with such unmitigated disgust—you would think that she'd stop trying to gain his affections.

Instead, she moved her purse to the floor and patted the empty chair beside her. I looked at Robert and waited for his reaction. He looked at me and reached for my hand once more. This time I let him hold it. *I'm going to find out what it is that she wants. I need to get to the bottom of this before she acts out again and I'm not here.*

I felt him squeeze my hand gently before he stood up and walked over to her, much to the surprise of my companions.

"He isn't really going over to her, is he?" Shawn asked in a low voice. "That's like throwing a small child to a lion."

"I was thinking shark. A rabid shark," Chad, the "Chips" in the trio commented.

"Can sharks even get rabies?" Dwayne asked.

"Dog sharks, maybe," Chad replied.

The four of us watched as Robert smiled at Erica and allowed her wandering hand to cover his. He didn't move, didn't even say anything. He just sat there, smiling at her while she spoke, her mouth moving a mile a minute, pausing only to see if his reaction would change with each one.

As Mr. Danielson went over a script that we were supposed to perform for our final exam, I continued to watch the one way exchange between Robert and Erica. I knew that there was nothing that she could say or think that could threaten my relationship with him but the insecure part of me that always felt intimidated by her couldn't help but start to panic as time went on and he didn't leave.

"Shouldn't you go and, like, take him away from her or something?" Chad whispered to me and motioned towards the two with his head. "She's probably already planning on what they're going to name their grandkids. She's psycho." He circled his ear with his index finger to emphasize his point.

I smiled and shook my head. "I trust Robert. He's not going to do anything to hurt me. He's just trying to find out what makes her tick."

Dwayne leaned forward and nudged Chad's head out of the way so that he could be heard more clearly. "I know what makes her tick, and he's not going to find it by listening to her talk about lip gloss."

I looked at Dwayne and pressed him for details. "She's got a boyfriend, one that she's been dating since before Graham. They never broke up, even when she and Graham were together. He's one of those über rich guys that are always traveling and stuff. She brought her car into my dad's shop one day and he was with her. She was all over him but he wasn't having any of it."

"What did he look like?" I asked.

Dwayne smiled at me. "What? You want me to describe him like a girl would?"

My eyes rolled at his question and he laughed. "He's okay I guess, if you like that blonde, muscular, super handsome type. All the girls I've gone out with prefer the dark and handsome type."

"So what happened with you? Charity date?" Chad piped in.

While the two of them started quibbling, Shawn squeezed in. "You're so very different from the other girls, Grace. My girlfriend would be screaming with jealousy if she caught me sitting next to any girl. It's a good thing she goes to a private school."

I laughed and sighed, turning my attention back to the two beautiful people sitting in the corner of the classroom. "I hear that a lot. The different part."

Shawn's head bobbed in agreement. "You're the good kind of different, though, and Robert's very lucky to have you. Don't tell him I said that. He might think I'm hitting on you or something. And forget I said the first part, too; you might get a big head and totally want my body or something."

My laughter continued, my face turning red with both amusement and embarrassment. "I give you my word."

He smiled and leaned back. "Uh-oh. I think Erica just got a bit of bad news."

I could see what he meant when Erica's face went from gleeful to devastated with just the few words that Robert said to her as he stood up to leave. I could have felt sorry for her, her face was that pained. But she focused her gaze on me and I saw the cold venom there and I knew that there wasn't pain there. It was a hurt pride.

"Well, that was informative," Robert said as he sat down next to me. "I feel like I've just been sucked through a vacuum bag that was filled with her entire life story."

Chad held his nose, as did Shawn and Dwayne as Robert spoke. I looked at them curiously and they all winked at me. Robert chuckled as he filled me in. "They're preparing for the pile of…well, you-know-what that they're fairly certain she told me."

Dwayne smiled and said with a nasal voice, "You got that right. That girl can drop loads like an elephant at a diuretic party."

I watched Robert's face light up as he saw Shawn's reaction to Dwayne's comment. "She did tell a few pretty outrageous stories, I'll say that much."

The bell began to ring, heralding the day's end and I jumped up and out of my seat, eager to hear what it was that Robert had discovered from what Erica hadn't said out loud. He gripped my hand and threw my bag onto his shoulder quickly. He said a polite goodbye to Chad, Shawn, and Dwayne and then pulled me out of the classroom with as much speed as he dared without appearing unnatural.

We were out of the school and on his bike before anyone else had exited. I didn't see the faces of any students as he sped out of the parking lot and down the street, heading in the direction of his home. He said nothing to me, leaving me alone in my thoughts as we raced past homes and trees until we came to the large, white walls that surrounded his house. The gates that kept the outside world at bay opened up and allowed us inside. I had once asked how exactly they did so without a keypad or some kind of remote control and he had simply smiled and wiggled his fingers.

He pulled the bike into the garage that was located on the side of the large house and parked it next to the black Charger that my dad had insisted I be driven in should Robert ever want to take me somewhere. A fine layer of dust covered it, a testament to the lack of use it had received since Robert had convinced my dad to allow me back onto the motorcycle.

I climbed off the seat and looked at the empty stall next to the car. "Your mom isn't here?"

He shook his head. "She's away."

I said nothing else. Over time I had learned that that two word phrase was all I would get as an explanation whenever she was somewhere I wasn't allowed to know about, answering her call. The small, white Honda that she drove was as inconspicuous as it got until it was parked next to the collection of ebony vehicles that Robert owned, so its absence was just as noticeable.

Robert's hand lashed out and he caught me by my waist, pulling me into his embrace. "Hold on," he whispered and before I could even process what it was that he had said, we were whizzing by walls and furniture, doors and windows until we were in his room.

He chuckled as he pried my hands from his jacket, my nails digging so far in they left little half-moons in the leather. "That wasn't that bad. I've put you through much worse."

This was true, but he'd never done so while taking me to his bedroom when everyone else was gone. Stacy and Lark would be together somewhere most likely and I doubted that Graham would suddenly appear out of nowhere to disturb us. "So what's with the rush anyway?" I asked as I felt my heart rate return to normal.

"I wanted to talk to you about what I learned, but I wanted to do it in private. You can't get any more private than an angel's bedroom, right?"

I laughed nervously and quickly shifted my focus to the wall behind the bed. He had been doing some redecorating, it appeared. "What's with the photos?" I pointed to a collage of photographs, all framed in black that were staggered and stacked in a large, asymmetrical grouping. Each photograph was of the two of us, shots from various outings and moments. Some I recognized, others I did not.

"When did this go up?"

He glanced negligently at the photos and shrugged his shoulders. "Probably right after fifth period started."

"You cut class to put up some pictures?"

He placed his hands on his hips in mock offense and scoffed at me. "As if I would ever do something like that!"

I rolled my eyes and sat on the edge of the bed near the collage. "This isn't one that I recognize. Who took this one?"

228

I was pointing at a shot of the two of us seated outside of the school, his arm draped over my knee, the two of us caught in mid-laughter. As surprising as the shot was, what amazed me more was the fact that the two of us looked like we belonged together despite the obvious differences between us.

"Lark did. She took all of the others, too," Robert responded, not even looking in the same direction. He was standing in front a small white box, his MP3 player in his hand. He fiddled with it before nodding, happy with whatever it was that he'd selected, and placing it into a slot that sat in the middle of the box. The room was soon filled with one of my favorite songs, the mellow rock beat bringing a smile to my face.

"I didn't know she took pictures, too," I said and gently stroked the two dimensional angle of Robert's cheek in one particular photo where he was staring down at me while I laid my head in his lap. I stood away to admire the different shots, each one capturing a moment of intimacy, regardless of the activity that was pictured.

"We're glowing in each one," I murmured as I noticed the bright softness that each photograph possessed. "It's like you're so happy, it's bouncing off me, like I'm the white to your black."

He walked over to me and pulled me to a standing position as one of my favorite songs began to play. "You make me happy. How could it not be seen?"

He placed my hand onto his shoulder and wrapped the other one around his waist. He rested his hands against my waist and we slowly rocked in a circle. "I could spend the rest of eternity with you, just like this."

I flashed him a wide grin. "I think we'd eventually get tired of this song after the first thousand plays."

"That's true, but I'm sure that by then we'd be singing our own song."

I stopped moving and tried to pull away. "Is that what this is about? You're still trying to get me to turn?"

Robert held fast and forced me to look at him as he argued his point for what was probably the millionth time. "We're destined to be with each other, Grace. Trust my divine knowledge on this one."

"I don't think that I need to remind you that even divinity has a flaw," I reminded him.

Sighing, Robert allowed me my need for distance. "Well, since we're not going to talk about our distant future, how about we talk about our near future instead?"

I nodded, liking that idea much better. "I want to know what you learned from Erica today."

Robert walked over and sat down near the foot of the bed. He patted the wide expanse next to him, the invitation obvious. When I hesitated, he groaned and I ended up sprawled on my back on the bed while he appeared as though he had never moved a millimeter.

"O-kay," I said with as much patience as I could muster. "Now that you have my undivided attention…"

The bed gently vibrated as he laughed softly. "I'm sorry. I'm just impatient today, aren't I?" He waited for me to nod in agreement, which I did enthusiastically, before he continued. "What I learned today was something I didn't expect. Her head was filled with the usual nonsense: movie stars, clothing trends, etc… What I didn't see there was what surprised me."

Robert laid down on the bed next to me and the two of us stared at the ceiling as he began to explain what made Erica tick. "Grace, she has no memories of her family. No memories that go past a few days anyway. There are sections in her mind that stretch back weeks, months, but they do not involve anything that would include her parents, any siblings. They simply don't exist. Not in her head, anyway.

"The entire area where one contains the memories of their loved ones is completely blank."

"How could that be? She goes home to them every single day. Graham's met them, spent time with them. How can she not have any memories of them?" The idea that you could not remember those who mattered the most in your life terrified me. How could I even exist if I had no recollection of my dad, or my mom?

"The void isn't a natural one, Grace. The human mind is capable of erasing itself, to be sure. Disease, stroke, trauma, even shock can all cause the brain to shut down and in an effort to protect itself, it'll dump memories, skills, even basic human functions. What I saw inside of Erica was something completely different; something that looked like someone intentionally erased the part of her that grounded her, made her, for lack of a better term, human."

I sat up and rolled over onto my side. "How is that possible?"

Robert turned over to face me, raising himself onto his elbow. "There are many ways. Medication, hypnosis, surgery to name a few."

"So you think that this was done by a doctor?" I asked, suddenly understanding.

"I don't have a definitive answer but I am fairly certain that her memory loss is due to medication. It's the only explanation to the recurring loss. If she's going home every day then she should form new memories of the people in her life, even if they come as a shock to her, but there is nothing," Robert explained. He reached his hand out and brushed a finger down the bridge of my nose. "She has a directed focus. It's a mentally visual mantra."

"To hurt me," I said quietly.

He nodded his head. "I cannot be assured that the thoughts that are in her head are genuinely hers but from what I have discovered, as well as from what I have observed, she views you as a threat."

"A threat to what though?" I heard the pitch in my voice grow higher as my confusion and frustration started to break through my stubborn calm. "How am I a threat to her? She's the beautiful one, the popular one, the rich one. As she keeps on pointing out, I'm the freak. How am I a threat?"

Robert's fingers trailed down my arm, ending at my own and intertwined with them as he replied. "You disprove every single one of her claims, Grace. You discredit her simply by existing and when you do so, you become a threat to everything she has built: her reputation, her popularity, her brand of beauty."

The idea that by "simply existing" I was taking down the monster that was Erica Hamilton sounded about as ludicrous to me as it probably would have to her had she been listening.

"Grace, open your mind and think about it. She calls you the freak, puts you down because of the way you dress, the way you look, ridicules you about who you are and who you associate with but ask yourself, if it came down to it, whose friends would save whom? Would those she calls her friends even bother to acknowledge her?"

I threw myself back down onto the bed and laughed. "That's cheating, Robert and you know it; Erica would be invincible if she had you on her side."

Robert moved over me and I looked down to see him hovering, his body just inches above mine. I lifted my hands to grab onto him but he raised himself out of my reach, the tips of his hair falling forward like black rain into his face. "That isn't fair either," I said, laughing.

"It's not supposed to be, but I think I can make an exception for you," Robert said in a low voice as he lowered himself down on top of me. He should have felt much heavier but I knew he was doing that on purpose to keep me from having to bear his weight.

"So do you really think that Erica's the way she is because someone is drugging her?"

Robert pushed his hands beneath me on the bed and, holding me, rolled over until I was perched above him, my hair now framing his face in mahogany ribbons. "I would be certain if there was a face that I could see there, or a memory of her receiving the medication, but I suspect that she wouldn't remember that either if such were the case.

"I hold out hope that this is from human interference and not from something else."

"Something else? You mean like another angel?"

232

His eyes grew dark, the glimmering silver turning to a dusky charcoal. "Not another angel. No angel would deliberately mess with another human's mind like that."

The hard edge to his tone coupled with the stony iciness behind his eyes caused my blood to run cold as I ran through the possibilities in my mind. "What else could it be then?"

Robert's sat up slowly, allowing me time to ease myself off him until the two of us found ourselves in a seated position facing each other, me—confused and slightly afraid, he—still and serious.

"I think it's time I told you about what it is that some humans become when angels try to turn them without permission."

MYTH

"How good are you with your mythology, Grace?"

The question caught me off guard. "What do you mean?"

"Well," he began, "more specifically, how well are you versed on mythological creatures?"

"That depends on what you mean by mythological. Are we talking Grecian myths, Scottish? Asian?"

The air around us turned very cold as his mood grew darker. "Have you ever wondered why so many cultures have different versions of the same type of myth? Angels, or winged people are described in various myths all across this Earth. You know the reason for that is because we exist everywhere. We're far too numerous to exist in the same area without drawing suspicions.

"The same can be said for those that we turn."

Puzzled, I frowned at his incomplete explanation. "Yes, and you said that you were going to tell me what exactly they are. Is there some kind of correlation between mythological creatures and the humans that have been turned?"

He nodded his head as the beautiful lines of his face grew harsh and hard, his mouth forming a grim line. "When the human being is turned by an angel, the change is usually very beautiful. Your body ceases

234

to age, your illnesses, weaknesses become nonexistent. You become immortal, with a heart that beats with the rising and setting of the sun and moon, unstoppable, constant. Your skin takes on a glow, nearly imperceptible by humans, and your eyes change color, usually to the same color as the angel that has turned you because that is how the angel turns you; he passes to you some of his divinity.

"But, when an angel isn't given permission to do this and he does so against the wishes of the Seraphim, his divinity is tainted, cursed by his disobedience. This affects the human he is trying to turn in different ways."

I listened intently and watched as he stood up to pace the room, his explanation demanding he be anything but still right now.

"I asked you about how well versed you are on mythology because a great deal of mythological creatures are the results of those cursed turns."

He turned to face me, needing to see me, watch my reaction as he spoke. "Nearly four thousand years ago, a poor, but beautiful farmer woman named Varmila was turned without the permission of the Seraphim by an angel who had fallen deeply in love with her. The turning seemed to go well. There was nothing outwardly different about her until she had an affair with a human and, surprisingly, became pregnant as a result.

"It should have never happened—the turned are incapable of breeding—but still, it did, and her pregnancy went on its normal course. Soon she became sick, and her appetite for normal food waned; she began to crave the taste of raw meat.

"With each subsequent child she bore, she grew hungrier and hungrier for the taste of blood until finally she began killing her own children, even as she continued having them. By the time she gave birth to her last child, the bloodlust had taken over her completely and that baby was born having been nurtured in her mother's womb solely on the blood of its siblings.

"The Seraphim had had enough of this and destroyed Varmila immediately after her last child was born. They then sentenced the angel who had turned her to a mortal life. This was the beginning of the new laws, the laws that required angels who turned humans without permission to destroy their…creations."

The way he said creations showed an extreme distaste for the term, as though it were too clinical and removed. He smiled grimly at my thoughts and nodded. He placed his hands behind him as he finished with his story.

"When Varmila died, the Seraphim didn't know what it was that she had given birth to. It looked like a normal child. Beautiful and sweet, very affectionate and without flaw, the angels could find no reason not to let her live. She was allowed to live with a family of Electus Patronus in a busy village until she reached an age where the Seraphim felt more able to deal with whatever it was that she would become.

"While she appeared normal on the outside, inside she was a different being. The time spent inside of her mother's womb, feeding on the innocence that her mother consumed changed her, altered her physically. Her heart beat slower than it should have; her skin, though beautiful and flawless was thick and tough. She couldn't eat what her human caretakers ate, but she never starved.

"And then it happened. The Seraphim and their entourage came to see for themselves what had become of their little charity case. What they found changed everything.

"When Varmila's angel turned her, it wasn't complete. The turn, the actual physical change continued as Varmila changed, as Varmila became a monster. When her daughter was born, the turn transferred onto her child. It was when the Seraphim arrived that the turn had finally become complete. Varmila wasn't the monster anymore. Her daughter was."

Robert walked closer, his voice growing lower as he revealed to me something that I had not expected.

"She called herself Miki."

"Sam's wing-bringer," I breathed.

236

He nodded. "He became instantly attracted to her, their connection so strong that his change occurred right then and there, like lightning striking the ground. Sam, not knowing what Miki was and believing her to be human, immediately asked for permission to turn her, but the Seraphim denied him. There was something about her that they did not like, something about her that they couldn't quite figure out."

I felt my forehead crease as I thought back to that night less than three months ago when Sam had told me about Miki. "He said that he turned her and that she became a monster that he had to kill."

Robert sighed as he saw the memory replay in my head. "He lied to you, Grace. He didn't kill her."

"What happened to her then?" I asked. "If he didn't kill her then she must be alive, right?"

He shook his head and began to tell the final chapter to this confusing and dark story. "When the Seraphim left Miki with her caretakers, they left her in a large town of nearly eight hundred people. For that time period, that was a metropolis. When they arrived back just twenty years later, a blink in our time, Miki was the only living person left.

"The Seraphim couldn't stand for that, they couldn't allow such enormous loss of life from one person who had been so closely tied to them. So they tried to kill her. But it was far more difficult than they had imagined because after twenty years, her thick skin had turned rock hard, she was fast and, like us, she could read minds. She knew exactly what was going to happen; she was prepared while the Seraphim were not.

"It was a battle, an epic battle of good versus evil. It was so large and destructive in scale that history couldn't keep it."

"How exactly could it have been difficult for them to kill her if she was the only one left in the village?" I asked, confused by the dynamics of this rapidly changing story.

"I said that she was the only living person left, not that she was the only person left."

My mouth popped open so loudly, the sound broke through the CD that was on its second rotation in the stereo. "The only *living* person?"

"Miki had killed everyone else in the village, but remember that I said that the turn was completed in her. She had become a monster."

My head started to hurt with all of the ups and downs of Robert's story and I laid down, my arm resting over my eyes to block out the light. "And what kind of monster is that?"

"Cruor Messor."

"What?"

"Cruor Messor; a blood reaper. Her mother's appetite for blood had transferred onto her while still in utero. Her strength, beauty, speed…even her immortality came from the angel who had tried to turn her mother. But ultimately, what made her the monster was the human side of her that manifested a virus that preyed on the weakness of the human body.

"She became an incubator for this virus, but because of her thick skin, it couldn't be transferred through from one person to the other the same way other blood-borne illnesses are, so her immortal body adapted the virus so that it could be transferred via a more readily available and easily distributable substance."

I bolted upright at his answer. I thought about every single vampire movie I had ever watched, every book I had read and I knew the answer before he had a chance to say it. "Her saliva."

"She wasn't a vampire, Grace. She was…she was their mother. She's the mother of all the monsters in this world that need blood to survive; vampires are simply the most well-known."

"Oh God."

Robert nodded grimly. "Miki had created her own little army of immortal creatures who were strong and fast like her, whose bloodlust was just as ravenous. And because of the residual power that existed in her saliva, some of them possessed the same abilities that the Seraphim did, although in a much weaker state.

"The Seraphim and Miki's army fought non-stop with no losses on either side for weeks-"

"Why didn't the Seraphim just snap their fingers or something? I mean, isn't that how it's supposed to work?" I asked.

"No. You can't kill the dead the same way you do the living. The Seraphim had never faced this kind of enemy before; they didn't know what to do. The fighting seemed endless; the divine versus the dead. And then Miki's undead soldiers became weak with hunger. That was one of the advantages that the angels had on them: we don't need to eat."

He paused to retrieve something from the trunk that sat at the foot of the bed, the one that held all of the important artifacts from his life. He placed a small red object in my hand and allowed me to inspect it as he continued.

"It took very little time after that to whittle down their numbers until only Miki and a few of the strongest of her children were left. She stood on the corpses of those that had fallen and laughed at everyone, especially Samael. She told him that though he had tried to turn her, she was the one who had turned him instead. She laughed because she knew the Seraphim couldn't destroy her; she was as divine as they were. She didn't need to feed, didn't need to rest. She felt nothing, she loved nothing. She was the epitome of death.

"The Seraphim began to doubt. The Seraphim never doubt, Grace. They're a combined intelligence; they are never wrong. But in Miki, they found they were wrong…a lot. She was smarter, she was devious, and she knew the weaknesses of the angelic mind. The Seraphim were losing to a monster of their own creation.

"Imagine how desperate the must have felt, knowing that they were losing—actually losing! But like all storms, they end. There was an elder named Avi who finally figured out Miki's greatest weakness. Over the weeks of battle with her children, Miki would only appear at night, disappearing just before dawn, only to reappear again at sunset.

"Avi knew then that as divine as Miki was, she was still part human, and during that time, many children in that area were born with a condition that made them sensitive to light. As it had her strength and her intelligence, turning had intensified this condition, turning a sensitivity into a deadly allergy. Avi learned that Miki was allergic to the sun, an allergy that passed on to some of her children.

"On the day Miki died, Avi blocked her escape towards shelter and, as dawn broke through and the morning sun began to shine on her, her body began to change. Her smooth, opaque skin turned angular and translucent. The sun's rays could be seen shining *through* her, and when her entire body was as clear as glass, she shattered like it."

He pointed to the object in my hand and I held it up. It was a dull, red piece of glass that felt unnaturally warm against my palm. "That is one of the various pieces that were passed on to each elder, a reminder of what happens when we fail to obey the rules that are handed down to us."

"So how did you come across it?"

"My mother."

I didn't know much about Ameila, and so I was captivated and secretly thrilled to know that I was learning something new about her.

"Ameila was a Seraphim?"

He nodded and removed the shard of glass from my hand. "Still is."

"But I thought that when you were born, when she had killed all those people…the Seraphim was going to punish her. How can they punish one of their own?" I asked as I watched him pass the shard across his knuckles with minor movements of his fingers, it moving along as though it were on a conveyor belt.

"The Seraphim aren't immune from punishment just because of what they are, Grace. If we cannot hold the guilty accountable simply because of their place of authority then we're no better than-"

"Us," I finished for him.

He shook his head in disagreement. "No. Humans aren't infallible, that's for certain, but they tend to find methods of regulation that often leads to fair and just results. No, what I was going to say that we're no better than animals."

My laughter was a foreign sound after such a dark story. "But animals can't see you. Why would you compare yourselves to creatures that don't even know you exist?"

"Because animals are as close to what we all could be if we weren't given the ability to understand and empathize. A bird cannot understand what laying an egg on a radiator will do to its embryo; a dog cannot empathize with a cat that lost a fight with another dog; a fish cannot forgive another fish who is trying to eat it. We can. It's a gift to us, your kind as well as mine." He grabbed my hand and pressed my fingers to his lips. "We are also given the ability to not just love, but to fall into it, stumble upon it, crash down until it surrounds us."

I felt the words he said against my fingers travel up my arm in alternating warm and cold waves, distracting me for a minute. Or two.

"Distracting you from what?"

I blinked as I drew a blank. "Um…"

He laughed and pulled me off the bed and into his arms. "Would you like me to refresh your memory?"

I laughed, although the sound was half-hearted at best. "I remember now. I wanted to know why, if the Seraphim destroyed the vampires and…the other things, why do we still hear about them? Why are there so many stories about them?"

"Because Miki had been alive for twenty years, Grace. All she had to do was infect five people, who would then infect five people and so on. She traveled; she utilized her freedom for trips to spread her mayhem and chaos to regions elsewhere. Think about how trusting people would have been of a beautiful young girl wandering all alone from village to village."

"So the monsters that died with Miki weren't the only ones."

"No, they weren't. Angels are capable of doing a great deal when gathered together, but we weren't about to risk killing off entire towns and villages just to destroy a few of Miki's offspring. Especially after the evil that had infected the first several generations began to weaken and many of their human sensibilities and traits returned."

I scoffed at that idea. "Monsters with human sensibilities? You mean like not getting caught murdering innocent people?"

Robert held me immobile as he stared down at me. "Grace, those creatures kill because it is necessary for them to survive. You think it is evil because their food source happens to be humans but you must remember that that evil was implanted by one of my kind. Which is more abhorrent, the monster or its creator?"

Rolling my eyes I quickly got down to my main point. "Okay, so now that you've explained to me all about Miki and her monsters—I still cannot believe I'm having this conversation with you—do you think that one of them could have erased Erica's memories?"

He nodded slowly, hesitantly. "I would like to think not, since I know all of those in the area, but I'm afraid that if this was being done by a supernatural being, it would be one of them and not one of the others."

"Others?" I gasped. "What others?"

Sighing, Robert began to answer. "Grace, you humans believe that you have incredible imaginations because of the creatures you read about in your books and see in your movies, but everything fictional to you is based on something real, something that exists among you that you simply refuse to see because that would mean having to admit to being wrong, that fiction is indeed fact."

"I accepted it. I accepted you. In fact, I listed quite a few of them before I even found out-" I argued but he held his hand against my mouth to quiet my words.

"And I keep telling you that you're different. Grace, I just told you that monsters truly do exist, and I'm about to tell you about creatures that you probably have never heard of, and you'll accept this because you are different. You're not like the rest of the people that live outside of those white walls and that iron gate.

"Do you think that Graham would be willing to accept that there are Sceadugengan that roam your front yard? That there are Mazikeen who move his keys around so that he thinks he misplaces them? That

242

there are Werewolves and Shape-shifters who watch movies while he's working?" he asked even though he already knew the answer.

When I shook my head, he asked the one question that he hadn't yet. "And, do you think that he'd be willing to accept what I am?"

This time I spoke up. "Yes—unequivocally. He knows how much you mean to me. He knows that you saved my life, Robert. He knows that you love me. He would accept you no matter what you were."

Robert smiled sadly and brushed away the tiny tear that had mysteriously formed at the corner of my eye. "And what about when he learns that I'm Death. Would Graham still accept me, Grace?"

I had no answer for him that wouldn't have been a lie. I didn't know what Graham would have thought about that.

"I'm a mythological creature twice over, Grace, and even those who are raised to believe in me have a difficult time accepting it when I appear to them. But that's not important. What I want you to understand is that my world is one where you exist among those you cannot see because you don't want to see them. Or, more importantly, you don't want to know who truly is and isn't one of you."

I opened my mouth to deny this, but how exactly could I do that? He had just described a whole other world that existed right beneath my nose, and I was oblivious to it. All I wanted was normalcy; it was what I kept telling everyone anyway. I was exactly the type of person Robert was describing.

"I'm sorry," he apologized, but I shook my head.

"No, you're right. You shouldn't apologize for telling me the truth. You just didn't know that you were describing me when you did it because you didn't know how deeply my need to be just like everyone else really ran. So, now that we've got that out of the way, can we get back to who might be the one tampering with Erica's memory?"

I needed the change of subject. I needed it like a hangover cure because the truth of Robert's words had started to spread like an ink stain in my head and I didn't understand why it bothered me so much.

Robert eyed me nervously, but obliged me. "I'm going to have to follow her in order to find that out, Grace. I cannot see a face or hear a name in her head that stands out other than your own, so I can only rely on real time revelations."

The thought of Robert following Erica, watching her as she went about her life in every way felt like I had swallowed a fishbone that had lodged itself in my throat and every time I tried to swallow down my annoyance, it irritated me more. "If there is no other way—I cannot believe that we're helping out Erica Hamilton!"

"I could ask Lark to do it, if that would make you feel better."

The suggestion burned like a bright beacon of hope for about one tenth of a second before the image of Lark strangling Erica flashed in my head. Robert saw it and laughed, shaking his head. "I guess not."

"If this is what it's going to take to stop her, I can handle you being around her for a day. *One* day. No more."

The air around us grew warmer as my concession pleased him. "You're very generous with your boyfriends."

I laughed at that. "Boyfriends? There's only ever been one."

"And who exactly would that be?"

"You, of course!" I exclaimed laughing as he nuzzled my neck.

"I'm afraid that you're incorrect," he whispered into my ear.

Stiffly, I pulled away, just the hint of him not being a part of my life enough to turn my mood instantly black. "What do you mean by that?"

Immediately he released his arms from around me and placed them on my face, cradling it like you would something precious, priceless. "I told you before, Grace. I'm your future. It gets no more permanent and intimate than that. Boyfriend is a temporary title."

I opened my mouth to argue but he lowered his face to mine quickly and pressed his mouth to my top lip. Instinctively, my bottom lip closed around his, and though I knew it shouldn't have happened, I gently stroked it with the tip of my tongue.

It had an immediate effect on me; my brain grew foggy and my ears filled with the humming of something I could only guess was my blood; blood that felt hot, heated to burning. It was all I could do not to force him to stay absolutely still so that I could savor him for as long as humanly possible. Instead, he pulled away and began apologizing profusely. "I shouldn't have done that. I knew better. I knew…"

"Why are you apologizing for kissing me?" I demanded. "It was a kiss. People do it all of the time. People who don't even like each other do it, and they do it in ways we never have…and probably never will."

Robert held me fast as I struggled to pull away. "Don't, Grace. Don't run from this just because you're angry."

"I'm not angry, Robert. You've got to learn to gauge your emotions better because what I'm feeling right now is disappointment and rejection, not anger."

"I'm confused. You're speaking to me as though you're angry. Your thoughts are full of anger," he stated, his words clinical in their lack of emotion.

"What you're seeing and hearing is the result of once again being rejected, Robert. I get your whole chaste-virginal thing. I do. But what I did there—that was a kiss. I wasn't throwing myself at you. I learned from past rejections not to do that anymore.

"But when you choose to pull away from my kisses; that hurts, Robert. When I see other couples who share in things that we never do, I feel like I'm losing out on something special. Even Donovan and Kendra kiss that way, and according to you, their relationship isn't real. No, I'm not angry, Robert. There's no room for that in me right now."

He watched me, searched within my thoughts to find the slightest bit of exaggeration, but I knew he'd find none. I pulled away from him and he let me go. I walked over to the stereo and pressed the stop button. "I used to love that song," I muttered.

I removed the CD from the slide that appeared at a press of the eject button and I placed it back into its case.

"When are you going to do it?" I asked as I put the case back into the void it had left behind when it was removed.

"When do you want me to do it?" he replied, his tone flat and emotionless.

"After you take me home."

"I don't understand you."

"What's there not to understand? You'll take me home and then you'll go and follow Erica around to see who is turning her brain to rat jelly."

Robert shoved his hands through his hair and groaned. "No. I don't understand *you*. You become aggressive and demanding when you want something, and when you're denied it, you become defensive and withdrawn while I become the villain when all I was doing was protecting your virtue-"

"Who asked you to?"

"And yet, when I have asked you to turn, to become immortal so that we can have nothing but time to be together, to finally be with each other in the way that we *both* want, *you* deny *me* and again become withdrawn and defensive. Why?"

I looked past him towards the wall where the collage of photos displayed two people who were blindly in love, who appeared to have nothing but joy and contentment between them. "Angels believe in myths, too you know. You have these beliefs that humans all feel the same way; that our feelings can each be categorized and labeled, everything all sterile and clinical-like and if they happen to change, you can simply offer up a substitution and we'll be alright.

"Well, let me fill you in on something, Robert. I'm human, which means I have human feelings, dynamic feelings that go beyond your black and white labels. And what I feel when you reject me and deny me the simple pleasure of kissing you, and then turn around and tell me that if I change for you, that you'd give me what I want, that tells me that who I am, the human Grace, isn't good enough for you or your angelic virtue. And what I feel is unadulterated, unsterilized hurt."

I walked towards the photos and pointed to them. "That is the sterilized version of us, Robert. It fits in here, in your room because that's what works for you. Everything has its place, its reason, its need. I have a place, too, a reason in your life. But the way you act sometimes, Robert…it makes me feel like that place belongs only in those photos."

I turned around on my heels and headed to the door. He reached it before I did and opened it, holding it for me as I walked past him. He said nothing as we walked out of the house and towards the detached garage. "Can we ride in the car?" I asked softly.

He gave me a puzzled look and I turned away from his gaze as we walked into the three car building. I didn't need to say it. I simply thought it, thought that with the way I was feeling, the last thing I wanted to do was spend the next few minutes with my arms wrapped around him.

He nodded curtly and quickly opened the car door for me. I climbed in and fought the tears that threatened to spill onto the seat. Robert climbed into the driver's seat and started the car, putting it into reverse and peeling out as though he were running away from something.

We remained silent the entire way to my house, my heart feeling heavier and heavier as each minute ticked by. When we pulled into the driveway, I saw Graham's car parked in its usual spot by the curb. He was sitting on the hood, waiting for someone.

"He's waiting for you," Robert said in a low voice.

I said nothing. I simply sat in the car and thought about what had happened over the past few hours. I'd learned some shocking truths, but it was that last one that caused me to tremble with fear.

"Grace, please…"

He reached over for my hand and I didn't pull away. *Grace, you're my entire world. I just didn't know that though this is your first relationship, I'm the one who has a lot to learn. Help me, teach me. I do want you, Grace. Know that I am telling the truth when I tell you that I fight against every natural instinct in my body that tells me to give in to you, to give in to myself not because I don't love you just the way you are, but because I'm trying to keep you safe, keep us safe.*

"What does that even mean?" I cried. "Safe from what? From each other? Aren't we hurting each other enough the way things are going now?" I looked out of the window and shook my head at the direction the conversation was heading. "We'll talk about this later when we're both not feeling so…different."

I began to open my door and felt it being pulled away from my hand. Or, rather, I felt myself being pulled away from the door. Robert had me in his lap, one hand pressed securely against my hip, the other holding my face still. "Grace, I do feel different, and I don't want that feeling to ever leave me."

He pulled my face towards his, holding me still as his lips found their way to mine. With infinite slowness, he gently cupped my bottom lip between his and I felt him tug at it slightly before the tender nerves that existed just below the surface lit up with activity, letting me know that he had just licked my bottom lip.

I took in a deep gulp of air, inhaling his breath as I did so. His eyes were wide, his pupils darker than I'd ever seen them and I felt myself fall into them, disappearing into inky blackness.

ᴄꙅ

"You're awake, finally."

I blinked at the light that shone brightly in my eyes and covered them with my hand. "Mmm. Robert…"

"I'm here."

I moved my hand and focused on the two heads that observed me from their seat on the coffee table of my living room. "What happened?" I mumbled as I rubbed the sting out of my eyes.

Graham snorted. "Robert suffocated you, what do you think?"

Robert, in turn, gave out a rather obnoxious laugh. "Graham is just upset because he had to witness us making out."

My hand dropped from my face and I sat up far too quickly, the dizziness causing me to sway. Robert and Graham both reached out to grab a hold of me. "We…were making out, weren't we?" I sighed.

Robert chuckled and nodded. Graham rolled his eyes. "It was gross. It was like seeing my little sister making out with the janitor or something. It looked like you guys were deep in conversation up until that point. What were you talking about anyway?"

I looked at Robert and he winked at me as he answered Graham. "Mythology."

BYGONES

Robert left less than an hour after I woke up. I walked with him, hand in hand to the door and instantly felt shy, as though this were the first time we were saying goodbye. He had laughed, but the moment we stood in that doorway, there was no room for humor.

"Thank you," I said shyly, heat suffusing my cheeks.

"For?"

I tried to say it, but the words simply would not reach my lips, and he smiled. "Oh. Well, you're welcome. And I should say thank you as well."

"For?"

He brought his free hand to my face, gently tracing the curve of my ear, my jaw, and finally the bow of my mouth. "For proving me wrong."

"Oh."

He chuckled and rubbed the pad of his thumb across my lower lip, still so very sensitive to his touch.

I'll be back by this time tomorrow. I promise you.

As much as I anticipated it, I wasn't disappointed when Robert did not kiss me goodbye and instead simply pressed his forehead to mine for a brief moment. After what had happened at his house and then in the car, I understood that he had gone beyond the boundaries that he had set for himself and needed time to adjust to that. I was willing to accept that because now I knew that it was possible to do so.

When I walked back into the living room, Graham had popped in my old copy of Rocky Horror and was waiting patiently for the iconic lips to start lip-synching to the intro. I plopped down next to him on the couch and together we watched the first ten minutes of the movie in silence.

"So, Grace—ow!"

I smiled smugly as I rubbed my fist, pleased that I had delivered the first punch after only ten minutes. "You were saying?"

Graham rubbed his arm and glared at me, having not expected that I wasn't going to allow him to break the rules simply because we had gotten off to a late start. "This is serious, Grace. Ow-ow, stop hitting me!" His arms flew out and grabbed a hold of my hand as I reared to deliver another blow, pushing me down onto the sofa cushions. "You psycho! I broke up with Stacy!"

Everything in me went on pause as I allowed his words to bounce around in my head. I slowly sat up down and looked at him, unsure whether his news was a good thing or a bad thing.

"You broke up with Stacy," I said, a statement rather than a question.

Graham nodded and gingerly let go of my arm, twitching in response to my every move, obviously fearful that I'd hit him again. "I guess I should be honest and say that we kind of broke up with each other after school. I had actually planned to do it a couple of days ago-"

"The day after I fell…"

"Yeah," Graham confirmed. "And I wanted to talk to you about it on the way to school, but then Robert showed up and…well, you know what happened. I gotta admit that I was a little jealous that you'd just forgive him for not being there for you, but I was more upset that I wasn't going to get to talk to you, ask you for some advice about what to do…so instead I just winged it. I went to her dad's school and we talked. It was probably the only time we ever had a conversation without arguing. Ironic, isn't it?"

"Very," I agreed.

"Stacy and I both like each other more now than we did when we first went out, but we know that we're not good together. Heck, the whole school knows that we're not good together," Graham laughed softly. "Stacy's a great girl, and despite all of the fights, I'm glad that we dated, Grace. I really am. I can see why you two are friends, and why you, Stacy, and Lark make such a good team. You guys complement each other. I always thought that Stacy was the oddball out of the group, but now I know that it's me."

His jaw set into a stubborn line as something crossed his mind. "I was such a jerk, Grace. I know I've told you before how sorry I was about how I treated you last summer, but Stacy made me see it from a different point of view. Not from yours, or from mine, but from hers.

"She told me about how it looked from her end, how hard it was for her to hear about what had happened from some of the kids that go to her dad's school, and to know that you were alone through all of it. She told me that I had apologized for what I had said to you. I mean, I apologized for what I had said to Erica, but I never apologized for leaving you alone.

"She said that I needed to think about how it felt to sit alone in my home when my dad was off on one of his benders and Mom was out perming and dyeing her problems away at the salon. She told me to imagine doing that and then having no one to call. I didn't fully understand that what I had done to you cut you off from everything, and I'm sorry. I'm probably the sorriest piece of crap you'll ever meet in your life. It's no wonder I'm such a screw up when it comes to girls, huh?"

I gave Graham a good once over, looking at him in a way that I never truly had before. He was still the handsome boy that I was proud to say was my best friend. He still had those rich green eyes that could make a girl swear off any other color for the rest of her life, and a smile that could kill you with dimples. And none of that did anything to mask what lay underneath. He was still cocky, but he was also humbled now.

He no longer had the picture perfect life. I knew now that he never truly did, that it was all an act that his parents had put on for show which he kept up because it was the only way he could keep himself, keep Graham from turning into a joke like his home life.

"Graham, we're in this together, right?" I asked him. When he nodded, I continued. "Well then, if we're in this together, as best friends, then you should know that you don't have to apologize to me over and over again for the same mistake."

Graham smiled at that. "That's funny because Stacy said the exact opposite. She said that I needed to make it clear, over and over again, that I was sorry for what I did to you, and that I wanted to make amends in any way I could."

We both laughed at the excess of Stacy's advice. "Her heart was in the right place, but I think that if you apologize to me one more time, I'll have to do some serious soul searching to try and figure out whether or not *I'm* the bad person."

He looked at me quizzically. "What do you mean figure out whether or not you're the bad person?"

"Well, if you said you were sorry one more time, I'd have to spend a considerable amount of time working one of the springs in this couch free so that it stabbed at you all night while you slept."

Graham slammed a pillow into the side of my head while I burst out laughing. "You're heinous, you know that?"

I nodded my head while I continued to laugh, the vision of him tossing and turning by one strategically placed spring doing much to undo the damage that the day's events had caused.

"I'm sorry," I said to him when I had regained my composure.

He brushed off my little display of hysterics and smiled as he put his arm around my shoulder and pulled me next to him, our heads resting against each other. "I tried to be a good boyfriend, Grace."

253

I stared at the television and attempted to find something useful to say. I could find nothing, so I just let him continue talking.

"I tried to be the boyfriend that she expected, but I'm no good at meeting expectations. You know that, Grace. Everyone always expected so much from me. My dad expected that I'd get some huge football scholarship, but look at me. Third quarter is almost up and the closest I've gotten to an interview with a scout was when Mrs. Goldman's granddaughter was selling Girl Scout cookies last week. My mom expected I'd turn out to be some kind of whiz kid and instead I blew all of the classes I'd have had with you this year on stupid and useless junk for Erica.

"And then there were *her* expectations. She expected me to completely stop thinking about you, to pretend that you didn't exist, but I simply couldn't do that. I couldn't ignore the fact that I had hurt you. I couldn't ignore the fact that you had always been there for me, always been my rock, and I left you to play with a stupid cardboard box, which meant that I disappointed you, too."

Graham pressed the pause button on the remote control and then threw the remote onto Dad's recliner with a raspy sigh of disgust. "That sounded stupid—I'm no good at this kind of stuff, Grace. I can't tell people what I'm feeling or thinking the way that I want to, it never comes out right. That's why…"

He stopped talking and though I wanted to ask him to continue, he didn't. He just sat back and stared at the television screen, the movie frozen in time just like our conversation.

As the digital clock on the VCR slowly moved ahead, I sat there and thought about what he had said about failing to live up to the expectations of so many people, myself included. It brought me back to the conversation that Dad and I had had on that first day back to school.

He had told me that I expected too much from people, that I had expected too much from Graham and that it was probably a good thing that our friendship had ended. I had left the house that day angry, hurt that he would suggest such a thing, and although Graham and I had worked things out, I still carried a small amount of resentment towards my dad for having said it at all.

Yet now I could see that he was right, and I felt an inordinate amount of guilt for putting Graham through that. Perhaps if I had been the better friend…

"Hey, I'm going to hit the sack. I work the day shift tomorrow and then I've got an interview at the sporting good shop next to the Dairy Queen so I need to get some sleep."

Reluctantly, I stood up and watched as he stretched himself out on the couch, his feet extending way past the arm. I grabbed the blanket that he had thrown onto the recliner and opened it up, carefully placing it on him, making sure to cover his feet. "Goodnight, Graham," I said to him softly as I climbed the stairs to my room.

"Goodnight, Grace," he called back just before I reached the landing.

I flipped the light on in my room and shut the door softly. I turned around and let out a softened squeal. Lark was sitting on my bed, her legs folded in front of her, a book in her lap.

"Jeez! Could you at least warn someone that you're going to be sneaking into their room?" I hissed. I walked over to my dresser and began rummaging for clothes; I needed to take a shower and wash off the wear of the day that was starting to feel like a second skin.

She didn't even move, didn't acknowledge that I had said anything at all. I shrugged my shoulders and, after grabbing some underwear and my usual pajamas, I left the room to head to the bathroom, flipping the light off as I did so.

I stayed in the shower until the water ran cold, and I shivered almost violently as I dressed, suddenly angry with myself for not choosing something warmer to sleep in. I wrapped my hair in a thick towel and ran to my room, anticipating the warmth that would soon build beneath my covers with Robert.

"Oh dangit," I said aloud when I entered my room once more and found that Lark hadn't moved from her spot in the middle of my bed, her eyes still glued to the book. "Are you going to be there all night?"

She finally looked up at me, her face eerily calm. "Robert's not going to be coming back tonight, remember?"

Oh.

"Oh? Is that all you can say? 'Oh'?" Lark tossed the book aside and stood up, her movements lithe and graceful. "You sent my brother to spy on Erica. You got him to tell you about the others. You got him to tell you about our mother. And all you can say is 'oh'?"

I started to back up as she approached me. "I didn't get him to do anything. I didn't ask him to tell me about any of that, Lark. He did it on his own."

She laughed, the sound of bells filling my head. The harmonious peal distracted me long enough for her to maneuver herself directly in front of me, blocking out any path of escape.

"You never have to ask him, Grace. He will always tell you everything because you mean more to him than any of us." She walked away and sighed, her head hanging low. "It's how it should be when you're in love."

"Lark, I-"

She held up her hand, stopping me from continuing. Her body began to float above the bed, leaving behind no impression that she'd even been sitting on it. "I didn't come here to argue with you about Robert. He's a big angel; he can deal with his own mistakes."

Angry, I folded my arms across my chest, tucking my hands away so I could hide the fists they made. "Mistakes? What mistakes? He-"

"He's spying on a human for another human. He's told you about a world that your kind isn't ready for or willing to accept. He's broken the rules because of you over and over again, Grace, and he's going to have to face the consequences for it sooner or later."

The idea that I was going to get Robert into trouble was enough to sober me up and keep me from interrupting her as she slowly drifted back down onto my bed, this time near the foot, and began pulling her legs in front of her, crossing them. "Come, sit. You must be cold by now."

I nodded and walked briskly to the opposite side of the bed. I climbed beneath the covers, muffling a shocked squeal from their icy smoothness, and settled myself against my pillows.

When I was still, Lark began to speak again. "You know that Graham and Stacy broke up."

I quickly bobbed my head down once, acknowledging her statement. She smile sadly and spoke, "I'm feeling very torn about it. The rational part of me says that I should be feeling mutual hurt for Stacy because she is my friend. It's what an angel should do. But there's a part of me that I don't understand that is telling me that I should be flying and singing with joy.

"I cannot talk to Stacy about this, obviously, and Robert won't listen to me speak about Graham at all, so I'm left with asking you why I feel this way. I consider you one of my closest human friends, Grace, and although you are Graham's best friend and at one point felt the exact same way that I do about him, I know that you are capable of understanding how I feel and can explain to me why it is that I feel this way in the first place."

I pushed the covers under my chin so that they wouldn't muffle my voice, and I looked directly into Lark's eyes as I began to speak. "You care about him a great deal. You care about Graham in a way that makes everything you know about logic and humans seem unimportant and unnecessary, and you like that because you're like that. You are a walking contradiction—flawed perfection. You're an angel who cannot see; at least, not in a conventional way, and that makes you different in both of the worlds you live in.

"Your feelings for Graham are the same way. They contradict what you're used to and you don't know how to handle it, so you choose instead to fight it, but it's like a Chinese finger-trap. You keep pulling away from it and it in turn just grows tighter and tighter when all you really need to do to be free is to push towards it."

257

Lark sneered at my explanation. "I give you an opportunity to help me and you give me metaphors involving a child's toy? I know I care about Graham. I care about Stacy, too. I cannot *help* but care about them because it comes with this whole angel thing I've got going on here, just in case you've failed to notice or anything."

The mocking tone of her voice felt like needles in my head as her words were repeated in my thoughts.

What I want to know is what can I do to stop this? I want to know how do I stop wanting to be with Graham? You did it. You stopped. Tell me how to do it so that I don't hurt Stacy. Tell me how to do it so that I can avoid hurting Graham.

My head turned away from Lark and I gazed out of the window. The very same window that Robert used to come into my room that first night, the window that he drifted into that first night I told him I loved him. "I fell in love."

Lark threw up her hands in annoyance. *There's that love talk again. What is with you humans and your incessant speeches about falling in love? Even Stacy said that she didn't want to date anymore, that she just wanted to 'fall in love' and be 'blissfully complete' for the rest of her life.*

I watched as a car drove down the street and smiled. "Humans may have long and fancy speeches about love. We might write stories or sing songs about it, watch movies about it and yes, we dream about it. But angels…you physically change because of it. Robert would never have grown his wings if he hadn't admitted that he loved me. You know this far better than I do, so quit trying to find reasons to hate it and instead find reasons to seek it out."

Lark glared at me, her pale sage glow growing deeper in hue until it reached a deep emerald. *You humans always think you know everything, but history proves that you're consistently wrong.*

I pulled my comforter down to my waist and glared back. "And yet who's the one coming to a *human* for advice?"

I saw the flicker of anger in her eyes in the same instant I noticed the muscles in her neck clench with frustration. Every instinct in my body told me to try and get as far away from her as possible, but I ignored it. This wasn't Sam I was facing. This was Lark. Confused and hurt though she may be, she was still my friend and I wasn't going to run away from her when I was the only person she had to talk to.

I misjudged you again it seems. Just when I think I have your kind figured out, you go and prove me wrong. You, Stacy, and even Graham.

Feeling brave, I finally asked her the question that had been weighing on my mind for the past few days. "Why did you tell Graham to come and help me?"

She looked up and I could see nothing but raw pain in her gilt eyes. *He's your friend. I knew Robert wasn't able to help you, and I couldn't lie about why I'd be there.*

My chin jutted out as I listened to her half-answer. It wasn't a lie, but it wasn't the whole truth, either. "You know there's more, Lark."

She stubbornly set her feet onto the floor and began to leave. I quickly grabbed her arm and tried to tug her back onto the bed; it was like trying to move a house.

I did it for you. I saw what was in your head. I saw what you were thinking and I knew you needed someone who could support you and help you. I knew you could count on Graham.

Lark pulled her arm out of my hand and faced me. I could see the twinkle of light reflecting in the corner of her eyes as small, crystal tears began to form there. They fell like snow drops onto the floor, first one, then two, and eventually twelve little spots of glistening crystal glittered there. It was the most emotion I had ever seen expressed by her that didn't involve anger.

"You also did it for yourself. You needed to see what was in his head, needed to see if he'd reject your voice or if he'd welcome it," I accused. "And when he didn't reject it like you had hoped, you knew that there was no excuse left to not admit that he's a good person, a good human-being and that there was nothing wrong with you feeling the way you do."

She turned away and stared at the blank wall opposite the bedroom window. *You know, for a human, you're a pretty good mind-reader.*

"You're easy to read…for an angel."

She laughed at that, but it was an empty sound. *It doesn't matter anyhow. Graham will graduate; he'll leave Heath and everything in it behind forever. There is no future for us. My past has already deemed it so.*

The finality in those last words jolted me. I began to ask her what she meant by that, but she was already fading away into a light gray mist.

"He is your future," I said softly as the last wisp climbed up over my window sill and out into the night sky. "Don't let your past dictate what you can and cannot have now, Lark."

COMPOSITION

When Robert returned to my room the next evening, the information that he had gathered by watching Erica told us very little. He had had to leave her for a short period of time in order to answer his call, and he admitted to being afraid that it was during that time that she'd had her memory once again erased.

He offered to watch her again, but Lark's words echoed in my head about breaking the rules and having to face the consequences—consequences that I knew nothing about—and I simply couldn't let him go through with it.

"Lark is being paranoid, Grace. I didn't violate any rules," Robert assured me.

"Well, I'd rather not take any more chances. You're more important to me than whatever is going on in Erica's head. There are only a few more months left of school anyway, and then I'm out of here."

I opened up one of my drawers to pull out a pair of sweats—it was very cold, despite it being on the cusp of spring—and proceeded to gather other articles of clothing in preparation to shower. I looked up and caught Robert's reflection in my mirror, his face filled with hurt.

"What's wrong?" I asked when I had turned around, immediately concerned.

"The way you spoke of leaving—you only mentioned yourself," he said stiffly.

"Well, yeah. I'm the one heading off to college in the fall. Or, at least, I'm planning on it. I don't expect Erica to follow me all the way to wherever it is I'm heading."

Robert glanced at the clothes in my hands and began to sit up from his position on the bed. "I'd better leave."

I threw my little bundle on the bed and reached for his hand. "Wait, why? What did I say?"

Robert pointed to the clothes that had fallen loosely apart. "Nothing, Grace. Nothing at all."

I tightened my grip on his hand and then felt my fingers curl into my palm as Robert disappeared into a plume of black mist. "You know, you and your sister are getting on my nerves with this-this poofing into smoke thing," I said, annoyed. "This is why humans date other humans. They don't just poof into nothing and run away!" I said that last part as the smoke disappeared out of my window.

I heard a knock on my door and felt relieved for the distraction. "Come in," I called out and then grabbed my clothes from the bed, tucking them under my arm.

Graham poked his head in. "Hey, Grace. Look, I wanted to know if you had any extra folder paper."

"Yeah. Sure." I grabbed my backpack and handed it to him. "There's some in my binder."

Graham thanked me as I walked past him towards the bathroom. I turned the shower on and allowed the bathroom to fill up with steam. I climbed into the hot spray and allowed it to beat into me a pattern of relaxation and calm.

I ignored the knock on the door while I washed my hair and soaped myself. The knock grew louder as I rinsed off, and by the time I was dry and fully dressed, the knock had grown so insistent I thought it would fall off its hinges.

"What?!" I demanded as soon as I opened the door. Graham stood in front of me with a blank sheet of paper and a pencil in his hand, a look of utter despair on his face.

"I don't know how to do this," he said sadly.

I looked at the paper and the pencil and eyed him out. "You don't know how to do what? Write your name?" I pushed past him and walked into my room, noting that he had at least put my backpack in the right spot.

"No. I don't know how to write a letter to Lark."

I pulled the towel out of my hair and began to rub it dry as I processed his words. "You want to write a letter to Lark?"

He nodded his head dumbly.

"And you don't know how?"

Again, his head shook up and down. I sighed. "What's keeping you from doing it?"

"I don't know how to put my thoughts down to paper. It's like with everything else, I'm alright, but when it comes to her…Grace, I tried this three times and the furthest I got was the D in Dear."

I grabbed the sheet of paper from him and sure enough, there were several indentations in the shape of a letter D marring its otherwise perfect surface. "What made you decide to write a letter to her in the first place?"

"I just have this feeling that if I'm ever going to tell Lark how I feel about her, it's got to be now. Spring break is coming up and mom wants me to fly down to Florida and spend it with her-"

"But you're going to miss the wedding!"

"I have no choice, Grace. I can't be sleeping on your couch while you and Janice do all that wedding stuff. You've got plans you have to take care of, and she's going to have a baby soon. It's time I started to think about the future—my future." Graham shook the piece of paper in his hand and tapped it with the pencil. "That's why I need you to help me with this. I don't want to leave Heath without letting her know how I feel about her, without giving it a shot.

"Thing is…I don't know how to do it. I need our help, Grace."

I admired him for his tenacity. He had never looked more determined before. Even when he was on the football field he still appeared slightly aloof, as though that wasn't where he truly wanted to be.

"Well, okay then. Let's get started on this letter."

He grinned at me like a kid who'd just been given a new toy, and I tried to smile in return with equal exuberance, but in the back of my mind I kept hearing Lark's words…

There is no future for us…

Graham was determined that there would be a future for him and Lark, and I was equally determined to help him prove Lark wrong.

ς

Spring break was almost here when Graham knocked on my bedroom door, a thin stack of papers in his hand. "Are those college applications?" I asked as I pointed to the disorganized piles that lay out before me on my bed. "I've got mine almost completely done; I've just got a couple of essays left."

"No. I only applied to one college," he replied. He handed me the sheets of filler paper, each one completely full of his semi-neat handwriting. "This is it."

"What is it?"

"The letter."

I looked at the first page closely and saw that indeed, this letter was meant for Lark. The time he had taken to embellish her name told me that whatever it was that he had written had also been done so with equal care and attention.

"That's nice," I said as I traced the L with my finger. I could feel the deep indentation and smiled as I realized what he had done. "You did this on purpose so she could feel it and read it."

He blushed at the truth. "You're too smart for your own good, Grace."

"Nah. I'm just a sucker for romance." I handed the stack back to him, but he pushed it away.

"I want you to read it," he said. "Read it out loud and tell me if this would be enough to tell you that whoever wrote it was in love with you."

"I don't think I should," I objected, trying to have him take his letter back but he stood up and walked away, putting as much space as possible between himself and the words that he had written.

"Please, Grace. I need you to read it. I need to hear it."

Sighing, I stared at the words on the page. Knowing that if I didn't, I'd sorely disappoint him, I began to read the composition that had taken him two weeks to complete.

"*Lark,*

"*I'm not very good at expressing how I feel, especially when what I feel is something that I've never felt before. I don't really remember much about the first time I saw you. I was living in a fog and I couldn't have appreciated you for all of your beauty and your charm.*

"*I do remember the second time I saw you, though. You were surrounded by some of the most beautiful girls in school, but none of them shined like you did to me. It wasn't a day that should have held any brightness, any kind of hope, and yet you stood there like the only star in the sky—meant to be wished upon. And I wished on you. I wished that one day, you'd remember my name.*

"*I know that sounds pretty stupid. Everyone remembers my name. I'm one of the biggest jerks in school. But I wanted you to remember my name for another reason. I wanted you to be able to say my name and be able to say 'Graham Hasselbeck is a good guy.'*

"*When I saw you again at the cemetery, I thought it had to have been fate that brought you there to my Grandmother's grave. Why else would you have been there? And then you said my name; you said it and I knew that my wish had come true.*

"*Every single day since then, I've thought of you. That sounds kind of stalkerish. I'm sorry. Let me try that again.*

"*Every single day since then, I have thought of how wonderful it's been just being around you and that light you seem to bring with you. I cannot think of a day yet where seeing your face hasn't made me happy.*

"*But happy doesn't begin to describe how good it feels. It sucks sometimes, not being able to see you, not being able to hear your voice. And I wonder if you might feel the same way. I had a chance with you, a chance to tell you how I felt, but my heart fumbled that ball and instead my head won out.*

"*I won't say that I regret my decision, because I don't. It helped me to learn more about myself and what I was capable of, both the good and the bad. It gave me a friend I didn't have before then, and it gave me an appreciation for knowing what I want and what I'm not willing to settle for.*

"*And what I want is to tell you that I don't see my life going anywhere unless you're in it because I love you. It's not the kind of love I have for Grace, because I love her, too. But this is something different, something that feels like a big rock is sitting on my chest and the only way to remove it is to see your face and hear your voice.*

"*And I hear your voice in my head, and I see your face in my dreams, and I know that if I closed my eyes for the last time, or if I never heard another thing for as long as I lived, those would be enough for me. The stupid poets who wrote those sonnets of love and devotion didn't know what they were talking about because they'd never met you. They've never known what it feels like to carry my heart in their chest whenever you walk by.*

"*They've never known what it feels like to have my legs whenever I smell your perfume. They've never known what it feels like to hear you say their name and see you smile when you say it.*

"*I'm not good at expressing my feelings, Lark. I've been so confused about so many things that after a while, they all start to blend into each other and I cannot pick out the differences anymore. But what I feel for you stands out like a wide receiver open in the last twenty yards from the goal. It stands out like a single flower on a gravestone covered in snow. It stands out like a quarterback writing a love letter to someone whose love he doesn't deserve.*

"I dream of one day being able to say these things to you in person, to have enough courage to be able to look into your beautiful face and not stumble on my words, but I can admit that I do not know any other way to tell you this than through this pencil and these sheets of paper.

"You've changed my life, Lark. No matter what happens between us, no matter what happens after this, I want you to know that besides Grace, knowing you has been the best part of my life, and the only part that I'll ever look back on without regret.

"Sincerely Yours,

"Graham Hasselbeck"

I quickly handed Graham the stack of paper with shaky hands. He looked at me, nervously anticipating my response. "Well…?" he asked while I dabbed at my nose with a tissue he handed to me.

"Well what?" I replied, trying to contain my emotions so that I didn't end up speaking like a cartoon character.

"What do you think? Do you think she'll like it?"

I looked at him, looked at his face and his wide, anxious eyes. I couldn't lie to him, and so I didn't. "I don't know, Graham. I honestly don't know if she will or not. Lark isn't like most girls. *I* love it, but then again, I'm not like most girls either."

He nodded his head as he digested my answer. "Well, could you give it to her?" He folded the stack of papers in half and then pressed the bundle into my hands. "Could you give this to her, read it to her and let her know that I don't expect anything from her. I don't expect anything at all."

I clasped onto the letter and nodded. "I promise you that she'll get it."

Graham smiled and wrapped his arms around me, hugging me tightly to his chest. "You're the best, Grace. And I meant what I wrote in there about you, too."

I laughed at that. "I know you did."

He loosened his hold on me and then pressed a sloppy kiss on the top of my head. "I do love you, Grace. You're my best friend. The best friend any guy could have. I don't know what I did to deserve you but I'm glad for it."

I couldn't say anything to him as he got up and left. I just watched him go, feeling incredibly lucky and guilty all at the same time.

As soon as the door was shut, I looked at the folded bundle in my hand, opening it up to once again run my fingers across the deep indentations of each letter.

"Did you hear all of that?" I asked softly, my hand starting to tremble as it reached the end of the last page.

"Yes."

Lark stood by my window, her hands clenched at her sides, her eyes shut tightly, as though it could keep out the vision of my holding the declaration that I held in my now violently shaking hands.

"Now you know for certain. Now you know exactly how he feels, without your charms, without anything but his own heart in each and every word. I didn't want to read this letter, Lark. I didn't want to read it knowing that you were here and he had no clue. That wasn't fair to him."

I stood up and grabbed one of her hands, shoving the papers into them. "You said that you two had no future together, but he thinks differently."

"He thinks differently because he's a silly human who doesn't understand the concept of time and-"

"And what?" I asked angrily. "And what? What doesn't he understand that's somehow so fantastical, so divine that only you can know? Huh? How can you stand there and be so self-righteous when you cannot even recognize love when it slaps you in the face?

"*He* knows what it is and isn't afraid to tell you, and he's the silly human, remember? He's the one proving to you that you're the one who doesn't understand the concept of time because you're wasting it trying to figure out an excuse that will prevent you from having to face the fact that deep down, you love him, too."

I stood nose-to-nose with Lark, my breath coming out in angry huffs while she remained calm and collected. But I could see that her icy exterior was beginning to crack.

You understand and see nothing.

"Oh no. I see a lot more than you do, Lark. I can see that you're scared, but what I don't see is why. Why are you so afraid of letting him love you? Why are you so afraid of loving him back?"

She turned her face away, the crystal droplets once again falling from her eyes. I bent down to collect them, each one a perfect teardrop. "You can cry tears, but you cannot accept the reason why you do so. You have his heart, Lark. What are you going to do about it?"

Lark opened my hand and removed the tiny crystals from my palm. She placed them into the folded letter and then returned it to my hand. And then she was gone.

FLEE

The last week of class before spring break held the usual amount of excitement that any vacation would bring. All throughout the school, everyone was talking about their plans for the upcoming week; everyone except for one small group of people.

"Do you know when she's coming back?"

Graham and I looked at Robert as Stacy asked him the same question for the third time today. "Has she spoken to you? Called? Anything?"

"Stacy, he's told you twice already that the answer is no. Could you leave the guy alone?"

Stacy's head snapped up to look at Graham. "Since when did you care about leaving Robert alone?"

Graham pushed the food on his plate around as he answered her. "Since you started hounding him three days ago."

As the two of them argued, I observed Robert, who appeared to have a headache. I knew that wasn't possible, but from all outward appearances, that's exactly what it looked like as he rubbed his temples with his fingers, his head balancing precariously against them.

"Just like they never broke up, huh?" I joked, looking for something to break the tension with.

He peered out at me from beneath his hands and snorted. "Just like they never started dating."

I couldn't fault him there. He was right. Though it had been a few weeks since they had broken up, Graham and Stacy looked exactly as they had when they were dating. The only real difference was that instead of sitting next to each other as they had previously, they now sat on opposite sides of the table, their seats as far away from each other as possible without being a part of a different table entirely.

"So…" I began, looking to change the subject, if only between the two of us.

"Yes, Grace?"

The indifference I detected in Robert's tone disturbed me. "Are you going to act like this for the rest of the school year?"

His face didn't show any reaction to my question at all, something that I had come to expect over these past few weeks. A part of me wondered why I even bothered asking him any questions anymore.

Robert threw his napkin onto the table and stood up abruptly. "I've got things I need to do."

He walked away from the table, not bothering to say goodbye to anyone. Not bothering to say goodbye to me.

"Are things okay between you and Robert?" Stacy asked in a low whisper. "He seems angry."

Graham left his seat and quickly sat in the one vacated by Robert. "What's wrong? What's going on with you two?"

"Nothing," I lied. "He's just…upset that Lark and his mom left on vacation without him."

Stacy nodded her head, wholly empathizing with Robert and the falsehood I had just told them, while Graham simply looked dejected. It wasn't a good look for him.

"Grace, do *you* know when they'll be back?" Stacy questioned cautiously.

I frowned and shook my head. "I know absolutely nothing, Stacy."

She bobbed her head in acknowledgement and then started to play with her mashed potatoes, disappointment written clearly on her face. Graham watched her with an equally gloomy expression on his.

In that moment I felt nearly ready to curse Lark for doing this to all of us. After she had left my room, Robert appeared, angry and upset. He told me that Lark had left Heath—and most likely the country. He accused me of not trying hard enough to keep her in the dark about Graham's feelings; that I had intended on her overhearing everything that was said between Graham and I in an attempt to play matchmaker. I was so hurt by the accusation that I had asked him to leave and never come back into my room again.

He abided by my demand, yet still showed up each morning to pick me up. He had neither apologized, nor offered an explanation as to why he would feel it okay to jump to such conclusions when he could have seen for himself that that was never my intent at all.

As each day dragged on, it felt like we were growing further and further apart as we spent less time together during school. Graham seemed to step in like a surrogate-boyfriend whenever I was left to walk to class or home alone, and this only fueled Robert's disenchantment even more.

Today was no different as the bell that announced the end of lunch began to ring. "I don't want to go to fourth period," Stacy groaned into her mashed potato and pea sculpture. "Hey, let's ditch school and go to the mall!"

"Are you out of your mind?" I asked her. "Your parents would ground you until you were old enough to collect social security if you did that."

"Ugh—I'm so tired of rules and regulations and restrictions and blah-blah-blah. I just want to live a little. Is that such a bad thing?" She grabbed her backpack and fished out her keys. "You guys coming?"

Graham looked away while simply I shook my head. "Sorry. As much as I despise Biology class, I need this credit in order to get into Berkley."

Stacy's eyes widened with surprise. "Berkley? So far away?"

"Yeah. I got my acceptance letter last week and I'll be able to pay my way through one of their student work programs; all I gotta do is graduate. They've got a pretty good journalism program there, plus I've seen their brochure. I'll totally blend," I explained as I slung my backpack over my shoulder.

"Well that's great, Grace. You're going after what you want. And-" she said with a flourish of her hand, "you might actually get some color on that skin of yours in the process. What about you, Graham? Where are you headed?"

Graham shrugged his shoulders. "Some place in Florida most likely. I'll stay with my mom so that I can get the residency discount and probably see if I can get a spot on one of the football teams as a walk-on."

"Well, I've decided that I'm not going to college," Stacy announced matter-of-factly.

"What? Why?" Graham and I asked simultaneously.

"It's complicated," she began but then turned around and started to walk away before finishing her statement. "Grace, I expect you at practice today—you're back in the beginner's class," she yelled out as she headed towards the exit.

Graham and I both looked at each other, confused and distressed at her announcement—and I was slightly nervous about the practice part. "Did she tell you about this before you broke up?" I asked him.

He shook his head. "She never mentioned it. I think I was too busy talking about my plans to really notice though, so I can't be sure."

"Maybe this is her way of rebelling," I suggested. "I mean, she joked that her mom wouldn't let her go to college alone, and if she did go, she wouldn't be able to pursue what she wanted—she's always done what they asked of her—maybe she's done playing the role of the obedient daughter."

Graham held the cafeteria door open for me as we walked out. The hallway was nearly empty; the bell was just about ready to ring. "I suppose you're right. She was always paranoid about missing curfew, always worried that if she didn't check in, her parents would ground her or something. I told her that she's eighteen, she can do what she wants, but she would tell me that 'Korean daughters don't act that way' and that she had to be a 'dutiful daughter'. I just hope that this isn't the case."

Our pace didn't pick up, despite the bell ringing, and we kept walking slowly towards our classes. "Why not?" I wondered.

"Because part of the reason why she dated me was to defy her parents and look at how well that turned out."

"Ahh," I realized. "She was testing the waters with you, and her parents didn't flip out."

A broad grin stretched across his face as he nodded. "Yeah. Her brothers did, though. All five of them."

My biology class was up first and I looked at the door with trepidation. "I'm up."

"Are you gonna be okay?"

"Yeah," I said with a half-smile. "I'll be fine. What about you?"

His smile faded a bit as he answered with the same reserved tone that I had just used. "Me, too. Wait for me here after class, okay? I'll walk you over to English."

"Alright," I agreed, and walked into the classroom.

ᗘ

School ended without any real fanfare. As I had expected, Robert wasn't in class. Graham had apparently expected it too, because he was there waiting for me as I walked past the double doors. "You need a lift home?"

"Yeah."

The two of us walked through the school corridors like nothing had happened these past eight months, nothing had changed between us. He nodded his goodbyes to some of the kids that called out to him, bumped fists with some of his football buddies, while I stood beside him quietly.

When the entrance to the school was far behind us and we were both in his car heading home, Graham finally asked me the question that I had been dreading because I knew that I would have to lie to him.

"Did she leave because of me?"

I had planned what I was going to say as soon as Robert had informed me four days ago that Lark had left, laying down the words and rehearsing them so that when today actually happened, I'd be able to say them without faltering and giving away the lie.

Instead, all I could do was stare at him with my mouth open, unable and unwilling to deny the truth that we both knew but didn't want to admit. It had been so much easier and less complicated to lie to Stacy, and I almost hated myself as I wished for that to be true for Graham as well.

But how could I tell him that Lark had indeed left because of him? He'd ask me why and I had no answer. I couldn't very well explain to him that she wasn't quite human and that for some reason unknown to me, she couldn't admit to anyone—especially herself—that she was in love with him.

The path to falling in love with an angel was a straight one—I knew that as soon as I accepted that I was in love with Robert—but it was paved with broken glass that you tread on barefooted. I had already shed my blood on it but I had done so willingly. Graham was in love with Lark the person. He knew nothing of Lark the angel, and I could only guess that this was the side of herself that Lark didn't want Graham to know about.

Of course, speculating did nothing to help either of us, and since Robert was far too angry with me to even bother explaining, speculation was all I had. And I was all alone with my theories since I couldn't very well discuss this with Stacy either. The vacation lie was so simple and convenient, and it fell out of my mouth so quickly and smoothly, Stacy had believed it without question which meant that I couldn't even hint at the root cause being boy trouble anymore.

"Grace?"

"Hmm?"

"You didn't answer my question. Did she leave early because of me?"

"I-I don't know, Graham," I managed to utter before my mouth shut down on me again.

His head jerked once, acknowledging my answer, but the promise of a more thorough inquisition lurked just beyond the woeful cast in his eyes.

"Did you want me to drop you off at practice?" he asked as we pulled up to the curb fronting his house. "I can do it on the way to work if you want, but I won't be able to pick you up."

"No. I don't think I'll be going today. I don't feel like getting my butt kicked by eight-year-olds."

This seemed to amuse him as he started to chuckle softly. "I'd actually like to see that. It might be worth calling in sick just for that reason alone."

I immediately protested against the idea. "You'll get into trouble with Robert, and I can't lie to him if he were to ask me if you were really sick."

The laughter faded, but my words hung like stale air around us in the car. Without intending to do so, and despite the current state of our relationship, I had just admitted to Graham that my loyalty belonged to Robert first.

"Wow. That's a reality check."

"Look, Graham, I didn't really mean it that way," I tried to explain but he brushed it off.

"No, no, Grace. You know what? If I were in your shoes, I'd feel the same way. I guess I was just hoping that I wouldn't have to deal with this for a little while longer…you know, like until you had your first kid or something."

We exited the car and walked towards my house. Graham stopped halfway up the walkway, his gaze directed towards his house. The blinds had been drawn back—the first time in over two months—and the chaotic mess that made up the living room could be seen from the outside. Graham seemed fixed to the ground beneath him, but I could tell that he was as curious as he was concerned.

"Do you want to go and check on him?" I asked him. When he didn't answer I didn't press the issue.

We walked through my front door and Graham groaned. "She's making tofu casserole again. That's it, I'm eating at work."

I grimaced as well. The aroma of cabbage and bean curd masked any pleasant odor that might have been detectable had we had anything but tofu and veggie-based faux meat products for the past few weeks. Our only saving grace was turkey bacon at breakfast.

"Is that you, kids?" I heard Janice call out from the kitchen.

"Yeah, Janice, we're home," I replied as I held my hand over my face.

Graham wrinkled his nose and shook his head. "You know, it always smelled like tofu and cabbage at Stacy's house, too, but at least her mom uses actual meat in her dishes. I didn't know that when I agreed to stay here that your future step-mom would try to turn me into a rabbit," he whispered to me as we walked towards the kitchen.

"Shh," I hissed. "Hey, Janice, what are you making?"

Janice was chopping vegetables for what I could only assume was yet another salad. Her large belly kept her at a distance from the actual counter, causing her to lean forward uncomfortably, but she still wore a fairly pleased smile. "I've got a Tempe and vegetable lasagna with cabbage noodles baking in the oven, I'm chopping up some bell peppers for a wild rice salad, and in about thirty minutes, I'll pop in a pan of organic whole wheat brownies for dessert. So, how was your day at school, kids?"

I turned to look at Graham, who was too busy looking green to answer, and sighed. "School was fine. We're going upstairs to do some homework before Graham has to go to work, so if you need anything…"

Janice waved her hand in the air, the kitchen light glinting off the blade. "Alright."

I grabbed Graham's arm and pulled him towards the stairs. We climbed up to my room and heaved a sigh of relief that the odor from downstairs hadn't made its way upstairs, too. "When is she going to start eating normal food again?" Graham asked as he threw himself onto my bed facedown.

I placed my backpack on the floor by the dresser and shrugged my shoulders. "I don't know. I hope that after the baby is born she at least lets me start cooking more than once a week."

"Yeah," Graham agreed. "At this rate, I'll be thinner than you by graduation."

"Hey, you know you at least get to eat out when you're at work. I'm the one stuck here every night eating tofu and bean sprouts while you're stuffing your face with pizza and hot dogs."

Graham threw a hand negligently into the air, his finger pointing at me. "Your fault. You could always tell your boyfriend to bring you something to eat, or take you out once in a while."

To that I said nothing. I unzipped my backpack and pulled out my binder to go over my homework, ignoring the photographs and notes that framed my dresser mirror. Grabbing a pencil from my bag, I sat down on the floor beside my bed and stared blankly at the French assignment from this morning.

"Hey, Grace?"

"Mmm?" I said, the pencil in my mouth preventing any articulate sounds coming out.

"Are you gonna tell me the truth about what's going on between you and Robert?"

I pulled the pencil from between my lips. "What do you mean?"

The bed began to shift behind me, the springs moving loudly as Graham hefted himself off and sat down beside me, our backs pressed up uncomfortably against the metal bar of the bed frame.

"I mean, there's something wrong between you two, and I don't care how many times you say that everything is fine and how it has nothing to do with Lark, because I can tell that everything is not fine, and that this probably does have something to do with Lark." He grabbed the binder from out of my hands and tossed it a few feet in front of us, soon followed by my pencil. "I'm your best friend, Grace, remember? If you can't talk to me about it, who can you talk to?"

I giggled nervously, the idea that I could talk to Graham about what had happened between Robert and I seeming so much more like a fantasy than the reality of Robert and Lark being angels we had both fallen for.

"Grace?"

I looked into Graham's eyes and I could see that there was genuine concern in them. He grabbed my hand and squeezed it reassuringly, something a best friend would do.

"We had a fight," I said, finally.

"About…?"

I looked at him and there was no mistaking what the reason was in my face. He put his head down. "Oh."

"Yeah, oh," I said with a downhearted laugh.

"But why? What's so wrong with me loving his sister? I mean, besides the fact that I'm obviously not good enough for her and that I was pretty big jerk to you? That shouldn't be reason for him to take this out on you," Graham argued, his free hand flailing around to emphasize each point.

"He thinks that I was plotting to get the two of you together," I admitted. Though not the whole truth, it wasn't a lie either and that was enough to save my conscience.

"Well, I only wish that were the case. You helped me out when I needed you, but you never pushed me towards Lark. You never tried to get me to break up with Stacy, even though you knew how I felt about her. You were being my friend, and he can't get mad at you for that. Not again."

I shook my head at Graham's reasoning. "You don't understand, Graham. When he accused me of these things, I got upset because I know that you're good enough for Lark; maybe too good. I know that you would make Lark very happy, and I told him, but I was so angry…I said some things I shouldn't have said."

Graham looked at me with surprise. "Like what?"

I turned my face away and whispered my reply.

"Well now that was stupid."

My head whipped back to face him, my mouth open in shock. "Thanks, *best friend!*"

He shrugged his shoulders. "What? It's the truth. You told him you never wanted to see him again, yet you take him up on his offer to drive you to school and bring you home? Talk about sending mixed-messages, Grace. He's in love with you, and yeah, he was stupid for saying what he did, but he did it because he loves his sister. You need to apologize to him, Grace."

I slouched beside him and stubbornly folded my arms across my chest. "He hasn't apologized either. What he said was wrong, Graham, and it hurt because he should have known better, he should know *me* better."

Graham nodded in agreement. "Yeah, he should have, but so should you."

"What exactly does *that* mean?"

"You know exactly what that means. You of all people know how overprotective Robert is when it comes to his sister—I'd probably think it was kinda creepy if I didn't know how much he loved you—so you should have known that he'd assume that if she was upset by something, it would be because of me. He was simply reacting the way a big brother would. Give the guy a break. He's only human."

"You have no idea what you're talking about, Graham," I huffed.

"I know more than you think," he retorted. "I know that sometimes I do and say some pretty boneheaded stuff, but trust me when I say that I know a lot more about being a guy than you do, Grace, and Robert was being a total *guy.*

"I also know that what you said to Robert was you running away from the argument, instead of dealing with it like you're supposed to when you love someone. I ran away from our friendship, Grace, so I know what running looks like. I know that it doesn't have to involve anything but

280

words, and that it can hurt you just as much as it does the person you're running from.

"You love Robert. He makes you happy and he loves you, so stop being stupid and just apologize to him."

I wanted to scream at him that he didn't know what he was talking about, that he was just as wrong as Robert was but there was no point. He wasn't wrong.

"Grace?"

"Yeah?"

"Hate me?"

"No."

"I'm sorry."

"Me, too."

☙

I was in the middle of washing the dishes after dinner when the doorbell rang. "Grace, Stacy's here," Dad called out from the living room.

I placed the last dish in the drying rack and wiped my hands on a dish towel as she walked into the kitchen. "Hey, Stacy."

"You didn't show up to practice. Again."

I grinned nervously at her stern expression. "Um…I'm sorry?"

"Can we talk-" she looked through the kitchen entrance at Dad, who was too engrossed in whatever it was he was watching on the television to notice us "-somewhere private?"

I pointed upstairs and she nodded. I placed the dish towel onto the counter and turned off the light as we headed towards the stairs. "I'm going upstairs, Dad," I called out. His hand waved at us casually; he was too involved with his show.

As we passed Dad and Janice's room, I could see Janice laying out some clothes on the bed. She lifted her head from her task and smiled at me. I smiled in return and then headed to my room.

"How goes the wedding plans?" Stacy asked once we were seated on my bed.

"They're going, I guess. I asked if I could help, but Janice said that she didn't have anything for me to do and that she'd let me know when she did. She and Dad don't talk about it much in front of me for some reason. I think that they feel I might not be ready to deal with it."

I looked at Stacy, who was dressed in a sports bra and what looked like gym shorts, and asked her what it was that she wanted to talk about. I should have known as soon as she started.

"Do you know when Lark is coming back?"

I shook my head. "I told you, Stacy. I have no idea."

She clenched her teeth, my answer obviously not to her liking. "You'd think that with all that money she'd at least carry around a cell phone that worked or something."

I laughed softly. Though Lark carried around one of the latest model cell phones, it wasn't operational, merely decorative. "Well, she does have something far better than a cell phone," I replied.

Stacy huffed. "Fat lot of good that does anyone when she treats that gift like people do cell phones; something she can just ignore when she doesn't want to be bothered."

"So what makes you think she'd be any different if her phone actually worked?"

"I don't know, but at least it would give me another way to get in touch with her without having to go through Robert."

I tucked my head down and asked in a low voice, "So you've asked Robert to try and get in touch with her?"

Stacy nodded. "Yes, and he said that he wasn't about to bother her for my human whims."

I glowered at the idea of Robert being so callous. "That doesn't sound like him."

"I know. He apologized immediately of course, but said that he still wasn't going to bother her." She started to rub her arms as the breeze that blew through my window took a sudden chilly turn. "I asked him why he was so agitated, but he wouldn't say. He just kept looking at you and then told me to leave you alone."

"Me? When did you ask him these questions?"

She looked out of the window and struggled with what she wanted to say, but finally turned her head to respond. "Just before I rang the doorbell. He was sitting on his bike and staring through the front window."

I leapt off the bed and ran to my window, sticking my head outside to glance up and down the street. I pulled myself back in and sat on the edge of the bed when I was convinced that there was no one there. "Did he say anything else?" I asked expectantly.

She shook her head. "He waved when I said bye, but that was it. What's going on, Grace? You two have been acting very weird lately. The only one who's been semi-normal is Graham, which means he's told me absolutely nothing."

"It's complicated, Stacy."

"I'm sure that this wasn't too complicated for Graham," she replied sulkily.

"I've known Graham since we were kids, Stacy. He lives with me. He's my-"

"Best friend—I know. He told me the same thing when I called him up at work to find out what's going on; he said you would tell me when you're ready, that you don't know any more than I do about what's going on with Lark, and that I should just leave you alone. Why is everyone telling me to leave you alone? What's the deal, Grace?"

"I think you should leave Grace alone, Stacy."

Stacy and I turned to see Robert sitting on the ledge of my window, the inky color of his clothes blending in with the darkening sky outside. Stacy looked at me with wide eyes. "Does he always do this?"

I nodded.

"Well," she began, turning to speak to Robert, "I'd say that was romantic, but seeing as you're probably not here in any romantic capacity,

I'll just say that you're being incredibly rude, which is pretty ironic considering that you're supposed to be an angel."

Robert stood up and moved very quickly, his body turning into a streak of black before disappearing near the closet.

The knock on the door caused both Stacy and I to jump. "Hey girls, we're heading off to bed now," Janice said from behind the door. "Stacy, don't stay too late, alright? I'd rather not be woken up again at midnight by your mother looking for you."

"Okay, Miss Dupre," Stacy called out.

"Alright. Goodnight, girls!"

"Night, Janice," I replied loudly, my eyes growing wide as Robert appeared again, sitting on the sill as though he had never left.

Stacy eyed Robert and waited until she heard the bedroom door across the hall shut before she launched into Robert. "What was *that* about?"

"It's one thing to have her friends know that I am in her room; it's another thing entirely for her parents to find me in here, alone or not," Robert answered woodenly.

"You couldn't just pop out of the window or, I don't know, disappear into smoke or something?"

"Hey," I whispered. "Could you two quit with the bickering?"

Stacy and Robert glared at each other but nodded, each one curt and matter-of-fact. "Thank you," I sighed. "Now, why are you here?" I said as I turned to give Robert my undivided attention.

Robert looked at me, his face still the most beautiful thing I have ever seen. I caught the flicker of something in his eyes, a slight softening that gave me a glimmer of hope that I didn't know I had needed or wanted. His mouth twitched and he quickly covered it with his hand, blocking the smile I knew he couldn't keep from appearing.

Stacy coughed, a rough, disturbing sound that caused the both of us to turn our attention to her. "I'm okay. Just a bug. That window needs to be closed."

Robert stood up and pushed the window down, leaving just a small sliver of space between it and the sill. "Is that better?"

She nodded and then dabbed at her eyes with the back of her hand. "So, before you and Grace start making up, could you please tell me when Lark is getting back?"

"No."

Stacy turned her head to me, her eyes wide with suggestion. I sighed and looked at Robert as I, too, asked him the same question. His answer was no less firm, although the look in his eyes had softened some more.

"I understand you're doing the whole big-brother-protective thing, Robert, but I really need to talk to her," Stacy insisted. "And *don't* try reading my mind to find out why. I don't want her learning why through you. That's not fair to her *or* to me."

"Stacy, reading someone's mind isn't something that is done by selection. It just...is. I can ignore most of it, but I cannot stop it from happening any more than you can stop yourself from blinking. Also, I resent the notion that I would listen to your thoughts in an attempt to undermine your right to divulge your little secret to Lark yourself."

"Alright. I'm sorry for that. Now, will you tell me where she is, or get in touch with her for me?"

Robert shook his head. "No."

"Well, what about for me?" I asked. "Will you tell me where she is?"

"I'm sorry, Grace. The answer is the same. Lark made it clear that she was to be left alone; I promised her that she would and that she could return on her own time," Robert insisted.

"Robert, I know that this phrase probably means absolutely nothing to you, considering that you've never had to worry about it or anything like that, but time is of the essence here," Stacy broke in.

"Perhaps Lark doesn't understand that your time doesn't quite flow in sync with our time," I added.

The softness that I saw hinted in Robert's face dissipated and was replaced with a new cold bitterness. "I'm very well aware that my time doesn't quite flow in sync with yours, Grace, and so is Lark."

"Okay, good. Could you please tell Lark that I need to speak with her then," Stacy interrupted, moving to stand between Robert and me. "This is important, Robert. I'm asking here. Please?"

He looked at me above Stacy's head as he answered. "I'll think about it."

"Thanks," Stacy sighed in relief. "This means a lot to me, Robert. Really."

He nodded brusquely, his gaze never leaving my own. "Stacy?" he said softly.

"Yeah?"

"Could you leave now?"

Stacy noticed where his gaze was directed and turned to look at me, the silent question written in her eyes. I nodded and she exhaled slowly, looking back at Robert before shaking her head. "O-kay."

She gave me a quick hug and waved at Robert before slipping quietly out the door. Robert and I stared at each other until I saw Stacy's car reverse out of the driveway and her red taillights fade away down the street.

"We need to talk," Robert and I both said at the same time. The look on his face and the look in mine reflected in his eyes told me that this was going to be more than just a simple talk.

FRAYED

"You first," I told him, wanting a bit more time to be able to word my apology just right.

"I was planning on doing so anyway," he insisted. "May I?" He held a hand out and motioned to the empty space on the bed that Stacy had occupied. I nodded and he sat down, carefully maintaining a safe distance between us.

I looked at him expectantly and waited for him to begin speaking. He kept looking at me, but said nothing. Every so often I would look behind him at the clock on my dresser as the minutes ticked by, but I didn't say anything about the time. I honestly had missed his presence so much; simply sitting here with him was enough. I didn't need conversation. I didn't need-

"Grace, I need to show you something."

I blinked. "What?"

His hand stretched forward to hold mine but before his fingers grazed my skin, he pulled his hand back. "May I?"

I looked down at his hand and blinked once more to adjust my vision. "Is your hand...shaking?"

Robert clenched his hand into a fist and pressed it against the bed, the force causing the bed to dip and the springs to squeal from the pressure.

My hand covered his, the contact meant to be reassuring. Instead, my mind was instantly filled with the unrelenting stream of information that Robert's mind contained, ever constant and unyielding to the limited capacity of my own. I started to feel the pressure build as each foreign memory began to stretch my mind until all I could see were the tiny pulses of light beneath my lids.

This had happened once before, the first time that Robert and I had consciously held each other's hand—a platonic gesture meant only to help me—and I had passed out as a result. My nose had bled, my mind felt like it had literally exploded, and Robert had stayed with me throughout it, despite only knowing me for less than a day. This time, however, I hadn't lost all consciousness and could still feel his hand beneath mine. The other was gently cradling my head that had dipped forward and then to the side as the onslaught of thoughts and visions took over, weighing me down with them.

"Are you alright?"

I opened my eyes slightly to see Robert's concerned face looking at me from an odd angle; his head was tilted to the side, his torso twisted towards me. I smiled at him and nodded my head.

"Are you sure?"

"Mmm-hmm," I murmured, just glad for the contact.

He looked at me, studied my face. As soon as he was sure that the dizziness had passed, he helped me to a sitting position. "You let me know when you're ready for this," he said as he wiped my forehead with the back of his hand.

"I'm ready."

"We don't have to rush this, Grace. Are you sure you're ready?"

"That depends on what it is that you have to show me. Is this about Erica?"

"No," he replied.

288

"Well. I guess I'll just have to wait and see then, huh?" I remarked.

My hand that was still covering Robert's lifted off of his as he removed it from the deep indentation that he had created in the mattress. "I'm sorry about the bed," he commented before taking a hold of my hand and pulling me close. "Don't move. No matter what you see, do not move," he instructed before lowering his head to mine.

Our foreheads touched faintly but before I had time to appreciate the cool smoothness of his skin against mine, I was no longer in my room. Instead, I was now watching two people leave the school grounds in a rusty green vehicle. I knew who they were instantly as the mixed feelings flared within me—I was now seeing things from Robert's point of view and his emotions were now my own, his anger and his hurt two distinct voices inside one cold and lifeless heart within him. As he watched the pair leave, his attention turned to another figure leaving the school.

The man was older, slightly portly with a noticeably hurried gait. His hair was disheveled and his brown suit was wrinkled where it had gathered while he sat. Robert watched the man walk across the parking lot towards a dark brown station wagon. The car was unlocked. The man climbed in and turned the key to start the engine. It was a sickly sound, as though the car were pleading with its owner to put it out of its misery, squealing like a wounded animal just before the final blow of mercy was to be dealt.

The car pulled out of its stall and rolled slowly out of the lot, its direction negligent. Robert was moving, too. His vision became foggy yet no less clear, an odd thing I noticed, as he followed the vehicle. Each second that ticked by, each simple increment of time seemed to turn the sky around Robert darker and darker as the car in front of him began to weave in and out of its lane.

Soon the station wagon was barreling down an empty stretch of road, the demand nearly too much for the tired engine to handle as it inched its way up to a terrifying speed. As the car weaved into the oncoming lane, I could make out what appeared to be the front end of a bicycle lying in the middle of the lane ahead.

The driver, however, did not. It happened in a split second. The car hit the bike at such an exaggerated speed, the frame split in two and went flying into the undercarriage. Though I personally knew nothing about the workings of a car, this was not my vision. This was Robert's, and I instinctually knew that the metal bars that made up the bike were about to do something horrifically disastrous to the rear axle of the station wagon.

With a loud, metallic snap, the remains of the bicycle tore through the rear of the car, the resulting damage causing the car to rise up above the pavement. Physics then took over as the car's mass forced it into a tailspin. The intense speed combined with the friction from the tires pulling against the asphalt caused the vehicle to jerk up, resulting in the car flipping over for several rotations, eventually coming to a rest on its roof.

Behind it, the road was a veritable battlefield of twisted metal and torn rubber. There were gouges deep within the asphalt with several distinct tracks formed by what would soon be tread-less tires and the remainder of the pipe that protruded now from the underbelly of the completely destroyed vehicle. Glass littered the road, though it looked far different from the type that would belong to a windshield or windows.

Robert approached the car, the fog lifting just slightly, though the darkness never receded. As he drew closer, the sight of blood on the ground was a sign that whoever was in the car had not escaped unscathed. Robert's hand grabbed a hold of the door where the window should have been, as though he were grabbing a thick book. He lifted his hand and the door peeled off of its hinges smoothly, effortlessly, like removing a slice of cake.

He tossed the door to the side, ignoring the screeching sound it made as it slid several feet away, and peered inside of the cab. He shook his head at what he saw, and I felt myself recoil at the image as I tried to place the somewhat recognizable face that belonged to the man who had been driving. The steering wheel was pressed up against his chest, pinning him to the seat of his now overturned car. His face was a mangled mass of torn skin and blood that sparkled with fragments of the same odd looking glass that lay out in the road behind him.

"Hello, Oliver," I heard Robert say in a soothing voice.

"Oh good. Someone is here to help me," the man named Oliver said in a garbled voice. He coughed as blood bubbled up out of his mouth and nose and landed on the ceiling of the car, mixing in with the sickly sweet liquid that had already pooled there. "I think my cell phone is still in my pocket. Could you call my wife?"

Robert's hand reached into the car and he gently touched the man's shoulder. An intense light filled the car in a quick burst of light, and then Robert was outside of the vehicle, the man named Oliver standing beside him, confused and disoriented. "How'd I get out here?" he asked before his eyes picked up on what Robert had already known.

"Hey, that's me in the car. But I'm right here… Wait—does this mean that I'm…dead?"

Robert shook his head. "No, Oliver. This just means that I'm not interested in having this conversation in the car while it's leaking gasoline and smelling of cheap vodka and whisky."

"Hey now, I don't know what you're talking about. I wasn't drinking. See? Perfectly sober," Oliver argued, demonstrating his point by taking several steps away from Robert and then spinning around on his heel, his balance perfect; the motion smooth.

Robert's hand flashed out, his fingers wrapping around Oliver's throat as he said in that same calm, soothing voice, "You're lying, Oliver."

The man held his hands up, his face turning a putrid shade of purple as he relented. "Okay, okay. Yes, I did have a drink. Just one th-" Robert's grip grew tighter around Oliver's throat and the man started to cough before managing to gasp out a quick "I drank half a bottle!"

Robert eased his grip on Oliver's throat, though he still had his fingers laced around his neck in a vise grip that I could eerily feel on around my own. "That's better. Now, Oliver. We're going to play a little game called truth or dare. I'll ask you a question and you'll tell me the truth or you'll dare to lie to me again and then we'll repeat what you've just experienced here, only I won't use my hands."

"Wh-what will you use?" Oliver stuttered.

Robert's lips curled back in a menacing growl and gnashed his teeth. Oliver began to shake with fear and understanding and obediently nodded his head.

"I'm glad that we understand each other. Now then, question one, do you know who I am?"

Oliver shook his head, the movement so small and quick, had I been looking with my own eyes I would have missed it entirely. Robert smiled at the man's answer. "You're telling the truth. Pity—I was hoping that perhaps you would. I rarely enjoy moments like these, but for you I'll make an exception.

"Who I am, Oliver, is your road to perdition. Or, I could be your road to salvation. The choice is yours."

The man's eyes widened with confusion. "I...I don't understand."

Robert pointed to the body that was slowly dying in the car in front of them. "You're not in that body, Oliver. You're standing beside me because I have the ability to allow you to live and make right the wrongs you've done, or I can allow this scene before you to play out and you'll die a very painful death that will be but a precursor to what lies in store for you."

Oliver looked at his lifeless body, obscured by the steering wheel that held him immobile and upside down, and then turned his focus to Robert, whose menacing appearance could be seen in the glassy reflection of Oliver's eyes. "What do I do? What do I do to make things right?"

"We play the game. Next question, Oliver. What is your worst crime?"

Oliver looked at Robert and then back to the car. His head kept swinging back and forth between the two, obviously deciding which fate was worse. Robert, having stared at the half-moons in his nails while Oliver decided, impatiently snapped his fingers. A slight spark flew out from between them and landed in a stream of liquid, igniting it in a bright blue flash of fire. The flame traveled quickly, hungrily seeking out more fuel as it headed directly towards the station wagon.

"No! Wait!"" Oliver cried out. He lurched forward but Robert held him back with the faintest of grips on his shoulder.

"Will you tell me?"

Oliver nodded his head frantically, his gaze fixed on the flame that streaked ever closer to his body and its would-be metal coffin.

Robert waved an indifferent hand in the air and a gust of chilled wind suffocated the determined blue wave of heat. "Now. Tell me."

Defeated, Oliver nodded. "I killed a girl."

Robert's body jerked at the confession. "You…killed a girl?"

Oliver nodded, his head hung low in shame. "I was on vacation with my wife and kids in Nebraska four years ago. I left them at the hotel to go and get some food from this take-out place we had read about in one of those tourist magazines, you know. I stayed longer than I was planning and had drunk a little too much while there.

"I didn't mean to do it. I didn't, I swear, but I couldn't see her on the road—it was dark and I didn't know where I was—and by the time I realized what had happened, it was too late. I tried to get her some help, but she was already gone. She was so beautiful and young, not much older than my own daughter was, and all I could think about was what would happen if I got caught? What would happen to my own little girl? What would happen to my wife? My son? I panicked and I left her there—my family, we left the next day."

Robert acknowledged this confession grimly, his ire and disgust turning his body cold. "There's more."

The man fell to his knees. "Yes, there's more," he replied. "I hit another girl a few months ago…here."

Robert's body grew ramrod stiff as he listened to the man on the ground begin to retell a story that the two of us were very familiar with.

"I've been having nightmares about what happened, about that girl that I killed. I didn't even know her name. I never looked it up on the internet or anything—I didn't want to get to know her, see her family, her pictures—but her face kept haunting me every time I closed my eyes.

"It became so bad that the only way I could get her out of my head was to drown her out. I started to drink more often; I couldn't function without it; I couldn't work, couldn't do anything unless I could no longer feel my legs or my hands.

"I was at a friend's house one morning—he was having problems at work, too—and we just sat around the house and drank can after can, bottle after bottle of whatever it was we could find. I saw the time and knew that I had to get going; my wife had made reservations for dinner with her parents and I had promised that I wouldn't be late this time.

"I was fine driving, I swear. I could have made it home without a problem. But then I saw her again, the girl I had run over four years earlier, riding her bicycle, and I thought…I thought that if I could catch up to her and talk to her, get her to forgive me, she'd let me go, she'd let me go to sleep. I thought I was putting my hand on the horn. I swear. I didn't know that I wasn't pressing the horn with my hand. I didn't know that I was pressing the gas pedal with my foot until I heard the bike beneath the car.

"I stopped. I did, I stopped the car and got out. I ran over to her, the girl, and I saw her—only it wasn't her; it wasn't the girl. I didn't know that first girl, but this one…I knew her, I recognized her face. I couldn't believe that I had done it again, and to someone I knew on top of that. I didn't know what to do…and then she started to speak, and I panicked again. I left her there. I left her on the road and I went home.

"I promised from then on that I'd never touch another drop if she lived. I swore to myself and anyone who was listening that I'd never drink another drop of alcohol if she made it. But I knew that she wasn't. I knew that she was going to die just like the last one because she looked worse. There was so much blood this time, not like the other one. She was bleeding everywhere; I had crushed her and her bike together. Oh, God."

Oliver threw his hands onto the ground and began to gag and heave. Robert stood there and watched him in stony silence, his frigid demeanor doing nothing to calm the ill man before him. Finally, he bent down and grabbed him by the nape of his neck and yanked him upwards. "You're not going to throw anything up. You're not in your body, remember? And even if you were, you already emptied your gut of everything in it the minute you crashed so I suggest you quit with the theatrics and get on with it.

"Now-" he released Oliver and watched him as he crumpled back to the ground with a soft thud "-finish your confession."

The man bobbed his head sickly and did as he was ordered. "I stayed up all night waiting for the news to say something about what happened. The Sunday paper had a small story about it, but it was the Monday paper that said that she had survived with minor injuries—minor injuries! I kept following the story in case she didn't make it after all, but she was fine. I kept to my end of the deal. I was good, I kept off the bottle.

"Then I started to worry about her telling the police about me. I kept thinking what if she saw me? What if she recognized me? The dreams started to come again, only this time I saw two faces instead of just one.

"I had to see for myself if she was okay, I had to know that she was fine, and so I did. She was more than fine. She was different, like everything had suddenly been fixed in her life while mine was falling apart. But then she looked at me, and for a second I thought she'd start telling everyone that I was the one, that I was the one that hit her. But she looked away. Like everyone else, she just looked away.

"That was too much for me. Two faces, one with no name, the other with a name and a history. I couldn't sleep again, I couldn't eat, couldn't do anything but fight with the nightmares. And so I found a bottle of gin that I had hidden away in the basement. It felt like I'd found liquid peace. I closed my eyes and their faces were gone. I couldn't put the bottle down after that. There was no way. I'd be a complete mess if I did, you have to believe me!"

Oliver stood up on his knees and clutched at Robert's shirt. "Please, please tell me you'll forgive me. Please."

Robert pushed the man away and took several steps back. He was shaking, the black anger turning his vision to a deep, blood red as it blocked out everything else that was good. "Tell me her name," he hissed at the man. "Say her name."

Oliver opened his mouth and blurted the name out quickly. "Grace. Her name is Grace Shelley. She's a student at Heath High School just up the road, one of mine, actually."

The name on the man's lips did nothing to calm Robert, and instead seemed to fuel the rage that boiled within him. I could feel something inside of him turning thick and hot, as though hell itself was simmering just beneath his skin and threatened to boil over and consume everyone and everything in its rage filled path.

"Wh-what are you?" Oliver cried as Robert towered over him, his menacing presence blocking out the last of the sun's rays.

"It doesn't matter what I am. What matters is that you turn yourself into the police and make right the wrongs that you have done."

"But I just did, didn't I? I did that by confessing, you said to confess! I fixed it!" Oliver protested.

"No, you didn't. Because of your cowardice, Grace turned in an innocent man, destroying his life and ruining her credibility. You nearly took her from me, nearly took her from her family, and the casualties keep piling up, Oliver. This is it, do-" Robert grabbed a hold of Oliver and dragged him back to the car. He stretched one hand towards the body in the vehicle and looked at Oliver once more "-or die. Make your decision."

Oliver looked frightfully at his body in the car and at the murderous expression on Robert's face. "What is she to you?"

"Who?"

"Grace. You said I nearly took her from you. What is she to you?" Oliver asked once more.

"She is my salvation. And she's yours as well," Robert replied, his voice nearly inaudible it was so sad. "Now...choose."

Oliver closed his eyes and gave Robert the answer that he had been waiting for. Robert's outstretched hand gently touched the body that hung limply in the car and once again, the blinding flash appeared, blocking out the scene before me.

As soon as the light dissipated, I was shocked to see that Robert was back at the school, his vision locked once more on a pair of students who were heading towards a rusty green car. He continued to watch as the car pulled out of the lot and then turned his attention back to the school.

A man appeared from out of the school. He appeared nervous, jittery as he headed towards his car, a dark brown station wagon that sat far apart from the other cars in the faculty parking lot. He looked around him, as though he were checking to see if anyone had followed him. When he was sure that no one had, he bent down and looked at the front end of his car. Robert focused his gaze and he could see the distinct dent in the front end that was littered with chips of paint that he knew came from my bicycle.

Robert jumped down from his perch, and only then could I see that he had been sitting atop one of the trees that fronted the school. He walked casually over to parking lot, his hands in his pockets, his jacket zipped up slightly.

The sound of his footsteps crunching against rocks and debris on the ground was the only sound as he made his way towards the man who still nervously flitted around his car. Robert's gaze traveled down and he nodded grimly as he took in the brown shoes with black laces. The man was kneeling forward, his pants lifting up and exposing the white socks beneath the brown slacks.

"What are you doing there, sir?" Robert asked in a steely voice.

The man jumped up and grabbed his chest in surprise. "Oh goodness, you scared me there, Mr. Bellegarde. Robert—your name is Robert, isn't it?"

Robert nodded calmly. "Yes, sir, it is."

The man looked relieved as he took in Robert's dark clothing and ruffled hair. "For a second there I thought you were someone else. Well, what can I help you with then, Robert?"

Robert pointed to the damage to the front end as he spoke. "That's a fairly large dent there. Did that just happen? Did someone just run into you and leave without offering to help?"

The man coughed as he shook his head, the question obviously making him feel quite uneasy. "Um, no. No, nothing like that at all. No."

Robert bent down to gently rub his fingers against the dented surface. "This looks pretty bad."

He looked at the man standing next to the car and watched him as he began to run through several different possible explanations for the dent, none of them being anywhere near the truth. Robert motioned with his hand, a quick, undetectable flick really, and something suddenly crashed into the side of the car.

"What was that?" the man shouted as he peered around the hood. "Is…that a…bicycle?"

Robert walked over to twisted lump of metal and shrugged his shoulders. "It looks like something that used to be a bicycle, sir."

The man heard the confirmation in Robert's voice and he looked about ready to faint. Robert stood up quickly, already concerned that his plan was about to fail. Instead, the man reached into his pocket and pulled out a small, blue cell phone.

He flipped it open and pressed three numbers before pressing the receiver against his ear. He looked at Robert and mouthed the words "I'm sorry" before he began to speak to the operator who answered the phone.

"Hi, yes, 911? My name is Oliver Frey and I have some important information regarding the hit-and-run accident that occurred near the Heath library back in September. What kind of information? Well, wow…I've never done this before so I don't know how to…I'm…I'm the one that ran that young girl over. Yes. That's right. It was my car. What color is it? Brown. Type? Station wagon. Yes, I'm at Heath High School, in the faculty parking lot.

"Am I alone? No. I have the young woman's boyfriend with me right now. Yes, ma'am. I won't be leaving. I've…I've run away from this far too long already."

Robert felt a slight sense of relief at Mr. Frey's words, but he couldn't keep the anger that had begun to fester within him from growing at the sound of relief in Mr. Frey's voice. He ground his teeth, the sound far too loud to be normal, but Robert didn't care.

Mr. Frey looked at Robert's expression and he handed the phone to him. "The operator would like to speak to you, to confirm that I haven't run away." He gave Robert his keys as well and then backed away from the car, his hand rubbing his chest as he looked at Robert with a pained expression. "There, now I can't leave."

Robert pocketed the keys and then placed the phone against his ear. "Hello."

"Hello Robert."

Robert lowered his voice so that Mr. Frey wouldn't be able to hear him. "Mother, are the police on their way?"

"They'll be there soon, son. This is a very good day for you, and for Grace, but Mr. Frey needs to complete his confession or else-"

Robert cut her off. "I know. Don't worry. It'll be completed." He hung up the phone and then handed it back to Mr. Frey.

"Thank you, Robert," he said as he took the phone and sheepishly stuck it back into his pocket. "I suppose you want to know why, right?"

Robert shook his head. "My guess is that you're an alcoholic who tries to drown your troubles with Russians, Scots, and the French."

Mr. Frey seemed shocked, but that shock soon faded as the reality of what he was doing, what he had done began to hit him. "I'm sorry, Robert. I should have done something other than run away, but I didn't, and I'm ready to accept the consequences for that. I only wish that I could tell Grace, tell her that I'm sorry for what I did."

Robert nodded brusquely at the apology and hid his clenched fists back in the pockets of his jacket. "You'll get your chance."

My homeroom teacher nodded with slow, sad movements. "I've been drinking for so long now; I use homeroom as my recovery time. It allows me just enough time to get over my usual hangover. I want you to know that I tried, Robert. I tried very hard after what happened to quit drinking, to give up this bottle of beast so that I'd never hurt another person ever again, but I couldn't. I wasn't strong enough.

"I don't know if I'm strong enough now, but it looks like where I'll be going, it won't matter. I'm done trying to run from this."

Robert's divine hearing told him that the police cars were on their way. Quickly, he asked the final question, the final phrase having not been said yet. "Do you have any remorse, Mr. Frey?"

The older man looked at Robert, looked at him with understanding eyes, and nodded. "Yes. Yes, I do."

Robert nodded and sighed with relief. "Good. It'll be easier for you."

Mr. Frey smiled. "Easier for me? You talk as if you know where I'm going, kid. I'm going to jail. They don't have special cells for guys like me; just special punishments. It doesn't matter; I've been avoiding this for too long, but at least I'll finally be able to stop running. Please, tell Grace I'm sorry. Tell her family, too."

Robert looked up as the sounds of sirens at full blast blared through the school's front drive. Three police cruisers crawled to a stop in front of him and Mr. Frey and he stepped back as several uniformed officers walked up to them. They cried out orders that resulted in the teacher raising his hands above his head and bowing his head down.

The commotion brought out the teachers and students that hadn't yet left the school building and they all gasped in shock as the mild-mannered, always comatose Mr. Frey was placed in handcuffs and then led to one of the awaiting police vehicles.

Several students approached Robert and the remaining police officers, all of them wanting to know what was going on. A handful of teachers were gathered near the teacher's entrance, their heads shaking at the scene. Mr. Branke stood off to the side, a cigarette in his hand…unlit. The word soon spread around campus that the man who had hit Grace and then fled the scene had finally been apprehended, and that he had not only confessed, but that it had been Mr. Frey.

"Robert, is it true?"

"Hey Rob, I'll bet you're glad that the guy who hit Grace is going to jail!"

"Wow, Mr. Frey? Did you know about this, Robert?"

Robert looked at everyone surrounding him, their questions all hanging on their tongues, their eyes expectant and curious. "I've got to go tell Grace," he said quickly, and the murmurs of agreement soon followed him. He did his best to maintain a human-like pace and climbed onto his motorcycle with the same forced passivity.

He took one look at the crowd that still gathered near the police cars and shook his head. Though none of them had dared to feel any sort of sympathy for Grace when she had laid injured in the hospital, or had sided with her when she had mistakenly implicated Mr. Branke for this very crime, they were all feeling quite glad for her now. He didn't understand the human idiosyncrasies that allowed them to be so apathetic time and time again over the same thing, and then suddenly develop an interest as if it were pulled magically from thin air.

He sped off towards the house that held the only human who truly mattered in this world, the only one whose life he valued above his own. He quietly pulled up to the curb and stopped his bike in the spot that should have been occupied by the same rusty green car that he had seen leave the school.

He looked towards the door and he saw her through the window as she stood in the kitchen. He watched her eat, watched her laugh, watched her clean up and put away the dishes from her meal. He could hear her, she was humming. He recognized the tune and he felt an uncomfortable burning sensation in his throat as memory after memory of moments spent with her while that very tune was playing began to stack up in his mind, replacing everything else of importance.

His hand stretched out as he saw her pull her ponytail out of its constricting band. His fingers itched to play with her hair, something he had not done in what felt like far too long despite it only being days. When she yawned and placed her hand over her mouth to stifle it, he raised his hand to his own, the mimicked motion somehow comforting to him.

"You know you could just walk in and ring the doorbell."

He looked down to see Stacy standing there beside him, her hair a sweaty mess, her clothing…missing. "You're in your underwear."

She looked at her clothes and shook her head. "I'm not naked, you dork. This is a sports bra, and these are my work-out shorts. Trust me; I'm wearing far more clothes than you'd see at the pool. So, why are you standing out here anyway, looking all stalkerish and crap?"

Robert didn't answer her and just kept staring through the window.

"Look, I know I'm being a real pain, but do you think that you could let me know how I can get in touch with Lark, or at least let me know when she's coming back? This is kind of important."

Robert turned his gaze to Stacy and replied, "I'm not about to bother my sister with your petty, human whims, Stacy." Though the words sounded callous, I realized that he had not said them to be so. He waved at Stacy as she walked towards the house, but did not follow her despite his desperate need to do so, to be able to see and hear Grace's voice, and to tell her that for now, at least, she was safe.

I opened my eyes as Robert pulled away from me, our contact broken, the vision gone. "Wow."

Robert nodded. "Yes."

"It was Mr. Frey," I whispered in disbelief.

Robert's eyes hardened into cold slate as he once again nodded his head. "He's been watching you this whole time, sitting there while you worried about who it was that did this to you. If I wasn't entrusted with

302

his soul, I'd tear his heart out and send it straight to Hell with his head not too far behind."

The dark anger in his voice should have frightened me—it would have frightened anyone normal, that's for sure—but I felt a fluttering in my stomach because I knew that his reaction could only be so strong if he still cared for me.

"Of course I care, Grace. I love you. That doesn't go away just because you or I are angry at each other," he complained.

"I know," I said softly. I had so much more to say to him, but this wasn't the right time, not when something more pressing was demanding our undivided attention. "What will happen to him now? I mean, with…you know…you?"

"He has confessed to me, and for that, he has earned himself some extra time, but he needs your help now, Grace," Robert said urgently.

I looked at him, confused. "Me? What can I do?"

Robert grabbed my hand and pulled me up. "You can save him."

FORGIVENESS IS DIVINE

"Me? How can I save him?" I asked as Robert pulled me towards the window. "And where are we going?"

"Grace, right now, what I need from you is to trust me. I'll explain everything to you, but you have to trust me, okay?"

With the millions of things I had stored up inside of me to say to him, the countless words and phrases that were all clamoring for a chance to finally be said, the only thing that came to my mind was "always".

Robert smiled at me and wrapped my arms around his neck. He scooped me up and then together we floated out of my window. He waited until we were several yards above my neighborhood before the dark, smoky mist began to appear at our feet, disguising our appearance in the night sky.

As we traveled past house after house, I kept feeling the need to ask him what exactly it was that I needed to do to save Mr. Frey, but I held my tongue. I didn't care what it was. Right now, all I wanted was to pretend that nothing had gone wrong between Robert and me, that no harsh words had been said, and that we were simply two lovers spending precious time together.

That time will come.

Four words had never sounded so sweet. For the first time in what felt like a lifetime ago, I rested my head against Robert's chest. The hollow sound that existed there provided me with a strange comfort, and I closed my eyes to it, allowing its silence to blanket me as we moved swiftly through the dark clouds.

As the lights below us grew brighter, it got harder and harder to ignore them. The noise as well became difficult to tune out and I knew that we were outside of Heath's city limits. I just didn't know where.

We're in Newark, just outside of the Police Station.

I braced myself as the ground drew closer, but Robert landed with perfect grace and skill. He had managed to bring us within feet of the building without being seen, but there wasn't any time to stop and marvel at such a feat as Robert lowered my feet to the ground and removed my arms from around him. He clasped my hand in his and began to pull me towards the main entrance, his feet moving far too quickly for mine to keep up and I tripped several times before we made it through the doors.

It was only then that I realized I wasn't wearing any shoes. I looked down at my feet and groaned at the damage my lack of speed had wrought.

"We can worry about your feet later. We have to help Mr. Frey," Robert whispered into my ear before dragging me down a long hallway.

He pulled me through a door on the right and we soon found ourselves in a small room that had a tiny window covered by a grate. "Wait here," he said in a stern voice that promised dire consequences if I were to disobey.

I wanted to ask him just where exactly I'd go with no shoes or clue as to where I was, but he had already left, closing the door behind him. In an attempt to make the time pass by more quickly, I began to inspect this room that Robert had brought me to, but it was as bare as my feet. Only a small, rectangular metal table and two cold, metal chairs decorated this room. The walls were gray, painted concrete with nothing adorning them to take away from the drab and dank atmosphere.

A florescent light hanging above my head was flickering in that annoying way that makes you certain that that's where headaches are born. I closed my eyes, pressing against my lids with my fingers in an attempt to block out the bright pulses, letting up only when I heard footsteps approaching...and then passing by as they continued down the hall.

I don't know how long I waited, but it was long enough for me to have fallen asleep on the cold surface of the table. I began to dream almost immediately, the cold and lonely room in the police station quickly morphing into the cold and lonely room in my own house.

I was standing in the middle of my bedroom, nothing having changed at all, yet everything was different somehow. I looked over at the bed; it was unmade and well slept in as usual, the covers pushed down to the foot of the bed, and a pillow had fallen to the floor.

I turned to look at my dresser, everything still piled carelessly on top, my alarm clock pushed to the far corner, a stack of books on the opposite end. I looked at the mirror and saw that my reflection showed nothing different about me. Same plain face, same brown hair and brown eyes. I began the short trip to my closet when something caught my attention.

Or rather, something that wasn't there caught my attention.

I turned to look once again to my dresser, and my gaze traveled to the bottom of the mirror. There was a sticky residue there, evidence that tape had been there, but whatever it was that it had been holding was gone. I looked at the top of the mirror and saw the same sticky residue, but no tape.

I tried to remember what it was that had been there, but my mind was foggy with thoughts that didn't feel like my own. The sound of a car starting up outside caused me to turn around and head to my window.

I stuck my head through the opening and smiled as I saw Graham's car pull away from the curb. He was probably heading off to work. A few seconds later, Richard came storming out of their house wearing a stained bathrobe, a frosted bottle filled with clear liquid in one hand, a glass filled with ice and an amber liquid in the other. He was shouting at the car as it sped away, the words too garbled for me to make out, but the tone saying more than the words could.

I called out to him, my anger at his behavior towards his son taking control, and chastised him for letting the alcohol once again take priority over sobering up for his son. He never turned to look at me, and instead took a swig from his glass and shuffled back into the house, the ratted bathroom slippers on his feet kicking up muddy slush from a spring snowfall that I did not remember onto the bottom edge of his robe.

A knock on the door caused me to jump. I hit my head on the window as a result and was rubbing the growing lump when Dad walked in. He was holding a basket of freshly laundered and folded clothes. "Hey, Grace. Did I scare you?"

I shook my head. "No. I was just looking outside. Richard was shouting at Graham and I yelled at him to stop, but it's like he didn't hear me."

Dad nodded his head and smiled. "Of course he didn't hear you, Grace. He's half-dead from all of the booze, and half-deaf from all of that yelling. I don't know how Graham puts up with it, but I suppose you can't help but worry about him, no matter what happened between you two."

"He's my best friend, Dad. It's kind of my job to worry about him," I joked as I began placing my shirts into my drawer. I stopped at the last one, the markings on it very familiar. I opened it up and puzzled as to why it was in my possession. "How did this shirt get in here?"

Dad patted my shoulder. "Grace, I understand that you feel a need to hold onto Graham despite what he's done to you, but his behavior and his treatment of you should be enough to tell you that he's not your friend. I cannot even say if he ever truly was."

Rolling my eyes at Dad's over-protectiveness, I shook the shirt in front of Dad's face to bring his attention back to my question. "Why was this shirt in the wash, Dad?"

He grabbed the shirt from me and looked it over before placing it on the dresser. "You always had a thing for smiley faces, Grace. I would guess it was in the wash because you wore it again, though I don't know why. It's a fairly ugly shirt. You'd think that there'd be more of a selection at that thrift store you like so much."

I stared at the shirt and opened my mouth to tell Dad that I hadn't worn this shirt in over six months, that it had been in Robert's possession the last time I saw it, but said nothing. That would have been very difficult to explain, and Dad would have automatically assumed the worst, which would have been even more difficult to reverse. I set it aside closed my drawers.

"How's Janice doing?" I asked as I began to put away some of the other items in the basket.

"Why are you asking about her?"

I turned around, a pair of socks in my hand, and took a good look at his face. He looked thinner for some reason, older. There were dark circles beneath his eyes, and the lines on his forehead seemed to have grown deeper and longer, engraving his face with an age that didn't belong to him.

"I wanted to know how she was doing," I said slowly.

"I don't know how she is, Grace. We stopped talking to each other after she moved, remember?"

My face wrinkled with confusion. "What do you mean, 'after she moved'? Moved where?"

Dad's mood grew sullen and he started to walk away. "Dad!" I called to him, and he turned around, his eyes sad, his mouth twisted in anger.

"You got your way, Grace, isn't that enough? She never had a chance with you, we never had a chance, and now that I'm finally starting to move on, move past this, you bring her up again. Is this some kind of twisted game you're playing, Grace? I get that you're still upset about Graham. I understand that you blame yourself for Stacy being the one hit by that car and not you, but do you have to act like everyone else's feelings are here for you to toy with because life dealt you a lousy hand?"

The words that came out of his mouths sounded foreign, they didn't make any sense because none of that happened. But then the memories, those strange memories in my head that felt like they didn't belong there…suddenly did.

I closed my eyes and I could see images that weren't mine, and yet were. The first day of school, the day of the accident, the aftermath…they were all familiar and yet different.

Dad had said that it was Stacy that had been hit by the car, but how? In my eyes, I saw the same road, and I was on it, but I wasn't alone. Stacy—she was beside me; we were walking, her car having broken down half a mile away, and we were headed towards the library to use their phone.

In every other way, the scene played itself out exactly the same, but this time it wasn't me that was hit. I heard myself scream as Stacy was jolted away from me. The impact of the car sent her shooting forward and landing on the asphalt several feet ahead of the vehicle which then proceeded to run over her before coming to a halt a few feet away.

The driver stepped out of the vehicle; disoriented and on shaky feet, he walked over to the crumpled and bloody heap that was Stacy. I ran towards them, my voice nothing but screams. The man looked up as I came nearer and then in a panic, began to run to his car. I screamed at him to stop, to come back and help, but he left. He got back into his car and drove off.

I looked down at Stacy and I shut my eyes to the image, opening them up once more in my room. "Stacy…" I whispered, and looked up at Dad's face; it was twisted with the same pain that I was feeling.

"She didn't suffer, Grace. The doctor told you that she died very quickly, that there was nothing that you could do."

I shook my head at the idea of Stacy dying. Healthy, ass-kicking Stacy? Stacy was the one hit by Mr. Frey's car instead of me? "This isn't real," I began to mumble to myself. "This isn't real. Stacy's not dead. I was the one hit by that car. It was me, not Stacy. Robert knows that it was me, he was there, remember?"

Dad shook his head and approached me. He placed two, strong hands on my shoulders and began to shake me, the motion too gentle to do anything but muss my hair. "Grace, what are you talking about? Yes, baby, Stacy is dead. Remember? The car swerved to avoid you and hit her instead. She died just a couple of weeks after school started. And who's Robert?"

"Who's Robert? What do you mean, who's Robert? He's my..." My head whipped around to the mirror, my eyes focusing in on the spots on the mirror that were conspicuously empty. "He's, he's..."

"Grace? He's what? Who is he?"

I turned to look at my dad's face and I couldn't answer him. I reached to grab the t-shirt that he'd placed on the dresser and noticed my hand—my right hand—was bare. I dropped to the floor and began searching the carpet, my hands running over and into the soft plush material, raking it with my fingers.

"Grace, what are you doing?" Dad asked, alarm tingeing his voice.

I didn't answer him. I simply knew a desperation to find the ring that wasn't on my finger, that should have been there because I never took it off.

"Grace," he shouted when I didn't answer him. "Grace?"

He began to shake me, and everything began to fall into place. Janice had moved away, just like he had said she would. Dad's attitude towards Graham was just as cold as it had been after Graham had ended our friendship, which meant that Graham and I had never made up. But we hadn't made up until after the accident...which killed Stacy.

"Oh God," I moaned. If the accident had killed Stacy, that meant that there was no Robert.

"Grace, what's wrong?"

"Robert..." I sobbed softly, closing my eyes and curling up into a ball on the floor, the pain of him not existing more excruciating than the idea of him simply not being in my life. I felt empty, hollow, my insides caving in around my wounded heart.

"Grace!" Dad shouted.

"Grace?"

I felt him shaking me, but I didn't want to open my eyes.

"Grace, open your eyes, it's okay."

I shook my head, unwilling to see a world that didn't possess the one thing in it that made everything else work.

Open your eyes, love.

I did so, but more out of shock than anything else. My head was no longer against soft carpet. Instead, it was pressed against cold steel. Mercury eyes, liquid and brimming with concern were staring at me from the edge of the table that I had fallen asleep on.

"Robert?"

He nodded his head, his hand gently squeezing mine. My eyes shifted to it and I spied the glint of silver around my finger. "Oh, it's back," I whispered.

"It never left," Robert said softly.

With a cry, I wrapped my arms around Robert's neck, the sobbing that had begun on the floor in my dream crossing over into my reality, only now with relief and joy that Robert was here, that he was real, that he was still mine.

"What's wrong?" he asked, concerned. He gently pulled me away just far enough so that he could look into my eyes. "Grace, what's wrong?"

"I dr-dreamt that y-you weren't r-real," I hiccuped, my fingers digging into Robert's shirt in an attempt to keep him from pulling me away any further. "Don't leave me. Don't ever go away again."

He allowed me to bring myself closer, his hand pressing against the back of my head, his embrace strong and comforting. "I promise, I promise you, Grace. It's okay. It was just a dream, I'm here," he cooed into my ear. I nodded my head, but didn't let him go.

A soft cough alerted me to the fact that we weren't alone. "Who's that?" I whispered into Robert's ear, unwilling to turn around, to leave the stronghold of Robert's arms.

"Mr. Frey," Robert replied. "He's here to ask you for your forgiveness, Grace."

I lifted my head from Robert's shoulder and looked at him in disbelief. "Are you serious?"

Robert nodded. "Yes. I am."

"But he nearly killed me," I hissed. "He left me to die on the side of the road, Robert."

"Yes, he did. But I told you that he needs your help, and it begins with this," Robert insisted, pulling me away once more to turn and face the man who had nearly destroyed my life. "He needs absolution, Grace. You can help him by doing this."

"How?"

"Listen to him; let him tell you about what happened."

I looked at him with disbelief in my eyes. *But I already know what happened.*

Robert reached for my hand and held it, giving it a gentle squeeze. "He needs to do this, Grace. He needs your forgiveness. And you need to listen."

"Fine," I conceded and turned to face the man who ran me down. "Tell me about what happened."

Mr. Frey looked at me and then at Robert. Seated in the chair opposite me, he seemed as confused as I did, but proceeded to tell me the same series of events that he had given to Robert, the details bringing forth different memories, each one from a different point of view to form a complete picture of what had happened to me. As the story reached its culmination, the scene in my mind changed. It was no longer my body on the ground. As I had in my dream, it was Stacy's body that lay broken and battered on the road as Mr. Frey drove off to escape the reality of what he had done.

I felt Robert release my hand and he turned me around to face him, his eyes searching, his mind probing as he, too, saw the image in my thoughts, leaving him perplexed and bewildered.

"Grace," I heard behind me. I turned to look at Mr. Frey, whose eyes had turned puffy and bloodshot, his nose large and red with the emotions that he had been unable to express to Robert when faced with his death.

I looked at him, took in the drastic change that had occurred since the last I had seen him, both in my own mind as well as Robert's, and I started to see something in him that I hadn't before. In his face, I could see my father's, aged and miserably lonely. His hand bore a white line on his left ring finger, but no wedding band. My hand clenched instinctively, feeling the press of the sapphire stone against my palm and relishing in its presence. There were no laugh lines around his eyes, though he appeared far older than Dad, and I knew that he had no friends who could offer him the solace of friendship.

"You live a very sad life, Mr. Frey," I told him. "You ran away from your problems to keep your family safe from it, and yet they left you anyway, didn't they?"

Robert and Mr. Frey gasped at my words, both shocked at what I had been able to discern, Robert amazed that I had learned something he hadn't. I stared at Mr. Frey and started to feel sorry for him as I thought about the girl who had died, and about Stacy, whose death in my dream felt just as real. "You've lost everything; your wife; your children; soon your career and your freedom will be gone, too. You killed that girl, and somewhere, her family is wondering the same thing that my father wondered about me.

"There is no reason on earth that would justify me forgiving you for what you did. You left me to die on that road. You knew who I was, knew that I had no one, and instead of taking even one moment to be the person you want me to be, you walked away. You left me there, all alone, scared, broken, dying. And then you let me accuse Mr. Branke, let him be arrested and watched as I ruined his life. There is no reason why I should forgive you, Mr. Frey. I shouldn't forgive you.

"But I will."

Mr. Frey began choking in disbelief and out of habit, I stood up to pat him on his back. He looked at me with wide eyes, his hands shaking, sweat pouring down the side of his face like he had just been doused with it. "Why?" he whispered, his voice cracking from the surprise.

"Because it was me," I said softly, sitting back down in the chair across from him. "It could have been someone else, someone who *would* have died, someone I care about very much, but it wasn't. For whatever reason, it was me that you hit that day, and that accident changed my life."

Robert knelt down beside me and I felt the burn in my throat as I saw so clearly what life had been like without him in it, even if only for a blink of time. His gray eyes grew dark and stormy as he saw what I did, knew what I had seen.

I blinked away some of the fresh tears that formed and took a deep breath, needing to finish what I had been brought here to do. "Mr. Frey, you have my forgiveness, but what I hope for you, what I pray for you is that you can forgive yourself. You have lost a lot because of what you did, and you will probably lose a lot more, but I know that you haven't lost what's most important—not yet."

Mr. Frey began sobbing and though I knew that I shouldn't, I felt a need to comfort him. I placed my hand onto the table, extending it out to him, palm up. He looked at it with skepticism, looked at me with confusion, but his hand slowly inched forward, and I felt it fit awkwardly into mine, the small contact opening up a floodgate of tears from both of us.

We sat there like that, hands extended, tears freely flowing until there was nothing left to give. No more tears, no more confessions. I felt emotionally drained when I stood up, with Robert nudging me and announcing that it was time to go.

"Thank you," Mr. Frey whispered to me as we walked out of the room, his hand pressed against his heart in sincerity. "You truly are an angel of mercy."

I laughed nervously at his words and looked at Robert, who shook his head and pushed me forward. We walked quickly past several police officers and loiterers who didn't seem to notice two high school students, one barefoot, haunting their halls well past midnight.

314

Only when we were outside did I ask him what it was that I had done, and why it had been so urgently necessary.

"You're the angel," he teased, but quickly grew serious as we reached the end of the sidewalk fronting the police station. Without stopping or even warning me about what he was about to do, Robert pulled me into his arms and pushed up off the ground, the movement sending us into the air.

I kept my face pressed against the warm column of Robert's neck, seeking to see nothing but him, smelling nothing but him; Mr. Frey wasn't the only person who needed absolution.

It wasn't long before the odor of damp, freshly mowed grass intruded in on me, breaking through the heady scent that was uniquely Robert. I raised my head just enough to peek over Robert's shoulder and see where it was that we were. The white wall was unmistakable, the large, white house instantly recognizable to me. "Why are we here?" my muffled voice asked into his jacket collar.

"We need to talk, and you need a place where you can yell."

I chuckled at that. "That might be true."

"Of course it is," he insisted.

He carried me through the doorway, the quiet only emphasizing the darkness that filled the house. Once in his room, he closed the door and placed me gently onto the bed. He removed his jacket and proceeded to hang it up slowly, something I had never seen him do.

"Are you stalling?" I asked, the question seeming silly for someone who had all the time in the world.

"To you it seems silly. To me, it helps to keep each moment with you from ending that much sooner."

I didn't know what to say to that. I always took for granted the fact that as slow as time seemed to travel for me, it went by at a rapid pace for him, and his movements—when they weren't being scrutinized by those who could discern the difference—were an excellent display of that lack of appreciation for time.

"Grace, before you say anything, before we start arguing again, I want to speak to you about what happened today-"

"At the police station?"

He didn't turn around, but I saw his head nod, the dark head moving up and down as he spoke. "Yes, at the police station. When you fell asleep, you dreamt...you dreamt about what your life would have been like had I never entered it-"

"Had you never existed," I corrected.

"I will always exist, Grace, but that is neither here nor there. It was explained to you that when you form a memory, it burns itself into your mind, branding you with the truth of it. Memories differ from other thoughts. They don't change, even if you think they do. They don't form independently."

"I don't understand."

Robert raised his arm up against the bedroom door and rested his head against it. "In your dream, we had never met, you had never regained your friendship with Graham, Janice never moved in, and Stacy—Stacy was the one who ended up being killed, right?"

I nodded then looked away, feeling stupid because he wasn't even facing me.

He sighed and continued, "You began to see things in your dream, remember things that you thought didn't belong there, right?"

"Yes.

"Grace, those are genuine memories. Those are things that are burned into your mind as though they actually happened to you."

I sat there with my mouth ajar, the idea sounding far more absurd each time I replayed it in my head. I tried to find something articulate to say, something that would contradict him without leaving any room for doubt. All I could come up with was "You're real".

He turned around and looked at me, his eyes a dark, shadowy gray, his mouth a harsh line that hinted at anger and hurt. "Do you not understand what I am telling you, Grace? Memories formed by dreams are tied to those dreams, forever linked to tell you that they are not real, just visions

316

of your subconscious—they are never independent of them. Your memories have no dreams."

"So what does that mean?"

Robert shook his head and grit his teeth, fighting the answer that struggled to be told. "It means that someone has been toying with your mind, Grace. I just don't know who, or even when."

I felt more confused than I was frightened. "How? How does someone just *put* a memory into my mind without me knowing about it?"

"I've told you how; it's just that I told you how it's done in reverse-"

Recognition dawned on me and my eyes grew wide in shock and anger. "You mean that what's happening with Erica…that's happening to me?"

He nodded slowly, my saying it seeming to finalize it somehow, and neither of us liked that idea.

"This doesn't make sense though. Why? Who?"

Robert grimaced. "I don't know. You're never alone anywhere except in your room, so that rules out any of the conventional methods, which means that whoever is doing this has the ability to get to you when you're asleep." He turned around once more and cursed under his breath.

I had never heard him speak like that before, the words sounding so foreign coming out of his mouth. I stood up and slowly walked over to him, my steps unsure, my hand shaky. He was shaking as well, though I could not discern from what until I placed a nervous hand on his shoulder and he spun around to face me.

"You're afraid," I said softly, easily recognizing the signs.

"I left you alone. You told me to and like an idiot I listened, and now someone is messing with your mind in a way that I cannot figure out. What if whoever did this had tried to do something else? What if they tried to hurt you?" Robert's hands grabbed a hold of my arms and gripped them tightly; my body started to shake and I realized that it was because he was trembling, his hands holding onto me because he needed *my* support.

I didn't know what to do; this was a situation that I wasn't familiar with. Robert had never shown fear before. At least, not in a way that would shake him to his very core. He had never looked more vulnerable than he did right then. I had watched him die, watched him writhe around in unimaginable pain, and yet he had always remained iron-willed and steadfast. Now I was the strong one.

I could not move, his steel-like arms held me at a safe distance, so I simply waited for him to loosen his hold on me. I looked at him, my eyes never leaving his, reaffirming that no matter how angry, how upset I had become over the words he had spoken, I was where I belonged, where I needed to be.

"Robert," I said in a soft, soothing voice. "I'm sorry for telling you-"

I was cut off from my apology by the swift pull of him bringing me into the tight circle of his embrace. My arms wrapped around his back with unspeakable and intrinsic need.

"Don't apologize for something that I made you do," Robert groaned into my hair. "Don't."

I shook my head, unwilling to be let off that easily. "You didn't make me react the way that I did. It was wrong of me to say what I did to you, regardless of how I felt. I regretted it as soon as I said it, but my stupid, stubborn pride wouldn't let me admit it."

"I should have been the one to apologize, Grace, not you. I'm the one who overreacted, who should have known better. My accusations were baseless and wholly reactionary, and it was my stupid, stubborn pride that wouldn't let me admit to it either. I am sorry, Grace." Robert's arms pulled me in tighter, something that I didn't know was possible, and I, in turn, tried to pull him as close to me as possible, needing to feel his warmth, his strength.

Only when my legs felt like they would give out from standing for so long did Robert finally pick me up and carefully place me on the bed. He sat across from me and pulled my feet into his lap. "You've got weird toes," he commented as he began to massage the soles.

318

"I do not!" I protested, and tried to pull my feet away, but he held fast. "They're normal looking toes. Besides, I don't recall ever seeing *your* toes."

Robert bent down to untie the laces to his black shoes, something I had never seen him do before, and watched, fascinated as he proceeded to remove the shoe followed by a long, black sock. Once bare, be brought his foot onto the bed and allowed me to inspect it. I leaned forward and reached for it tentatively.

"What?" Robert asked as he took in my hesitancy.

"It's just that…well, whenever Graham would shove his foot at me, it was always sweaty and smelly. I just—I assumed that yours would be the same way," I admitted sheepishly.

He let out a loose, carefree laugh as he wiggled his toes. "I don't sweat, and I'm fairly certain that you're aware that I don't…smell. Not badly, anyway."

I looked at him with doubt in my eyes, but allowed my hand to take a hold of his pale foot and true to his word, it wasn't sweaty or foul smelling. To my surprise, it actually gave off a pleasant odor not dissimilar to the one that you could pick up when he spoke to you.

"How weird," I murmured as I looked at the smooth skin on the sole of his foot. "Can I see your hands?"

Robert held out his arm and I grabbed his palm, searching for what I knew would be absent when I got to his fingers. "You don't have any fingerprints!" I exclaimed in shock. "Why didn't I notice that before?"

"Because you just assumed that, aside from the obvious differences, I was just like you."

"Oh."

"Grace?"

"Yes?"

Robert removed his hand from mine and brought himself closer to me, his face mere inches from mine. "Are we…okay?"

I nodded in response, too afraid that saying anything would make it anything but. Robert smiled. He was so close, I could feel his warm breath on my face and I greedily inhaled it, the intoxicating scent doing things to me I knew no drug ever could. Robert's smile grew ever wider as he leaned in closer until finally our lips were just a millimeter apart. I looked down and felt my breath catch in anticipation—it had seemed like forever since I had been this close to him—his lips still parted in that devastatingly handsome smile causing my heart to skip noticeably.

"You're more excited than usual," he commented with a slight laugh. "Perhaps this is too soon-"

"No!" I cut him off sharply and pushed myself forward, closing the microscopic distance between us until my lips were pressed firmly against his. It was a defining moment for both of us; the ever running current of electricity that sparked out between us turned into a living, breathing entity that ignited something inside of us; and for an altogether too brief of a moment, we both lost control of ourselves.

Robert's hands came up to hold my face steady as I struggled to bring his own closer—he could never be close enough, I decided—and with a kind of mad urgency, he began to deliver the kind of hard, biting kisses that I had never known I needed. It wasn't soft and gentle, sweet and endearing like all of the others were. It wasn't even scintillatingly arousing like our last kiss had been. This was a desperate, almost message sending kiss that brooked no doubt in how much he needed me.

And I needed him. I needed him more than air or water or light. He was every emotion, every thought I possessed. I felt waves of heat flow to every limb, my fingers tingling from the fierce push of it. The world could have died, the universe imploded in on itself, and nothing would have ever altered my life the way he did when his mouth opened beneath mine and I tasted him. It was all I could do to keep from promising him anything and everything if only he'd never stop.

But he did, his breathing just as ragged, his trembling just as strong as my own. I felt the extreme disappointment replace the heat almost instantly. "Don't stop," I panted.

Robert shook his head as he tried to regain his composure—I liked him all rattled up—and held onto my shoulders, though whether it was to support me or himself, I didn't know. "We cannot, Grace. It's not right, this is not the right time."

Frustrated and disappointed, I sighed. "It's never the right time."

"Grace, please," Robert implored. "You won't have to wait forever. I promise."

"You keep saying that but I keep finding it harder and harder to believe you."

We sat up, separated by the things we wanted to say, and the things we wanted to do but couldn't. We were supposed to be moving forward, we were supposed to be growing as a couple. Instead we were moving backwards, and we both knew what that meant.

Even if we were too afraid to say it aloud.

SPRING BREAK-IN

With less than a week left before Dad and Janice's wedding, I found myself with absolutely no time to do much of anything. Graham had taken it upon himself to stay as far away from the overly anxious pregnant woman and all of the wedding finalizing as possible. That meant, of course, that I'd seen very little of him these past few days.

When he learned that Robert and I had resolved our problems, he seemed relieved, but refrained from asking me about Lark again from that point on. I felt conflicted because for whatever reason, it seemed that by mending things with Robert, I had effectively barred myself from any conversations with him about Lark and Graham, and that didn't seem fair to me at all.

The last day of school was also the day before Graham took off for Florida to spend Spring Break with his mom. Knowing that he wouldn't be attending the wedding, he chose to give Dad and Janice their gift early. He presented it in the morning, its wrapping quite crude and with far too much tape, but once Janice had managed to remove the yards of cellophane, she was awed by what she found.

"Oh Graham, this is wonderful!" she exclaimed as she pulled out a white, leather-bound photo album. It wasn't the type that you'd find in your photo section of your local big-box stores, of that I was certain. "Where ever did you find something like this?"

Graham smiled proudly. "I ordered them from a shop my friend Donovan's dad owns. He runs that antique store down by the old coffee shop and he had this catalogue from a company that makes these hand-made photo albums. I thought that since Grace got you guys that scrapbook for the baby, why not add something for your wedding?"

"Did he do the embossing, too?" Janice asked as she ran her fingers across hers and Dad's initials that were gilded in gold leaf across the front, just below an oval shaped external frame.

"Yeah. I didn't ask Grace what the colors of your wedding were because…well, I'm a guy—we don't do that kind of stuff, and I'd just forget anyway. So I just chose white, if that's okay," Graham admitted sheepishly.

Dad reached over to take a look at the album and marveled at its weight. "How many pictures do you think we'll be taking at this wedding," he quipped. As he opened the book, he realized why it was so heavy.

"These pages are thick! And they've got actual photo corners, like the old ones we have for some of our old albums in the attic. I think there's one of your mom's up there, too Grace. Thanks a lot, Graham. I'll probably be one of those 'admire-them-from-a-distance' kind of husbands when it comes to this sort of stuff, but you chose something that we can hand down to the baby when he's older. Thank you, very much!"

Graham seemed pleased with the praise he was receiving, and I felt immensely glad that he was here with us, instead of at his home with his father. "You're welcome, Mr. Shelley. You guys have gone out of your way to help me out, and I don't know how I'll ever repay you for it, but the least I can do is get you a gift that you'll actually use."

Janice laughed as she took the album back from Dad and flipped through the pages herself, touching the raised photo corners and admiring the vellum page separators. "You're Grace's best friend, Graham. I think I speak for both of us when I say that you're a part of this family; we care about you very much and appreciate you being in our lives as well as Grace's."

Graham's cheeked turned red at all of this affection, something he was not used to receiving at home, and he quickly turned his attention back to his breakfast. "Hey Grace, is Robert coming to pick you up this morning?" he asked, trying to change the subject to alleviate his discomfort.

"Yeah, he'll be here in a few minutes," I replied as I finished the last bite of my toast and yogurt. "Why?"

Graham pushed his eggs around his plate before answering. "I needed to give him something."

I stared into my empty yogurt cup and nodded. He wasn't going to tell me, not wanting to cause any more strife between Robert and I, and I felt both grateful and resentful at the same time. It shouldn't have to feel this way, but it did and I hated it.

"Do you think he'd mind if I brought you back home? I have to go and grab a whole bunch of clothes from my house, and I thought you could help me out—you know, pick stuff out for me so that I don't look like a total dork."

I looked up and smiled, shaking my head. "He'll be alright with it, but I'm pretty sure he'd rather you take him along because we all know my taste in clothing bites."

"Well, how about the both of you come then?"

I stared at him in shock. "Are you sure?"

"Yeah—you're a package deal, and if that means a better sense of style, I guess I've got no complaints."

I laughed at that, lightly punching his arm and laughing even more when he pretended it had hurt. "We'll all just meet back here after school."

"Sweet."

Dad coughed and I turned to face him. "Yeah, Dad?"

He glanced between Graham and I and let out a deep sigh. "I was just wondering when you and Robert became a 'package deal', and why

324

Graham is suddenly so okay with it. It just reminds me that you're no longer seven…and I'm going to be starting all over again."

Janice began to laugh this time and patted his shoulder reassuringly. "It's alright, James. Boys are supposed to be easier."

Dad chuckled and pointed to the layered shirt and jeans ensemble I had on. "I didn't raise a prissy princess—or even a regular princess. Grace has always been independent, self-sufficient, and just plain easy. It's just-" he seemed to struggle with the words as he looked at me and then quickly away "-watching her grow up has been one of the best experiences in my life. And to see her make her own path in life, rather than follow the ones that others want her to…it would have made her mother very proud—it makes me proud."

"Aw, Dad," I groaned and brushed my hand against my eyes, desperately trying to hide the moisture there.

The doorbell ringing alerted us to Robert's arrival and I jumped up, embarrassed at my obvious glee that he was here, but also anxious to see him and speak to him about Graham's plan.

"I'll get it," Graham said and pushed me back down into my chair.

"Oh," I huffed and watched him walk off towards the door.

Dad chuckled. "You didn't actually think that Graham was going to let you speak to Robert first and tell him that he needs help picking out his clothes, did you? Coming from the queen of the fashionably challenged?"

I rolled my eyes and slouched in my seat, knowing that Robert had already heard everything that we had said; and what he didn't hear voiced, he surely had seen in our thoughts.

Graham and Robert walked into the kitchen together several minutes later and I had to blink a few times to reassure myself that I was seeing the same two individuals who had always seemed at odds with each other, even when there was no reason to be. They were laughing and joking about something that I obviously wasn't privy to, and I felt…jealous. I closed my eyes and reopened them once more in shock—was I really jealous?

Robert looked at me, an amused and slightly smug smile on his face. My eyes narrowed. "Are you ready to go, Princess?"

My mouth gaped and my gaze whipped to Graham who blushed red with guilt. "You. Are. So. Dead."

Robert, Graham and Dad burst into raucous laughter and I turned to look at Janice, hoping for a little double-x chromosome help from her, but she shook her head and tried to stifle her laughter with one hand while the other rested protectively on her belly. "Sorry, Grace," she apologized between giggles. "Matthew is making me laugh." She patted the mound of baby beneath her hand and I shook my head.

"He's not even out of the womb yet and he's already laughing at me. Some big sister I'm going to make," I sighed.

"You're going to be a fantastic big sister," Janice insisted, and Dad nodded, though his continued laughter did little to convince me of his sincerity.

Graham bobbed his head as well and grinned at me. "He'll just get all of his sports advice from his Uncle Graham and his fashion advice from his brother-in-law Robert."

The sudden quiet spoke volumes.

"I went a little too far, didn't I?"

When no one answered him, he nodded his head slowly and then pointed towards the living room. "I think I'll go and get my stuff to head out."

I looked at Robert and then at Dad, who appeared as though he had just swallowed his coffee mug whole...with scorching hot coffee still inside. "Okay, I think it's time we went, too," I announced nervously and grabbed Robert's hand, pulling him outside before an unnecessary questioning began.

We were on the bike and halfway down the street before Robert finally asked me what was wrong. I pressed my forehead against his leather-clad back and sighed. "He just got through nearly breaking down over me growing up. Can you imagine how he must feel now after hearing that comment about you being my baby brother's brother-in-law?"

Robert said nothing to that and remained quiet as we rode to the school; I was too busy thinking about what it was that Graham had given to Robert to notice the expression on his face.

❦

"So the wedding is just a few days away," I said casually while staring at Janice's little SUV sitting in the driveway while waiting for Graham to arrive after school.

"Yes," Robert replied.

I fidgeted with my feet, my fingers doing a mad dance of nervousness as I tried to word the question right in my head, unsure of how exactly to go about doing this without sounding so…dorky.

"Yes."

I looked at him confused. "What?"

He smiled and tipped my chin up with his fingers, gently running down the length of my jaw with the tip of his thumb. "Yes. I'll be your date for the wedding. That's what you were going to ask, right?"

"Um…yeah," I answered, embarrassed. "Wow, that was easier than I thought. I've never asked anyone out on a date before—I've never had an opportunity before—and I thought maybe you'd feel uncomfortable being asked by a girl."

Robert's hand trailed up to my ear and he gently squeezed the lobe between his thumb and forefinger as his other fingers tickled the nape of my neck. "You can ask me anything, Grace."

I nodded uncomfortably. "I just thought that maybe you'd say no."

"And pass up an opportunity to see you in a dress again? Never," he kidded, his other hand rising to brush against my cheek. "You are going to wear a dress, right?"

"I don't know," I said, shrugging my shoulders. "Janice has something hidden away in a bag that she won't let me see. I think she feels if I don't see it until the day of the wedding I won't be able to think of any excuses not to wear it."

Robert smiled and looked over to the house. I watched as an expression of deep concentration crossed over his face, soon replaced with one of surprise and then blatant pleasure. "Ahh," he said, smiling.

"What?"

He turned to look at me, his smile doing funny things to my insides. "Even if you could come up with a viable reason to not wear it, I wouldn't let you."

I gasped at his little disclosure. "You saw it!"

Nodding, he laughed. "I did, but I won't have the pleasure of seeing you in it again until the wedding, so we're both going into this blind."

I turned my back to him, fuming. "I cannot believe you get to see it before I do. No—you don't get to see it before I do—you stole a peek in Janice's head to see it." I spun around to face him again and glared at his obvious amusement. "That's not fair."

Robert bent down to kiss the tip of my nose. "You're adorable when you're left out of the loop."

There were a few choice words that I would have liked to say to him but I put them aside as two cars pulled up. The rusted green car I recognized; the other I did as well, but didn't want to see.

"The police are here to speak to you about Mr. Frey," Robert announced as he stood in front of me protectively.

"What about?" I asked. Though it had been a week since Mr. Frey had turned himself in, the police had yet to announce the arrest and I wasn't about to announce anything to anyone, since I wasn't even supposed to know.

"It's not good," he replied as two officers approached me, one with what looked like an envelope in his hand.

"Grace Shelley?" the one with the envelope asked. When I nodded, he handed me the envelope with a grim expression on his face. "I've come to formally notify you that we've arrested the individual who ran you over in September. You'll recognize his name; it's Mr. Oliver Frey, your homeroom teacher."

Pretend you're shocked.

I looked at Robert and then at the officer, trying my best to appear surprised by the news. "Wow—Mr. Frey? He-he was always so…quiet," I said with as much excitement as I could manage.

"What's this about Mr. Frey?"

We all turned to see Graham and Stacy standing beside Robert— Stacy with a large, empty duffel bag slung onto her shoulder. She looked at me and then at the envelope in my hand and gasped. "It was Mr. Frey?" Her surprise was a testament to how small our circle was—the whole school knew and yet Graham and Stacy managed to remain oblivious to it all.

The officer who had been empty handed came forward and wedged himself between his partner and me. "Miss Shelley, in that envelope are some forms that we'll need you to sign. We also have to speak to your father, since you were a minor when the incident occurred, to go over a few details that are described in those forms."

I opened the envelope and pulled out the packet of papers and began to go over it, nodding as each detail that had been voiced to me by Mr. Frey himself was listed. I saw the signature at the bottom of his statement and then proceeded to the next page.

"What does this say?" I asked the officer, pointing to the sheet in front.

"That's an incident report, Miss Shelley," he replied. "While in custody, Mr. Frey somehow managed to leave his jail cell. We were afraid that he had escaped and were prepared to alert you to his involvement, but he was discovered an hour later in a back storage room that we sometimes use for interrogations.

"He was dead."

If I had to pretend shock before, there was no need to now. "Dead? From what?"

The officer looked at his partner before pointing to the same sheet of paper. "It's listed right there. We didn't come sooner because we wanted to be sure that our report to you was complete."

I skimmed through the descriptions of the discovering officer and found the final sentence at the bottom of the page. "Pulmonary embolism?"

"What's that," Graham asked behind me.

"His heart blew up," I responded, my voice so low, I wasn't sure if he heard me.

Stacy sucked in her breath while Graham's whooshed out as they both took in the shock of the sudden confession and equally sudden death.

Robert wrapped his arms around me and it was the sudden stillness in my body that made me realize that I had been trembling almost violently. I looked up at him and he shook his head, a warning not to ask the question that was threatening to come out in a loud scream.

"Hey, Grace. You gotta go and talk to your dad about this. We'll go and deal with my things," Graham said quickly, pulling Stacy along with him. I nodded my head stiffly and turned to look at the police officers who stood dumbly beside us, simply waiting for me to invite them into the house.

As Graham and Stacy walked towards his house, Robert and I, followed by the officers, walked towards mine.

"Dad?" I called out upon opening the door, stopping only when I didn't recognize my own voice. "Janice?" I said aloud, hoping for a different result. I cringed at the near whiny tone that came out of my mouth.

Janice appeared from the kitchen, her ever trusty dish towel busily soaking up whatever it was she had on her hands. "Grace, Robert, I thought you were—oh, the police are here." She stared in shock at the two strange men who stood behind me and walked back into the kitchen. I heard the back door open and her voice call out for Dad.

When she reappeared, he was by her side, and the two of them immediately came to me, Robert stepping aside to allow them to flank me as they prepared for what the officers had to tell them. We sat on the couch, a united family unit as once more, the officers went over what happened. I handed Dad the papers that contained Mr. Frey's signed statement detailing the incidents that led up to the accident as well as afterwards as the officers spoke.

When they came to the incident report that described Mr. Frey's "escape" and subsequent death, Dad let out a roar of complaint. "How could you let him escape? And then to just die before without even being punished for it? My daughter has been through Hell because of this man, and he didn't even spend a single night in jail?"

Janice placed her hand on his knee—an effort to calm him, I suppose—and took the papers from his hand. "He went very quickly if this report is correct. The stress of having to bear this secret must have been too much for him."

Dad looked at Janice incredulously. "Stress of not wanting to be caught!"

Janice ignored that last bit and then looked at Robert. "It says that you were with Mr. Frey when he called the police. Is that true?"

I looked at Robert, who nodded his head stiffly. "I was the first person he confessed to. I stayed with him while he dialed 911, and then remained with him until the police arrived. I came and told Grace as soon as I could, but didn't want her to tell anyone else because it wasn't official yet."

Dad's face had turned a distinct shade of crimson as he glared at Robert while his voice once again roared with anger. "You knew this whole time, knew and didn't tell me. And you-" he pointed an accusatory finger at me "-you knew and kept this to yourself. How could you, Grace?"

I opened my mouth to reply. *Don't.* I looked at Robert and saw the quick shake of his head, my mouth closing and my head hanging low with shame and guilt.

"Mr. Shelley, I told her not to tell anyone, not even you, because if Mr. Frey was lying, I didn't want her telling you and then having to deal with feeling like she was disappointing you all over again—especially after what happened with Mr. Branke."

Robert's explanation seemed to calm Dad down as he continued. "I told her to wait until the police showed up with a written statement. I'm sorry if you feel betrayed, but this was what was best for Grace. I only ever had her welfare in mind."

Dad looked at Robert and then at me, his head tossing and turning like he was witnessing a silent tennis match. Finally, he threw up his hands in defeat. "Fine."

Janice let loose a sigh of relief, and I followed suit.

The radio attached to one of the officer's shoulder started blaring and the officer stood up to respond. He walked towards the door and then turned back to look at his partner who had heard the entire exchange.

They both turned to look at me, a silent accusation in their eyes.

Robert grabbed my hand and a flurry of thoughts and images passed through my head. I gasped, and Robert squeezed my hand tightly, a signal to say nothing.

"Um, we've got a report of a robbery taking place next door. Isn't that where your friends went?" one of the officers asked. "And wasn't the girl carrying a very large, very *empty* bag?"

The two officers looked at each other and they both rushed out towards Graham's house, Robert and I on their heels. As the four of us crossed over the front lawn to Graham's front door, I could hear the argument going on inside and looked at Robert, whose eyes were narrow slits as he heard with incredible clarity the horrible things that were being said behind the door.

To my dismay, the police officers both placed their hands on their weapons, unsnapping the band that kept it secure, and called out to the voices. "Open up! This is the police!"

Robert, seeing my panic and fear for my friends inside, became angry. A sudden chill came over us and the officers began to shiver as they stared at each other with puzzled looks on their faces. Robert held my hand and I felt the warmth travel through him into me, keeping me from the icy blast that seemed to only target the officers.

The sound of breaking glass inside caused me to jump and the officer who had been holding the envelope squeezed the trigger of his weapon, the report of the gun louder than I had expected and causing a steady buzzing sound to fill my ears. I screamed, and Robert's growl of anger was the only warning as the officer soon found himself on the ground, his weapon mangled in his hand. The other officer, having seen nothing but his partner fall, looked at him in shock.

"What are you doing? You're acting like a second week cadet! Get up off your ass—we're going to be doing paperwork for a month just to deal with your gun going off. And how are we going to explain that?" He pointed to the metal lump that had never left his partner's hand.

Before he could answer, the door opened and Graham emerged with a very shaken Stacy. They jumped back in shock at the sight of the two police officers—one with his hand on his gun, the other on the ground with something that might have been a gun at one point in his hand.

Graham looked at me and shook his head. "Dad called the cops when he heard me getting my things. He said that everything in the house was his, and then he tried to hit Stacy."

I looked at Stacy, who appeared slightly winded but altogether fine. "Did you...?"

She nodded. "He's old and drunk—no offense, Graham—which made it pretty easy."

I looked at the police officer who still stared incredulously at his partner and then at Robert, who was quietly seething at the officer's clumsiness. "This is my friend's house, Officer-" I eyed his nametag "-York. He was just grabbing some clothes for a trip he's taking tomorrow down to Florida to see his mom. It must've upset his father; he's got a drinking problem. There is no robbery; just an angry and drunken man who doesn't want his life to change."

A moan from inside followed by a loud belch caused Officer York to turn his head towards the door. He peered inside and stood aback as the depth of the situation was finally revealed.

Strewn all across the floor were empty take-out containers of food and cans of beer, mixed with the occasional empty bottle of whisky or vodka. The stench that flowed out was nauseating and I could see why Stacy had been so upset. I covered my nose with my hand, a motion that was mimicked by everyone else with the exception of Robert.

"Is that your father young man?" Officer York pointed to the lump lying on a pile of crushed boxes bearing the labels of several alcohol brands.

Graham nodded solemnly and turned away, upset at over the circumstances that led to this most recent confrontation. "Yes, sir—that's my father."

The other officer, who had by now regained his composure and was still busy trying to figure out what had happened to his gun, coughed and indicated with a flick of his head that we were attracting an audience.

I turned around and saw the neighbors from across the street, as well as those in the house on the other side of mine all standing in a huddled group, staring and speaking in low tones, their heads shaking with distaste.

"Graham, I think you should go into Grace's house and wait for the officers there," Robert said in an authoritative tone.

I watched silently as Graham nodded and walked towards Dad and Janice who were both standing in front of the door. Janice opened her arms to Graham and embraced him while Dad shook his head and patted Graham on his back. He looked up at me and I saw the disappointment written there. Richard had been one of his closest friends, and now…

"Grace, you should probably get inside as well," Robert insisted. When I opened my mouth to refuse he pressed a finger against my lips. "Please. Your best friend needs you."

I turned to look at Stacy who nodded her head in agreement. "He won't talk to me about this, you know that. You're the only person he trusts."

"But who's going to tell them about what's really going on here?" I asked and motioned towards the two perplexed officers with my head. "They don't know-"

Robert once again held his finger to my lips. "I'll tell them." Robert pressed his forehead to mine briefly. "I'll be there as soon as I'm done here."

He turned me around and gently pushed me towards my home. I didn't look back as I approached my front door, Dad standing there waiting for me.

"It's a good thing he's leaving tomorrow, kiddo. I'm beginning to question whether it was a good idea to allow him to continue to stay here in Ohio," Dad said as he welcomed me with a comforting hug. "This is some day, huh?"

My muffled reply into his chest brought out a soft chuckle. "I don't know why these things keep happening to our family, but you've got yourself one heck of a guardian angel there in Robert. Most guys—especially eighteen-year-old guys—would tuck tail and run if they had to deal with what you've had to in this past year, and I have to hand it to him—he's stuck by you through the hit and run, Graham, me...there's no getting around it, Grace. Robert is good for you."

I already knew that. Sometimes it felt like I had been born knowing that. "Don't tell him that though, Dad. He might seem like he's got the patience of a saint, but he's got an ego and that's all I need, for him to start strutting like a peacock because he has your approval."

Dad began to chuckle again, and I felt his body rock as he shook his head. "Just because I believe he's good for you, that doesn't mean I approve of him. He's done some stupid things, too, like removing your casts and not telling us about Mr. Frey—why didn't you at least tell me, Grace? I wouldn't have thought you were telling me anything but the truth, you know that. You've never lied to me, so there are no trust issues between us."

Though he waited for me to respond, I couldn't. Dad said that I had never lied to him, but he was wrong. I had been lying to everyone I cared about for the past six months, lied to everyone that I loved, and it was starting to wear on me, but the rapid pace of events wasn't giving me much opportunity to dwell on it.

Dad pulled me into the house and led me to the couch, where Graham was currently seated, a phone pressed to his ear, one hand covering his eyes in apparent exasperation.

"Mom—no, you don't have to come, I'm okay. Yes, I'm still getting on the plane tomorrow. I don't know. I don't know, Mom. No, no he didn't. Yes, yes but no-" The conversation continued like that for several more minutes.

When Graham's call ended, Janice took the phone from him and returned it to its cradle. Dad coughed uncomfortably and I looked down at the floor, unsure of what exactly to say.

"So," Graham began, sighing as he did so. "I convinced Mom not to fly up here. She's pissed, but she's not coming."

"And tomorrow?" Janice asked.

"I still leave in the morning. Stacy is going to be dropping me off so you won't have to disrupt your wedding preparations," Graham replied. "I'm really sorry for all of this-"

"Ugh—don't apologize, Graham. You didn't do anything wrong, and even if you did, you didn't do anything to deserve what just happened," I shouted, cutting him off. After several minutes of silence I looked at him, puzzled. "Did you say that Stacy is taking you to the airport?"

He smiled and bobbed his head once. "Yeah. Weird, isn't it? We never got along before we started dating, barely got along while we were dating, and now she's doing favors for me." His head snapped up and he looked towards the door, a nervous expression crossing his face. "You don't think that the police will arrest her for assault, do you?"

I shook my head. "No. Robert is going to take care of everything. He'll make sure they don't arrest her *or* you; if anyone gets arrested, it'll probably be your dad. It might actually do him some good."

"Grace," Dad interjected, "why don't you and Graham go up to your room. I'm going to go back outside and speak to the police myself."

Graham and I looked at each other and both stood up. I followed him upstairs and together we walked into my room, both of us collapsing onto the floor beside the bed in emotional defeat.

"Things are going to be okay, Graham," I said reassuringly.

"I know. Dad's just doing this to try and prove a point to my mom; that she still cares about him. I told him that she already has a new boyfriend, and that's when he called the cops."

Shock kept me silent.

"What? Oh, I didn't tell you. Yeah—she's dating this real estate agent. His name's Roy. He's alright I suppose. I met him at Christmas. He and mom apparently met at some sort of Realtor convention she went to last year and they really hit it off."

My eyes were large with this new bit of information. "You mean your mom and he…"

Graham sighed. "Yeah. I guess in Mom's mind, it wasn't cheating since she and Dad hadn't really been together-together, you know? I'm not bothered by it, even though I know I should be. If I were my mom, I wouldn't have stuck around either."

I placed my hand over his and patted it. "But you did."

The low laughter filled the quiet of my room as he nodded. "Yeah, I guess I did. Don't get me wrong, I love my mom, not like I loved my nana, but she's never really been…a mom. She's always tried to be more like my friend, always showing me off, her handsome, football star son. Ever since homecoming though, she's been pretty much okay with keeping me out of her spotlight."

"Because we lost the game," I muttered.

"Basically, yeah. That game was a big let-down for her, but it was one of the best days of my life."

I turned my head to look at him. "The other team got a triple-digit score…in football. How in the world was that one of the best days of your life?"

Graham's hand beneath mind flipped over and he twined his fingers with mine. "We started to hang out again, remember? You won that stupid costume contest, and Lark…"

"Graham, what did you give to Robert?" I asked when his voice trailed off.

"I gave him my word that I'd leave Lark alone."

My fingers clenched around his as I railed into him. "You did what? How could you do that? You love her!"

"Ow—yes, I do—ow, Grace! Ow! Let go!" Graham pried his fingers free from mine and began to rub his hand. "Geez, you'd think I just told him that I'd leave you alone or something! Look, I'm not going to get anywhere with either of them if I keep hounding him. He's got to know that I respect his decision to take care of his little sister, to protect her-"

"But she doesn't need protection from him!"

"I know she doesn't. I just…it just felt like the right thing to do. It was bad enough having to deal with five disapproving brothers with Stacy. If Robert and I can't come to some kind of mutual understanding, there's no hope for Lark and I, and that's only going to make things harder for the two of you. I can't accept that, Grace. I've caused too much pain in your life already."

"Only when you weren't in it," I said in retort, though softly.

"I suffered, too."

We sat there in silence until a soft knock came from my door. "Come in," I responded.

Stacy and Robert walked in, followed by Dad, a look of satisfaction on all of their faces.

"Well, no charges will be filed…against *anyone* for what happened today," Dad announced. "Graham, your dad has agreed to go to a treatment facility in Mason in exchange for Stacy not pressing charges against him for assault. He's very lucky that Stacy agreed to this because it looks like your father was the one who supplied Mr. Frey with all that alcohol the day that he hit Grace."

My eyes bulged and I heard Graham's grunt of surprise.

"What?" we both said in unison.

"According to Richard, Mr. Frey was here drinking all morning on the day that you were hit, Grace. Your teacher didn't admit to that, apparently trying to keep his friend from getting into trouble, but Richard didn't know that. The police aren't going to charge him yet, and might not either if he continues with his rehabilitation, but nothing is set in stone. He wants to say goodbye to you, Graham," Dad finished.

I looked at Graham and saw the crack in his strong exterior as he turned to face me. "It's not your fault," I said to him quickly, seeing where his train of thought was leading him. "You didn't know; this wasn't your fault."

Graham shook his head in defiance. "I don't want to see him."

"Graham," Stacy whispered, "He's your father. He did some pretty stupid things, but you're going away for a week and he's going away, too. You're going to hate yourself if something happens and the last thing you said to him was 'get off her you drunken bastard'." Stacy popped her head up to look at us. "What? That's what he said!"

"I'll go down with you," Robert spoke up. I looked at him in surprise. He kept his eyes focused on Graham. "Stacy is right. Say goodbye to him."

Graham gave in and, after standing up, walked downstairs behind Robert. I shook my head at the odd picture they made. Dad smiled at me and then made his way out of the room as well. "Thanks, Dad," I called out to him before his head disappeared.

"No problem, Kiddo," he replied.

"Stacy?"

"Yeah?" she answered as she sat down next to me, occupying the spot that Graham had vacated.

"What did you do to Richard?"

She broke out into a fit of giggles at my question. "Nothing. I guess Graham told a few stories about me to his dad or something because as soon as I took a step towards him, he began to flip out and tripped over the trash on the floor."

"Oh."

"Why?"

"I just thought that it would be something that you could tell your grandchildren one day—how you took out both your ex-boyfriend *and* his dad."

Stacy smiled half-heartedly. "Yeah. That would be something."

I nudged her with my elbow and laughed. "What a start to spring break though, huh?"

Her smile widened as she nodded. "No doubt."

ROLES

The following morning, Graham had packed everything he had with him into two large duffle bags. I woke up early to make him a breakfast of actual bacon and eggs, and we spent a good hour just talking before Stacy arrived to take him to the airport.

"You're my best friend, Grace," he said before he left. "I don't think I could have made it through any of this without you."

I jabbed his arm with my fist lightly, not knowing what else to say or do at this point. His smile was warm and comforting, and I felt relaxed knowing that, for the next week at least, he'd be spending more time worrying about his tan and how to keep from drowning than anything going on here.

"I'll see you in a week!" he shouted from the car. Stacy's small hand waved at me from the driver's seat just before they pulled out.

It was still dark so I decided to head back up to bed. Robert lay there waiting, his arms open in a warm invitation. I crawled into them and snuggled up against his chest, hiding my tear streaked face against his shirt and hoping I didn't cause too much damage to the expensive fabric.

"You know I don't care about those things, love," he said softly against my hair. "I'm only concerned with how you're feeling. If you need to cry, cry. I understand."

"Why? Why are you being so understanding about Graham now?" I sniffled.

A long sigh, followed by a soft chuckle disturbed the quiet. "Because when he had a chance to use his own misery against everyone, he chose not to. He's a lot like you, you know. He's different from a lot of the humans here who would use their problems as an excuse for their behavior. Instead, he's gone out of his way to do and be everything but."

"What do you mean?"

Robert's hand began to stroke the back of my head as he explained. "You've been through a great deal of trauma in your life, endured the scorn and ridicule of your peers, and yet you're still warm and welcoming, loving and generous. You've never blamed your circumstances for your actions, and have always treated everyone fairly, even if they haven't done so to you.

"Graham has shown me that he is the same. I admit to having misjudged him on many occasions, but yesterday he did something that no human has ever been interested in Lark has ever done without being threatened to do so."

"He gave up," I concluded for him.

"He told you."

"I asked," I admitted.

"Well, yes. He gave up. I didn't expect it, to be quite honest with you. There are two people who fill his thoughts on a daily basis; you are one of them," Robert told me. "You're constantly in my thoughts, too, but for me, I view you in the same way that he views Lark, and I know how difficult it is to be without you, how suffocating it feels to not have you near me.

"You're the air that I need to breathe and the heartbeat that keeps me alive. In those false memories you have, you said that I didn't exist; that's true. If I had never met you, Grace, I *wouldn't* exist. I know that with unwavering certainty. And if *I* feel this way, I know that, even if only in a human capacity, Graham must feel something like this, too."

Something stirred inside of me, something that I didn't know had been lying dormant and undiscovered that love hadn't touched yet. "You're truly amazing," I whispered.

"Why? Because I'm a stubborn angel who took too long to realize something that you already knew?"

I laughed, the sound burying into his chest. "No, because you've made me see something that I didn't know I wanted."

"And what is that?"

I shook my head and kept my secret to myself. "I'm not telling you."

Robert groaned as he came up against the mental block that he had helped me to master. "I'm beginning to think that all of those moments where you claimed you didn't know you were hiding your thoughts were just ruses."

I continued to laugh as he prodded me to tell him what I had learned, but I remained steadfast. "You're not learning anything from me until I'm ready," I vowed, and giggled when he shifted his body quickly, flipping me over onto my back, his torso pressed up against mine.

"I can make you tell me, you know," Robert teased.

"I look forward to it," I said with a sly smile.

Slowly, he lowered his mouth onto mine, our lips molding to each other's. The simple contact was enough to turn my heartbeat into its own little drum machine and the pace of my breathing matched its speed as Robert began to push against my mouth, nudging my lips open with gentle persuasion. I heard myself moan and reached my arms up to try and keep him from pulling away before I could taste-

"Grace?" A knocking at my door caught my attention and I groaned in disappointment. Robert was gone.

"Yes?" I answered, not bothering to hide my annoyance at the disturbance and what it had cost me.

"Did I wake you from a good dream?" It was Janice, her voice sounding amused.

"Better," I mumbled and, with a grunt of disapproval, climbed back out of bed. I opened the door to see Janice standing in front of me, a long, white bag hanging across her arm. "What's up, Janice?"

She saw the direction of my gaze and smiled. She pulled the bag off her arm and handed it to me. "I thought that we could talk, and that I could also give you your dress."

I took the garment bag and walked over to my closet, slowly opening it up, hoping that Robert wasn't standing in there—hiding. With a sigh of relief, I saw that he wasn't, and hung the bag up next to the other one that held the tattered remains of the only other dress I owned.

"You can look at it if you want," Janice insisted, sitting down on my bed. "I admit that I was kind of paranoid that you'd see the dress and then not want to wear it if I showed it to you too early. But since it's so close to the wedding, I thought that if you didn't want to wear it, you deserved to have at least some time to find yourself something different to wear."

I shook my head and smiled at her as I sat down next to her. "I'll wear it."

"Even if it has ruffles?"

I eyed her, my mouth turned down in distaste. "You didn't buy a dress with ruffles, did you?"

She laughed and shook her head. "No. Trust me to at least know what you like and don't like, Grace."

"Whew," I said with a rush. "I was worried for a second."

Janice suddenly sobered up and I did so as well in response. "I wanted to ask you something, Grace. I didn't do it when I should have, and I know that I'll regret it if I never do, so you're going to have to humor me while I do this, okay?"

Confused, I nodded. "Okay…"

Looking into my eyes, Janice reached for my hand and held them in her lap. She smiled at me nervously, and I returned a smile of encouragement, something that, surprisingly, came very naturally.

"Grace, I wanted to ask you for permission to marry your father. He's been all yours for such a long time, so I know that the idea of sharing him might be something that you're not quite willing to accept, but I do love him…immensely, and I promise to keep on loving him for as long as these old bones of mine allow."

I looked at her with surprise. "Janice, I wasn't expecting this. Wow. Usually you hear about the groom asking the bride's family for permission, not the bride asking the child."

Janice laughed. "Well, these aren't usual circumstances."

I joined her in laughing as I replied, "No, you're right. These aren't the usual set of circumstances. Not here, anyway, but yes, you have my permission to marry my dad."

Janice's arms went around my shoulders in an initially awkward embrace that grew more sure as my own went around her. "You're something special, Grace. Your dad always said that about you, and he's right. You're one incredible young lady."

"I try," I said jokingly as we separated.

She smiled and patted my leg. "I wanted to also talk to you about my role in this family, Grace. I wanted to make sure you understood that I'm not looking to replace your mother, or even become your step-mom. You're eighteen now, and far too old to be gaining a new mother. But I would like to know that when your father and I do get married, that you'll consider me your friend."

This was something new, something I hadn't expected, and it made me feel incredibly grateful that she was the one that my father had finally chosen to move on with. "Janice, that really means a lot to me. And I know that you're not trying to replace my mom, but it still feels good to hear you say it."

Janice's smile was sincere. "I know your mother was an incredible woman, and I know that I can never take the place of her in your father's

345

heart—I don't want to. I'm just glad that he's made a place for me inn there; I can only hope that you'll allow a little in there for me as well, because I do care a great deal for you.

"I know that you might not be able to believe this, but when I was your age, both of my parents remarried. My mother married this really wonderful man, Gregory, who loved my mother. He never tried to take the place of my dad and always made it clear that his role was as the spare-father, instead of the step-father. My sister and I grew to love him very much, almost as much as we loved our father

But when our dad re-married, his new wife Iris was a different story. My sister Katie and I used to call ourselves the Cinder-twins because of how she treated the two of us.

"She assumed that we'd automatically take a liking to her; obviously she forgot what it was like to be a teenager. When we didn't give her what she expected, she did her best to turn our father against us." Janice looked at my face and began laughing. "Oh goodness, that does sound overly dramatic, doesn't it?"

I nodded my head, my eyes wide with speculation.

"I'm sorry, Grace. Unfortunately, it's the God's honest truth. Iris told my father that my sister was pregnant when she started to gain weight, and my father forced her to take a pregnancy test to prove that she wasn't. It was very humiliating for Katie, but it didn't matter as long as Iris was adamant that Katie had done something she shouldn't have.

"Thankfully, I was old enough to leave home. Katie only saw our father on weekends, and soon she, too was old enough to leave. We never spoke to our father again after that. We had Gregory, our spare-father. He was more than enough for us, we learned, and it was because he allowed us to welcome him in, rather than forcing us to accept him whether we liked it or not. I promised myself that that was how it was going to be with you."

"You were actually considering calling off the wedding if I said that I didn't approve?" I asked Janice incredulously.

"Yes. You deserve a happy home just as much as anyone does, Grace, and I don't want to bring Matthew into a home where his mother and his sister don't get along. He deserves happiness, too," Janice insisted.

"And what about Dad?"

She took a deep breath and sighed, nodding her head in understanding. "That would have been hard. But our first priority is to our children. His to you, mine to Matthew."

I shook my head at her answer. "Matthew is his son, too—I might as well just change my name to Erica if I made Dad choose between him and me. I guess it's a good thing we don't have to think about it, huh?"

Janice laughed and nodded her head once more. "Very. I'm glad that we had this talk, Grace. You're definitely a very special young lady, and I'm going to be very proud to know that Matthew has you for his big sister."

"Me, too," I replied. "I'm glad that you're going to be my spare-mom, and not my step-mom."

I saw the gloss of tears start to form over Janice's eyes before she stood up quickly, her hands dabbing at their corners. "Well, I'll leave you to take a look at the dress and get—oh dear."

She turned to look at me and I saw a nervous smile cross her face. "I forgot to ask you one more thing."

"What?" I asked, concerned, my eyes flicking down to her belly.

"Oh no, it's not time yet," she laughed.

A huge sigh of relief left my lungs as I joined her laughter. She grabbed my hand and, when her laughter died down just long enough for her to form a coherent sentence, began to speak. "Grace, I wanted to know if you'd like to be my maid of honor."

My eyes grew wide with surprise. "Me? But what about your sister? Or-or-or your co-workers?" I asked nervously—I didn't know what a maid-of-honor did—how was I going to be a decent maid-of-honor for a pregnant woman?

"Katie is walking me down the aisle, so in essence, she's taking over the role of my father since Gregory passed away several years ago, and my mother a year after that, and I just think that you'd be perfect for this role, Grace."

My cheeks pinked up at the thought of taking on such an important job for someone whom I once hated, but I nodded my agreement just the same. "Yes, I'll do it."

Janice grinned from ear to ear and hugged me once more, her torso twisted to the side so that she wouldn't smash her belly between us. "That makes me the happiest bride in Heath, Grace."

"I'm glad," I said, smiling uncomfortably. She saw that and asked me what was wrong. "But…I don't know what a maid-of-honor does," I admitted, embarrassed.

"You just show up," Janice insisted and hugged me once more before leaving.

I made a mental note to Google the responsibilities of the maid-of-honor later, and then glanced over at the closet, dreading what lay behind the door. "Two dresses," I muttered to myself. "I now own two dresses."

ℜ

Janice had a final dress fitting after dinner, which confused Dad and me to no end, so for the first time in months, Dad and I were alone in the house. He took a shower early and proceeded to sit down and watch the news while I cleaned up in the kitchen.

"Hey Grace, when you're done in there, could you come over here and sit down with me?" Dad called out from his chair.

"Sure."

I finished putting the dishes away and turned the light off. I walked over to the sofa and plopped down, looking at Dad's wearied face and wondering what it was that he had to discuss with me. I didn't have to wait long.

"Grace, I know that Janice spoke to you this morning, but I wanted to talk to you about what my marrying Janice means," Dad said as he pressed mute on the television's remote control.

I sat up and leaned forward, my hands clasped together and resting between my knees. "Dad, I know what it means: you're going to be happy, you're getting back the life that you lost when Mom died."

Dad shook his head, leaning forward and taking a hold of my hands. "Grace, you seem to think that marrying Janice is somehow giving me a whole new life. That's not the case. Since the moment I met your mother, I swore that my path in life was set. I knew it deep down to my bones.

"And then you came along and everything changed; I learned that you never set foot on any path until your first child is born, that the time you spend before that was simply you preparing for the journey. And I have to admit that I didn't expect to be so enamored of you and this path of fatherhood that you took me on, and yet you had me hooked from day one.

"When your mother died, I thought 'that's it, my life is over', and then I learned that you were alright and I knew that my life, though wonderful and full with your mother, wasn't tied to her. It was tied to you. You're what keeps me going.

"So no, Grace, Janice isn't giving me a whole new life because I already have you. She's simply adding to it, and when Matthew is born, he'll make this life that much richer. I just wanted you to know that after the wedding, I'm still going to be your dad, and I'm still going to love you and your mom. None of that is ever going to change."

I blinked back my tears. "Thank you. And I love you, too."

"Well," he said, blinking back his own set of tears, "I think you know that Janice cares for you very much."

"She told me so this morning."

He smiled and squeezed my hands. "Your mother would be very proud of you, you know that?"

I shook my head. "I don't know what she'd think, honestly. I try to, but I don't remember much about her. Stacy's always talking about what having a Korean mother is like, but I don't remember anything like that, and what I do remember is limited to a few smiles and a few conversations that have very little to do with what I'm going through now."

"Well, trust me when I say that she would definitely be proud of you. I imagine her thinking about what a beautiful young lady you've grown up to be, and how thankful she would be, knowing that you have wonderful friends in your life who care about you and appreciate you for who you are and not what they want you to be. And...I think she would even approve of Robert. She might even go so far as to call him 'handsome'." Dad managed to choke out that last part and I giggled at the absurdity of Dad calling anyone handsome.

"I know that you might think this callous of me, Grace, but there are moments when I am glad that she's not here. If she were, I don't think you'd have grown up to be so much like her."

I stared at him, speechless. It took me a few minutes to finally arrange the words in my head so that they'd make sense. "Are you trying to say that if Mom hadn't died, I'd have ended up more like you and that there's something wrong with that?"

Dad nodded his head and laughed. "Yes. I've always said that your mother was more than just my better half, she was the saint I'd never be, and I knew when you were born that if you ended up half as wonderful as your mother was, you'd be three times a better person than me. I was wrong, of course. You've actually exceeded your mother in greatness— Abby didn't exactly have a great sense of humor."

"Dad," I groaned.

He laughed louder. "See? Abby would have thought that was funny. You know a bad joke when you hear it."

He sat there laughing in the quiet while I watched him, glad that he'd had Mom to laugh at his bad jokes and listen to his weird CDs, and thankful that he now had Janice to do these things for him.

Suddenly the quiet became too...quiet.

"Grace…"

I frowned at the tone in his voice, the quick change in his demeanor worrisome.

"Grace, why didn't you tell me about Mr. Frey?"

I stumbled for an answer, something that wouldn't sound as absurd and ridiculous as Robert was Death incarnate who'd received Mr. Frey's confession just hours before his death, and then snuck into my room to share what he had learned with me by sending his thoughts and visions into my own mind by intimately pressing his forehead against mine.

"Because I didn't know anything for sure, and I didn't want to get your hopes up again," I finally said, the words almost convincing enough to fool myself.

"Grace, I'm your father. I don't need anything but your trust," he insisted.

"Dad, I'm sorry that I didn't tell you, and I'm sorry that you had to find out the way that you did, but that doesn't mean that I didn't trust you—that I don't trust you. It's just that I don't trust myself. Being wrong about this cost Mr. Branke his reputation. It doesn't matter that I was wrong, or that Mr. Frey confessed. All anyone ever remembers is that first accusation."

Dad seemed to grasp what I was trying to say when he nodded, his hand raising to rub his forehead. "I just don't want you to think that you can't tell me everything; that I won't understand, because I will. I may not be the hippest dad-"

"Dad, I'm not into the trends and whatnot, but even I know that the kids my age don't use the word 'hippest'"

Dad smiled at my interruption. "Okay, I may not be the most *trend*-following dad, but I do love you, and want you to know that you can trust me, Grace, even with yourself."

"Thanks, Dad. I appreciate hearing that, I do."

"So…"

I looked at him and saw the wearied look return. "What, Dad?"

"Are you going to tell me?"

Puzzled, I asked him what he was talking about. "Grace, yesterday, Graham referred to Robert as Matthew's brother-in-law-"

My jaw dropped as I finally realized what he was so worried about. "Oh dear bananas, Dad! No, no-no-no-no-no! Graham was being a dork! Oh God, I'm gonna kill him," I moaned, closing my eyes, mortified.

"It's okay, Grace. If you and Robert have already made a commitment, I'm alright with it—okay, maybe not exactly alright with it—but if this makes you happy, if Robert is the one you see spending the rest of your life with, I'll support your decision. You are an adult now, after all," Dad affirmed.

I removed my hands from his to hold my head—it was now pounding a rhythm that sounded way too much like Wagner's Wedding March—and I groaned. "Dad, I have no plans on getting married any, I repeat *any* time soon. I'm still in high school, for crying out loud! How crazy would I have to be to even consider something like that?"

"Oh, well, that's good then! Phew!"

My head popped up and I looked at him through hooded eyes. "Was all that you just said a lie? Were you only saying it because you thought I was engaged to Robert?"

Dad shook his head, his hands waving in front of him in emphasis. "No, no Grace. I meant it. It's just…well, judging by your reaction, even *you* find the idea of getting married so young to be a pretty bad idea. I was merely saying that if you were to decide on it, I'd support you."

I placed my head back into the cradle of my hands and sighed. "Dad, I love Robert. Do I see myself spending the rest of my life with him? Yes, but marriage? Dad, the only wedding I want to think about right now—and for a long, long, *long* time afterwards—is yours."

Dad sighed in relief and I couldn't help but laugh. "Grace, remind me the next time I see your best friend to put him in a headlock for aging this old man sooner than necessary."

"After I get through with him, you can do whatever you want. I promise, Dad."

"Grace?"

"Yes?"

"I think Robert would make an excellent son-in-law, just for future reference."

"Thanks, Dad."

"Love you, kiddo."

"Love you, back."

WEDDING MARCH

The morning of the wedding, I woke up feeling strangely sad. Things were happening so quickly and it felt like if I blinked, I'd miss it all. Robert had left long before the sun had come up, his call demanding more and more of his time, and so I didn't have him to help figure out what exactly it was that was bugging me.

I stared up at the ceiling, wondering how long I'd have before I had to start getting ready, and what it was that I was expected to do. Googling the responsibilities of a maid-of-honor hadn't given me much useful information. I was supposed to help her get dressed—how was I supposed to do that when I needed help getting into a dress myself? I was supposed to help her keep her make-up and hair from getting mussed, but I couldn't even keep a pony-tail from turning into a tumbleweed.

The only task that didn't seem so daunting was holding her bouquet during the exchanging of rings, although I was fairly certain that if I were given enough room, I'd manage to screw that up, too.

My eyes traveled to the closet where my dress hung, hidden away behind doors and a vinyl bag lining. I hadn't bothered opening the closet door since I had placed the dress in there, and there were no urges to peek now.

354

"I wonder if anyone would notice if I wear jeans underneath," I said to myself.

"Grace, are you awake?"

I rolled over and sighed. "Yeah, Janice."

The door opened and Janice, her hair in rollers, a layer of green gunk completely covering her face, walked in. "My sister Katie is here and she's offered to do your hair and make-up, if you don't mind." She handed me a white box and smiled.

"Well, since I'm pretty hopeless when it comes to doing any of that, I guess I don't mind," I replied, taking the box from her. "What's this?"

"I forgot to give those to you the other day. Those are the shoes for the dress. I borrowed one of those sandals that Robert had bought you and took it with me when I picked those up—just to get the right size, mind you."

I removed the lid of the box and pushed aside the tissue that covered the mystery footwear. Beneath a double layer of tissue and several useless packets of desiccant, I found the burgundy peep-toe pumps. I pulled them out to inspect them and to my dismay, saw that the heels were much higher than anything I was used to, which was nothing at all.

"Thank you, Janice," I managed to say with a smile.

"You're welcome. Now, I know that I've kept you out of the loop as far as the wedding details go, but that's only because I know that all of this would probably bore you half to death. But I think I should let you know that the wedding starts at noon. You, Katie and I will be driving to the Bellegarde Family Retreat in about an hour and we'll be getting ready there."

My head cocked to the side as I took in what she had just told me. "The wedding is being held there?"

She nodded gleefully. "Yes, Ameila offered your father and me full use of the grounds at Christmas and we accepted. She offered to set up two tents and seating for the ceremony and reception, as well as one for getting ready which saved us an incredible amount of money, I cannot even begin to tell you, Grace."

My mind rushed rapidly through the hope that if Ameila was here, setting things up for Dad and Janice's wedding, perhaps Lark was with her as well. "Well, I'm glad that Ameila was generous enough to do this for you, Janice. Wait," I paused and looked at her carefully, "you didn't tell her she could cater the wedding, too did you?"

She shuddered and shook her head. "Oh no. Your father had only one request when I was planning the wedding, and that was that he choose the caterer—I guess he thought I'd be too nice to say no to Ameila had she offered."

"So she didn't offer," I asked.

Laughing, Janice shook her head once again. "No, she didn't offer at all, which was great, because that meant I didn't have to turn her down. Robert has a wonderful mother."

I bobbed my head in agreement. "Yes, he does."

Janice's eyes flicked to the clock on my dresser and then gasped. "Oh goodness, you'd better get in the shower, Grace. Katie is downstairs putting some stuff in the car. You can meet her when you're done."

She looked at me, as though deciding something, and then grabbed me in a brief and uncomfortable hug. I didn't have time to return it when she let me go and rushed out, a curler coming loose as she did so.

I placed the box that was still in my hands and reached over to my nightstand. I pulled its only drawer open and grabbed the phone that lay inside. Quickly, I dialed Stacy's number and waited for someone to answer.

"Uh, hello?" a rough voice answered on the other end.

"Hi, this is Grace, Stacy's friend—could I speak to her please?"

I heard a shuffling sound and a few thumps before I could detect the muffled voice of Stacy on the other end.

"Give me the phone, you jerk!" she snapped.

"You heard mom, no phone calls before ten. You're so going to get-ow!" the other voice replied before the sound of the receiver dropping on the floor caused me to pull my own away from my ear.

"Grace? Is that you?"

Putting the phone back against my face, I responded. "Yeah, it's me."

"What's up? You have to be quick—my mom has this rule about the phone ringing before ten in the morning," she said hurriedly.

I spoke as quickly as I could, hoping to get everything out before Stacy's mother discovered her on the phone. "Janice just told me that Ameila offered to hold the wedding at their family retreat, which means that she's going to be here. If she's here, there's a chance that Lark might be as well."

"Do you know for sure?" Stacy asked before a distinct click ended our conversation.

"Stacy? Stacy?" I called into the receiver, but the beeping sound of a disconnected call confirmed what I knew. "Ugh, why don't you have a normal mom like everyone else?" I grumbled to myself before hanging up the phone and shoving it back into the drawer.

I glanced at the clock and, sighing with resignation, got up to get ready for my shower.

⚃

Katie, Janice's sister, was exactly what I had expected: a shorter, somewhat younger version of Janice with bottle-dyed blonde hair and sparkling blue eyes. She was very adept with a set of rollers as she somehow managed to turn my perfectly disastrous head of hair into a mound of curlers and pins in a matter of minutes.

While I sat and stared at my lumpy, almost abstract-shaped head, Katie was busy putting the final touches of spackle onto Janice's face. I had to hand it to her; she was very quick and skilled when it came to transforming someone into someone completely different. Janice looked ten years younger, her skin flawless, her lips miraculously fuller than they had been this morning.

"The trick is brushing your lips first with a toothbrush before applying those new lip plumping glosses they have out now," she told Janice who apparently had asked what it was that she had done to create such an illusion.

"I won't look like I got punched in the mouth, will I?" Janice asked with concern as she gently touched her bottom lip.

"Oh God, no, Jan; you'll just look like you got some work done but no one will know how," Katie laughed.

I looked at Janice's lips once more and pulled my own in, tucking them beneath my teeth—I did not want to look like I had been punched in the mouth; wearing a dress I hadn't seen yet was bad enough. I spied Katie looking at me from the corner of my eye and I quickly turned my head in the opposite direction, not wanting to get her attention—the longer it took for her to get to me, the better.

"Grace, have you taken a look at your dress yet?" she asked me from behind Janice. I turned my head to look at her, unsure how exactly to go about answering her without drawing her into a conversation.

"No."

"Well, let's take it out so that you can see it and try and figure out what you want for your makeup, alright?" she said as she reached for the smaller white bag that hung across a garment rack. We were in a small tent several feet away from where the reception ceremony would be held, the sound of activity quietly humming just beyond the canvas walls.

"I helped Janice pick this out, but she thought the original color was all wrong, so she ended up choosing something different—oh, Jan, this will look beautiful on her."

I couldn't help it; I turned my head to look. The bag had been pulled away from the dress, allowing me to see it in its entirety. It was another strapless number, this time in a dark, almost blood-red shade. The bodice was a mass of shirred, shimmering fabric that ended in a cinched, empire waist, accented with hundreds of tiny, matching crystal beads, the skirt falling down beneath them like a waterfall of red wine. "Wow," was all I could manage to say.

"Do you like it?" Janice asked, a tinge of worry easily detectable in her voice.

"Yes," I whispered as I stood up to take a closer look. The dress draped to the ground, and I now understood the necessity of the suicidal heels. "I was afraid—I thought you'd get me something pink…with ruffles," I admitted as I touched the glimmering little beads sewn into the dress. "It's a stunning dress, Janice."

Katie clapped her hands and Janice sighed with relief at my response, obviously worried that my distaste for dresses would automatically cause me to dislike the dress.

"Alright, well now that we know that you like it, let's talk about makeup, Grace," Katie said as she began to pull a few bottles and jars from the large bag she had brought with her. "Do you want a dramatic eye or something more natural? If we go natural, we'll have to do a darker, dramatic lip and vice versa."

I stared at her in utter confusion, the words sounding more like a foreign language than anything I had ever heard before. "What?"

Janice coughed, a blatant attempt to mask her laughter as she tapped her sister on her arm. "She doesn't use makeup, Katie, so asking her about it really won't help. You're going to have to take the reins on this one."

Katie nodded in understanding and began to pull out a few more items from her bag, including several brushes and tubes. "Well, since it looks like I'm being given complete liberty here, I'm going to give you a fabulous new face."

I opened my mouth to argue but Katie quickly pushed my chin up, closing my mouth and effectively silencing me with the swipe of a brush. I sat there for the next twenty minutes as she began to dab and sweep, brush and buff my face into something completely unrecognizable. I watched the progress in the mirror that had been set up and tried my best to hide my fear that by the time she was done, my face would be caked with so much gunk, I'd be too top heavy to even make it down the aisle.

"Okay, and we're done!" Katie exclaimed when she stepped away to allow me to admire her work.

"I don't look like me," I uttered as I turned my face side to side, the makeup heavy and completely masking the face that I had grown up seeing every day in the mirror.

"Yes, that's the whole point, Grace," she said, exasperated. "I'm going to go and do my makeup and then it'll be time for your hair. Do *not* try to undo anything that I've done," she warned.

I nodded grimly and then turned my glaring eyes to Janice, who looked extremely apologetic. "She can get a little carried away—I'm sorry, Grace. Would you like me to help you wipe some of that stuff off?"

Shaking my head, I closed my eyes so that I wouldn't have to see myself in the mirror anymore. I walked over to the entrance of the tent and peeked out at the activity going on outside. Two large tents had been set up, one near the gazebo where the ceremony would take place, and another in the open field for the reception.

Tables and chairs had been set up in there, the chairs wrapped in ivory material with a large bow in the same color as my dress accenting each back. There were flowers everywhere, their scent masking the smell of freshly mowed grass, and workers were busy hanging up large chandeliers from the top of the tent.

I could see nothing of Robert or Ameila, though if they were indeed helping to set up, I wouldn't have been able to see them anyway; their movements were so quick. I tucked my head back inside and looked at the bag that I had brought with me. I had packed the corset that Lark had picked out when Robert had purchased all of the items for our first date, as well as some of the jewelry items that Robert had bought, though even I knew that they wouldn't match the dress.

Knowing that I'd have to be dressed first so that I could help Janice, I grabbed my dress, ducked behind the changing screen that was set up in the room and began to remove my jeans and shirt. I opened up the bag and pulled the corset out, then stared at it dumbly. "Janice," I called out.

"Yes, Grace," she answered, coming over to stand on the opposite side of the screen.

"Um…could you help me put this corset on?"

I heard her soft laugh as she walked around and nodded. "Of course." She helped to loosen the laces and slipped the corset over my head. She then tightened and tied the laces, being careful to leave enough room for me to breathe.

"Thank you," I said with gratitude and she smiled with affection. "You're welcome, Grace."

She left me alone to change, and I hurried, quickly pulling the gown up over my hips and then zipping the dress up as far as I could before my arms became too short. I walked out, carefully lifting the hem of the dress off the ground and presented myself to Janice for her approval.

"Oh, you're beautiful," she exclaimed, her hand covering her mouth as she took in me wearing her dress for the first time. "That color suits you so well," she said, her eyes glassing over. "I am so glad that the sales woman at the store said that someone like you deserved a color fit for a queen. Merlot—that's the name of the color—is definitely fit for you, Grace. And the style suits you with those beautiful shoulders of yours."

I blushed at the compliments and patted my cheeks to try and tamp them down. I pointed to my back and asked if she wouldn't mind zipping me up the remaining few inches.

"Okay, I'm all done, so let's get started on your hair, Grace," Katie said from her chair in front of the mirror. She turned to look at me and grinned with an almost child-like enthusiasm. "I don't know if you have a boyfriend or not, Grace, but if you don't, you will by the end of tonight!"

I looked at Janice who shook her head, and I grinned. "Can you get my hair done quickly so that I can help Janice get dressed?" I asked her.

"Oh yes, I already know what we're doing to your hair."

I looked at Janice, panicked, and groaned when I saw the bobby pins being pulled out of the now endless bag of Katie's. "How many of those are you going to stick in my head?"

Katie laughed rather maniacally, and pushed the bobby pins to the side. "I'm only going to use a few. I thought I'd play up that whole Asian side of yours with some chopsticks!"

My eyes grew wide and I looked at Janice once again, my face too stiff with makeup to do anything but mouth a silent question.

Janice nodded and quickly grabbed her sister's hand before it emerged from her bag with the eating utensils. "Katie, how about we just put Grace's hair in a nice little half-up, half-down up-do?"

Katie shook her head at that idea, obviously set on styling my hair to look like a bowl of brown noodles. "I've got a theme going on here, Jan. It's going to look fabulous. Trust me; look at what I did with her face!"

Janice looked at my struck expression and forced Katie to drop the chopsticks. "She doesn't want her hair styled that way, Katie. Just do a nice and simple up-do, alright?"

Katie looked at my panic stricken face and sighed. "All right," she conceded. "But if no one asks you to dance, that won't be my fault."

I took solace in that and allowed Katie to turn my mass of curlers into a river of chocolate brown curls, some piled on top of my head and draping off to the side, while the rest flowed down my neck and back. I was surprisingly pleased with the result and made sure that I let Katie know, if only as a consolation for not allowing her to use her chopsticks.

I turned to look at Janice, who also seemed very pleased with the outcome of my hair, and proceeded to grab the remaining garment bag from off the closet bar. I pulled down the zipper and gently removed the ivory gown from its vinyl enclosure. It was another strapless gown, beaded with sequins and crystals all along the bodice, followed by a beaded trim, ending in a flowing shower of gauzy material.

"Isn't it beautiful?" Janice cooed as she looked at it from over my shoulder.

362

"It is," I agreed, carefully removing the support straps from the hanger. "Is this meant for pregnant women?"

She nodded happily. "I've always loved this particular designer, and I cannot begin to tell you how pleased I was to find a maternity wedding dress in just this style. With my blimp of a belly, I need something that can drape over it but not make me look like I'm wearing a tent."

"Well, I don't know much about dresses, but this definitely won't look like a tent on you," I agreed.

With Katie's help, we managed to get Janice into her strapless slip, and then together we slipped the wedding dress over her head, carefully pulling it over her belly and hips. I tugged the zipper up behind her and tucked the pull into the cleverly designed seam.

"What are you wearing on your feet, Jan?" Katie asked, turning around to look for Janice's shoes.

"Nothing."

"Nothing?" Katie exclaimed, shocked at the idea of walking down the aisle barefoot.

Janice nodded. "My feet are the size of boats, Katie. Nothing I tried on looked right or fit, and since my feet seem to grow more and more bloated each day, I figured if I wanted to be comfortable on my wedding day, I'd be better off going barefoot.

"I already spoke to Ameila about it and she said she'd take care of everything, so I'm not wearing anything."

Katie snorted and shook her head. "How bohemian of you, Jan. I guess it'll make for an interesting story to tell your grandkids, but I can't help but wonder what mother would have said."

"I would think she'd be too busy complaining about my pregnant belly to care about my bare feet, Katie. In any case, help me get my hair out of these curlers. I don't want to be late for my own wedding!"

Katie and I began to unpin the rollers from Janice's hair and I watched as Katie quickly brushed out the tight spirals and began to pin them into lovely waves framing Janice's face. She tucked and tugged until every single strand of Janice's hair was pinned up in a soft, upswept style that complimented her heart-shaped face.

"Okay," I said once Katie stepped aside to admire her handiwork. "I don't know much about what else I'm supposed to do, but I wrote this part down." I grabbed a pen and a piece of folder paper from my bag and began to go down the list that I had written out. "Now that I've helped you dress, I'm supposed to make sure that you've got the four traditional gifts a bride is supposed to have before she goes down the aisle. Something old, something new, something borrowed, something blue."

Katie began to fasten something around Janice's neck and then nodded with satisfaction. "There's your something old, Jan: Mother's cameo choker from Gamma Barbara."

I looked at my list and crossed that out. "Okay, your dress is something new-" I crossed that out as well "-now all we have to do is get you something blue and borrowed."

Janice laughed and pointed to the back of her legs. "I've got blue covered—varicose veins aplenty behind my knees."

"That doesn't count, Jan," Katie scoffed. She turned to look at me and I saw her gaze lower to my hand. "That's it! Right there, on your finger—you could loan Janice that ring of yours, Grace! It's blue and it'll be borrowed. That's perfect!"

I looked at my hand and saw that she was speaking of the ring that Robert had given me, its deep blue stone shining brightly, even in the poor lighting of the tent. I looked at Janice and saw that she disapproved her sister's suggestion, but I saw the sound reasoning behind it. I wiggled the ring off my finger and handed it to her. "Here, Janice. It's exactly what you need and I don't want you to start off your wedding missing anything."

I saw Janice shaking her head, her refusal on the tip of her tongue, and I pushed the ring into her hand. "Don't say no, Janice. It's my job to make sure you get everything you need to make this day perfect, so don't help me fail."

364

Katie grabbed the ring out of Janice's hand and began to push it onto her fingers, searching for one that would allow the small silver band to slip on. It finally slid down the pinky finger of her right hand and Katie and I sighed with relief. "There," Katie said, smiling, "everything is perfect."

The flap to the tent pulled open and one of the most beautiful women I have ever seen stepped through wearing a simple gray dress that would have looked drab on anyone else, but on her, it looked like she was a walking thundercloud, demanding the attention of everyone around her.

"Janice! Aren't you a vision!" Ameila declared, her hands extending to take a hold of Janice's. "I do believe that James is probably the luckiest man on Earth."

"Ameila, I want to thank you from the bottom of my heart for all that you've done for me," Janice said with sincerity. "I don't know what we would have done without you."

Ameila waved her hand at that. "Stop—after you went out of your way to invite my family to your home for our first Thanksgiving and Christmas here, the least that I could do was offer you my hospitality. Besides, we're family, are we not?"

Janice smiled and nodded, and the two women embraced in a friendly hug.

Ameila turned then to look at me and smiled softly. "Grace, as always you eclipse everyone. I commend your future step-mother on choosing such a fitting dress for you, and in such a striking color! Just wait until Robert sees you in it. He promised to be very good and not peek—it will definitely be worth the wait."

Finally, she turned to address Katie, who seemed too shocked to do anything but stare in awe of the ethereal beauty that was Ameila. "You must be Janice's sister, Katie." When Katie only managed to nod, Ameila grabbed her hand in a reassuring gesture. "I am Ameila, a family friend."

I bit back a snicker when Katie couldn't muster anything other than a squeak and then looked at Ameila. I suddenly felt the urgent need to ask her about Lark jump to the forefront of my thoughts. And then I saw it—it was so fast, I would have missed it if I had been as entranced by her as Janice and Katie were—she shook her head quickly, a warning not to broach the subject. I frowned, but nodded in understanding.

"Well, I just wanted to check on the bride and let you know that your groom is waiting for you," Ameila said with a forced smile that still managed to take your breath away. "Grace, when you hear the music start, I want you to walk out of the tent and follow the white runner towards the gazebo, alright?"

"Alright," I agreed.

"Katie, since you're walking Janice down the aisle, I want you to count to twenty after Grace leaves and then it'll be your turn. Take slow steps so that the guests can appreciate Janice's dress." When she noticed Katie's downcast expression, she smiled at her and added, "We also want everyone to take notice of her hair and makeup, since you did such an excellent job on hers." She made it a point to emphasize "hers", and then turned to leave.

"The next time I see you, you'll be Mrs. Janice Shelley," she said with a wink just before she exited the tent.

Janice beamed at those words, a delighted glow appearing on her face. I took heart in that and waited for my cue. As soon as I heard the music, my legs pulled me forward, and I was nearly out of the tent when Katie cried out, "Your shoes!"

Quickly, she found the box and helped me slip them on, helping to steady me as I teetered dangerously. "Are you okay?" she asked after a moment, and I nodded. "Good. Now, hurry!"

She gave me a good shove and I stumbled out of the tent, my arms flailing like two demented windmills. I would have fallen flat on my face in front of the guests had it not been for the strong hand that managed to grab a hold of one flapping arm just before my nose made contact with the white runner beneath my feet.

"You, my dear, are in need of an escort."

I stared down at a pair of perfectly polished shoes and knew instantly who it was that had rescued me from making an utter fool of myself. "You must be addicted to saving me," I said jokingly as I raised my head to stare into his pewter eyes.

"I might be the one in need of saving by the way you take my breath away," he replied, helping me to stand upright. "However, there's something that's just not right." With lightning fast hands, he pulled out something from the pocket on his jacket and began to wipe my face. Though he was quick, he was also infinitely gentle.

He stood back, scrutinizing me with a sight I knew could detect even the most microscopic of flaws, and sighed in satisfaction. "That is much better. I don't like it when I cannot see your freckles—they are some of the most beautiful things I have ever seen."

A head popped out from a slit in the tent and we both turned to stare at Katie, who looked furious that I hadn't managed to take one step beyond the tent yet. "Why are you still here?" she snapped before turning to look at Robert. Instantly, her demeanor changed and a smile began to spread across her face. "And who are you," she asked in a sultry voice.

I decided right then and there that I didn't really like Katie very much.

"Hello," Robert greeted, the smile he gave in return turning her cheeks bright crimson. "My name is Robert Bellegarde; this is my family's retreat, and this-" he looked at me with loving eyes "-is the love of my life."

I choked on his words, and he gently patted my back, the smile never leaving his face. Katie's did, however, and for a split second I was reminded of another bottle-blonde who hadn't taken the news that Robert had chosen me to fall in love with that well.

"The music has started—you should get going," she said to me curtly before pulling her head back through the slit.

Robert chuckled as he held his arm out to me and I took it obligingly, grateful for his help and glad that he didn't like the new and improved me; the old me suited him just fine.

I looked towards my dad standing at the top of the gazebo, anxiously awaiting his bride, and I nodded. "Yes."

We began walking, Robert's pace matching mine step for step, and I smiled—a silly, goofy, weird and altogether un-Grace-like smile—and I didn't care. My dad looked so happy and young that I could almost picture what he had looked like when he had married my mom. I saw Stacy sitting in the second row, her pale face glowing from her own brand of happiness. She winked at me and nodded to her side. I looked to the seat beside her and felt a burst of joy within me as I saw Graham sitting beside her, a coy smile on his face.

I turned to look at Robert, whose wide grin was enough to draw forth a rush of heat to my face that had nothing to do with the people staring at the odd couple we made. Robert led me to my designated spot below the steps leading up to the gazebo and then took a seat next to Ameila, the only other unoccupied seat. I felt a slight twinge of dismay, but as the melody playing changed to a more romantic tune, I shook the thought out of my head. This moment was all about Dad and Janice. There would be time for questions later.

IN YOUR DREAMS

Having never been to a wedding before, I had no basis for comparison when it came to how the vows and the ceremony went for Dad and Janice. But from what I saw, what I heard, and what I felt during the brief ceremony, I knew that Dad and Janice had just shared one of the most happiest moments in their lives.

I'd never heard Dad speak so lovingly about anyone other than Mom before, and though a part of me still felt some sadness that he was saying these words to a different woman, I also felt wholly grateful to Janice for finally being the person that made him fall in love again.

It also helped that she totally did not mind, and in fact laughed when the song that played when they made their way down the aisle after they had been pronounced man and wife was none other than a meowing version of "Celebration".

The reception began with typical fanfare, though I was too busy staring at everything that had been done since I had popped my head out of the dressing tent to peek at the preparations. The chandeliers that had been hung from the top of the tent were blazing with light, their crystal facets dangling down, sparkling with an almost impossible amount of sparkle. I pointed to them and looked at Robert, who winked, knowing exactly what I was thinking—of course he would.

Stacy and Graham found us rather quickly and I threw my arms around Graham, still shocked that he had flown back home to attend a spring wedding in Ohio rather than a bikini party in Miami. "You have got to tell me how you got back here," I told him as we sat down at the table that had been reserved for us. "Did you know you were going to come back?"

He shook his head and began to drum his fingers against the table, a sure sign that he was nervous. "I didn't know what I was doing until I got on that plane, to be honest with you. I just couldn't deal with sitting at my mom's place and wondering what's going on here. I told my mom that I had to come back, and she didn't argue—she changed my ticket and I flew home."

Stacy grinned at me and nodded her head. "I called him this morning—after ten—and of course his mom was telling me that he wasn't there, that he'd left to come home and why wasn't I at the airport picking him up—I was a wreck when I picked him up, let me tell you—I must have broken about ten traffic laws and about a dozen laws of physics just to get to the airport."

Graham laughed and pointed to Stacy's hair. "She has hair just like yours when you wake up, Grace. It's hysterical! She came racing up to the curb to get me and jumped out of the car with her hair looking like some kind of Medusa head or something and I swear, she scared some kid standing next to his mom. Poor kid just started screaming like she was going to eat him or something."

I began laughing as Stacy started to pummel Graham's arm, her fists missing their mark more often than not because she was too busy laughing to concentrate, and even Robert found this amusing enough to join in.

Graham began nodding his head and grinned at me once the laughter died down. I stared at him, my mouth pulled up on one side in a smirk, and asked him what he was smiling about.

"You. Who'd have thought that Grace Shelley would be sitting at a wedding wearing a fancy dress and high heeled shoes? And looking pretty darn good, too, if I do say so myself—no offense, Robert—which would make quite a few girls at school mighty jealous."

I rolled my eyes at his comments, but Robert nodded his head and grinned as well. "I helped," he said cockily. He pulled out the handkerchief that he had used to wipe my face and threw it at Graham. "That contains nearly three-quarters of the makeup that was plastered onto her face. For a short while, she was a completely different person."

Stacy grabbed the handkerchief from Graham's grasp and opened it up, gagging as she realized the amount of makeup that had been on my face. "Good grief, what was she trying to cover?"

I chuckled and pointed to my face, as though that were explanation enough. Robert pushed my hand down and clicked his tongue in disapproval. "You know that's not true," he insisted.

"I know that she put so much makeup on me if I had leaned forward too far, I'd have fallen over. Actually, I *did* fall over."

Stacy snorted and threw the handkerchief up into the air, shaking her head as it landed onto the table with an audible sound. "I've heard of being top-heavy, but never when it came to someone's face."

The conversation died then as guests started to fill up the tent, each one stopping by our table and the one occupied by Dad and Janice to congratulate us on the marriage, or to compliment us on our clothes, our hair, and so on. It was rather tedious to pretend that I appreciated their comments, because in truth, I was more embarrassed than pleased, my face burning with it. As each person or couple filed past us, I became more and more convinced that I was never going to get married if getting married resulted in so much attention.

"I'd love to see you in a wedding dress one day," Robert whispered into my ear as he nuzzled it with his nose, breathing in the scent of my hair—I hope he enjoyed the aroma of four cans of hairspray.

"Dream on," I whispered back, never breaking my smile as the last few guests paid us a visit before heading back to their tables.

"Why?" Robert asked, his whisper sounding more like a hiss. "You speak of wanting to spend the rest of *your* life with me, yet don't see yourself getting married to me?"

I looked at him and frowned. *I'm eighteen years old—the last thing I want to talk about is getting married. I understand that it's natural for people to want to think about it at weddings, but not me.*

Robert pulled away and stared at me, his expression one of puzzled annoyance. In an effort to distract myself from his glaring eyes, I grabbed my napkin and unfolded it slowly, almost methodically. I shook it out thoroughly, as though doing so would somehow erase the creases that had formed in the thick linen before placing it on my lap.

"Are you sure you shook out all of the wrinkles?" Stacy quipped as she laid hers onto her lap with careless speed.

"I'm just trying to make sure I cover up enough—I don't want to spill anything on this dress," I improvised quickly.

Graham held his glass up to be filled with some pinkish looking beverage and grinned. "So, what's on the menu?"

"I have no clue," I replied truthfully. "Janice let Dad choose the caterer—I didn't even know the wedding was going to be here until this morning, so you can imagine just how much I know about the food."

Stacy pulled up a little card that had been lying on her plate and began to read it out loud. "This afternoon's late lunch has been catered by the Angels' Street Mission." She held it out to Graham who took it and began to read off the menu.

"Appetizers—Asparagus Wrapped in Bacon—hey, that's my kind of appetizer! Soup—Lentil and Ham with Roasted Butternut Squash—great, more rabbit food. Main Course—Your Choice of Wild Rice Stuffed Chicken Breast or Warm Steak Salad with Blue Cheese Vinaigrette—I feel cheated, totally cheated by this menu."

Robert grabbed the menu from Graham's hand and completed the listing. "For Dessert, White Chocolate cake with Blackberry Filling with White Chocolate Ganache Frosting prepared by the ladies at the Angels' Street Mission."

He placed the card onto his plate and smiled, obviously appreciating the name. "I think that that was a wonderful idea—having the mission cater this wedding."

Stacy nodded in agreement. "We give the kids there free lessons on the weekends. This was an excellent idea."

"I didn't know your dad knew anything about that place," Graham said as he watched while servers carrying overly large trays piled with plates of Asparagus began to walk towards the tables. "But I don't care either—bring on the grub!"

I rolled my eyes and looked over to my dad, his face beaming as he watched while everyone was being served. I didn't know how much he and Janice had intended to spend on this wedding, but with Ameila taking care of most of the costs, the majority of their budget was available to do with as they pleased and it made me feel inordinately proud that Dad had chosen to help one of the charities here instead.

"Are you going to eat that, Grace?"

I turned around and saw Graham staring at my plate hungrily. I looked down and saw that a serving of the appetizers had been placed in front of me. Shaking my head, I handed the plate to him. "Here—I'm not a fan of asparagus."

Robert handed his plate to Graham as well, giving him the excuse that he wasn't a fan either. He then turned to look at me, using this opportunity to continue the conversation that I had wrongly assumed was over.

You need to explain to me why simply talking about marriage sounds so abhorrent to you.

I looked away as I responded, not wanting to see the reaction in his eyes. *I'm not that girl—the girl who spends her childhood thinking about the guy she would marry, the guy who would rescue her from her prison tower. The only time I ever thought about who it was that I wouldn't mind getting married to, it ended up being Graham.*

I waited for the response, but when none came I felt a slight panic come over me. I turned around, afraid that he wouldn't be in his seat when I did, more afraid that he would be.

Still here.

I giggled nervously, quickly covering my mouth with my hand. He grabbed it and pulled it down, pushing my chin up with his fingers, a warm smile on his face. *You don't have to worry about what I think anymore, Grace. I know what you felt for Graham, and I'm okay with it. You two have a history, a very long history that cannot be erased simply because I've entered your life.*

I shook my head and lowered my head, suddenly shy. *There's only ever been you.*

"Hey, are you two lovebirds just going to make googly-eyes at each other or are you going to actually eat?" Graham grumbled from his seat.

I looked in front of me and saw that a small bowl of orangey soup had been served. "How does it taste?" I asked, as my eyes took in the orange lumps that floated just beneath the liquid's surface.

Stacy snorted. "He apparently enjoys it a lot more than he thought he would because he's already tried to take mine."

Robert handed over his bowl to a grateful Graham, then turned to look at me once more. "Aren't you hungry?"

I shook my head. "No."

"Why not?"

"I haven't really been that hungry lately," I admitted. "I guess I've been too concerned over all that's been happening."

"You need to eat, Grace. Your human body needs sustenance to operate."

Graham grunted his agreement. "You should eat more, Grace. You've lost a lot of weight these past few weeks—of course that might have more to do with Janice's cooking, but this soup is good; you should at least try some."

Stacy grinned. "Yeah, Grace. You should try it. Who knows, you might like it so much, you might be serving this at your own wedding someday."

I glowered at her, sinking into my chair as she laughed at my reaction. "Why is everyone so obsessed with me getting married?" I grumbled, not understanding the fascination with the idea.

"Because it's a wedding, and you're the next natural choice—you and Robert aren't going anywhere, not from what I can see, plus it makes sense," Stacy said between spoonfuls. "Besides, it's not like we're suggesting you get married right this instant. That would just be dumb."

Graham and Robert nodded, both of them grinning like loons, causing me to roll my eyes. "I'm not the next natural choice. You could meet Mr. Right here tonight," I remarked to Stacy, and began searching the crowd for someone to prove my point.

"Don't bother—I tried," she laughed. "Everyone here is either too old for me, works at your dad's Grocery store—which would make it too weird—or happens to be Graham, and we know how that went the first time around."

"You know, there's nothing wrong with getting engaged early and then postponing the wedding for a few years," Graham chimed in.

"Traitor," I hissed at him.

"What?" he said as he guffawed. "You know if you're trying to get Robert to propose, that's not exactly the best way to go about doing it."

That was it, the last straw—I had had it with the innuendos and the jokes. I stood up, threw my napkin into the bowl of cold soup, and stormed out of the tent, losing my shoe somewhere between the table and the last tent pole as I headed towards the park bench that seemed to be calling out to me.

I pulled off the other shoe so that I wouldn't look as ridiculous as I felt walking barefoot in a bridesmaid's gown, and, lifting the hem, closed the distance between me and the bench.

"Ugh," I grunted as tried to sit down without damaging the dress and stumbled, landing on the bench roughly, the hard surface sending shooting pains down my legs. "This wouldn't happen if I were wearing jeans," I complained as I pulled the skirt up and tucked it between my legs, assembling what could only have been the most pathetic attempt at a pair of makeshift pants anyone has ever seen.

"You know your friends were only kidding, right? The last thing on their minds is you and I getting married."

Robert sat down next to me, his eyes filled with humor, the smirk on his face quickly fizzling out the annoyance in me and replacing it with something warm and bubbly.

"I know," I replied. I tossed my head back and looked up at the sky.

"What are you doing?"

"I'm trying to find a star to wish on."

He watched me as I searched the still sky. When I finally spotted a familiar twinkle, I closed my eyes and silently made a wish.

"What did you wish for?" he asked me, gently lifting me from the cold, uncomfortable bench and placing me into his lap.

"It's a secret. Besides, couldn't you have just heard it yourself?"

He shook his head and laughed, his head tilting back to stare at the same shimmering light above us. "No—your wishes are your own. I only ask because I think you just wished on Venus."

I squinted and focused on the speck of yellowish-white light that I had pinned my latest hope to. "Are you sure?"

He shrugged his shoulders, his body still shaking from his laughter. "I could be wrong, but just in case I'm not, don't you think you should wish on something else? An angel, perhaps?"

"I don't think so," I said, laughing along with him. "I want to keep this one to myself for now."

His arms wrapped around my waist and he tugged me closer to him. Though I was sitting in his lap, his head still came above mine, which he used to rest his chin on. "Well, would you like to know what I wished for?"

"Did you wish on Venus, too?"

"So you do believe me!"

I chuckled. "It's the thought that counts, not the actual object you make your wish on, silly. And no, your wish is your own, just as mine is my own."

"Well then no, I didn't wish on Venus. I wished on that star over there." He pointed to a twinkling light closer towards the horizon and I burst into laughter.

"What?" he asked, taking a closer look at what he had just pointed to and then smiled. "Oh. I guess if you can't wish on Venus, I can't wish on a 777."

I shook my head, my laughter turning into hiccups as I watched the twinkling light he had wished on slowly move towards the Newark Airport.

"I wished that you would change your mind."

I stopped laughing.

"Change my mind about what?"

With a lone finger, he began to trace the line of my collarbone, slowly scraping across the rise of my chest, landing at the opposite end. "I thought you didn't want to know."

"Too bad; you opened your mouth, now you have to tell me," I argued.

His curious finger climbed the length of my neck, stopping to memorize the quickening pace of my pulse before moving up towards the curve of my jaw. One finger turned into two as he lifted my chin up, forcing my eyes to look up in order to gaze into his.

"I wished that you would change your mind about not turning, about not getting married, about a lot of things."

"I wished the same thing about you."

He chuckled, and smiled sadly. "See how well we suit? You are the yin to my yang, my perfect fit."

I frowned at the tone his voice took on, almost regretful. "What does that mean, exactly? I know what the words mean, so don't try to patronize me by giving me literal definitions—I want to know what you mean when you say those things to *me*. I don't want to hear the doublespeak you give to everyone else."

His eyes searched mine, the edges of his pupils pulling in and out as he sighed with such resolute sadness, I could almost taste it. "Just that whenever I think about what my life would be like without you in it, I see nothing."

"What do you mean by nothing?" I asked, turning my body around to face him, my hands placed on his shoulders to steady myself.

"I mean just that—you want to spend the rest of your life with me, right?" He waited for me to nod before continuing. "What happens, Grace, if the rest of your life means the next twenty minutes?"

I laughed at the absurdity of the suggestion—how could I die within the next twenty minutes if I were seated in the lap of Death himself?

Robert's hands gripped my arms and he shook me gently, the motion enough to put an end to my humor. "Grace, this isn't funny. Don't you see? I cannot be with you all of the time—I listened to you and stayed away from you, and now your mind is filled with memories that don't belong there. What if whoever put them there had chosen to do something else to you? I've seen your heart struggle to beat, seen your body battered and bruised, but dying comes in all forms and I can only put it off for so long before the consequences become too grave."

"What do you mean, put it off? Put what off?"

He looked away, his mouth set in a stubborn line, his eyes shut, as if to block images that I knew he could never fight away. "Your death."

I stared at him—the accusations, the gratitude stuck in my throat. He pressed his hand against the side of my face, pushing away some of the hair that had slipped from their pins and fallen into my eyes. "Each time I changed your fate, I lied to myself and said that it was because your father needed you, your friends would miss you, you didn't want to die—the truth is that I did it because I couldn't lose you. I refuse to.

"But, I cannot keep doing that, Grace. I cannot keep you from harm much longer, and the longer we stay together, the more dangerous life will get for you."

The threat in his words caused a shiver to run through my body and for the first time, I felt the chill spring air against my skin. I looked at him and I could see the raw fear in his eyes. "I've already been hit by a car and nearly strangled to death by your best friend. I nearly froze to death waiting for you on New Years, and now someone is messing with my mind. How can life get any more dangerous than that?" I joked.

He didn't laugh. "Grace, I have already gone against my call to keep you alive after Sam, but even if that weren't an issue, there are those of my kind who don't appreciate our type of relationship—they believe that by my loving you, I am breaking rules that were set up to protect both of our kinds. While I do not believe that they themselves would do any-thing deliberately to harm you, there are...others who feel the same way-"

"Wait...others—you mentioned them before—shape-shifters and werewolves—you were serious?"

Robert placed an arm beneath my legs, another around my back, and then lifted me as he stood up. He began walking further away from the wedding party, towards the line of trees that acted as a perimeter of the park grounds. He continued walking as the darkness loomed towards us, the cover of the trees turning a bright, spring afternoon into something sinister and dark.

Though there were thousands of leaves and twigs scattering the ground, I didn't hear a single snap or crunch as Robert had stopped walk-ing and simply floated through the maze of evergreens and oaks. I inhaled the scent of moss and wet soil, and something that I knew could only be described as green. It filled my lungs with its clean odor and, though I knew I should have been feeling nervous or slightly fearful, instead I felt giddy.

We finally stopped moving when I could barely see the light from the edge of the trees that promised sanctuary from all this darkness. I gasped as Robert lowered me to the ground, my bare feet landing on the spongy and crackling earth beneath me.

"Why are we here?" I asked, taking his hand and holding it securely in my own.

"You'll see," he replied.

I waited, but for what? I didn't know what to expect and tried to keep an open mind.

A snapping sound caused my head to whip around, and I stared, puzzled at an odd empty space to my right. I peered at it, the shadows seemingly not quite right. My hand reached out and I took a few steps forward before being tugged back by Robert, his head swishing back and forth in warning.

A soft laughter crept forth from directly in front of me and I watched in awe as the odd shadows started to blur, movement bringing the darkness of deep greens and browns closer to me. I gasped as a silhouette formed from the hazy jumble of colors, undistinguishable at first, but slowly melding together into something distinctly recognizable.

Within a few short moments, the figure of a woman stood directly in front of me. Her long hair was thick and mossy, the variegated green strands covered with tiny pink and violet blossoms that opened and closed as she breathed. It draped over her nude body like a living curtain, moving and flowing about her to hide the parts that would have made me blush. Her eyes were dark as tar—there was no white to them at all, making them stand out like two holes in the pinkish green of her face. She smiled at me, her pearl-like teeth the only part of her that didn't fit in the forestry of her body.

"Silly child," she said in an oddly musical voice that was too raspy to have been beautiful. "Do not be afraid of me—have you never seen a nymph before?"

I shook my head roughly, which made the tree-like lady laugh, the sound seemingly coming from everywhere and nowhere all at once.

"N'Uriel, I am surprised at your current choice of human—she's not at all like those vain creatures your Sam used to bring along for fun," she said to Robert, the lilt in her voice teasing, mocking.

The ground beneath her feet moved, pulling her forward though she herself never took a step, and stopped just millimeters from him. She was tall, I hadn't realized just how much until I saw her stand, nose to nose with Robert. "Pity he tried to rid you of her, otherwise he might still be here to talk to me. Your sister hasn't come to visit in far too long, and your mother has been busy with her little project."

She turned to look at me, her smile growing wider until it looked almost cartoonish in its size, the corners of her mouth reaching towards two leaf-like appendages that jutted out from the sides of her head that I could only assume were ears. "Perhaps now that we have met, you will stay and talk to me, tell me of things that go on in your world, yes?"

"Grace is not here to become your companion, Bala," Robert said woodenly.

The nymph slid back several feet, her smile fading, her dark eyes turning into jet black slits on her face. "Then why *did* you bring her here?" she hissed.

"She needs to see what else exists in this world, what else watches her when she thinks no one is looking."

Bala's lazy smile returned. "Ahh, so you came to frighten the poor child—but how afraid of dying can she be with Death as her soul mate?"

Robert turned to face me, a severe expression on his face. "Bala is a wood-nymph—hardly dangerous to you or me, but she can be very, *very* annoying."

I turned to look at the nymph Robert called Bala and bit back a gasp when she winked at me—it was like watching a piece of onyx disappear behind a leaf—and then slowly retreated towards her original location, speaking as she did so in a voice that sounded like the rattling of leaves against a piano wire. "Be careful, young one. He doesn't know what he's setting into motion by bringing our world into yours. He cannot protect you forever—you must learn how to protect yourself."

"How?" I asked before she disappeared once again, fading into the greenery around her.

"It's written in stone…" her voice sang, the sound disappearing into the rustle of leaves.

"Was that it? Was that what I have to be afraid of?" I asked, turning around to face Robert. "Robert?" He wasn't there.

"Robert?" I called out, spinning around in place, my head whipping back and forth, looking for any sign of him amongst the greenery. "Where are you?"

"He's watching you."

I turned around upon hearing the gravelly voice behind me.

"Uh-uh-uh, not over there either," the voice taunted, this time to my left.

I spun around, my heart starting to pick up speed. "Who are you?" I asked softly.

"Why don't you guess, and then I'll tell you whether or not you're right?"

I shook my head. "This isn't a fairy tale and you're not Rumplestiltskin."

I heard a low rumble coming from directly behind me and I slowly turned around, my fear intensifying by what I saw. A pair of eyes with scarlet rimmed, phosphorescent-jade irises stared out at me from the dark canopy.

They were deeply set in a face that should have been human but had lost its way somewhere, instead pulled down, long and narrow like that of a horse, but with a vaguely human nose and distorted mouth. That mouth, the lips grayish with cracks of deep black edging around them opened in a sick smile, baring horribly gray teeth that looked like they had been deliberately filed down to points.

"You're right about that for they never write about my kind in your fairy tales. I'm too real."

Something inside of me, something that I would later wish would have just shut up, forced me to stand up straighter, pushing my shoulders back and raising my chin—I stared at the creature defiantly as it approached me. "You're not original enough to read about," I said snidely as I took in its entire figure.

Though its head was like a horse, its body was more human-like, with a muscular torso that extended into two hairy arms with claw-like hands at each end. It wore a dark cloth over the majority of its lower half with only its large, club shaped feet peeking through, the toenails curling upwards, almost like some macabre form of living, elfin shoes.

"Interesting? I'm not *interesting*?" As if to prove me wrong, it began to shake, its body vibrating so rapidly it gave off a slight hum. I forced my feet to stay glued to the ground beneath me, unwilling to run away and leave my back exposed to whatever it was.

The smell of burning hair began to mix with the scent of the forest around me and I wrinkled my nose, slowly raising my hand to cover my face in a poor attempt to block the pungent smell from turning my empty stomach. The humming grew louder, transforming into a high-pitched whine before it simply stopped.

"Am I interesting now?" it said in a familiar voice and I screamed.

The once muscular arms were now lithe and graceful, the claws transformed into feminine hands that gently pushed its dark hair from its face. The cloth, though still draped over its body, did nothing to hide the womanly curves beneath it, the dainty feet peeking from beneath the hem completely belying what they had been just moments before.

"You're not-" I gasped, looking into the eyes that had changed from jade to a deep brown with a faint, nearly imperceptible crimson ring surrounding it. "You're not my mom," I whispered.

"No, I'm not, but I can see her in your face, I can see that she lives in your dreams, and that as frightened as you are, you're slightly grateful to me for showing you a pleasant image before you die."

I watched, horrified as the creature drew closer to me, but I remained rooted to the ground, determined not to show him the fear that threatened to send me bolting into the dark forest behind me. A dark fog began to surround us and I shuddered with relief as the creature stopped his approach, instead staring with curious eyes as the smoke began to swirl around me, thickening, deepening until an arm was pushing me backwards and Robert stood between the two of us.

"Hello, N'Uriel," the creature said in a perverted version of my mother's voice, contempt dripping from every syllable.

"You overstep your bounds, Erlking," Robert bit out.

Erlking laughed, a feminine laugh that brought tears to my eyes, it was so beautifully familiar and yet so frighteningly different. "You left her here for the sole purpose of frightening her. I have done my part and now I want payment. I haven't eaten human flesh in over a century, N'Uriel. I have behaved, I have followed your rules—let me have her; you owe me this much!"

Robert growled a warning, his arm pushing me behind him, his feet firmly planted to the ground, bracing for something—I did not know what. "I owe you nothing—she is not yours."

"She is not yours either, or have you forgotten the laws?"

Robert shook his head. "I have forgotten nothing, but you obviously have. You threatened a wing-bringer, Erlking. You know what the punishment for that is."

Erlking's eyes changed color, the brown quickly being swallowed up by the dark red rings as it began to shake with rage. "You did this deliberately! You used her as bait to get me to-"

It roared in unrestrained anger and charged, its hair and cloak blending into a frighteningly familiar halo of black hatred.

Everything that followed happened with blinding speed, and yet I didn't miss anything. A hand pulled me backwards as Robert flew forward, crashing into the figure that still looked so much like my mother I fought several times to keep from screaming out not to hurt her, the sound of the impact reminding me of an egg falling onto the floor. I struggled against the restraints that held me back, the sudden fear for Robert's life replacing every other emotion in me as the sound of scraping and crunching assailed my ears.

Suddenly, a high-pitched keening replaced all other sounds and I screamed Robert's name, needing him to hear me above everything else. The fight was over before I had gotten the last syllable out of my mouth, before I'd even managed a single blink.

Robert straightened while the black cloaked figure crumpled to the ground, more liquid than man. I felt the binding around my chest loosen and I flew forward, rushing to Robert without any thought save him. He turned around and welcomed me into the cocoon of his arms, the strength in them doing everything to reassure me that he was okay.

"Shh," he whispered into my hair. "I'm okay. It's alright. I was never in any danger, Grace. He never even touched me."

I didn't believe him—I began to examine him with my hands and eyes, rapidly moving them around his body, looking for any signs of injury or damage and seeing that nothing on him was even out of place—it was as if the entire scene that took place before me hadn't even happened. The only hint that alluded to anything having taken place was the odor of decayed foliage on his jacket. And...

I peeked around him, needing to see that whatever it was that had attacked him wouldn't do so again. I felt myself choke as the eyes of my mother stared out at me, her mouth moving slowly.

"Don't listen, Grace," Robert warned, but it was too late.

"He killed me, Grace. He killed me again, just like he's going to kill you," my mother's voice said as it slowly faded.

I shook my head and looked away, not wanting to see or hear any more.

"Bala-get rid of the body," another voice ordered.

My head picked up, and I stared in shock as Lark approached me, her hair flowing around her face wildly, her glow a fiery red. "You're here!"

"Of course I'm here—if I weren't you'd probably be missing a limb right about now, you stupid, reckless human!"

Her tone was as course as her words, but her face told a different story and I rushed to hug her, not realizing just how much I had missed seeing it. "Thank you," I whispered to no one in particular. "Thank you."

Sighing, she wrapped her arms around me, returning my embrace, albeit a bit stiffly. "I don't understand your kind. I insult you and you hug me."

I laughed, not caring how many insults she threw at me, just grateful that she was here and that she was alright.

"She's not alright. She shouldn't even be here," Robert said, glowering, picking the words out of my thoughts like a snowflake out of the air.

"And you shouldn't have tried to pull that stupid stunt of yours," she countered, motioning towards the slowly disappearing body of Erlking, who was sinking into a pile of dead leaves and branches, the earth swallowing him whole right before our eyes. "Honestly, Robert, an Erlking? You think that frightening Grace into agreeing to turn is the best route? She could have been killed!"

."*An* Erlking?" I questioned. "I thought his name *was* Erlking."

"We don't call them anything but what they are—Erlkings, shape-shifting creatures who feed on people," Robert informed me. "Another one of Miki's children; they can take on the shape of anything, any person, but unlike the typical shape-shifters that live freely in society, their natural form is grotesque and deformed, a result of their...diet."

I looked at him in horror. "You left me alone with him in here, just like he said...as bait."

He nodded. "Yes, but you were never alone, Grace. I was always here—he even told you that I was watching."

Lark clucked in disapproval. "That was irresponsible of you, Robert...but there's no time to discuss this now—we have company."

Robert and I turned around to face whoever it was that was approaching, each of us silently promising to deal with what just happened as soon as possible.

DECLARATION

"Grace! I came looking for you when you didn't come back and then I heard you scream—Robert, what happened—Lark…"

Graham's jacket was covered in dirt and bits of leaves as he approached us, ducking out of the way of a branch that I knew had not been there just minutes ago. "Whoa—" he shouted as he slipped on something, landing on his backside with a squish.

I rushed over to help him, hoping that whatever it was that Bala had done to the body of the Erlking wouldn't be discovered anytime soon. I began to laugh as I realized that in his haste to find me, Graham had forgotten to remove the napkin he had tucked into his pants.

"Great. I'm lying here in the mud, looking like an idiot while you stand there laughing," he muttered, yanking the cloth from out of his waistband.

Robert moved in front of me and offered Graham a hand, which he gladly accepted. "Thanks," he said, eyeing me. "You know, no offense, but this is a really terrible place for a family reunion. Why are you in here anyway? And why were you screaming?"

"I saw a…bug," I improvised quickly when I saw the struggle in Lark and Robert's eyes as they fought the urge to reveal the truth.

"A bug. You screamed because of a bug." Graham said suspiciously.

"It was a big bug," I replied stubbornly. "Huge. You would have freaked out if you had seen it, too. Where's Stacy? I find it hard to believe that you'd come here without her wanting to join you."

"Oh, she had to go to the restroom. She said she'd come and find us when she was done. Hi, Lark."

I turned around to look at her reaction to Graham's greeting. It was the first time he had spoken to her since before she left, the first time she had seen him since she'd overheard the words he had written down, his heart drenching several sheets of paper, line by line.

"Hello, Graham," she said shyly.

I turned around to look at Robert, worried that he'd interfere; terrified that he'd assume that I had somehow managed to set this up as well. His eyes narrowed, a frown burning creases into his forehead.

Not wanting to continue to face his scrutiny, I turned to look at Graham. He should have looked captivated; he should have looked lost in Lark's beauty and presence. Instead, he looked just as angry as Robert did. I opened my mouth, hoping to drive some sense into him, into both of them that this was not a moment to start fighting, but Robert pulled me away, my mouth shutting in surprise.

"Why did you leave?" Graham asked as soon as I was out of the way.

"I had to," Lark replied, her words heavy with hurt and guilt.

"You didn't have to. You could have stayed."

She shook her head defiantly. "No. I couldn't. I know what you want to say, Graham, but-"

"No, you don't know what I want to say. You don't have a clue what I want to say because you never stayed to hear them," Graham argued. "But you're going to now. You're going to hear how the minute I knew you were gone I couldn't think about anything else but where you were and if you were okay. You're going to hear about how difficult it was for me to write that letter to you, how hard it was for me to admit to things that I've never felt before, and how afraid I was that after finding out what it said, you'd think I was an idiot and too stupid for you to bother with.

"But most importantly, you're going to hear how painful it is to wake up every single day and not know how you feel. I can continue to love you forever—I didn't think that was possible and always thought Grace was being stupid for even saying stuff like that—but I cannot keep going around not knowing how you feel about me.

"It's pretty selfish of you, if you ask me, to not tell me how you feel. If you don't feel the same then okay, I can accept that. But at least tell me, dammit. I'm a big boy—I can take it. But if you do feel the same way, if you do care about me the same way that I care about you then you could at least let me know so that I don't have to keep repeating myself here."

Graham's breathing was thick, his chest rising and falling heavily as he finished, sweat starting to bead on his face from nervousness. Lark stepped forward and placed a hand against his forehead, slowly dragging the moisture away.

"I do care about you," she said softly. "I don't want to. I don't want to feel these things for you because it isn't right."

"Why isn't it right?" he asked in a low voice. "Why isn't it right for you to love me, too?"

"Because I promised I'd never love anyone else," came her whispered reply.

Graham's body stiffened…for a moment. And then his features softened as he realized something. "You loved someone else. I'm not the first."

She nodded slowly, sadly. Her eyes brimmed with tears that bided their time, waiting for just the right moment to fall. "I loved someone very much—someone who was taken away from me too soon—and I promised him that I'd never love anyone else, never feel that way ever again. I broke that promise the moment I met you and no matter how much I might feel for you, it doesn't erase the fact that it still hurts knowing I betrayed him."

"You shouldn't feel guilty for something you had no control over, Lark," Graham countered, his hand extending to her, seeking her acceptance.

"You don't get it—it physically *hurts* me, caring for you, missing you…loving you," Lark whispered before turning away, rejecting his outstretched hand. "I promised, swore on the very hope that it would be enough to last me forever that I'd never feel again what I felt for him. He accepted his fate because of that. We both did."

Graham approached her and placed his hands on her shoulders in gentle solace. "Who was he?" She shook her head and he tenderly pressed his cheek to the top of her head, a loving gesture that forced her head to bow with something I could not decipher—shame? Hurt? It was enough to cause Graham's arms to surround her shoulders, pulling her against him, and she did not resist. Instead, she allowed him the small gesture, and he asked her once more to reveal who "*he*" was.

With her head held down, she began to speak, her voice low and flat, the choir of caroling bells gone, replaced now with the sadness of empty hope.

"His name was Luca. He was my friend, my confidant. He knew all of my secrets—the ones I could keep, anyway—and he never shared them with anyone, no matter how desperate or dark they were. He was just like me—independent, free-spirited, and cynical of everything and everyone. We didn't see the reason or the purpose behind what it was that we were, what it was that we were meant to do, meant to be. He felt that our existence wasn't just about duty and obligation—that was going to happen no matter what. Life, he said, was about living. With all that we can do, why do we not let everyone know what we're capable of, he asked. What good was being able to do such incredible things if we had to keep it to ourselves?

"Together we disrupted the careful balance that had been set up by millennia of those who came before us. We went wild, running around like two love-struck individuals with more power than we deserved and too poor judgment. We terrorized everyone and everything.

"We created what was destroyed, destroyed what was created—we had no care for life, for thought, or for love save our own. It was the most exciting and thrilling time in my entire life; he made me feel alive, feel for the first time that those invisible chains that hold all of our kind down with inherent rules and restrictions were loosening their hold, that we could break them and finally be free.

"By the time the Seraphim learned of our havoc, several decades had passed and we had done much to ruin our image in the eyes of the humans who should have been able to turn to us for help—now they ran away from us, seeking aid and solace in other things. Almost too late, I started to realize that what we did was wrong.

"We were hurting not only others, but ourselves as well. And the worst crime imaginable had been committed time and time again: We had caused the humans to lose faith in us, in our kind. My mother—though she was gravely disappointed in me— convinced the Seraphim to give me another chance, to have the faith in me that I had stripped from others. But…Luca had no one to speak out for him.

"He was stripped of everything; his abilities, his strength…even his beauty. He was sentenced to live a mortal life among the very people that we had terrorized. This is as close to a death sentence as one can get for our kind—it is the cruelest of punishments and the worst of fates.

"I chose to stay with him, having found no justice in his being allowed to die while I remained healthy and alive. I watched him age, watched his human body suffer illness and wear, and I did it while enduring his never ending rage against me for not doing more to help him, not doing more to convince my mother and the Seraphim to be as lenient and forgiving with him as they were with me….not suffering with him.

"The slowest time period in my life spanned less than a year—I knew that the human mind, when aged and allowed to decay, could turn vile and angry; what I did not know was that *our* minds could as well.

"Luca's anger grew uncontrollable and violent, with him never realizing that his lashing out never hurt me…just himself. His once divine flesh, so strong and beautiful, bruised horribly, his bones breaking like glass thrown against a stone wall. He forgot who I was after a while, resorting to calling me 'girl' whenever he needed me to help clean him up after his body had lost all ability to control its functions.

"The more difficult it became for him to survive without help, the angrier he became, and I was always the target for his rages, though after a while they became more verbal than physical as he weakened even further.

"When at last Luca's mortal heart gave out, when God finally took pity on him and called him home, only then did he remember who I was, and he made me promise that no one else would ever mean as much to me as he did. I promised him that there would be no one else, that for the rest of my existence I would only feel that way for him. I lied to him and it's killing me."

"He did not love you, Lark-" Robert ground out. "He used you to fulfill his sick, perverted games. He hurt humans for fun, destroyed countless lives all in the name of rebellion that served no purpose other than to amuse. He lied to you to further his deception. Love doesn't deceive-"

"Love doesn't deceive you say? You're one to talk, brother!" Lark snarled. "When will you confess to Grace about your own deceptions?"

"What? What deceptions? What does she mean?" I asked, my heart thudding loudly in my chest at the implication in her voice.

"Wait a minute-" Graham cut in.

The three of us turned to him, just remembering he was there.

"What are you talking about?" he said with nervous laughter. "You're speaking like you're a lot older than sixteen, Lark—what's this about several decades? Powers? Humans? Watching someone grow old? What is going on here? What are you talking about?"

Lark and Robert looked at each other, their eyes wide with shock, their mouths stubbornly set in defiance.

"Will someone tell me what's going on? Lark?" Graham snapped, his arm releasing Lark and turning her around to face him.

"Graham, now's not the time to-"

Graham turned to face me, his eyes blazing with anger. "Shut-up, Grace!" he barked, cutting me off. "I've always known that I wasn't exactly allowed into your whole 'circle of friends' thing here—not after what I did to you last summer—but this has got to be some kind of twisted joke, right? All this talk about powers and Seraphim and…mortals—is this some kind of obsessive fantasy game scenario you guys have cooked up or something, because right now, that's the only thing that makes any sense."

I looked at Robert, whose head was turned away, refusing to answer. Lark was also stubbornly looking the other way, her lip trembling with hurt and…fear. "Are you guys just going to let him keep asking?" I shouted at them. "Lark, you let him hear all of that, but you won't tell him anything else? You won't even explain any of it?"

She turned her head to glare at me, the tears that sat at the base of her bottom lid threatening to spill at any moment. "He wanted to know—I told him the truth."

I shook my head angrily. "No. No, you didn't tell him the truth—you told him *part* of the truth. He deserves to know everything. He poured his heart out to you and you weren't even *there* when he wrote that letter, so you know that this has nothing to do with charm or-" I looked at Robert, a fissure of pain starting to wind its way through my heart "-deception. You know that what he feels for you is real. Tell him the truth. He deserves that much."

Graham looked at me with hurt in his eyes, and then switched his gaze to Lark, whose tears finally fell forward, tumbling down her face. Graham reached out to catch one and then gasped as the cold stone hit the palm of his hand.

"What…?" he breathed.

"There you are!"

Stacy stumbled through the thick brambles, her shoes in one hand, the hem of her dress in another. "I swear, if I knew you three were planning on going hiking, I'd have worn a better outfit; this dress is totally ruined—my mother is going to kill me when she sees it. What's going on? Why all the glum faces? Lark…"

Lark and Robert remained mute. I glanced over at Graham who was, in turn, staring at the minute crystal that sat cooling in his palm, a tiny rainbow glimmering from within it as though it possessed its own inner light.

"Oh God," Stacy whispered as she realized that something was wrong. "You didn't tell him, did you?" she cried, her eyes flitting between the four of us.

Graham whipped around, his fist closing in around the teardrop. "You knew?"

"I-I...I..." Stacy stammered, looking at me for help.

The desperation in her face was so acute, on reflex my mouth opened and the truth began to flow out. "Graham, Lark is a-"

The final word was caught in my throat as I felt a hand clamp over my mouth, a strong arm pulling me back, away from Graham, away from my friends.

"Lark is a what?" Graham asked. "Let go of her, Robert! Tell me what Lark is!"

"No, don't!" Stacy shouted. "Don't tell him, Grace. Please!"

Graham grabbed her arm, his grip ungentle, his eyes filled with anger and betrayal. "Don't tell me what?"

Stacy's eyes began to water and she looked at her arm, Graham's fingers already leaving reddish bruises on her pale skin. "It's not right for us to tell you; Lark's not ready to tell you."

"Ready for what? How can she not be ready to tell me about whatever *this* is but she could tell you?" he asked as he shoved his hand beneath her nose, the crystal in his palm screaming out a silent accusation. "My *best* friend has been lying to me for God knows how long; you, my ex-girlfriend, have been lying to me, despite making *me* promise on my grandmother's grave to keep your secret to myself!

"And for some obviously selfish reason, neither of you could find it in yourselves to trust me enough to tell me about any of this until *after* I happen to pour my heart out to Lark, who in turn tells me that she's in love with some dead dude who she watched magically grow old and senile. And after all of that, she's *still* not ready?"

He let go of Stacy's arm and pointed to the shimmering stone in his hand. "If this is what she's not ready for, you're mistaken, Stacy. And, just in case you were wondering, I'm *more* than ready for whatever this is, because whatever *this* is, it doesn't change how I feel. I've been feeling it for far too long and far too deeply for it to simply just go away."

Stacy grabbed Lark's arm, surprise and hurt shimmering in her eyes, and shook her head. "You knew…you knew about how he felt about you and you still let him ask me out."

Lark, having remained silent all this time, stepped forward, an explanation ready to burst from her mouth, but Stacy held up her hand to stop her. "No, don't—you don't have to explain anything to me. What you did, you did because you were my friend. You kept the truth from me because you didn't want to hurt me—I understand that."

She turned to look at Graham, a sad smile on her face. "I told you we weren't suited for each other."

Despite the tension in the air, Graham managed to smirk at that. "Well, you don't get to hear this from me that often so cherish this moment—you were right, Stacy."

"I know I'm right—I usually am."

Graham shook his head; Stacy was always going to be Stacy. "I need to know what's going on." He looked at Lark, and then at me. "Grace, I need to know. Whatever it is, whatever the hell all of this is, I'm ready for it."

"Are you, Graham?" Robert asked, his voice overflowing with doubt. "Are you certain you're ready for this?" He stepped towards Graham, pushing me behind him as he did so. I choked on my response when I saw the back of his jacket begin to push upwards, bulging from the activity beneath it.

"Robert, no!" I cried, already too late.

"You think the truth is going to make all of your questions go away," Robert said, a statement more than a question.

The sound of ripping fabric and Stacy's gasp were lost in the sound of the darkening forest coming alive at the appearance of Robert's ebony wings, nothing but black, branch like protrusions at first, followed by full plumes glistening like wet onyx. He expanded them, their tips reaching out well beyond our little circle to touch the trunks of trees several meters away.

"What…what the hell are you, man?" Graham breathed as he took a step back, his eyes widening in shock, his breathing speeding up from fear.

"I'm the truth that you've been looking for, Graham, what you've been so desperate to know," Robert said snidely as he stepped forward to close the distance between them, his wings fluttering as they folded inward. "You wanted to know the truth, you wanted to see what Grace has been lying to you about. Here it is."

"Robert, stop," Lark finally shouted.

Graham's head whipped around to look at her, as though seeing her for the first time. In truth, it was.

"If he's a…a bird, then what are you?"

Lark shook her head angrily. "He's not a bird, Graham. Take a good look at him with open eyes—see him for what he is."

With great difficulty, Graham turned to face Robert, the two of them making for a striking study in contrast; Robert, with his dark hair and pale skin was almost a negative of Graham's blonde hair and tanned skin. "I don't know—I don't know what you are. You've got wings, man! What the hell kind of person has wings? Birds and bats have wings— you're a manager of a movie theater, for Pete's sake!"

"Astute as always, Graham," Robert said mockingly.

Stacy grabbed Graham's hand and pulled him towards Lark. "You aren't helping, Robert. If you cannot figure out what Robert and Lark are by looking at him, Graham, then take a look at her—really look at her for who she is, without pretending, without pretenses."

"What's a pretense?"

"God, just forget that and look!"

Graham's gaze became glued to Lark, his eyes taking in her silver dress that matched exactly the light silver of her eyes. He watched her as the last glint of light disappeared from the cracks of the canopy above us, night finally settling in. The increased darkness revealed to Graham what it was that he could not see in Robert, what death had not robbed from her.

"Holy wow," he breathed, as the soft glow that emanated from her began to stretch out. "That's incredible…it's like you're some kind of angel or something." He stepped closer to her and stroked at the diffused light, his movements making it seem like he could actually *feel* the light itself.

"That's because that's what I am," Lark admitted in a shaky yet hopeful voice.

"I've always known that," Graham replied with a soft laugh, though his face revealed nothing but wonder and amazement.

Lark took a hesitant step closer to him, her eyes cautious. She raised her hand up, her palm facing out towards him. His hand lifted to press against it, his gasp coming out in a stuttered burst as the connection became complete and the truth that couldn't be explained in mere words began to flow between them. "Awesome," he whispered as his gaze locked with hers.

Stacy and I held our breaths as we waited, my heart racing, speeding up with each deep breath that Graham took in. His eyes grew wider with every minute that went by; recognition, confusion, and understanding blinking in flashes, something that the two of us were very familiar with.

Lark's face seemed to grow brighter as she shared with him things that I knew were only for him, things that she had never shared with anyone…not even Luca—I don't know how I knew this, I just did. Perhaps it was the sly smile passing over her lips that was quintessential Lark; maybe it was the way her pupils grew darker as the light silver ring that was her eyes grew thinner and lighter, telling me that she was pleased, inordinately pleased.

I only knew that when she finally attempted to lower her hand, and Graham refused to let it go, there wasn't anything else left to fear from him learning the truth.

"This is incredible," he breathed, his free hand lifting to touch the velveteen steel that was Lark's face. "Freaking amazing, even."

"Are you certain?" Lark asked hesitantly.

"I'm more than certain," Graham nodded enthusiastically. "How can I not be? I'm in love with a flippin' angel!" He sobered up immediately as he realized that Lark wasn't beaming like he was, her smile still sad, despite his acceptance of who she was.

"What's the matter? Isn't this supposed to be a good thing? I know the truth now—no more secrets."

Lark shook her head. "It's not that."

Graham looked at her and grimaced as he saw the pained expression in her eyes. "Then what is it?"

"I told you—it hurts to know what I feel for you. It hurts to *feel* it."

Graham looked at her with stark confusion. "I don't understand."

I dodged around Robert and grabbed Graham's arm. "Graham, there's something you need to understand about Lark and her kind. They cannot tell lies—it hurts them."

"What lie did she tell?" he asked, his confusion only deepening.

"She told you—us, actually—she promised to never love anyone else, feel anything like that ever again." I looked at Lark, finally understanding why she had never been able to talk about it without looking so troubled, so pained by it all. "Loving you wasn't what she had planned— love isn't ever something you plan out, you can't ever promise to never feel it—so when you became a part of her life, she became a liar, and loving you physically hurts her."

Graham's face drooped as realization began to dawn on him. "You mean that by feeling the same way about me that I do about her, she's in pain?"

I nodded, sadly. "Yes, but..." I looked at Lark and saw the despair in her eyes. "But something's not right."

Everyone's gaze was focused on me as I began to go over the past events, the moments where lies had done nothing but been mild irritants, and where assumed lies had been actual truths. "Lark, you promised to never feel for Graham what you felt for Luca, right?"

She nodded, her confusion now matching Graham's. I looked at the two of them and then I looked at Robert. "Remember when I had received that note from Sam and I thought it had been from Robert? You kept getting those annoying pains because the note was a lie—you just didn't know it was a lie at the time, which is why it hurt so much."

"Yes, but what does that have to do with this? I know what I felt, Grace. I did love Luca, very much—you do not mistake those feelings for simple juvenile affection," Lark replied.

"Yes, I know. That's not what I meant. Ugh—why is it that when I don't want you in my head, you're always in there and when it would be easier if you were, you choose to stay out?" I shook my head and grabbed Lark's hand, removing it from Graham's. "You're feeling hurt because you're lying to yourself, Lark. Don't you see?

"You're not feeling the same thing for Graham that you did for Luca because it's *not* the same thing. It can't be. Graham loves you, genuinely loves you, which is something that Luca did not, and you feel the same way. If Luca did love you, he wouldn't have demanded you make that promise in the first place. He would have wanted you to move on and be happy. He wouldn't have wanted you stuck on pause, denying yourself happiness and love all because he was gone. That's not love, Lark; that's control and manipulation."

Robert came to stand beside me and took his sister's hand from mine. "Little sister, I've no reason to help you and Graham be together…except that I can see it would make you happy. Grace is right: you've carried this burden, this false love with you for too long. You've let it eat at you and destroy what love should mean, what it should be. Let the past die. Let it find peace with Luca."

Lark's eyes began to shed sparkling tear after tear, each one falling and disappearing into the debris below our feet. Her glow shifted through the array of colors that each spoke of a different mood, a different feeling as she shed tears over her past for the last time.

"I'm amazed," she said to me when the storm of crystal had ceased, "that your ability to see things with your own mortal eyes surpasses what I can see with mine, blind though I may be."

"Hey, I don't have the ability to read minds so I've got to make up for it by being observant," I joked.

"What you are," Robert said as he released his sister's hand and reached for mine, "is amazing."

"I'll say," Stacy chimed in.

"That's the truth," Graham said, laughing.

"Agreed," Lark announced.

SONG BIRD

I grinned foolishly before I suddenly remembered something. "Stacy! You had something important to tell Lark, remember? She's here—what better time than now to tell her what it is?"

Stacy looked at the four of us, her smile suddenly falling. "I think it can wait."

Graham shook his head. "No it can't, Stacy. You don't have time for secrets."

"It can wait, Graham. This isn't the time for something like this," Stacy argued. "This time is for you two."

"What is it, Stacy?" I asked, curious now. "All I've heard come out of your mouth for the past few days as been 'I have to tell Lark something' and 'I have something that Lark needs to know'. I think it's only fair that after putting us through your constant hounding, you tell her."

Lark's beautiful smile should have been enough encouragement as she nodded in agreement. "Please, tell us what it is."

Stacy shook her head, and then pressed her hands to her eyes. "I can't."

Lark's smile vanished as she looked at Stacy with a puzzled expression taking its place. As if lightning had struck, her entire body jerked still. She gasped, her eyes quickly moved to Robert—they were filled with fear.

"Is it true?" she asked him.

Robert looked at me, as though waiting for my approval. "Is what true?" I asked him. "What's going on?"

Stacy eyed the three of us warily and then turned to question Lark. "Why are you asking him if it's true? Why would he know any more than you do?"

Lark ignored the question and then turned to face her brother, repeating the question she had asked him. "Is it true? Tell me."

He nodded once and I flinched as I saw Lark's eyes turn jet black with rage. Lark's face began to crumble as she turned to face Stacy, her hands gently rubbing the bruises that were left there by Graham's angry fingers. "It'll be okay," she said reassuringly. "I don't care what he says; it's going to be okay."

"What is going on?" I asked desperately.

My head whipped around to look at Graham and then at Robert. "Will someone tell me what's going on, since I'm apparently the only one out of the loop on this one?"

I looked at four separate pairs of eyes, each one trying desperately to avoid direct contact with my own, as though they were each guilty of something that couldn't be admitted to.

Robert's grim voice broke through the silence to answer me. "Stacy's dying, Grace."

"Don't be ridiculous. She's not dying—she's only eighteen. Besides, if she were, you'd tell me, you'd warn me, right? Right, Robert?"

When no answer came, I knew what it was.

"You already knew, and you kept it from me." I backed away, a hard pain sitting in my throat.

Lark began to shake with anger, her body vibrating so violently, Graham was unable to hold her without harming himself. He quickly backed away and then looked at me with guilt in his eyes.

"I'm sorry. Stacy made me promise not to tell and—I gotta be honest here—she scares me."

I nodded to him, but my eyes traveled back to Robert's, who didn't look apologetic at all. "And you have nothing to say?"

"This is more important than you, Grace," he replied before forcing me to turn around. "This is more important than you or me."

Stacy stood mere inches away from Lark as she spoke, her voice clear and steady, despite the gravity of her words. "This wasn't how I wanted to tell you… You don't need to ask Robert or Graham or go digging through the minds of the doctors in the oncology department at Licking Memorial or Newark or whatever else you're planning. My cancer is back—it's been back for a while actually, but I didn't want to say anything because I didn't think it was that big of a deal—and the doctors and I have been fighting it.

"Things were looking good, too…my markers were down and I was feeling fine. I didn't think anything about it or spend any real time worrying about it either; the doctors had me on what appeared to be a pretty successful treatment regimen. It was shortly after Halloween that my markers started rising again, and by Christmas, my oncologist told my parents and me that there wasn't much more they could do and so we're kinda just winging it."

I was glad that I wasn't the only person who was shocked by her cavalier attitude when I saw Lark's hands grab Stacy's arms roughly and began to shake her—or maybe it was that Lark's own shaking was transferring onto her. "Are you crazy? You're dying! Do you know what that means?"

"Actually yes, I do. It means no more spending countless hours in the hospital feeling so sick that it's almost impossible to believe that whatever it is that the doctors are doing to me is actually helping. It means no more watching my mom get her hopes up when the tests come back showing that instead of going down, my markers have gone up.

"It means knowing that I don't have decades ahead of me to screw up in life—I've got a few months, maybe a year to do what I want, how I want without the excuse of 'that'll kill me' or 'that's too dangerous and reckless' getting in the way because my life is already going to end.

"I'm okay with this, guys. Really, I am. The doctors told me when I was seven that I might not even live to be ten; I proved them wrong for over eight years. That's pretty good from where I'm standing."

Lark shook her head, as though unwilling to accept what Stacy already had.

"This isn't right. This isn't fair. Robert, you have to do something, you have to change it," Lark implored her brother.

He reached out towards his sister, sadness weighing on him heavily as he told her what she already knew. "I cannot. I don't get to decide these things, Lark, you know this."

"No. You've saved Grace's life, you've defied her death over and over again—you can do this for Stacy. Do this for her, Robert. Or for me. Do it for me, please." She pulled on the lapels of Robert's torn jacket, tugging at it with such strength its seams finally gave up and fell apart in her hands.

I closed my eyes and pressed my hand to my mouth, unwilling to accept that Lark was actually begging her brother for something, even if it was to keep Stacy alive.

"I am tied to Grace, Lark. You know this—I can no more allow her to die than I can myself," Robert tried to explain, but Lark wouldn't hear of it, her head shaking roughly, her movements causing Stacy to shake as well.

Graham and Stacy watched the exchange between brother and sister with utter disbelief written on their faces.

"No. It's not supposed to be this way," Lark cried before falling to her knees in weak defeat, her hands releasing Stacy, her arms falling to the ground. "It's not supposed to happen like this."

I didn't understand what she was saying but as she bent over, I knew immediately what she meant. I grabbed Stacy out of the way and looked at Robert who already had his hand on Graham's shoulder.

"Let go of me, Robert. Something's wrong with her," Graham shouted as he struggled futilely against the iron hold that Robert had on him.

"Nothing is wrong with her, Graham. Everything is right—trust me on this."

"Trust you? You've been reading my mind for the past six months, digging through my head and...aw hell, you've got wings, man. I'm not exactly sure who I can trust at the moment, but I'm fairly certain I'm not supposed to trust a guy with wings—and what's with the black? Angels aren't supposed to have black wings, man! Let me go!" Graham struggled but Robert effortlessly pulled him away from Lark, Graham's feet leaving deep drag marks in the soil.

"Graham, relax," I hissed. "You're going to miss it."

He glared at me but allowed Robert to pull him towards Stacy and me. "Miss what? She's losing it over there, Grace—I can't let her do that alone!"

I shook my head and pointed to the silvery-white lines curling and stretching across Lark's back, like thin fingers pushing up against her flawless skin. She tried to sit up but the pressure of what was growing beneath her flesh was too much and she doubled over, her mouth open in a silent scream.

Seeing the pained look in her face caused Graham to once again rush to help her. Robert's hand darted out and grabbed Graham's jacket. Graham shrugged out of it and landed on his knees in front of Lark, one hand trying to raise her head, the other rubbing the growing protrusions on her back.

"What's wrong? What's wrong, Lark?" he asked in frantic concern. "What's happening to you? What's going on?"

"She's growing her wings," Robert replied coolly. "You need to step away from her, Graham. She's never done this before and sometimes it can be very...violent."

Graham shook his head in defiance. "I'm not leaving her."

Robert shrugged and walked away. I looked at him, shock registering on my face. "How can you leave him there?"

"He won't die," Robert said nonchalantly.

"Sure…but even if he were, you wouldn't tell me, would you?" I retorted, turning my head away to watch the couple before me, still fearful for Graham's safety, though a lot more confidant now that I knew he wouldn't be seriously harmed.

"Like I said, this isn't about you, Grace," was all he said.

Though I had seen Robert's wings grow at least half a dozen times since he had gained them, he had never shown just how painful their emerging was, never given any indication that he felt any to begin with—his face was always so calm and still, a small smile always on his lips, as though he actually enjoyed it.

Lark, on the other hand, was in obvious agony. Her hands were digging into the soil without any resistance, her palms pulverizing whatever lay against them. As the branches on her back began to fan out and her skin began to stretch, her mouth opened once again, but no sound came out.

No sound that anyone could hear, anyway. No one but Robert, who visibly flinched.

And me.

The piercing shriek that filled my ears was much like the one that had come from Sam as he lay bleeding from the wounds I had inflicted, only this time the frantic and desperate cry sounded like a dying choir, the chords slicing and stabbing at me with an eagerness that cut off my ability to scream. I slammed my hands over my ears, futilely trying to block the sound from reaching the deepest recesses of my mind, but there was no stopping the onslaught from the deadly song.

The force of each shrill note reaching me was like a hammer slamming into my mind, and I fell to the ground, my knees cushioned by the leaves and soft earth. Stacy and Robert were at my side immediately, Stacy unaware of what was going on, and Robert, frightened and confused.

The haze of red began to sweep in and cloud my vision; I heard Stacy gasp. "Her eyes are bleeding! Robert, do something—she's bleeding all over, oh God, what's happening?"

Robert grabbed a hold of my head, his two hands pressing against my own as they clamped down over my ears, and he looked into my eyes. I saw his face, so beautiful, and yet so strange. I could see the thoughts in his head as he frantically tried to see what was wrong with me. I smiled at the glimpses of the two of us together that mixed in with everything else, though the pain continued to beat into me as the song continued. I felt the weight of something on my chest, and I peeked down to see what it was, but saw nothing there.

Feeling weak, I felt my head loll to the side despite Robert's hold, and I caught a glimpse of Lark, the branch-like appendages fully extended now, the tiny buds of feathers quickly forming and blooming into pristine white plumes that only further proved to me that she was, indeed, the most beautiful girl in the world. Her eyes locked with mine and only when her mouth closed did the song stop.

I breathed a sigh of relief, only to begin choking as the pressure in my chest finally loosened its grip, sending up a hot rush of metallic tasting liquid from my mouth. I could hear the voices of my friends as they all grew increasingly alarmed over what was happening to me. I couldn't move, couldn't speak to tell them that I was okay. I could only see the darkness pulling me down, covering everything with a deep, red stain…and then suddenly growing paler, a faint, yellow glow was encompassing me and becoming more and more opaque as the warm river of liquid continued to flow from my mouth.

Soon the voices became nothing but warm, soothing notes in the soft symphony that was now playing in my head, replacing the dirge filled choir that had brought me down. The darkness was completely gone now, replaced by a massive expanse of glowing light that stretched beyond what I could see, beyond what I knew existed.

"Hello, Grace," a strangely familiar voice said to me.

I blinked and stood up, the movement oddly quick and easy. I reached my hand out to comfort my friends, but they weren't there. No one was there—I was standing in nothing but light for as far as I could see, and I was completely alone.

"Not alone, silly."

I spun around, expecting to see the owner of the voice standing directly behind me.

No one was there.

"You remember this game, don't you? Follow the voice, Grace," the voice teased.

"Who are you?" I asked. Quickly, my hand went to my mouth, pressing down on my lips as the sound that came out was foreign.

Laughter reached me from what I assumed was a far corner and I proceeded to walk towards it, my hand still pressed against my mouth, refusing to let another unfamiliar sound come out. I walked until the soles of my feet began to ache. I raised one hand above my eyes to scan for the horizon, needing to see something that would hint as to just how much farther I had to go before I finally reached...something. I squinted, hoping to see that faint line that spoke of an actual end to my walking but the glare was too bright.

"This is ridiculous," I said to myself beneath my fingers. "And why does my voice sound like this?"

A whisper of breath blew across my ear. "Because that's what you sound like, silly!"

I swung around, my arm flailing out defensively.

No one was there.

"Ugh—this is getting to be incredibly annoying. And I do not sound like this...all, bell-like and...girly!"

I looked around the vast empty space around me and shook my head. "I cannot believe I'm standing here in the middle of nowhere, arguing with nothing."

"I'm not nothing."

"So says the voice that's coming out of thin air," I said in retort as I turned around.

"I don't think your father raised you to speak in such a manner."

My lower jaw swung open, the movement so quick, I could have sworn I heard the creak and pop of the sudden motion. Though her voice had been familiar, I simply hadn't heard it often enough or recently enough to have recognized it without it being placed with a face.

It was one that I was instantly connected to, one that spoke of a history that I had never known, that had never been given an opportunity to be shared with me. She wore a dazzling, if not sly smile, the mouth small yet with no loss for the delight that could be read on the lips that curled upwards, revealing a small, almost impish dimple in perfect, ivory skin. The eyes were a strange, umber shade with flecks of brilliant gold deeply embedded inside the irises. They were warm and inviting, the obvious joy in them paling in comparison only to my own. Her arms were extended with welcome, her dark hair tumbling over her shoulders like soot-filled waves.

"Mom?"

"It's me, Abby."

"Are you sure you're not just another Erlking or something?"

"Do I smell like an Erlking?" she murmured as I approached her, her scent the oddly familiar aroma of warm amber, soil, and fresh-cut flowers.

"I don't believe this is happening," I whispered as I literally inhaled memories from my childhood.

"Believe what?"

I raised my head to look up at her, and smiled. "Well, this; you're here, in my dreams, and you know who I am."

She laughed, the sound beautiful and heartbreaking all at the same time. "Grace, how could I not know my own child? You look like me! Far too much, I think. And how else am I supposed to visit you?"

"That's true, I suppose, but I always thought I looked a lot more like Dad."

She wrinkled her nose and shook her head. "It doesn't matter. Now then, we've got a lot to discuss before it's time for you to go."

"Go? But I just got here...right?" I asked, confused and disappointed that I would be waking up soon.

"No, Grace, I'm afraid that you'll be waking up far sooner than I'd like. That Robert of yours is persistent."

"He is. Almost to a fault."

"Well, his type usually are, dear. Goody-two-shoes are always persistent when they should be exactly the opposite, but that's not important right now."

"Then what is?"

She turned me around and I frowned in confusion. The never-ending expanse of white was gone, replaced now with the wooded backdrop I had left upon blacking out. A scene was playing out in front of me, a scene that I would have missed out on otherwise.

"I cannot believe it—I didn't expect it to be me," a female voice said in surprise.

"It wasn't you, it was me," a male voice argued.

I shook my head. "They never seem to be able to do anything other than argue."

Stacy and Graham stood mere inches apart while facing each other, both of their faces pinched with annoyance, their jaws jutting out in stubbornness while Lark stood mute between them.

"I know more about this than you do, Graham—if it was anyone, it was me. She didn't change until I told her about my cancer," Stacy argued, her finger jabbing into Graham's shoulder forcefully.

"She was already stressing out before you told her, and that was because of me. It happened because of me," Graham countered, swatting away Stacy's finger.

Off to the side I could see Robert on the ground, my limp body cradled in his lap, his arms gently pressing my head to his chest. "Did the two of you ever stop to think that perhaps it was both of you?" he asked, annoyance and aggravation oozing from his tone.

Stacy gasped, her face indignant. "I will *not* share this with him. Besides, it wouldn't be fair, he knows about her for less than twenty minutes and he gets to be her wing-bringer? I don't think so. It's got to be me. I'm her best friend. He's just eye-candy."

410

Graham scoffed at her insult. "Eye-candy? I think it's been established that I'm more than that. And I thought you were okay with Lark and I being together; why the tone?"

"I *am* fine with it. I just don't think that you suddenly becoming a couple automatically constitutes wing-bringer status. I'm the one with the deeper emotional bond—you haven't had time to form that yet. And I still say that it happened because of my news and not because the two of you admitted to sharing hormones," Stacy said, brushing his comment aside.

"It wasn't either of you," a soft voice said with surety.

Three pairs of eyes turned towards it, each one wide with surprise.

"What do you mean, it wasn't either of us?" Stacy demanded.

"Yeah, what she said," Graham concurred.

Lark shook her head and walked towards Robert, squatting down to push aside a stray curl from my face, her snowy white wings fluttering softly as they adjusted to her new position. "I don't know how it happened, or why it happened, but it wasn't either of you."

Robert looked down at my blood streaked face, his smile sad. "She's going to be quite upset about that—she's losing the battle to be normal if she's causing your wings to grow by doing nothing other than existing, little sister."

"It wasn't her simply existing that did it, Robert," Lark snapped before standing up and turning around to stare at Stacy, a forlorn look upon her face. "How could you know about being sick for so long without me finding out?"

Stacy shrugged her shoulders, and grinned. "Well, I told you, I don't think about it. You're not trying to dig into my head for my deepest darkest secrets—you're just listening for the stuff running through at the surface, right?" At Lark's nodding, she continued. "See, if you were a bit nosier like your brother, you might have known a lot sooner."

Graham coughed, and looked over at where I was lying. "Shouldn't she be waking up by now?"

Robert shook his head. "She's very sensitive to the sound of our pain, and with all that blood loss, it's going to be a bit longer before she awakes. I don't think she'll do so not knowing, however. Her mind, even while unconscious, is very active." Robert frowned at his own words, his brows squeezing together as he thought over what it was he said.

"Well, I don't like it," Graham said, matter-of-factly. "There's a lot I don't understand yet about how your kind works—I'm still tripping out about the wings…dude! Black!—but I know that we're not supposed to just start bleeding out of our eyes and vomiting blood for no reason."

"It wasn't for 'no reason'," Robert started to argue, but sighed and shook his head, the argument simply not worth it to him. He grabbed a handkerchief from the front pocket on his jacket and began to wipe away some of the dried blood from around my mouth, a worried frown marring his face.

"Robert, I know you can do that whole healing thing with people, so couldn't you try that with Grace? I mean, she's been out for a while, and even I know that's not a good thing."

"I can heal her body, Stacy, but not her mind. Physically, she's fine. Mentally, she's somewhere else, and that's something that she'll have to fix on her own."

I couldn't help but chuckle as I realized that mentally, I was right here. "Can't he even feel that I'm here?" I asked aloud, turning to face my mother.

"No, he can't. Angels are special creatures, but even they have their limitations. They can hear the thoughts of those sitting around them, and some, like Lark, can hear the thoughts of those miles away. They can heal, they can hurt. They are capable of some of the most amazing feats of strength and skill, but they're still lacking in many areas that humans have mastered. Like feeling, for example.

"He's tied to you emotionally, Grace. I'm sure you are well aware of that. But he's not tied to you physically. Not yet, anyway."

I looked at her and frowned. "What do you mean?"

She pointed to the way that Robert held my head, pressed closely to his chest, yet his body seemed strained, as though he were fighting to pull away just as his hands brought me closer. It was something that I wouldn't have been able to see had I been awake.

"He fights with himself when he's with you: He loves you, he wants to be with you to the point where it is physically painful to stop himself from doing so, but he does. He doesn't know how to cross that barrier, Grace, and he's afraid that once he learns how, he won't be able to stop himself from doing just that. He's as new to this as you are, but you weren't born with built-in limitations like he was. You can help him conquer that obstacle and learn to control how he feels and finally form that physical bond that your relationship is lacking."

"Are you suggesting that Robert and I…"

Her nod sent a hot flush to my face and I turned away.

"Grace, I'm your mother. If anyone is allowed to speak to you about such things, it should be me," she chided. She placed a cool hand beneath my chin and lifted my face. "Now, pay attention. This is important." She turned my face to my friends, their conversation growing heated as the topic returned to who it was that had become Lark's wingbringer.

"I don't understand why you're so upset about Grace being the one to make your wings grow." Graham stood off to the side, his hands shoved into his pockets as he watched Lark and Stacy, their hands held in front of each other, one face solemn, the other slightly annoyed. "If she's the one who did it for Robert, it makes sense that she'd do it for his sister, right?"

Stacy rolled her eyes while Lark's frown turned into a full-blown grimace. "It's like I'm being punished," she whispered. "I lost Luca, and now I'm going to lose the two of you as well."

Graham and Stacy instantly attended to her sudden grief, unsure as to what she was referring to. Robert hissed, understanding and sympathy quite clear on his face. The sound caused me to flinch as a sharp pain shot across my forehead.

"You're not going to lose me," Graham said with fierce determination in his voice.

"Hey, I've got some time left," Stacy said with a slight laugh.

Recognition suddenly dawned on Graham and he wrapped his arms around Lark, burying his face into her dark hair. "I didn't understand. I thought...never mind what I thought. I'd give anything to be able to stay with you forever, but I'll take what I can get. Fifty plus years with you is far better than a single day without you."

Lark's angry laughed shocked all of us. "You don't get it, do you? Of course not; you have no clue. If it hadn't been Grace, it would have been one of you, and then I'd have been stuck having to decide whether or not to turn you while leaving the other to wither away and die."

"What do you mean by 'turn'?" Graham asked, confused.

Stacy, too, seemed perplexed by Lark's words. "Yeah, I don't get it either."

Lark's laughter grew louder as she pointed an angry finger in my direction—or at least, the direction of my body. "She's Robert's wingbringer. Because of that, Robert can now ask permission to turn her, to make her immortal. Instead of accepting this, she turned him down, over and over again, knowing what it will do to him when she dies and simply not caring. And now, now there are two people whose lives could have benefitted from being my wing-bringer.

"Instead, it's her, the one person who would turn down immortality because it goes against her whole ridiculous plan of being 'normal'."

Graham looked at my body and then at Robert, seeing the grief that was on his face as the truth of Lark's words touched home. He looked back at Stacy, whose eyes had turned red with unshed tears, her face growing pale as she realized what she had lost. "What caused it—your wings to grow? Do you know?"

"Of course I do," Lark replied, her eyes whipping around to glare at Robert, who growled angrily in response. "I saw what's going to happen when Grace learns the truth about Robert, and her pain, her heartbreak at

414

that betrayal is what triggered my change because I'm just as tied to her as he is."

Graham and Stacy both threw accusing looks at Robert, whose lips were curled back as his growl grew deeper.

"You've said enough, Lark," he hissed, and I fell to my knees, the pain cutting through my head like a torch.

"No, I haven't, but I'm not going to be the one to tell her, Robert. You will," Lark said firmly.

"What did he do? What did he do to Grace?" Graham asked, his hands clenched into angry fists at his side as he stalked towards Robert.

Lark and Stacy both grabbed him, Lark being more successful. "That's not for me to tell."

He tried to shake his arm free, but Lark's steel grip minimized the motion so that all you could see was his shoulder twitching. He turned to stare at Lark, incredulity written on his face in deep lines. "You know this is going to hurt her, break her heart, and yet you won't tell her? She's my best friend!"

"I cannot break the laws of my kind," Lark argued.

"But you can skirt around them?" Stacy asked, her eyes wary as she took in the gravity of the scene before her. "I know you're not supposed to tell Graham and I what you are, but you did anyway. You broke all of those laws of your kind when you were with Luca, and now you decide that the rules can't be broken or even bent a little because it involves Grace?"

Lark's head began to shake in denial. "No, that's not it at all. What I saw, these are visions of the future, things that I see only because I can see the thoughts of others who can, and I know that when they happen, Grace will be shattered."

Lark's words caused me to turn to face my mom once more, shock and anger coursing through me.

"This is what I needed to hear? That Robert's betrayed me somehow?" When she nodded, I scoffed at the response. "Why?"

"Because the choices you make afterwards will affect not just your-self, but everyone else around you. What you decide once you wake up and hear the truth cannot be undone. Your decision will affect the genera-tions to come. You must remember how much he means to you, how much you love him. Remember that; promise me, Grace."

I looked away, unwilling to promise anything to anyone, not with the fissure that had opened up in my heart starting to groan under the weight of what it knew was coming.

I closed my eyes and pressed my fingers against their lids, the throbbing that had remained long after the shooting pains had gone only increasing as I did so. I could see in my mind the sadness that took over Graham's face as he realized that his life would one day end, while Lark's would go on. I could see Stacy's understanding that she could have had a chance at beating her disease had it not been for me. I could see Lark, her pain from realizing this future loss so acute, it physically hurt to acknowl-edge it.

And I could see Robert. Stubbornly holding onto whatever secret he had hidden away amongst the other secrets that were kept from me, secrets that would break my heart, that would cause a pain so great, simply seeing it had been enough to cause Lark's change to happen.

I opened my eyes, needing to ask Mom one more question, but in-stead, I saw the worry filled eyes of Robert staring down at me.

"Oh thank God you're alright," he breathed, his mouth bending down to press against my forehead, his cool hands and lips pressing against my skin.

I pulled away.

"Grace, what's wrong?" he asked, concerned.

I looked at Lark, Stacy, and Graham, their faces expectant. Only Lark's eyes held pity.

"Tell me," I managed to whisper. "Tell me the truth."

He pulled back suddenly, shock causing his body to turn stiff and hard, making my position in his lap uncomfortable, like I was sitting in a crevice made of sharp rocks.

"I can't," he said with finality.

"You mean you won't," Graham snapped, offering his hand to me.

I grabbed it and pulled myself up. "Tell me the truth, tell me what you've been keeping from me, what Lark saw," I demanded, trying but failing to keep the minute vibrations in my hands from traveling up my arms.

He shook his head and looked away as he stood up, dusting the debris from his pants. "I can't. I've seen what it'll do to you. I cannot do that to you."

"You've already done it," I accused. "You owe me the truth now that it's been done."

He turned his face towards mine, the silver in his eyes nearly blocked out by the jet black of his widened pupils. "I promised not to hurt you."

"You lied."

THAT OLD FAMILIAR STING

"When I first saw you, when I first came in contact with you, it was like a bolt of lightning had struck me directly in my heart and set fire to everything I ever knew about what it meant to be what I was, what it meant to love someone. It seems cliché, especially among your kind, but I knew from the moment I saw you that you were the one, not just my wing-bringer, but the one person that I would love above all others, above myself.

"I saw in you something, something unlike anything else I had ever seen in another human being in all my fifteen hundred years."

"You're fifteen hundred years old? You cradle-robbing bastard!" Graham shouted, lunging once again toward Robert. Lark's unnaturally quick hands managed to keep him at bay, her head shaking.

"I'm sorry you feel that way, Graham," Robert said sadly, never taking his eyes off me. "I love Grace. And my age was never a problem with her; her opinion is the only one that matters."

"I still say that's pretty sick!"

Stacy grunted. "Lark's over five hundred years old, Graham. What does that make you? A dinosaur hunter?"

Graham choked at Stacy's words, and quickly initiated a quiet conversation with Lark while Stacy rolled her eyes, continuing to chuckle at the turn of events.

Robert walked towards me, his hands extended. I pulled mine away and hid them behind my back. He saw this and stopped, understanding what it meant and continued with his confession.

"I wanted everything to be perfect for us, I wanted things to feel more like a fairytale, but I didn't understand that fairytales are impossible for humans—it's why your kind dream about them so often. Instead of a fairytale, we fought—almost immediately—and I could see my future with you fading.

"When you were hit by Mr. Frey, I saw that as a second chance for me, saw that as an opportunity to brand myself into your soul. I told you, Grace, that I've been fighting to keep you alive, fighting against the very thing that makes me who I am to keep you here.

"On the night that you were hit, you were supposed to die; Sam…Sam was there to end your life. When I got there, we argued over you. He told me that allowing you to live was going against his call…and mine. I told him that it didn't matter to me; you were my life, the call be damned."

"What *is* your call anyway?" Stacy asked, curious.

"You know that I can't-" Robert began.

"Tell me, yeah, I know," Stacy sighed in defeat, cutting him off.

"Thank you," Robert acknowledged. "I don't think you'd like me much if you knew, though."

"If what you're going to tell Grace is as bad as Lark's making it out to be, I don't think it'll make things any worse," Stacy quipped before turning away.

Nodding, Robert returned to his explanation.

"Sam finally relented when he saw what I was going through for you, and he left you with me so that I could save you. I didn't show you that part because you weren't allowed to know who Sam was, or what he was to be more precise."

"And yet you introduced me to him at Hannah's wedding?" I asked, surprised.

"Of course. He was my mentor, Grace. Whatever he was supposed to do, I was the one who prevented it from happening. He was doing what he was meant to—I'm the one who went against the rules."

I threw up my hands, unconvinced by his sudden defense of Sam. "He went against the rules, too, when he left you with me, didn't he? You're sticking up for him—why?"

"Because I cannot ignore the fact that by preventing him from taking your life, I also prevented him from fulfilling his call. You must understand how dangerous that is, not just for you, but for my family as well."

I couldn't argue with him about that. I had never put too much thought into the calls of the other angels, Robert's being enough to deal with. But knowing how important it was to each and every individual angel, and how each one correlated with each other, I had no choice but to understand and appreciate how denying one angel what they were born to do for his own, personal reason could cause trouble for Robert, Lark, and Ameila as well.

"Does that erase what he tried to do?" Lark questioned, her voice tinged with anger.

"Tried to do what?" Stacy and Graham both asked, their heads turning back and forth between Robert, Lark, and I.

"A lot more has been going on than what you've been telling me," Stacy announced, her tone miffed.

"Hey, I haven't been told anything—what's going on? And who is this Sam person you keep talking about?" Graham questioned.

"This is not the time for twenty-questions, Graham," I muttered.

"How about just one? Who's Sam?" he said in retort.

"Technically, that's two," Stacy said before repeating his question. "Who's Sam?"

Knowing that neither Lark nor Robert would answer her, I sighed and told them with as few words as possible who exactly Sam was.

Graham, as expected, didn't take this news too well. "Your mentor is the Archangel of Death? And you introduced him to Grace after he tried to kill her, like they're supposed to become best buds or something?" he shouted angrily.

"He was doing what he was supposed to do—what he was born to do. I was the one in the wrong when I stopped him," Robert argued. "I think I've explained that already."

"So you were wrong to keep him from killing Grace?" Stacy asked, her arms folded across her chest, her foot tapping with growing annoyance.

"Yes—no. I was wrong by the rules that govern my kind. I was right by the rules that govern my heart. No matter which path I chose, I would have been wrong in someone's eyes. I just chose what was right for me," Robert sighed. "And why am I explaining myself to you? This isn't about you; this is about Grace and me."

He turned his back to my friends and grabbed my hands, holding them tightly between his own. "Grace, if what Lark has seen has to play out, if it is indeed the future, it is what I will deserve. I don't want to keep anything from you anymore. I love you too much, need you too much to keep anything between us."

I braced myself, taking a deep breath and exhaling slowly as his confession began once again.

"Whatever Sam had done or had been prevented from doing when I introduced you to him was nothing that could have been stopped beforehand, by me or anyone else, and could not be held against him by me because of that. He simply was what he was. But I did have a reason for him meeting you, him seeing and speaking to you. I wanted him to know who you were, see how much you meant to me—not just hear it—so that he could understand why I needed you to live, why I would risk everything to ensure your survival.

"I didn't expect him to build such resentment towards me, or you for that matter. When he suggested that I lie to you about not loving you, I balked at the idea. I already loved you. If loving you wasn't enough to bring my wings, then what would? The pain of the lie was what would do it, he told me, and of course I trusted him. I had no reason not to—he had never sought retribution from the Seraphim for my preventing your death—I felt he had only my best interest at heart if he had been willing to allow you to live.

"When I saw you with Graham that night, I made the decision to follow through with Sam's plan. I knew that even if you didn't forgive me the lie, you wouldn't be alone and I took comfort in that, even though it caused such a strange pain in me to acknowledge it. When you asked me if I loved you and I told you "no", it was the hardest thing for me to do—the pain had begun long before the question had even been asked—but that pain was not what hurt the most. It was seeing your face when I lied to you that killed me.

"If I had doubted that I loved you, even in an infinitesimal amount, that moment would have erased it all. And it's remembering how I felt, watching you leave me that kept me from telling you the truth because there is only one thing in this world that frightens me, Grace, and that's losing you."

He paused, and I saw the trembling, felt it as he struggled with the words that were damming up behind his closed lips, his eyes closing, too, as if doing so could slow down the truth that he was so afraid to tell me.

He took a deep, needless breath, and sighed. His eyes opened, his face grim as he began to speak once more.

"Grace, when I first saw you, when I first met you, I could see your past, just as easily as I could see your present. I saw the events of the previous weeks, the previous months, and years. I saw everything that went on in your life before I had even breathed a single word to you.

"But what I saw most clearly was the most significant moment in your life, the moment that ensured just what type of person you would become."

"You saw my mom's death," I acknowledged. Of course he had. He had even allowed me to revisit it, my own way of remembering and saying goodbye. I had thought it a gift.

"It wasn't a gift, Grace. It was a lie."

I felt my throat grow dry and my tongue grow fat at his words. "A...lie?"

He nodded slowly, his hands squeezing tightly around mine, preventing me from pulling away, even as I felt my body struggle to be as far away from him as possible. "Yes, though what I showed you was true, there were parts that I hid from you because I thought doing so would protect you, and in effect, protect us, the us I wanted to exist."

"What could you have seen that I would need to be protected from?"

"Can you not guess? We're talking about the day your mother died. Can you not figure out what it was that I saw that could pose such a danger to you?" he asked me, though I knew that he hadn't exactly expected the answer he received.

"You saw Sam..."

"Yes."

I felt my knees buckle at the implication, the impact of the omission causing me to stumble and fall, though I never touched the ground; Robert caught me before I had a chance to hit the soil.

"Tell me," I whispered, my voice hoarse from the silent scream I was holding within me.

"Grace, I-"

"Tell me! For God's sake, don't talk to me about truth and honesty and then deny them to me! Not now, not about my mother!" I shouted.

Robert flinched at the harsh sting of my words, but didn't hesitate to continue. "Sam's call led him to the road you and your mother were traveling on that night. He had two names, two lives he had to end who would be in the car that would be coming down that road at just that moment—your mother's car. He thought a crash would have been enough to have killed you both; he was so angry when you both survived, despite his knack for causing such...artful destruction. He took that as a sign that you were mocking him and he became enraged.

"He caused the car to explode, knowing that whatever the damage, it would finish his task and he'd be allowed to move on. He did not know that you were not in that car when it exploded, Grace, otherwise you wouldn't be here right now. For whatever reason, he thought you had died with your mother. Perhaps it was the rage that clouded his vision, or perhaps he simply underestimated the human spirit that resided in your mother, but whatever it was, he left you alone.

"I saw that you remembered very little of this, and you certainly didn't remember Sam. His presence could only have been detected by someone like me, and so I made the decision then and there to never reveal any of this to you, or to Sam. It was the only way I could ensure your safety.

"When you were hit by Mr. Frey, I feared that Sam had recognized you, realized who you were and was simply trying to finish what he had started. Instead, you were just a number to him, just one of countless numbers on his list and Mr. Frey was unknowingly along for the ride. Had Sam known, had he realized who you were, he would have killed you on the spot, and no amount of pleading on my part would have prevented it. I thank God that he was ignorant about who you were."

I scoffed at this last bit, and managed to pry myself away from him as my anger finally began to form the words that had been trapped inside of me, too jumbled and confused to do anything but stew in my own building resentment.

"And yet you felt it was perfectly okay to leave me alone with him at Hannah's wedding. You knew, *knew* that he killed my mother, that he had tried to kill me—not once, but twice—and yet you didn't stop to think about bringing me where you knew he would be. And then to introduce the two of us as though we'd somehow become friends!

"Was that what you were hoping? That he and I would hit it off and like each other so much that he'd simply forget the whole not-being-able-to-kill-me-twice thing?"

When he didn't reply, I threw up my hands in frustration, fighting the urge to ball them into fists and beat him. "How could you do that to me? How could you risk my life like that? And when he told you that it would be a good idea to lie to me, you went along with it, knowing all along just how vindictive he could be, knowing how it would hurt me. You actually went along with it, like some stupid guy trying to fit in with the cool kids.

"After all that talk about loss and suffering, I was the one who suffered. I was the one who had to listen to your lie and believe it. It wasn't your heart breaking that night, it was mine! I was the one who watched you die, thinking I'd never see you, never hear you tell me that you loved me again. I was the one who lost then, not you. You don't know anything about loss or suffering. You've never lost a damn thing in your life!"

"Wait a second—dude, you're…dead?" Graham asked, his voice a strange and unwelcome interruption.

"Now is *not* the time to start catching on, Graham," I lashed out.

"Sorry."

"Sam came after me, made up that stupid sob story about his precious Miki, who I find out later is the mother of all vampires, and he tells me it's because if he's not happy, you can't be either, and like some stupid sap, I believed it all. It's like you guys lied about the lying; you lie all the time and don't care who it hurts. And now you tell me the real reason why he came after me was because he was simply trying to finish what he started eleven years ago."

"Did you say vampires?"

"Shut-up, Graham," four voices shouted simultaneously.

"Grace, you don't know that he remembered who you were that night. He was crazed, you saw that. There were a lot of things going on with Sam that I have yet to understand, but I fully believe that our friendship meant enough to him to keep him from killing you solely to finish what he started," Robert argued.

"But the fact remains that he did try to kill me, Robert. He did try to finish what he started and he would have succeeded, too. You made sure of that."

Robert shook his head in denial, his voice steely and determined. "No. He wouldn't have succeeded. I wouldn't have let him."

"You put me on a silver platter for him when you introduced us at the wedding. You left me alone, knowing who he was and what he had tried to do. You weren't there to stop him when he finally had me. And then…after everything, you had Lark take me home so you could take care of Sam. You could have left him there to rot after everything he'd done, not just to me but to you and your family as well, and instead you made the choice that you had been making from the moment we met. You chose Sam. You were more concerned with him, even after he tried to kill me, to kill us."

I felt my eyes start to sting as those words hit me like a brick to the chest. "You never did tell me what happened to him."

"I told you, he's gone."

I looked at him, the tears still clinging desperately to my lids. "Yes, but what did you mean by that? Gone as in dead, or gone as in not here?"

He turned away, refusing to speak the words out loud. I turned to look at Lark and I could see it in her face as well. I nodded in understanding and allowed my tears to finally flow freely down my face, watching in blurred waves as they fell to my feet.

"He was never punished, was he? He hadn't done anything wrong; he was just finishing the job he started."

When no arguments came I nodded in mute understanding once more. I felt my heart burn as I continued. "I guess there's no real point then, is there? He wants me dead, I'm supposed to be dead…it's only fair that he get his shot."

"No!" Lark and Robert both cried out, their voices cutting off as they each heard the other, their anger towards each other causing their wings to ruffle and bristle with tension.

"I won't let him harm you, Grace," Lark vowed, her eyes boring holes into Robert.

I laughed mockingly. "You won't let him harm me? No one can protect me. Even Robert knows I'm supposed to die. It's a sure thing now that everyone knows I was supposed to die eleven years ago and didn't. It's

426

why Robert's been bugging me to accept being turned. And you said it yourself that it was selfish of me to deny him this, knowing how much it would hurt him to see me die, Lark."

Her eyes grew wide, her mouth forming an "o" of surprise at my words as she nodded hesitantly.

"Yeah, I heard every single word of your conversation, Lark. And just so you know, there can be no greater example of selfishness than your brother demanding that I turn for him simply so he could escape ever having to deal with me finding out the truth. That's the reason, isn't it? The entire reason for wanting me to become one of those who-knows-what out there? If I became one of them, Sam couldn't kill me, and the secret would be safe, right?"

Lark looked over at Robert, her eyes still wide. He shared the same surprised look, their thoughts shared quickly between the two before they both turned to look at me.

"Grace, how did you know that I said those things?" Lark asked nervously.

"I was here. When I was passed out, I saw my mother. She brought me here to listen to you guys all argue and talk. She said that I needed to hear something important. She was right."

Lark and Robert once again stared at each other, their eyes flickering so rapidly as they shared a private conversation, I felt dizzy just watching them.

"Stop it!" I shouted. "If you have something to say, say it. I'm done with all of this secrecy, mind reading crap. I'm sick of it."

Lark shared one last apprehensive look with Robert and frowned. "We weren't speaking when we said those things, Grace. No one uttered a single word during the conversation you're talking about. Everything that was spoken was done in our thoughts—we didn't want to disturb you or draw any more attention to our location than we already have."

Stacy and Graham both nodded their heads, while Robert looked on, pleadingly.

"I heard you speaking," I countered, but bit back the rest of my words as Lark shook her head.

"You know that I cannot lie, not even a little, and I'm telling you that no one was talking, Grace."

I turned my gaze angrily towards Robert, waving off Lark's denial. "It doesn't matter who said or didn't say anything. The fact remains that I know what was being discussed, and I know that you've got it wrong; I'm not being selfish for not wanting to change who I am. If I could, I'd give any and all chances I had at immortality to Graham and Stacy because they have a genuine reason to want to live forever, they have someone who deserves to have them around forever, who *wants* to have them around forever."

I felt the burn in my heart and the ache in my throat as I let the final words slip past my lips, my eyes fixed on Robert's as I uttered them, feeling that fissure in my chest blow wide open as I did so. "I don't."

I grabbed the hem of my dress and began walking towards the twinkling lights at the edge of the woods. Robert grabbed my arm, but I yanked free. "Don't touch me," I hissed.

"Grace, please. I did this to keep you safe, to keep us safe because I love you," he pleaded.

"Don't. Talk. To. Me. About. Love!" I growled. "You don't have a clue what love is. You view love like it's a toy you can play with, and I'm merely the stupid box that it comes in. You don't view me as an equal—you never did. I've always known it, but I just haven't accepted it until now. It's why you waxed poetic about virtue and patience—I'm simply not good enough, not for that and certainly not for the truth.

"And you can go ahead and blame all of that on you being a naive angel who's never experienced what love truly is until you met me, and that you're still trying to understand it. But I'll know it's just another lie because I've never before experienced a single ounce of what I feel for you with anyone else. Not with Graham, not with anyone, but that not knowing has never caused me to keep from you anything that would have changed our relationship the way you just did.

428

"I never asked you to change who you were, despite all of your differences. I didn't care that you could read my mind, or could fly. My God, I even looked past all of the death stuff because I love you! But you couldn't accept me the way that I am—you kept trying to get me to agree to turn, and you couldn't even be honest about why.

"You brought me here to frighten me into turning, to try and scare me with my mortality by having monsters threaten my life, yet the danger is far more closer to home—Sam is still alive, he hates me more than ever, and it's all because of you."

I could hear my voice shaking and stuttering as my tears brought on hiccups. "You know the worst part about this? You did all of that to try to convince me to turn when you didn't really need to. I would have agreed to it, Robert. I was ready to tell you before all of this started, ready to tell you that I wanted to spend forever with you because I knew that if it took forever for you to finally want to be with me the way that I wanted to be with you, I would have gladly waited that long. But now that'll never happen because I can't trust you; you—an angel. And if I can't trust you then I can't be with you. Not now, not ever."

I started to walk away, but Robert's hand once again grabbed my arm.

"Grace, don't do this."

"I'm not, Robert," I replied simply through a thick curtain of tears and hurt. "You did it all on your own. Congratulations. You've finally learned how to be human." I jerked my arm free of his grip once more using my entire body weight and stormed away from him, each step feeling heavier and heavier, a complete contradiction to the exaggerated feeling of emptiness that was inside of me as I approached the ever brightening glow of the mocking lights that encircled the tent of merrymakers.

I quickly brought my hand to my face to wipe away any residual blood and tears before running into anyone that might recognize me. I heard the sound of footsteps nearing me from behind and I turned around, ready to sound off on Robert once more, but instead I saw the comforting face of Graham and I collapsed in his arms with a pitiful wail of sobs pouring out of me.

"Shh, it's alright," he cooed as he held me tightly against him. He did not move, did not stir as my body was racked with seemingly endless sobs. Instead, he smoothed my hair that had fallen out of its pins, stroked the nape of my neck, and allowed the slow beat of his heart to seep in to steady the erratic beat of my own until everything had calmed down.

When my violent sobs made way for the soft tick of hiccups, he finally spoke. "Stacy's gone to tell your dad and Janice that you're not feeling well and we'll take you home, okay?"

I nodded beneath his now impossibly dampened shirt, thankful for his presence. I muffled my gratitude into the soggy mess that I had created and felt him chuckle.

"You can thank me later by washing this shirt. Come on, I'll walk you to the car."

With one arm around my waist and the other one cradling my hand, we walked towards his green Buick, him gently patting my hip as I renewed the sobbing, though it was silent now. He pulled his keys out from his pocket and fiddled with them until he found the right one, then proceeded to unlock my door, pulling it open and helping me inside. He waited outside for Stacy to return, and when she did, she motioned for me to roll down the window.

"Okay, so I told your dad that you weren't feeling too well and that Graham was going to take you home. He said that he'd call you from the car when they were heading off to that resort place they're going to for their honeymoon. I'm going to call my mom from your house and tell her that I'm staying over with you, is that alright?"

I nodded mutely, the words making sense…and then not.

"So what are we waiting for then?" Graham asked as he walked over to his side of the car. He opened the door and pulled back the seat to allow Stacy to climb in but she remained on my side of the car.

"Lark. She doesn't want Grace going home alone."

"She's going to be with us. How can she be alone?"

I couldn't see Stacy's face, but I could tell by her tone as she responded that she was annoyed. "You don't really listen too well, do you? She's not going to have Robert there to watch her, not willingly anyway, and that's not safe for her."

"Because of that Sam guy?"

"He's not just that Sam guy, Graham."

I heard Graham's fist pound the roof of the car and I winced. "I know he's not just that Sam guy. I could kill Robert for bringing a guy like that into Grace's life. What was he thinking?"

"He didn't bring Sam into Grace's life, Graham. Sam was a part of her life before Robert was. Robert is the reason she's still alive—as heinous as his actions were, we have to at least acknowledge that."

I heard Graham sigh, followed by a muffled "I know" before he straightened his body. I turned to look out of my window and saw the silhouette of Lark standing just outside of the perimeter of the woods.

Grace, you know that he loves you.

I turned away from the window. "How utterly unfair, to not be able to avoid a conversation even this far away," I mumbled to myself.

He was stupid, he was wrong, he knows it. Please, give it some time and think things through before you go writing him out of your life forever. You don't know what he's gone through.

I stared at the gear shift and tried to ignore the musical notes that echoed with each word. I snorted as the last one seemed to echo in my head. "Forever isn't a term that exists with humans, remember? And you saw this happening. You knew it was going to happen…it's too late to stop it now," I whispered, knowing that she would hear me.

Whatever your decision, you must know that he's never going to leave you alone, right? He might have been foolish enough to trust you with Sam once, but he knows much better now. He has been actively trying to keep you safe, especially now. Whatever his faults, he loves you, Grace, and would gladly give up his life to keep you safe. Please, if nothing else, at least remember that.

I turned to scowl at her, but she was gone.

"Okay, Lark's going to meet us at the house. Let's get going," Stacy said as she slapped the car's roof.

"Hey, watch it, that's my car!"

"Oh please, you just punched it just a few seconds ago, you big baby."

"Well yeah, because it's *my* car."

"Well, I'm the fairer sex—what more damage can I do to it that you haven't done?"

"Fairer sex my—"

His response was muffled as Stacy climbed into the back seat and pulled the driver's side seat down. She scooted behind my seat and wrapped her arms around me.

"I'm sorry. I...I'm just...sorry."

I patted her hands and stifled a sniffle. Graham reached over and placed his hand on mine.

"I'm here for you, Rocky."

I smiled through my tears.

"Thanks, Frank."

Stacy's head popped between the seats and she looked at the two of us as though we had lost our minds.

"Did you guys snort something while I was gone? Rocky? Frank?"

Graham pointed to the ornament that hung beneath his rearview mirror—a cluster of different key chains, all bearing logos or images from our favorite movie.

"Oh. God, why didn't I notice that before; you guys really are weird, aren't you?" Stacy commented as she reached her hand forward to examine the odd collection that Graham had gathered over the years.

"We must be if we're hanging out with you," Graham quipped as he started the car.

"So says the guy dating the angel," Stacy laughed sadly.

Graham said nothing as he pulled out of his stall. He put the car in drive and the silence in the car followed us as we headed towards my house, the dark streets hiding what I knew the others couldn't know, couldn't feel.

Leave me alone, Robert. Stop following me and just go away.

The air around us turned cold and I watched as Graham flipped the heater on, his breath coming out in puffs of vapor despite the sudden blast of hot air.

I stared out of the window and pressed my head against the glass, watching the reflection of my tears trail down my face as my body slowly began to shiver from the sudden chill.

I love you, Grace Anne Shelley.

I rubbed the tears with the back of my hand, knowing that it was a futile gesture, but not caring. I closed my eyes and the warmth started to slowly return as we neared my home.

The lights were on, a familiar figure stood in the doorway, waiting for us.

"She's fast," Graham muttered, his tone flat.

"Yeah. If you thought it was bad with me, you're in for a rude awakening," Stacy quipped. "Now hurry up and get out—I have to pee."

Graham quickly opened his door and climbed out of his seat, pulling the lever to release the chair's back to allow Stacy to exit the back. He left and came around to the passenger side, opening the door and offering me a hand.

I took it and stepped out, realizing for the first time that my arm was throbbing. I apparently wasn't the only person who had noticed that my arm was injured when I heard three equally shocked gasps as the extent of the damage to my arm was revealed in the porch light of the house.

"Oh goodness, look at your arm," Stacy said, her fingers shaking as she reached out to gently touch the odd peacock-hued pattern on my bicep.

"What the hell did that? Did that come from Robert?" Graham asked, shocked by what he saw.

I looked down at my arm and frowned. The same, strange honeycomb-patterned bruising that had covered my hand after I had hit Lark last year now filled up half of my arm. I looked at Lark's surprised face and she shook her head in confusion.

"I don't think he intended to do that," she said quickly when she saw the anger in Graham begin to grow exponentially.

"I don't care if he intended to do it or not. He's hurt her and he's allowed others to hurt her." He turned to face her, a sudden thought coming to him. "How long did you know about all of this?"

Lark bit her lip and shook her head, unwilling to answer, but knowing that she couldn't help it. She fought against the instinct to tell the truth, finally giving up just before her voice turned into a scream.

"Since the day she came home from the hospital."

Graham nodded his head, his expression becoming hard, his eyes cold, and turned away, walking with me inside of the house. Stacy followed, as did Lark, who closed the door behind us, unable to look at Graham again after his response to her answer.

Wordlessly, I walked upstairs to my room and began to collect my things to take a shower. I left sodden, muddy footprints all over the carpet as I did so, but I really didn't care. I headed to the bathroom, passing a worried Stacy, and closed the door behind me.

I removed the dress and undergarments, making great ceremony of ripping the corset off from the front, popping each little hook and eye, before tossing it to the ground.

I stared at myself in the mirror and watched as I slowly crumpled inward, all barriers gone, all inhibitions disintegrated into nothing as I finally allowed myself to cave into the hole that now made up who I was.

I felt my tears, hot and unrelenting, fall down my face and splash onto my chest, my belly, my legs. I stared at myself as my eyes and nose grew redder with each passing moment, unable to handle the constant tide of tears and everything that coincides with them. I saw my lips begin to tremble and flutter as the once silent sobs started to grow in intensity, the sounds resembling those of a wounded animal.

I ignored the knocks and the calls of concern that came through the door, and when my body began to shake, the spasms of each painful acknowledgement of the betrayal that Robert had dealt me, only then did I wrap my arms around myself, a pitiful effort to keep that last vestige of restraint in place.

I stood there for what felt like too long and yet not long enough. My eyes had grown grotesquely puffy by the time I finally headed into the shower to wash the muck out of my hair and body.

I remained in the shower only long enough to soap up and rinse off. I dressed quickly and opened the bathroom door to see three anxious pairs of eyes waiting on the other side.

They said nothing as I walked into my bedroom and closed the door behind me. I could hear them crowd around my door, silently contemplating whether to open it or leave me alone.

I threw my dress into the hamper beside my dresser and glanced up at the mirror that was raised above it. Stuck to the side were photos—images of happier moments—or simply blissfully ignorant moments of Robert and I.

I reached up to remove them, the movement slow thanks to the pain in my arm. When my mirror was clear of any reminders, I walked over to the closet and pulled out the shoe box that held the sandals Robert had bought for me to wear to Hannah's wedding. I removed them and placed the photos beneath the tissue paper. I replaced the shoes and topped it with the lid.

Sighing, I walked over to the trashcan beside the nightstand next to my bed and placed the box in there. I continued to make these small trips until the small receptacle was overflowing with items that had been given to me by or reminded me of Robert.

"This is going to be hard enough with you still in my head," I whispered. "I don't need to see these things, too."

I crawled onto my bed and placed my head against my pillow, feeling the tears begin anew as I stared through the dark windows, imagining a pair of silver eyes staring through at me, sadness and remorse saturating each glimmering iris. I shook my head at the image. "It's too late," I mouthed, and then pressed a closed fist to my lips, stifling another sob.

When my eyelids finally fell from the weight of exhaustion and sleep, they did not do so before my mind tricked me into seeing those eyes once more, this time the silver replaced by golden rings.

EPILOGUE: ALBUM

I woke up the next morning in a fog, feeling strangely weightless as the scent of flowers drilled through my nostrils. I opened my eyes to see my room turned into a sea of bright yellow as every single inch was covered by a pot of lilies. Note cards stuck out of them like little white flags, each one bearing the same two-word phrase: forgive me.

I asked Graham and Stacy to help me remove them, telling them to take them wherever they wanted to, as long as they were nowhere near the house. For the next two days, I woke up to the same cloying aroma of the bright pink and white flowers and each time, Graham and Stacy silently carried each pot outside into awaiting cars. Finally, on the fourth day, I simply asked them to move the pots outside.

Surprisingly enough, while Dad and Janice were away on their honeymoon at a destination spa in Rockbridge—another gift from Ameila—Stacy and Graham somehow managed to be around each other without starting a single argument. Lark, somehow sensing that her presence reminded me far too much of Robert, kept at a distance. Her relationship with Graham had taken a sudden U-turn after he discovered that she had known nearly as long as Robert had that Sam had tried to kill me, and so she never came into the house again after that first night.

I tried to get Graham to understand her reason for doing so, but he couldn't accept it. He was loyal to a fault, I realized, and the guilt that I bore from knowing that he was preventing himself from being happy simply because he didn't want to betray me too was difficult to stomach. Stacy kept her opinion on the subject to herself, even from me, though I was certain she'd had several discussions about it with Lark during the moments she wasn't with me.

The bruising on my arm which had angered Graham and shocked Lark and Stacy had vanished that first morning—I didn't bother pretending that I didn't know how. I just didn't think about it at all.

It was during one of the rare moments when I was alone—Stacy was at a Doctor's appointment while Graham was attending his first day waiting tables at the diner near the mall after quitting his job at the theater—that I decided to finally go up into the attic to grab some of the things for the baby that Janice had written down.

I took a flashlight with me, as well as a spare bulb in case the light up there wasn't working. I pulled down the ladder in the upstairs hallway and climbed up into the dusty space, covering my nose with my hand as I did so. I pulled on the chain attached to the overhead lamp and nodded knowingly as the familiar crackle of a broken filament sounded. I slowly unscrewed the bulb and replaced it with the fresh one, applauding myself as the numerous boxes and sheet covered objects were illuminated in the bright, faux-daylight glow.

"Now then, which one contains all of my baby stuff?" I asked out loud.

I placed the flashlight near the edge of the opening and began to walk around, inspecting the dusty boxes with careful eyes, reading each label in the smooth, graceful strokes of my mother's hand, and the brisk, short strokes that belonged to my father.

I soon made out the outline of a crib—or at least, parts of a crib—beneath a grayish-pink sheet and lifted the dusty cloth off of it as gently as possible. The cloud of dust was minimal, and the light sufficient enough for me to see that the sheet had been covering the four sides that made up

438

the basic frame of what had once been my crib. I ran my fingers down the smooth curves of the white wooden rails, trying to see if I could ever remember being behind them. I couldn't, of course, but it felt good to try to remember something pleasant.

I pulled the rails out from its hiding spot and maneuvered them to the ladder. I began climbing down, bringing each one down with me, one-by-one. When all four were out of the attic, I dragged them into the bedroom that would soon be Matthew's. Janice had been busy painting the walls several different colors—each wall was a pale, pastel shade of blue, yellow, green, and orange—and arranging matching patchwork curtains against the lone window that mirrored my own facing out into the street.

I repeated this trip several times with more items and boxes I discovered and could move on my own, making sure to uncover the items that I couldn't so that they could be moved later without having to do any re-searching. When I was done, I finally sat down in Matthew's room to go through a box that had been labeled "Grace" in my mother's handwriting.

The tape gave way quite easily, and I pulled out several tissue wrapped pieces of clothing, including a bonnet and a dress that I could only have guessed was what they used to bring me home in. I carefully rewrapped them and placed them to the side as I pulled out several more objects that appeared to have been stored as I exited infancy and entered toddlerhood. There was even a pacifier that looked so mangled, I wasn't sure if it had belonged to me or some mystery dog my parents might have owned before I was old enough to remember.

A metal rattle that felt far too heavy for any baby to carry was resting in a box, along with a lock of dark brown hair tied together with a pale green ribbon.

"I hope there was some left on my head when this was taken off," I groaned.

Another package of tissue revealed what I assumed was a traditional Korean dress that I would have worn on my first birthday. I had seen pictures of it somewhere around the house, though Dad had long since packed most of the photos of my childhood away.

A soft, sage and lavender chenille blanket, folded into eighths rested over an album that lay at the bottom of the box. It was an unusually large album, judging by the cover, and I had to tilt the box on its side just to pry it loose from its tight wedging. Once I had it in my lap, I began to examine it, admiring the deep, textured grain in the black leather cover. The pattern was unusual, and reminded me of a heavy snake skin.

I lifted the cover to read the inscription on the inside.

"*How priceless is your unfailing love! Both high and low among men find refuge in the shadow of your wings.*"

The writing was the same flowing script that I knew to be my mothers, and I couldn't help but trace each letter with my fingers, trying to imagine her sitting with this book in her lap, writing these words down as she prepared for my arrival. I felt the twinges of anger and resentment start to build up within me when I stopped for a second to recognize that she wasn't here to explain to me why she had chosen what she had written, what its meaning was, its significance to her...to me.

As with the album that Graham had purchased for Dad and Janice, this one had a thick sheet of vellum between each page, and I lifted the yellowed, translucent page to reveal an aged photograph of several strangely-garbed women seated around a black, rectangular table just a foot off the ground. Their dark hair was pulled back in tight knots, their faces—what I could see of them anyway—were very serene.

One of them wore a sly smile beneath a swatch of lost pigment, everything but her smile gone forever. Beneath the image my mother had written several names, including one that read "Great-Great-Grandma Ahn Bi". I immediately adopted the woman with the missing face, save for the smile as my great-great-grandmother. That was the type of smile I would have loved to have inherited—spectacular all on its own, needing no other ornament—even the rest of a face—to enhance its beauty.

I turned the page to see another aged image, this time of several men seated around a bar. They varied in ages, though none appeared older than Dad. Their names were listed beneath each of them, but only one bore any particular title: "Great-Uncle Llehmai".

He appeared the most prominent one in the group, his strong, handsome face standing out the most clearly. His hair was dark, but not the darkest. His face was handsome, his mouth lifted only on one side as if he knew that was all he needed. He did not look Korean, but he wore the same style of clothes that the other men in the photos did.

"Maybe he was adopted."

I continued to flip through several pages, stopping at each one to inspect and admire the various vintage photographs of individuals given labels ranging from "Aunt This" and "Cousin That", the faces all so similar looking, varying only by slight degrees in height or slant of the cheekbones, tilt of the smile. I could see myself in the faces of these family members, just as I could see myself in Dad's face, and I felt comforted somehow, seeing that my family ties extended beyond just my mother, even if only through some old photographs.

I got to the last two pages in the album and frowned. The second to the last page contained an image of me as a young girl, wearing a dress that I didn't recognize, holding the hand of someone I did.

My eyes were raised up, instead of looking towards the camera. I was smiling, happy, my gaze focused on the person whose hand gripped mine nearly as tightly as I was gripping theirs. Though the photo was in black and white, I could see that my dress was probably green—mom liked to dress me in green for some reason—and my hair was pulled back with two clips that looked like they were made out of feathers, topped with flowers. I was missing teeth, and my gap-toothed grin only accentuated the deep dimple in my cheek.

I turned my attention away from the image of me to the one of the individual who was staring back into the camera. Her smile was incredibly bright, as though it were creating its own flash. In her eyes I could see hints of my own, and in her hair she wore matching clips, looking ridiculous but not caring as she beamed for whomever it was taking the picture.

Her dress looked to be of the same shade of green as my own, but hers was cut to flaunt the figure that I was somehow not blessed with. I laughed as I realized that our feet were both bare, our toes pointed towards each other, despite the obvious appearance of snow on the ground. Without her shoes on, I could tell that mom was a fairly short woman, my head coming up to her chest quite easily, despite my youth.

Beneath the image was a caption written in mom's clean penmanship: "Grace and I at Mother-Daughter day, February 7th".

It was the last picture that had been taken of my mother and me, one of the last things she did before she died, and I felt a need to keep this photograph with me. I gently pried it out of the metal corners that had kept it in place for over eleven years and turned it over, half-expecting to see nothing, and half-expecting to see something—anything—and feeling a sense of disappointment when all I saw on the back was the brand of photo paper used.

I chuckled and shook my head. I took a quick look at the last page, the empty photo corners there now matching the ones on the page directly next to it. I closed the book and proceeded to fit everything back into the box when something urged me to return to the photo album.

I again flipped through the images, the family that I had never known all welcoming me back with their familiar eyes and smiles. It felt good.

And then I reached those final two pages once more, this time both empty.

But also both with something written beneath the photo area in the little caption box provided for notes.

I re-read the one my mother had written describing our mother-daughter day. The photo in my hand was proof that it had been there.

Then my eyes glanced over to the page that I had assumed would be blank, its page free of a picture and thus, a comment.

But a comment was there, in Mom's handwriting, describing an image that wasn't there…and simply couldn't have been.

"Grace and Maia: Mother and Daughter"

Six words had never brought out such a non-reaction from me before as I stared dumbfounded at their implication. Had my mother done the unthinkable and began planning her grandchildren before her daughter had reached puberty? Was this some misplaced page, and there was another family member whose name was Grace somewhere in my mother's family tree?

I lifted the page to inspect the back, but saw that it was completely bare, no photo corners, no area for writing notes. It was a simple ending for what was a simple album.

I placed the page back down and stared at it, trying to figure out what my mother's intentions had been when she wrote this particular caption. Her words to me in my dream started to echo in my head, and I slammed the album shut, hoping the loud clap would be enough to snap me out of it.

Instead, my mother's voice grew louder and the only thing I could think to do to escape its incessant hounding was by distracting myself. I stood up and pushed aside the curtain in Matthew's room. I could see the countless pots of lilies still sitting in the lawn, slowly withering away in the sun from the lack of care they were receiving.

In the fresh light, I quickly repacked the box of things that had been intended for me by my mother and carried it, as well as the picture I removed from the album back to my room. I placed the box on my bed and approached the mirror. The residue of tape from the pictures that I had removed was still visible on the glass, the outlines of the images clearly formed in dust against the reflection of the afternoon sun beating down in my room.

I stuck the photo of my mother and me to the very top of the mirror, and smiled at her face, almost imagining that while the seven year-old me gazed up at her from the eleven year-old picture, she was more interested and pleased with seeing the eighteen year-old me looking back at her.

I glanced quickly at my own reflection and sighed at what I saw. There was no way a mother would have been pleased at seeing what was reflected at me in the mirror. My skin looked waxy and gray, my eyes puffy from endless nights spent crying and days spent sitting in denial. I had bitten my lips so hard trying to keep my sobbing to a minimum so as not to disturb Graham that they were now cracked and scabbed over. I hadn't taken a shower since coming home and it showed in my hair, which lay on my head like a tattered blanket.

My clothes needed to be changed, but with Dad gone, laundry hadn't been done in almost a week and I didn't have any clean shirts left. The one that I wore hung on my body like a sack and I bit back a hysterical giggle as I saw that it was a shirt very similar in style to the one that I had worn on the day I had first met...I couldn't even bring myself to think his name.

I shook my head and turned towards my bed. I moved the box over and crawled onto my comforter, wrapping my arms around my poor pillow—it had taken far too much abuse this past year by way of my tears and would soon need to be put out of its misery.

I stayed that way as the sun crossed over the sky and began to set just beyond my window. My room became a kaleidoscope of colors as the bright, white glow of daylight twisted and warped with the oranges, pinks, purples, and finally blues of dusk creeping into the still quiet of twilight.

I didn't move as I heard a soft knock on my door, and remained silent as I heard the door open and then softly shut. My bed creaked as the weight of another body forced the springs downward. I felt a hot teardrop pool in the small hollow that formed between my nose and the inner corner of my eye as I remembered that it had never once made a sound whenever...*he* would do the very same thing.

A pair of strong, sure arms wrapped around me and pulled me against a solid yet giving chest, my back feeling the unmistakable rhythm of a beating heart, and soon the tiny pool began to overflow.

He held me, content to let me cry as long as I needed to, for whatever reason. He didn't move or complain about stiffness or cramping, and I started to feel guilty.

"You shouldn't have to lay here and deal with me like this," I sniffled.

444

"Bah. You're my best friend. Besides, after what I put you through last year, I think I owe you."

"You don't owe me anything, Graham."

"Just shut-up and let me comfort you, okay?"

We lay there in silence for a little while before my mouth started moving again.

"You should be talking to Lark. It's not her fault, you know—none of this is."

He let out a long sigh. "I know. Stacy's been hammering me on this every day since all of this happened. It doesn't matter, though. She still knew and didn't say or do anything—I don't think I can accept that, Grace. You're my best friend. I can't see living my life without you there with me, and knowing that she and Robert almost guaranteed that that's not possible with this Sam guy on the loose…I just can't deal with that right now. And neither should you."

My heart pained at the idea of Graham already contemplating losing me, the grim reality that I had a target not just on my life, but on my very soul suddenly turning every precious moment together into something much more than just time.

"Stacy's going on some kind of trial drug program to see if it'll help fight off the cancer, and she's using that as a reason to tell me that I'm being stupid for not giving…*him* a second chance—that if she can fight for what she wants, why can't I. The problem is that I don't know what I want anymore."

Graham's breathing slowed as he contemplated what I said. "Well, the only way to figure that out is to go over the things that you could have. Do you want to work things out with Robert?"

"Work what out? What kind of relationship did we ever have if it started out with him lying to me?"

Graham nodded in understanding, and squeezed his arms around me even tighter. "I don't like the fact that any of this is happening, Grace. I was genuinely starting to like the guy—I love his sister something crazy—

and I know that despite all of the stupid things he's done, he loves you just as much I love Lark—perhaps even more."

"Are you actually suggesting I think about forgiving him when you're not even willing to talk to Lark?"

"I just think that if there's anyone out there who can keep you safe from this Sam guy it's him. I'll deal with hating him for everything else silently if it means that he'll stick around and keep this Sam person from hurting you again."

I shook my head at the suggestion. "I can't. I don't trust him anymore, Graham. I *can't* trust him. It's not like he dated someone else behind my back, or lied about his age."

"I know that, Grace. He put your whole life in danger, but he's also kept you safe, kept you alive all this time. As much as I hate him, I gotta admit that if not for him, I wouldn't be able to talk to you like this."

I didn't want to acknowledge the truth in his words. I couldn't do that, because doing that would mean taking that first step towards something that I no longer recognized.

Graham's chin lifted and pressed down against the top of my head, his voice filling in the silence. "This is so much more complicated than dating a normal person. Hey, next time, choose a human to date, alright?"

I felt an odd sensation in my chest and marveled as it crawled up to my throat and came out in a sound that was similar to a strangled bit of laughter.

"I tried that once, remember?" I told him. In that moment, an unbidden image formed in my head of two smiling faces, their bodies positioned in the same manner, their faces much, much older.

I could see their hands still clasped against her chest, his arms wrapped around her middle protectively, comfortingly. They were staring at a series of images of what looked like joyous times together, memories captured in wooden frames lining the walls and shelves, as though each one had to make up for those that were missing somewhere else.

The smiles grew sad as their eyes traveled the veritable globe through those photographs, and I realized with sudden clarity that they were the only people in each one. A lifetime of photos of just them, their smiling faces growing older with each progressing frame.

There was an obvious happiness in their faces. But I could see something missing, something that felt strange, an almost mysterious emptiness. I heard a shudder of breath and I watched as together their chests stopped rising, their bodies forever locked in a loving embrace. I looked on as the room grew frigid at a frighteningly quick pace, and a familiar dark mist began to fill the room, swirling around slowly until from beneath its dark layer, Death himself appeared, his magnificent ebony wings extended, taking up nearly the entire room, turning it dark and foreboding.

His beautiful face was pinched in agony as he reached a hand to touch the softly lined cheek of the woman, his thumb caressing the now blue-tinged lips of her mouth. He lowered himself to his knees and laid his head against her chest, sobbing as the sound he longed to hear did not greet him as it had always done.

He clutched at the bedclothes, his sharp nails turning them into strips of useless cloth as he tried to contain the emotions that roiled within him. He cried out, and my hands instinctively covered my ears, but I heard nothing this time.

The glass in the frames began to shatter and rained over the entire scene, landing on the bodies and mixing with the crystal droplets that had begun to collect on the ground beneath the dark angel. He angrily pried the man's arms away from her body and pulled her up into his own.

He pressed his lips against her cold face, over and over again, each time whispering something to her, desperately waiting to hear her respond, but of course she never did. He pulled something out of his front shirt pocket—a scrap of paper—and rubbed the surface with his thumb. His wings blocked my view of seeing what exactly was happening to that piece of paper, but as soon as he was done, it burst into flames.

He sank to the floor, her body in his arms, and he slowly began to change, his hair changing color, becoming lighter until it was void of any color at all. His skin began growing sallow and loose. I held my hand to my mouth, horrified as I watched the pewter irises began to turn into onyx, the silver running out with the tears that continued to flow down his face. His wings began to wither, the deep, midnight color fading to a dismal gray before disintegrating into a fine ash that blew into the cold, disturbed air.

He brought the woman's hand over his chest where his cold, motionless heart had lain dormant for what appeared to be decades, and smiled. I cocked my head to the side as I saw a faint ripple beneath the thin fabric of his black shirt, my eyes opening wide in shock.

"I'm coming, Grace. I'm coming."

He closed his eyes and I bit back a sob as I watched the rise and fall of his chest cease, the beating of his heart fade away like his wings.

My chest grew cold, the living heart inside sputtering at the shock of such an enormous, significant loss. "No," I breathed. The sob I had held back finally tore through me. "No!"

"Grace?"

The darkness of the room felt like the lights had just been flipped off as I blinked rapidly to adjust my vision to the sudden change. Sweat began to bead on my forehead and in my hands as the temperature of the room was now considerably warmer.

"Grace, are you okay?"

"What?"

"You kind of freaked out on me for a second there, got all stiff and…cold."

I began to giggle in nervous relief when I realized that the vision was gone, and my body was not laying in the arms of my dead angel, but rather those of my best friend.

"Well at least you're laughing."

I shook my head. "I'm sorry, Graham."

"Don't apologize. I kind of miss your dorky laugh. It reminds me that you're not dead."

At that, my laughter turned semi-hysterical, which in turn reminded me, too, that I wasn't dead. At least…not yet. "Don't insult my laugh—it's unique."

448

"Yeah, like a hyena."

I maneuvered my arm just enough to elbow him in his ribs playfully and we were both consumed by laughter as he feigned a mortal injury to something other than his pride.

When we both calmed down, our laughter subsiding into the quiet of the darkened room, I heard him sigh into my hair. "Grace, are you going to be okay?"

"I don't know," I told him honestly. "I've got a lot of thinking to do—I've avoided it these past few days, but I can't keep doing it. I can't run from this, and I definitely can't hide from this, which means that I can only face this head on."

"I'm going to face this with you, Grace," Graham said reassuringly. "You're not going to do this alone. I'm here for you. I'm not running away this time."

"I know," came my somber reply, but I also knew that whatever the end results, I didn't want Graham to have to face this alone either. "Graham?"

"Yeah?"

"Could you do *me* a favor?"

"Anything."

"Talk to Lark."

I grit my teeth and held my breath as I waited through his silence for a response. Finally, after a long sigh, I felt him nod his head. I exhaled in relief and allowed the first genuine smile to cross my lips in days.

"Grace?"

"Yeah?"

"Could you do *me* a favor?"

I hesitated answering him, fearful of what it was that he'd want from me in return, but he was my best friend and whatever he wanted, I felt compelled to at least consider.

"Anything."

"Could you take a shower? Because, no offense, but you reek!"

"Oh!" I gasped, and twisted in his arms to begin pummeling him, our laughter mixing in the dark room, filling the house with the first sounds of happiness in nearly a week.

"I'll let you get your stuff," Graham said after pinning me to the bed and proclaiming himself the winner when I finally relented and agreed to take a shower.

"See, that's a problem. I haven't done any laundry since before the wedding—my dad usually does it—so I'm clear out of clothes to sleep in."

"Hold on," he said and ran downstairs. A few minutes later he reappeared with several items in his hand, one of them being his old freshman wrestling shirt. "Here, you can wear that and these." He handed me a pair of boxers.

"Ugh! You want me to wear your underwear?" I gasped.

"What! They're brand-new. Mom bought them for me in Florida, but I never got a chance to wear them because I came straight back here. You can roll the waist so it'll fit you better, but at least you won't have to do laundry tonight, right?"

I nodded and thanked him begrudgingly. I quickly grabbed a pair of my own underwear and then headed towards the bathroom. I placed the clothes on the bathroom counter and turned to close the door.

"Ouch!"

I jumped onto the counter, nearly falling into the bathroom sink in the process, and grabbed my foot. It was bleeding from several tiny cuts. I peered down onto the floor and stared in shock at the tiny, reflective glass shards that covered the tiled ground.

"Grace? Are you okay?" I heard Graham ask from behind the door.

"Graham, did you use this bathroom at all this week?" I called out.

"Uh…no. I've been using your dad's. There's a tub in that one. Why?"

"I think Stacy might have dropped something in here—there's glass all over the floor."

I heard him groan at the sound of Stacy's name. "Are you bleed-ing?"

I nodded then laughed when I realized he couldn't hear a nod. "Yes. Could you get the broom and dustpan for me, please?"

When he didn't answer, I assumed he had already left to go and get them. A loud knock followed just a few minutes later.

"Are you decent?"

"Yeah," I answered.

He opened the door and immediately began to sweep the floor to-wards the shower stall, stopping only to begin sweeping the little razors into the dustpan. Once he was sure he had gotten everything off the floor, he squatted and began to examine my feet.

"This is pretty bad, Grace. They're all in your feet."

"No, really?"

We spent the next hour laughing and cursing as he plucked sliver after sliver of glass from my feet, placing each bloody one on a napkin next to me on the counter. By the time he was done, he had removed almost thirty tiny shards from the soles of my feet. He quickly bandaged my still-bleeding feet and carried me back to my room.

"So much for that bath," I joked.

"I'm going to kill Stacy when I see her—forget cancer. She's going to have to deal with me now," Graham growled as he stalked back towards the bathroom to gather the dustpan and the napkin.

"I hope it wasn't expensive," he called from across the hall.

"Hope what wasn't expensive?" I shouted back.

"Whatever it was that broke."

I shrugged my shoulders. "We don't really have anything expen-sive in this house. You know that."

"Yeah, well, last I heard, crystal was pretty expensive. Plus, it does a number on your feet."

I looked at my bandaged feet and then groaned as I saw the famili-ar honeycombed bruising start to form across them. "Oh, Robert...what did you do?" I breathed.

"What?"

I looked at Graham's confused expression and shook my head. "Nothing, just talking to myself," I said to him with a half-hearted smiled.

"Okay. As long as you don't start having full on conversations with yourself or anything," he chuckled.

When he walked away, I looked out of the window and felt the sadness that had retreated slowly start to return. My emotions were a jumbled mess, my feet were hurting, and I had seen a glimpse of what my life might become, a life that I once thought I wanted but now knew wasn't the right path for me.

Things were becoming far more complicated now that the truth was out in the open, in every aspect, and I just couldn't help but wonder what would happen when Spring Break was over, school started back up, and the lies fell back into place again. How would I be able to pretend that I was whole when half of me was gone, and the other half had shattered?

How can a heart hate someone so much, and love them even more?

Angel…

ACKNOWLEDGEMENTS

To every single person who hounded me non-stop to continue Grace and Robert's story. Your love and interest in their story has given me more than enough reason to keep their journey going.

About The Author

S.L. Naeole spends most of her time writing, reading, and living life to the fullest with her husband, four children, and Fuzzgut the cat in her home in the Aloha State.

CPSIA information can be obtained at www.ICGtesting.com
Printed in the USA
236400LV00001B/183/P